JENNIFER DUGAN

G. P. PUTNAM'S SONS

G. P. PUTNAM'S SONS
An imprint of Penguin Random House LLC, New York

Visit us online at penguinrandomhouse.com

Library of Congress Cataloging-in-Publication Data
Names: Dugan, Jennifer, author.
Title: Verona comics / Jennifer Dugan.
Description: New York: G. P. Putnam's Sons, [2020] | Summary: Told in two voices,
cellist Jubilee and anxiety-ridden Ridley meet at a comic con where both of their families
have booths, and begin a relationship they must hide from their parents.
Identifiers: LCCN 2019034212 | ISBN 9780525516286 (hardcover) | ISBN 9780525516293
Subjects: CYAC: Dating (Social customs)—Fiction. |
Anxiety disorders—Fiction. | Musicians—Fiction. | Cello—Fiction. |
Comic-book stores—Fiction. | Lesbian mothers—Fiction.
Classification: LCC PZ7.1.D8343 Ver 2020 | DDC [Fic]—dc23
LC record available at https://lccn.loc.gov/2019034212

Printed in the United States of America
ISBN 9780525516286
1 3 5 7 9 10 8 6 4 2

Design by Suki Boynton
Text set in Dante MT Pro

To RJP, who always cheered the loudest.
I miss you every day.

CHAPTER ONE

Jubilee

"YOU LOOK LIKE you're being tortured," Jayla says. "This is supposed to be fun."

Easy to say when you're the one on the other side of the tweezers. I squeeze my eyes shut as she picks them up again, a tinge of fear washing over me when I smell the glue. I can't move my head while Jayla's working on my eyelashes, something she's stressed to me about a dozen times already in increasingly frustrated tones, so I try to distract myself by practicing the prelude from Bach's Fifth Cello Suite in my head. I tap my fingers against the cold bathroom counter, pressing imaginary strings and feeling homesick for my instrument.

Feather eyelashes and fancy dresses are worlds apart from the chunky sweaters and ballet flats that I prefer. But this is for the greater good, a part of my weekend of "pushing the boundaries and embracing life for the sake of my music," which has somehow turned into letting my best friend dress me up for FabCon prom after an already long day at the convention, selling comics with my parents.

"Can I open my eyes yet?"

"No," she says. "You have to relax. Remember what Mrs. G said."

Right. I've been instructed (read: forced) by my private instructor, Mrs. Garavuso; the school orchestra teacher, Mrs. Carmine; and *both* my parents to "let go" and take a weekend off from my instrument. On a technical level, Mrs. Garavuso says I'm the best cellist she's ever had. But apparently I've been, and this is a direct quote, "playing with the passion of a robot lately." Mrs. Carmine, traitor that she is, agreed wholeheartedly. Not exactly what I want to hear as I prepare for the biggest audition of my life—the summer program at the Carnegie Conservatory, where I'll get to study with Aleksander Ilyashev. He's been my dream teacher ever since I heard him play Beethoven's Triple Concerto with the Boston Symphony. And if I want a shot at getting into Carnegie for real after high school, a summer of his advice and guidance is the biggest boost I could possibly get.

"You think too loud." Jayla sighs, so close I can feel her breath on my cheek. "Seriously, get out of your head."

"I'm not in my head."

"Lies," she says, but I can hear the smile in her voice. "Respect the rules. I bet you're breaking at least two right now."

The rules, right. Jayla and I made a list of them on our way to the con. I've been mostly focusing on the first three, with varying degrees of success. Rule One: I can't practice cello, nor can I do any homework this entire weekend. (Half credit; I've been practicing this whole time, but only in my head.) Rule Two: When not helping my parents in their booths, I can't sit in my room obsessing over the audition. (Okay, she's got me there; I'm totally failing at this one.) Rule Three: I have to try a new food at each restaurant we eat at. (Switching from Sprite to Cherry Coke counts. Fight me.)

"You're going to flip when you see yourself," Jayla squeals, pressing another feather to my eyelid.

"In a good way, or . . . ?" I fake cringe, and she smacks my arm.

"Yes, in a good way. Now sit still."

Not that I really doubted it. Jayla is to makeup and fashion what I am to music—top tier, the best of the best, no apologies—except nobody would *ever* say her work lacks passion. She's been planning on going to FIT her entire life, and her new obsession with cosplay has given her an extra excuse to flex her fashion muscles.

"Annnnnd done," Jayla says, and I open my eyes.

I blink twice. I look . . . *amazing*. My dark brown hair is piled high on my head in an elaborate updo with long feathers streaming out in different directions. She's blended shimmery teal and green eye shadows together around my eyes and added little dots of eyeliner to accentuate the corners, and then there are the feathers. The feathers! Tiny little teal things, curled to perfection, adorn each eyelid, transforming me into something more akin to a magical forest creature than a cellist. I've disappeared completely into Mora, the badass peacock-inspired leader from my stepmom's famous *Fighting Flock* comic series.

Jayla turns back to putting the finishing touches on her

own makeup in the mirror, gently dabbing bright white spots onto her dark brown skin. "Go get your dress on. I'm almost done."

"Yes, ma'am," I say, hopping off the counter. I grab my emerald-green dress off the hook and disappear into the bedroom to get changed. I bought this dress for a school dance a few months ago—Jayla said the color "really popped" against my fair skin—but she's modified it pretty heavily since then, changing the cut, adorning it with feathers, and just generally turning it into a gown fit for peacock royalty.

I glance at the time and groan. "Prom started fifteen minutes ago."

"We're supposed to be fashionably late," Jayla calls back through the bathroom door.

"If you don't hurry, we're going to be the unfashionable kind," I mutter, zipping up my dress. I'm still struggling to tie the crisscrossing green and purple ribbons up my arms when Jayla finally steps out of the bathroom.

"Here, let me," she says, coming over, and I do a double take. Gone is Jayla, and in her place stands the best Shuri cosplay I have ever seen in my life. She's wrapped her braids into a massive bun on her head, and while it's not quite Wakandan-princess level, it's close. Add in the makeup and the warrior outfit she's been crafting for months and—

"Holy crap," I say, and she laughs.

"Yeah," she says, holding her arms out and twirling.

"You're definitely going to win tonight. You know that, right?"

She shrugs. "I better, after what happened earlier." Mean-

4

ing when her Harley Quinn cosplay came in second place, which she rates as a major underperformance, even though there were nearly 150 people competing and there was no way she was beating someone in a life-size replica of Hulkbuster armor.

"Stop, you did awesome," I say, but she shakes her head.

Jayla's always intense with this stuff, partially because she's super competitive (see also: only being a junior and already the co-captain of her club's soccer team), and partially because people will find any excuse to tear down a black girl that dares to also cosplay white characters. Jayla can't just be good; she has to be *great*, and even when she's great, she still gets crap for it. It's gross and annoying and one of the things I hate most about the comics community.

"Ready?" she asks, cinching the last ribbon.

"Yeah, I just have to strap myself into these death traps," I say, sliding my foot into a shiny green stiletto. I thought Jayla was kidding when she showed up to my house with them. Spoiler alert: she was not.

Jayla offers me her arm as we head out when it becomes clear that an ultra-plush carpet adds an additional degree of difficulty to super-high heels. "Everybody's gonna love those death traps." She laughs. "There is absolutely no way you're leaving that dance without checking off Rule Four."

Ah yes, Rule Four, aka the Final Rule, aka the only thing I have yet to even attempt, despite the fact it would probably be the most inspiring for my music: I must experience a con crush.

Con crushes are kind of Jayla's thing—find somebody

nice, spend the weekend flirting, and then go back home, no muss, no fuss—or they were, before she started casually seeing the *other* co-captain of the soccer team, Emily Hayes, a few weeks ago. I was supposed to pick up her slack on that front, but no luck so far. It's not that I'm not open to it . . . it's just that nobody has caught my eye.

Jayla stops at the door next to ours and I knock. My mom opens the door, her bright red hair shining in the hallway light as she blinks hard. She's probably just waking up from a nap, and I don't blame her. After working in the shop booth all day so Vera could sketch and talk to fans in Artist Alley, she's got to be beat.

"Hey, Jubilee." She yawns, but I can tell the second she really looks at me, because her eyes widen and then her eyebrows scrunch together the way they do whenever she's pissed. "Nope."

"Is everything okay?" Jayla asks all innocently, like she doesn't already know.

"Vera," Mom yells over her shoulder, pulling the door open wider. "Look at these kids!"

Vera's sitting on the edge of the bed, pointing the remote at the TV and lazily flipping through channels. She looks over at me and Jayla and nods appreciatively. "Are you evening-gown Mora? Amazing! And wow, Jayla, incredible detailing on the Shuri chest plate. That must have taken forever!" She sounds utterly delighted. My mom is going to kill her.

"Thank you so much," Jayla says with the most wholesome smile she can muster.

"Vera." I can only see the back of Mom's head now, but I

6

know that tone. I get that tone from her all the time. It's the "you're lucky I love you, because you make my life nearly impossible" tone. "Jubilee cannot go out dressed like that."

"It's prom," Vera says. "Give the kid a break."

"It's not real prom—it's comic-book-people prom, which is worse. And she looks twenty-five."

"It's my winter-formal dress," I point out. "You were fine with it in December."

"See, it's her winter-formal dress, Lillian. It's fine." Vera smirks like that solves everything. I hope it does, but I also know Mom way, way better than that—and Vera should too. They've been together four years now, which means she's had forty-eight months to learn what I've known for as long as I can remember: when Mom stands with her hands on her hips, her pinky finger tapping ever so slightly, it means trouble's definitely brewing.

"No, it *used* to be her winter-formal dress, but now the back goes down to her butt and the leg slit goes up to her elbow! What message does it send to have the creator's own kid turning Mora into some kind of pinup girl?"

Vera drops her head back, pulling her jet-black hair into a ponytail that shows off her undercut before walking over and kissing Mom on the temple. Even when they bicker, I swear they're still the poster children for happily ever after. It's perfect and gross all at once.

"Lil," she coos, and my mom visibly softens. "So they took a little artistic license; it's fine. And the message it sends, if that's *really* your concern, is that people shouldn't have to choose between being feminine or strong; they can be both. And may I remind you that this is an all-ages, dry event—"

"Exactly. *All* ages, Vera," Mom interrupts. "Which means it's not just kids that will be there. All the pervy dinosaurs might show up too."

"They're not going to let people in to party with the kids," Vera says. "You were there last year; the only adults allowed were sponsors and chaperones."

"I still think she should at least wear a shirt over it," Mom says, crossing her arms. "You know what teenage boys are like."

Vera arches an eyebrow. "And I think it's bullshit to make women cover up instead of holding men accountable for their actions."

Mom purses her lips. "I hate when you're right."

"You know, I could have just stayed home and happily rehearsed all weekend."

"You needed some sunlight, kid," Vera says. I don't bother pointing out that there is literally no natural daylight in this hotel–slash–casino–slash–convention center. "Go. Enjoy yourselves. Let me take care of your mom." She winks, which makes my mom blush, and ugh, gross. Shouldn't the lovey-dovey newlywed stage be over by now?

"Okay, yuck, bye," I say, grabbing Jayla's hand.

"Bye!" Jayla calls as I drag her down the hall, and we hear my mom giggle and say "Vera!" as she shuts the door. "Wow," Jayla says. "You know they're probably gonna—"

"Don't even finish that sentence."

By some miracle, the elevator doors are open as we

round the corner, but thanks to these ridiculous shoes, we don't have a prayer of making it in time . . . which means potentially being trapped on this floor for several more minutes. Several more minutes, during which either one of my parents could decide to run out and change her mind about letting us go alone or making me wear a T-shirt. Somehow I don't think "pushing the boundaries of my experiences" means going to FabCon prom with my mothers. Again.

"Hold that door!" Jayla shouts, dropping my arm and sprinting the rest of the way. Thank god for battle-ready outfits. She slides in her arm just as it closes, and the door bounces back open. She grins as I stumble in after her, laughing hard. I lean against the rail to catch my breath and realize with a start that we're not alone.

Batman stands in the corner, head tilted, taking in the sight of us. Well, a smaller, teenage-looking version of Batman, anyway—in a white dress shirt, a skinny tie, and dark fitted jeans. Okay, fine, so it's basically just a dude in a mask. But it counts.

I can tell Jayla is probably about two seconds away from monologuing about the undue appreciation the comics industry shows for mediocre white boys and how this boy in a mask is case in point because he'll probably take prom king just for showing up. It's her favorite topic, and she's definitely *not* wrong—but it *would* make for an awkward elevator ride. I'm a little bit relieved when she just rolls her eyes at him and bustles to the opposite side of the elevator car, mumbling, "What's up, Office Batman?"

He bends down and picks up a feather I must have lost

while sprinting into the elevator, spinning it around in his long fingers. *Piano fingers,* I muse. I have a habit of reducing everyone down to the instrument they should play. Jayla would be a saxophone; my other best friend, Nikki, is a flute; my ex, Dakota, is an out-of-tune harpsichord. Vera is a—

"Lost one," Batman says, all quiet. And yeah, that mask and the scrape of his voice and the way he's sliding up his sleeves right now are kind of working for him. The idea of "pushing the boundaries" just got a lot more interesting.

"I guess I did." I smile and reach for it, but he just keeps twirling it, like he's in no hurry to give it back.

"She must be molting," Jayla deadpans. She pushes the button for the first floor, even though it's already glowing.

"Are you going to prom?" he asks.

Jayla widens her eyes, like *obviously, dude,* and nods.

"We are." I elbow Jayla. "Are you?"

"Nah." He reaches across and hits the button for the second floor, which is odd considering he had to have been the one who hit the button for the first floor to begin with. "I like your dress, though," he says, a little bit quiet, as the elevator doors ping open. He holds his hand out, offering me the feather.

"Keep it," I say, and a blush rises to my cheeks as he turns to leave.

CHAPTER TWO

Ridley

I BOLT AROUND the corner, shoving up my Batman mask and sliding down the wall before the elevator doors even shut. Okay, breathe in, hold it, breathe out. Repeat. This shouldn't be so hard. Wait. Do I hold it for one beat? Two? Three? Oh god, now it just feels like I'm drowning.

pullittogetherpullittogetherpullittogether

A cute girl dressed as my favorite comic character should not have this effect on me, but.

breathebreathebreathebreathebreathe

It used to be I could tell the difference between excitement and anxiety. It used to be I could handle crowds and small talk. It used to be a lot of things . . . but now it's not.

I take another gasping breath, replaying the moments in my head. The way her cheeks turned pink when she told me to keep the feather twisted me up in interesting, not terrible, ways. And yet.

And yet.

I dig my fingers into the carpet and stare up at the ceiling,

ing to ground myself before this panic attack spins too far out of control, but seriously, fuck this. Fuck being seventeen and wired so wrong that a person smiling at you can spin you into heart failure.

A door clicks open and a couple—drunk and sloppy like the rest of the casino crowd—steps out. I slide my mask down and shove myself through the door to the stairwell across from me, a welcome escape from their questioning looks.

It's one flight down to the dance or eleven up to my room, but I start to climb anyway, wishing there was a delete button in my brain. I don't know why I opened my mouth at all. So yeah, I should go. To my room. And probably never come out. Because reasons. But I still have this feather and—

My phone buzzes in my pocket, and I pull it out, sighing when I see Gray's name pop up.

"Ridley, where are you?" she asks. It's nearly impossible to hear her over the background noise.

"In a stairwell," I say.

"For good reasons or bad reasons?"

"Are there good reasons?"

"Yes. Come to the ballroom and I'll tell you all about the time I made out with your favorite superhero in the stairwell at RICC."

"Never happened," I snort.

"Okay, fine, it was his stunt double. On the escalator. Still counts."

I laugh; I can't help it. Two seconds ago I couldn't breathe, and now I'm laughing. Gray is magic like that.

"Are you trying to make me meet you or run away faster?"

I ask, but I've already started trotting back down the stairs.

"Ha ha, baby bro," she says. "Seriously, get down here. I can only cover for you for so long."

I let out a long breath. "I'm on my way," I say before hanging up.

There aren't many things that could get me to change directions when my head is like this. In fact, there's only one—Grayson Nicole Everlasting, Gray to me, heir apparent to the family business, the golden child to my black sheep, and the best big sister I could ever ask for. Not that I'd admit that last part. She's got a big enough head as it is.

I hit the bottom of the stairs, and Gray texts again to make sure I'm coming, the buzzing phone equal parts accusation and encouragement. I drag the heavy door open, focusing on the pinch of the mask's elastic strap behind my ears and the prick of the feather in my hand to keep from freaking out even more. The sound of slot machines and the smell of cigarettes waft through the air, and I try not to cough.

My parents don't usually bring me along to this stuff, since I kind of suck at being social, something that seems to frustrate my dad on a cellular level. But once a year, FabCon comes around, and with The Geekery being its biggest sponsor, my dad insists our presence is required. So Mom and I fly in from the Seattle house and he drives over from Connecticut with Gray, and we all fake being a happy little family for seventy-two torturous hours.

I skirt around the edge of the casino floor on my way to the convention center, holding my breath, with a smile pasted on my face. Mom spent the whole plane ride reminding me to hold it together in front of her Very Important Friends and to not piss off my father, so that is THE GOAL. All caps. Because I would give anything for this fake family reunion to be real, for just once my dad's hand on my shoulder to not pinch.

I take a long, deep breath when I finally cross into the no-smoking area—god, I hate cigarettes—and come to a stop in the hallway outside of FabCon prom, undoubtedly the most ridiculous part of this whole weekend.

There's a giant banner on the wall with my family's logo under the words PROUDLY SPONSORED BY written in the biggest letters imaginable. I don't know whether to tear it down or high-five it. Everything my father does is big, bigger than big, like a superhero from one of his favorite books. You kind of have to respect it.

"Ridley!" my sister calls, leaning over the railing the bouncer put up. She's dressed like—I don't even know. Poison Ivy, I think, but with a masquerade mask, I guess. Not like I'm in any position to judge. What did that other girl call me? Office Batman? Cool, cool, cool.

"Get in here before Allison tells Dad you were late," she says, frantically waving me over. She's right, but I roll my eyes anyway.

Allison Silverlake is Dad's assistant, spy, and latest hookup. Like it's not even a secret; he literally moved her into the Connecticut house with him. When my mom heard the news, she just raised an eyebrow and said, "Really, Mark," mildly exasperated, like he had called to tell her he got a speeding ticket or forgot the milk or something. I assumed finding out your husband of twenty years was shacking up with his mistress in your old family home would warrant a bigger reaction, but nah. That's not how my supremely fucked-up family rolls.

I squeeze the feather tighter between my fingers and start to head inside, but the bouncer, a big burly guy with a shaved head, puts his leg out, blocking me from getting in. "You got a ticket, kid?"

I reach into my pocket to pull out my lanyard, which says THE GEEKERY STAFF, EVENT SPONSOR in big block letters, but before I can show him, my sister reaches across his leg and grabs my arm.

"He's with me, Jake."

The bouncer drops his leg with a big smile because Gray always has that effect on people. "You all have a good night," he calls after us.

"Doubtful," I grumble, which makes her punch me in the shoulder as she pulls me through the crowd. Everybody thinks Gray is this perfect lady, but for the record, she is not. I mean, around other people, sure, but I've wrestled her over a slice of pizza before and that girl leaves bruises.

"Hey, Bats," someone calls out, and I whip my head around just in time to see the girl in the peacock dress walk by with her friend.

I want to say hi back, but *hi* seems too simple now that she's upped the ante by assigning a nickname.

thinkthinkthinkthinkthink

Calling her Mora like the character seems so formal. But what do I say? *"Hey, bird girl"*? Nope. *"Hey, Peacock . . . Lady"*? Nah. *"Hey—"* But the moment's passed, and she's still walking, and the tightness is back in my chest, and my sister is holding my wrist, which helps, but it also probably looks like she's my date. I shake my hand free, even though the loss makes my heart rate spike back up.

"Who was that?" Gray asks, stepping behind a long table. She shoves an armful of T-shirts and glow sticks at me, all adorned with THE GEEKERY in big letters, as if she expects me to go through the crowd like a proper host and hand them out. I raise my eyebrows right as the music kicks up a notch, the DJ jumping around to try to get the crowd pumped up. I can't believe how many kids are here, 150 at least, and this room isn't even that big.

Gray flashes me an apologetic look. "You're probably not up to handing those out, right? You doing okay, though?"

"Well, I haven't jumped off any houses lately, so."

"Not funny," she says, taking everything back and pulling the feather loose along with it. Gray picks it up, examining it in the purple and blue lights. "What's this?"

"Nothing," I say, snatching it from her and smoothing it into a slightly wrinkled version of its former glory.

She taps her chin, narrowing her eyes. "This wouldn't have anything to do with a certain peacock that's strutting around tonight, would it?"

"No," I say, dropping into my seat.

"Okay, great. Because I think the way you were stroking that feather just now was weirding her out."

I shove my hands under the table and scan the crowd.

She ruffles my hair. "Relax, Ridley. I'm messing with you."

"Ha, good one," I deadpan.

"I'm just saying, if you're going to become lovebirds"—she looks me up and down—"or lovebats, you need to step up your game. As in, like, put the feather down and at least say hi back when she talks to you."

"I'm not going to be love anything, with anyone, ever again," I grumble.

"Ridley . . ."

"Don't you have shit to hand out? God forbid a single person doesn't have something with our company name on it."

"Don't be like that."

"Can we just get through this night so Allison tells Dad I was here? Where is he, anyway?"

"You know him." She shrugs. "Always someone to schmooze at our events."

"Right, so why don't you follow in his footsteps. You'll be the delightful hostess, I'll watch the table, and we'll never mention my personal life again."

Gray rolls her eyes. "She wouldn't have talked to you if she wasn't at least a little bit curious."

"She didn't talk to me; she called me Bats."

"Same thing."

"Drop it, Gray," I say, because my leg is already bouncing as fast as it can go, and if she keeps it up, it might bounce right through the table.

"Fine." But then she scrunches up her nose, and oh no, I know that look. I hate that look. It's the look she gets when she thinks she's being clever.

She unties a balloon from the table, grabs a bunch of free-soda coupons and glow sticks, and pushes herself out into the crowd. And okay, maybe I was wrong. Maybe it was just her "time to get down to work" look. Maybe I can survive the next two hours in relative peace and then hightail it back up to my room without any more drama. Maybe I'll do such a good job that tomorrow I'll get invited to breakfast with my father . . . and maybe tomorrow pigs will fly.

I slouch in my chair. The bass line rumbles through my chest like an extra heartbeat, and I dig my fingers into my knees, reminding myself that I'm here and Gray's right over there and it's all okay. Someone comes to the table, and I shove some coupons and a glow stick at them, grateful for the distraction.

I spot my sister weaving through the crowd again. She looks over and gives me a little wave, and I know, I *know* whatever is coming next, I'm not going to like it. And shit, there she goes, right up to that girl in the feather dress, handing her the balloon and some coupons and leaning toward her ear.

Peacock girl—Peak, I decide, is the name I would have settled on if I'd thought of it when she first walked by—laughs and my heart twists. Peak and Gray talk for a bit, a few pointed looks cast in my direction. I slink lower in my seat, fiddling with a glow stick. I don't realize Gray's come back until she kicks my chair.

"Hey," she says, dropping into the seat beside me.

"What was that about?" I shout over the din of the music.

"I told her I was your sister."

"What?"

"I told her I was your sister," she shouts even louder.

"No, I heard you. I meant why."

"So she didn't think I was your date."

I tilt my head, glaring at her and swallowing hard. "What did you do?"

"Look." She points toward the middle of the dance floor. I can't see Peak anymore, but I see the yellow balloon bobbing along over the crowd like a latex buoy on an ocean of sweaty teens. "I just gave her the balloon so she'd be easier to spot. I thought it would make you feel better if she couldn't sneak up on you."

My anxiety kicks back up a few notches as Peak gets closer to the exit. "She's leaving, Gray." I shouldn't feel so disappointed, but I do.

dosomethingdosomethingdosomethingdosomething

Gray cranes her neck, leaning over the table to see better. "I don't think she is."

The balloon disappears, and now I'm standing up and leaning too. I watch Peak take a Sharpie from the bouncer and scribble something on it, and then she looks over at me and smiles.

I turn toward my sister, my eyes going wide. "What else did you say to her? Jesus, Gray, what did you do?"

"Okay, okay, I may have also mentioned that you could probably use a little encouragement." She scrunches up her shoulders. "Sorry?"

"I'm gonna kill you."

"Are you, though? Look."

I follow her gaze to where Peak stands. Over her head bobs the bright yellow balloon again . . . only now there's a crudely drawn bat in the center of it.

"What the hell is she doing?"

"Flashing you the Bat-Signal, dumbass. And it's friggin' cute." My sister laughs, giving me a shove. I stumble a little, my heart pounding in my chest, in my feet, in my tongue. The music isn't helping. Not at all.

"Go," my sister shouts behind me, and I do.

I do.

CHAPTER THREE

Jubilee

I FEEL RIDICULOUS holding this balloon, especially when it looks like he's desperate for an escape hatch, but there's less than twenty-four hours left at this con, and as much as I've been trying to "push my boundaries," I'm still con-crushless.

As a chronic overachiever, I will not be satisfied unless I check off every box on Jayla's list. As a chronic worrier, I don't want to leave any stone unturned on the off chance everyone's right and my music *can* be cured by a weekend of costumes, crushes, and tasting food I didn't even know existed before now.

For a second, Jayla was all "nope, no way, not this one, you can do way better than a skinny white kid in a crappy mask," but she got on board fast when his sister came over trying to talk him up. Jayla has a soft spot for awkward nerds, even if this one does happen to be a boy.

Plus, Bats is the only person in this entire place who's made my heart do a somersault. Also, bonus points to him for being bashful.

I pull at a little piece of my hair that came loose and wait for him to make his move. After an eternity, he comes over, practically destroying his lip with his teeth. The fact that he's so flighty somehow makes this whole interaction seem like more of an accomplishment than it probably should, but I like it.

I say hi, and he says something I can't hear over the music. I laugh and say, "What?"

He leans in even closer. "I said, 'Nice balloon.'"

And the way his breath brushes against my neck sends a little spark down to my toes. He smells like clean skin and soap and expensive deodorant that probably doesn't use half-naked women in its ads. He leans back, and I'm standing there slightly flushed over this good-smelling boy in a cheesy Batman mask. It's kind of ridiculous. I get a little dizzy off the whiteness of his teeth when he smiles, and all my plans go out the window, replaced by a song instead.

"Dance with me?" I say, or shout, really, over the music. He shakes his head, and I arch an eyebrow, surprised and a little confused. He stares down at his shoes, Checkerboard Old Skool Vans that look brand-new. He doesn't say anything else, and an awkwardness settles over us until I can't take it anymore.

"I'm gonna—" I say, gesturing vaguely in the direction I came from. He's worrying his lip again, and this isn't going how I expected, so it seems safer to just melt back into the crowd, preserving his piano fingers and stolen glances for my music and not having them spoiled by the reality of the boy behind them.

I turn and dance my way toward where I last saw Jayla. She was singing along with a group of girls on the edge of the stage, flexing her ability to build a squad from scratch in five seconds flat. She's not where I left her, though, and I stop quick to reorient myself in the crowd. Someone thumps against me and I nearly tip over, thanks to these damn shoes. I spin around to shout . . . but it's Bats standing sheepishly behind me. I crinkle my forehead. I'm usually a better judge of character than this, and now he's thrown me twice in the span of three minutes. He shrugs and flashes a shy smile behind his mask, a single dimple appearing and disappearing on his left cheek. It shouldn't work but it does.

There's a break in the music then, DJs switching out or something, and the room goes eerily quiet before bursting with conversations. Finally, we can hear each other. Sort of.

"Can we just—?" He gestures toward the exit, and I raise my eyebrows.

"Are you trying to get me alone?"

"Yes," he says, completely serious. "I hate crowds."

"If you hate crowds, why did you come to prom?" I ask, but then the music picks up again. People crowd all around us, jostling us with their dancing. He looks exceptionally uncomfortable. "Fine."

I nab the edge of his sleeve and pull him along behind me. He stiffens at first but relaxes into it when I shift our path over to the door. I let my fingers slip lower, smiling when we link our hands.

"No reentry," the bouncer says, lifting his foot up across the aisle, and okay, there goes my plan to come back and dance, I guess. I glance behind me and see Jayla, but she's talking and laughing with a group of cosplayers we met today. It'll be faster to just text her when I get out in the hall.

"Got it," I say, shifting past.

Bats drops my hand once we're out of the room. His kind of hovers for half a second, like he doesn't know what to do with it, before he shoves it into his pocket. I walk a little farther down the hall, but now we're almost to the lobby, which is nearly as busy and loud as where we just left.

"This way." He tilts his head toward a nearby hallway.

"I'm not going to your room," I say, because away from the music and the lights, it's becoming clear that—pushing the boundaries or not—this was not my best idea. Flirting in a relatively supervised crowded room is one thing; disappearing into a casino with a stranger in a mask is another.

"I'm not asking you to," he says. "There's this lounge thing around the corner. It's usually pretty empty."

Empty. Empty is a double-edged sword for any girl. I mean, on the one hand, it lowers the risk of my parents seeing me—let's be honest, if they walk by right now, I'm toast—but also, I don't know this guy. Like at all.

Maybe I'm just being paranoid or maybe this is what Jayla means when she says I'm afraid to take risks. Worse comes to worst, I could probably stab him with these shoes—which are killing my feet, by the way—plus there's pepper spray in my clutch. Mom doesn't let me leave home without it.

"One sec," I say, holding up a finger. I pull out my phone and fire off a text to Jayla, letting her know I left and who I'm with, and reminding her that his sister is running the merch table.

She writes back almost immediately: **OK, check in when you get where you're going so I know.**

"Ready?" I ask, sliding my phone back in my purse, and he nods, pushing off the wall he was leaning against, the one covered with a giant ad for The Geekery. I fight the urge to flip it off but can't manage to hold back the scowl.

"Everything okay?" Bats asks, following my gaze.

"Yeah, sorry, I know that's your boss or whatever. Gotta love our corporate overlords, right?" That's about as polite as I can be about our enemy number one.

It was bad enough when The Geekery was just famous for running indie shops out of business, but now that they're actively trying to take over comic lines like Vera's too—just, yikes. I didn't even know it was possible to hate something so much.

Plus, Vera and The Geekery's owner-slash-CEO, Mark Everlasting—by the way, could his name *be* any more pretentious?—have been trading barbs every chance they get since they paneled together a few cons ago. The moderator made some comment about them repping both sides of the industry and asked if they would ever collaborate. Mark said he would definitely be open to bringing her on board, and she responded by literally laughing in his face . . . which he deserved. I mean, if Vera is the Princess Leia of the comics scene, then he's Palpatine for sure. But yeah, her reaction went a little bit viral, and now their mutual dislike has ramped up to a full-on war.

"Come on," Bats says, pulling me away from the sign and leading me down the hallway.

CHAPTER FOUR

Ridley

THE LOUNGE AREA is nice and empty, which is good considering we're a peacock and apparently a middle-management bat. I found this place the other night when I was stress-pacing around the hotel and have been sporadically hiding out here ever since. Other than hotel employees or a few random stragglers, no one ever comes in.

I drop down into an oversized red velvet chair, and she sinks into the one beside me, kicking off her shoes and tucking her feet up underneath her. She's sort of half sitting on her knees thanks to the tightness of her dress, and I try not to stare at the way the slit on her thigh creeps up a little higher than it's meant to. I squeeze my eyes shut, trying not to be a creeper.

dontstaredontstaredontstaredont

My hands are all sweaty, which is the only reason I let go of hers in the first place, and I rub them on my jeans, trying to be discreet. I'm trying to be as casual and seem the least freaked out as possible, but.

"Are you going to take that off?" She flicks my mask, dragging my attention back to her face.

"I don't think so?" I say. I don't mean it as a question, and yet. She kind of makes a face, and a fresh round of self-consciousness washes over me. "I can, if you need me to."

"I don't know if I *need* you to—"

"Okay, great," I say, and she makes another kind-of-confused face that makes me feel like I missed something. And I probably have. I miss a lot when my head is spinning out with nerves like this.

"Are you ever going to answer me, though?"

I scrunch up my face; didn't I just?

"How'd you end up at the prom if you hate crowds so much?"

Oh. That. I shrug. I could tell her the truth, that it's my father's event and my deep-seated insecurity about my place in my family has left me desperate for approval and validation that never comes, but that seems too heavy to drop on someone whose only real conversation with me so far has been when I said "Nice balloon" and she said "What?"

Time to deflect.

"Why'd you leave if you love it so much?" I don't mean to be blunt, but I also really want to know.

"I wanted to talk to you more," she says like it's no big deal. Like she didn't just dump a shit ton of dopamine right into my brain, making it hard to think.

"Same," I lie, or half lie, really, because it seems like the right thing to say, but also because in this moment I can almost believe it's that simple.

dontfuckthisupdontfuckthisup

I shake my head a little, and she leans forward to catch my eye.

"Are you okay?"

My leg is bouncing again, the urge to run nearly overwhelming, but this is fine, I'm fine, I got this. But man, it would be nice if my bullshit could come off a little more low-key.

"Yeah," I say, but my voice sounds strange. She sets her hand on my knee, and I jerk it away, not because I want to, but because I have to. "I just get—I don't know. Sorry." I feel my cheeks heat furiously and pray my mask is hiding it.

"Hey," she says, and I snap my eyes to hers. I should have just gone to my room. I should have never tried to pull this off. I— "Did you know that peacocks are omnivores?" she asks, and that shuts my brain up real quick.

"Huh?"

"They're omnivores. Most people think they just eat seeds and vegetables and stuff, but they eat bugs and frogs and anything they can catch, really. And they roost in trees so that tigers don't get them while they sleep."

"Okay?" I sort of say-ask, narrowing my eyes.

"Did you also know that bats have belly buttons?"

"What are you talking about?" And it's possible I found the one person on this earth who's even weirder than I am, because what?

"They do; they have belly buttons because they're mammals, not birds. In fact, not only that, but they're the only mammals capable of powered flight. Pretty wild, eh?"

"They have belly buttons?" I ask, tilting my head. I have no idea what's happening right now, but the idea of bats flying around with little bat belly buttons is somehow both cute and disturbing.

"Yep," she says, and the smile is back, that goddamn smile. And that's when I realize my leg has stopped bouncing and I can breathe again. This weird-ass girl and her random facts just talked me down from the mother of all panic attacks. That's . . . new.

I take a long breath and catch her eye again. "Thanks," I mumble. "Like, a lot."

"For schooling you about bats and birds?" She ducks her head. "You're welcome, I guess."

"No, for—"

She waves me off. "My mom used to tell me random facts whenever I got nervous before recitals. We had a giant book of weird facts she'd cart around—worked like a charm every time."

"Recitals?"

"It's a long story. So, was it the dancing or the crowds?"

"Crowds." I wince. "But I also can't dance."

"Can't or don't?"

I shrug. "Is there a difference?"

"There's definitely a difference." She laughs and pulls her phone out of her tiny purse thing. "Hang on, I promised Jayla I'd tell her where we went. If I don't, she'll have the police swarming the place. So, if you're, like, a secret murderer or whatever and this was all a trap, you should probably just go now."

"I'm not," I say, trying hard not to overthink the fact that it's probably exactly what a secret murderer would say. "But I'm in awe that you essentially implemented a dead man's switch during our two-minute walk to this lounge. Very impressive."

"Yeah, well, I'm nothing if not resourceful." She smiles again, and it's a little bit contagious. "You have a dimple," she says, like it's something new and noteworthy.

"Nothing gets past you," I answer, and then bite the inside of my cheek. Was that rude? I was going for playful. Did she think it was rude? She probably did. I should stop talking. I should go.

"I like it," she says, and leans forward to poke her finger in it. I pull back, not because I don't like it. I just . . . wasn't expecting her to touch me.

"Sorry." She shoves her hands under her knees, and no, no, don't make that face. It was fine, maybe. I don't know. But nothing really comes out, so I just sort of shrug.

"You're fine," I say after too long because I'm awful at this. "It just caught me off guard."

"I find it hard to believe that you're ever off guard."

"I'm trying to be. Right now, anyway." I shake my head again. "I suck at meeting new people, sorry." Wow, nice, Ridley, nothing says flirting like dumping your social anxiety all over someone you just met.

"Same," she says, which seems fake, but okay. She waves her hand in front of me. "I'm digging this whole shy, stammering thing you have going on, if that helps you relax any."

I laugh; I can't help it. "You are definitely the first person who's ever said that."

"Well, it's true."

I narrow my eyes, looking for any hint that she's lying, and finding none. "I'm really glad you lost that feather."

"I'm really glad you picked it up." She leans forward and flicks the side of my mask again.

And I know she wants me to take it off. Hell, I even sort of want to take it off—like it's probably really fucking weird that I haven't—but it still feels safer in here. Like I'm watching it unfold somehow. Like maybe there's a chance I won't overanalyze every second of this conversation after it's over, because it happened to Office Batman instead of shithead Ridley. Also, I probably have those annoying red indents all over my face from wearing it all night, so.

We sit in silence for a second, just looking at each other—her through her feathers and me through my mask—but it doesn't feel weird. It feels . . . nice? Until she clears her throat and sits a little straighter, and I stare down at my shoes, willing my foot not to tap.

"How did you end up working for Satan's Comics with your sister tonight? Is it some kind of, like, sibling purgatory program or something?" she asks. "Did you do something really awful?"

"Satan's Comics?"

"Sorry, sorry, The Geekery." She rolls her eyes. " 'Satan's Comics' is just our little family nickname for it."

My stomach tenses. Right, she hates us, like everyone

else. Shit, even I do, and I own shares. Or will own shares someday. Maybe. If I'm in the will. Which I might not be, actually, but. "They aren't that bad, are they?"

"Oh my god." She frowns. "They've brainwashed you. Don't worry, I can help. Hurry, let's run away together. I'll introduce you to some real artists and a good comic shop, and we'll do our best to deprogram you before our evil overlords ever find out."

I do this snort-chuckle thing that I will definitely be cringing over for the rest of my life and shake my head. "Come on, they can't be as terrible as all that."

"You poor thing," she says, clutching her heart in mock horror. "Yes, they are. Do you know how many people they've put out of business? Not to mention the sort of events they promote." She makes a gagging face. "Plus, the way they go after Vera Flores now. I mean, come on."

Shit. Of course she would know about that—she's dressed as one of Vera's characters. She's probably as big a fan of hers as I am. If this girl finds out who my dad is, I'm totally screwed.

thinkthinkthinkthinkthink

"They do a lot of charity work," I point out, which sounds pathetic, but.

"Probably just for the PR," she says, which, fair. I should probably care that she's trash-talking my family's legacy, but the way she gets all animated and her eyes get all sparkly while she rants is a little bit addicting.

"Seriously, if you ever want to run away . . ." She laughs.

"Watch out, I might take you up on that," I say, the words just slipping out, and she smiles the kind of smile you can't fake, with the tip of her tongue sneaking out between her teeth. And I feel happy and sad at the same time and wish I was anyone else, because anyone else would be going in for the kiss right now, and I'm just sitting here staring.

Her phone dings. She reads a text message and frowns. "Shit. I have to go."

"You do?" I ask, trying to swallow the disappointment that's building like bile in my throat.

waitwaitwaitplease

Music starts playing—violins, maybe?—and it takes me a second to realize it's her ringtone. Which is surprising. I don't know what I expected, really, but I guess not classical music.

"Hello?" she says, wincing as she answers her phone. "Mom, I'm fine. . . . No. No! You do not have to come find me. Why are you even at the prom? . . . Uh-huh, sure, drink tickets, I completely believe that. I'm fi—okay, okay! Ten minutes? . . . Fine, five. Five. I'll be there. . . . Love you too. Bye."

"Everything okay?"

"Apparently, my mom showed up at the prom to 'give me drink tickets' and was pissed that I left without telling her, so now I have five minutes to make it to my room before I'm grounded for life."

I scratch the back of my neck, guilt turning it crimson. "I didn't mean to get you in trouble."

sorrysorrysorryyoucangopleasestay

"You didn't," she says, raising an eyebrow. "I knew what I

was doing when I left. This was basically an experiment anyway, so there was bound to be a learning curve."

"Experiment?"

whattheactualfuck

"Yeah, it's called 'stepping outside of my comfort zone.' You should try it." She pulls a pen out of her purse and scrawls some numbers up my arm. "Text me. Okay? I'm here all day tomorrow. I'll be working a booth, but maybe I can sneak out for lunch or something."

"Okay," I say, and then she leans forward and kisses me quick on the cheek before grabbing her shoes. I sit there stunned, my stomach doing a little flip as she runs off.

holyshitholyshitHOLYSHIT

CHAPTER FIVE

Jubilee

"GET UP," VERA says, flinging the curtains open wide so the sunlight slaps me in the face. I guess I'm still in trouble for yesterday. She's probably been hearing it all night since technically she's the one who went to bat for me. Still, this reversal of my parents' usual good cop/bad cop roles is slightly unsettling.

"I'm up, I'm up," I say, dropping my arm over my eyes. Jayla groans from the other bed. A quick glance at my phone tells me it's only eight a.m. "Why am I up, though?" I moan. The only time I willingly get up early on a Sunday is for string quartet . . . and this is not that.

"Because VIP hours start at eight thirty, and your mother and I decided that you will be helping us with that today, thanks to that stunt you pulled. God, Jubilee, what were you thinking? You know better than that. I trusted you to be where you said you were going to be."

Trust. Vera is huge on trust, and I definitely feel a little bit bad that she sees this as a violation of that . . . but also, come on. "I didn't go far, and Jayla knew where I was. I was being safe!" I push up onto my elbows. There are feathers and streaks of makeup on my pillow, and I don't even want to imagine what I look like right now.

Last night, I collapsed into my bed and fell asleep after spending an hour being lectured about everything, even though Jayla was still up watching *American Murderer*. We didn't even have time to dissect my speed date with Bats or the fact that—judging by the crown she came home with—she definitely won prom queen . . . and we probably won't until the car ride home either. Not if my parents keep this up all day.

"Safe? Safe is not wandering around a casino full of drunks by yourself late at night."

"I wasn't alone!"

"Oh, you think leaving with a strange boy makes it better?" Vera asks, turning to face me, and I realize my mistake too late. "Do you know how badly that could have gone for you last night? You just happily followed some rando out to a deserted hotel lounge! You could have been killed!"

"I said I was sorry." I groan, flipping the blankets back and storming into the bathroom. "What else do you want me to do? It was a bad decision. I get it!"

I slide the door shut and flip the shower on, hoping Vera will take the hint. A solitary feather still clings stubbornly to my eyelid, and it dangles in my line of vision with every blink. I pull it off and set to work wiping off the smeared green eye shadow, which is currently making me look like some kind of disco panda or something.

I step under the spray of the shower, trying to shove out the thoughts of how badly the night ended in favor of how well it began. Bats was so cute and nervous, and I've always had a weakness for dimples.

Jayla walks into the bathroom, letting out the steam and bringing a blast of cool air in with her. She flushes the toilet, scorching me under the water.

"Jayla!" I shriek.

"Sorry." She yawns. "Forgot."

I flick off the water and reach my hand out for a towel, which she tosses at me, and then she goes back to brushing her teeth. "Was it worth it?" she mumbles around her toothbrush.

I wrap the towel around myself and then grab a second one for my hair. "Was what worth it?"

"You and Office Batman."

"Maybe," I say, trying and failing to keep the grin off my face. Her forehead crinkles as I dart past her to get dressed.

"Oh my god." She spins around. "Another *boy*?" she teases. "That's two in a row, Jubi."

"I'm allowed to like boys," I remind her, tugging on my leggings.

"Technically, no one should be allowed to like boys," she says, grabbing her own clothes off a hanger and dropping them onto the bed. "But you do you."

"Stop it," I snort.

"Jubi, I love you and always will, but boys are gross. Don't come crying to me when he's all sweaty and smelly and just wants to talk about bacon and hot girls and Axe body spray."

"Okay, but that's like half of *our* conversations now." I laugh.

"We do not talk about Axe body spray," she says, looking scandalized.

"But the rest—"

"It's different." She smirks.

And it is. Sorta. I mean, not the bacon thing. I'm pretty sure straights and queers have the same proclivity toward bacon. Probably. I can't say for sure, though. Neither of us are straight, technically. Jayla has a strict no-boys-allowed policy, and I'm . . . flexible on the topic. I haven't really put a label on it. I've only had one real boyfriend and I've never actually dated a girl, but I've had some pretty serious crushes, plus that one brief and glorious make-out session with Kai, Nikki's ridiculously hot nonbinary cousin. There are just certain things that make me turn my head, regardless of who they're attached to. Like, I'm endlessly fascinated by dimples and good hugs and people who can surprise me—which Bats did last night, repeatedly.

I'd be lying if I said I wasn't hoping to run into him today. But still, something nags at me that I can't quite put my finger on. I know Jayla was just joking about the two-boys-in-a-row thing, but a part of me is still wondering, *Is that okay?* I know I like more than just boys, but does it count if I haven't seriously dated anyone but?

CHAPTER SIX

Ridley

I KEEP HOPING she'll come by. That she'll run up to the booth and find me, with a big grin on her face. That the spark from last night will catch fire, burning down everything around us. That satellites will fall, wars will end, and life will become infinitely less shitty.

But it doesn't go like that.

In fact, I don't see Peak at all, just an endless stream of people asking if we're out of the con-exclusive Funko Pop. Which, yes, so stop.

I consider texting her anyway, cracking some joke about her just being in it for the Bat-Perks. I even pull my phone out of my pocket, my fingers curled tightly around it, her number burning up my arm where the ink stains my skin. It's right there, and she's right here, somewhere. I could try to find her or hit send on my phone or do anything to push down that first domino, but I don't.

Because it's pointless. Tonight, I'll be with my mom on

a plane back to our Seattle house, and . . . she'll be off to god knows where.

I hate Seattle. It's dreary and damp, and despite living there for years, I don't really know anybody. I had someone, a good friend, actually, okay, more like an almost boyfriend, but that . . . didn't work out. And Mom's never home, too busy running the West Coast offices, so I just sit in a house with too many windows, watching anime alone. It will never feel like home the way the Connecticut house did before my "incident," as my family calls it. The irony that I survived a backflip off the roof, only to lose my whole life anyway in the form of a cross-country "fresh start," is not lost on me.

Dad still lives in the old house, with Gray in an apartment nearby. They're only an hour or so away from this con, and every time I do this one, a part of me hopes we'll skip the hotel rooms and stay at home, or at least that he'll invite me back for dinner or something, but nope.

So yeah, it's pointless.

But also, maybe it isn't.

I let my mind wander, imagining what it would be like to get up and find Peak myself. To not cower in my dad's shadow, waiting for whatever happens next. I shove up my sleeve and jab her number into my phone, typing out a text message: **It was nice meeting you last night.**

Oh Jesus fuck. It was nice meeting her last night? Why did I go with that? I drop my phone onto the table in front of me and run my hands over my eyes.

stupidstupidstupidstupidstupidstupidstupid

My phone vibrates and my breath catches, the tiniest

bit of hope forcing its way into my chest. Maybe she liked my message. Maybe she's into awkward losers with anxiety issues. Maybe.

I flip it over only to see a text from my mother with my flight information. There's a forced apology saying that she'll be coming on a slightly later flight but she's arranged a car for me when I land in Seattle. It's fine. I mean, it's not, but it has to be. Yay, three-hour layover in a strange airport by myself.

I stare down at the screen for a few more seconds, waiting just in case. Allison crosses her arms and frowns at me from the other side of our giant corner booth. I flash her the most sarcastic smile I can muster. "I'm taking a break," I say.

"A break from what, staring at your phone?"

I scratch the side of my eye with my middle finger and walk away. My dad catches it and narrows his eyes—because of course this would all go down during the one moment he deigns to show up at the booth instead of schmoozing in the casino—and god, can I just not disappoint him for five seconds?

His jaw ticks as he walks toward me, and shit, this is going to be bad. This is going to be really bad. Dad's temper is never that great, but Dad's living-in-a-casino-and-partying-around-the-clock-for-three-days temper is next level. As in, last year he made half our teardown team cry because they parked to the right of the loading dock and he said to park on the left, so.

But right when he gets to me, right as he opens his mouth to let me know exactly how much of a fuckup I am . . .

one of his buddies walks up, and Dad's whole demeanor changes. His face softens and he looks welcoming, almost happy, as he clamps his hand onto the other man's shoulder and says, "Chuckie, where have you been hiding?" And off they go back out to the casino. To the casino *bars*, more accurately.

And okay, nice. Crisis averted, I guess? As long as I don't think too much about how he must not even care enough to yell. It's fine. It's whatever. It's not like today can get any shittier anyway. I have a long flight alone ahead of me, and Peak never texted me back or even came to see me—unless she did, and that's why she's not writing back, which sucks worse. And what right does Allison have to question me, anyway? I'm an Everlasting, at least by blood, and she's just my father's latest lay. So yeah, maybe I flip her off again, just once more, as I disappear into the mass of people around us.

For once, I think I have something better to do.

• • •

The crowd in the convention center is suffocating, all the jostling and the pushing, and there are so many crying kids because Sundays are always half-price family day. My breathing picks up, and I start mapping my escape routes, fighting my urge to run. But I'm a man on a mission right now: I'm gonna finally talk to my comics idol, Vera Flores.

I've been too chickenshit to ever approach her before, double so now that she's officially my dad's nemesis or whatever. But having a cute girl dressed as one of Vera's characters tell me I should try stepping out of my comfort zone kind of felt like a sign. And judging by the fact said girl didn't return my text, it clearly wasn't a sign that she and I were meant to be.

So maybe it meant this.

Peak said it was an *experiment*. Like going to meet Vera is an experiment, one that currently has me on the verge of hyperventilating on the showroom floor, but.

I squeeze my hands until my nails pinch into my palm, and then cut a corner toward Artist Alley. The booths are smaller there than over on the vendor side, more crammed together. It's where all the artists and writers sit, clamoring for attention and shouting things like "Hey, you like scary books?" There are a bunch of Marvel and DC dinosaurs all in a row, and a pile of indie artists across from them. I stop at a table with a giant squirrel banner, which, okay, weird, but I take a bookmark anyway.

I relax a little when I finally see it.

Her banner is large but unassuming. It's got the cast of *Fighting Flock* in an action pose and her name written across the top in block letters. I take a breath, hold it, and then exhale. I got this. I can walk up to her and tell her that she's amazing and that her newest comic about an immortal teenage superhero who just wants to stop, to rest, to be done, speaks to me on a level that no book ever has.

dontscrewthisup

Vera Flores—well, Vera Flores-Jones since her wedding a couple years ago—has been my favorite person on the scene for a long time, even before her newest book.

43

Everything she puts out is super diverse and often queer as fuck, which I guess is to be expected when the business is run by a gay Latinx, but still. She is the future personified, and I love her for it. And I'm intimidated by it. And technically, she's the enemy and my dad would kill me if he found out I was over here. Which is why I'm standing back and gnawing the shit out of my lip, watching her line move without me in it.

This should be easier, I think. As the kid whose parents own one of the biggest comic-store chains in the country, the son of "the man who helped make comics mainstream," I should be able to meet anyone, right? Like, I shouldn't be so goddamn freaked out right now. Sometimes, sometimes I can. I've eaten pizza with the guy who plays Captain America in the movies, brought water to the people who created Ms. Marvel, shown Stan Lee and his assistant where the bathroom is. So yeah, I should be able to. Except.

Except.

Vera Flores-Jones is different. She makes her own way and tells stories that actually say something, that actually *matter* to me. She's the self-made person that my dad pretends to be, and he'll always hate her for that, but I don't. I could never.

"Hey, kid, you okay?" someone asks. It's the artist across from Vera, and he looks a little worried.

"Yeah, great," I say. "I'm just in the middle of an existential crisis because I disappointed the one person whose approval I'm most desperate for, and I met a girl who won't text me back, and tonight I have to fly across the country by myself, and I'm spiraling into a deep depression, and my anxiety disorder is *not* helping with that. How are you?"

"Uh, good?" he says, and wow, yeah, I've got to get that whole trauma-dumping thing under control.

"Awesome," I say. "Well, I'm just gonna get back to it, then." The guy gives me a confused nod, and I inch closer to the edge of Vera's table to check out the prints she's selling. I linger as long as I can without making it weird, before slotting myself in line behind the others. I'm three people away and still torn on my print—a fish guy with some girl underwater or a creepy clown—when somebody gently pushes past me.

"Sorry, excuse me, sorry," she says, not even looking at me, and holy shit, it's Peak. Of course she'd be here; she's probably the biggest Vera Flores fan on the planet, based on her cosplay last night.

And I didn't even get to talk to her about it last night, since I was so busy freaking out. I bet she even has the original Kickstarter editions of the books like I do, I bet she's memorized half the comic scripts, I bet she knows it all. And I swear to god I will drop to one knee and beg her to leave with me right now if she'd only turn around and recognize me—even if she did cut in line.

Except Peak doesn't stop in front of the table when she gets to it; she goes behind it and hands Vera a bottle of Gatorade and a protein bar. It's almost my turn at the table, and I don't know what is happening, and now I can't decide whether to walk away or pray she looks up.

"Mom said to make sure you eat something. Do you want me to watch the table for a while so you can take a break?

I can tell people to come back later," Peak says like it's no big deal. Like she isn't sitting beside *the* Vera fucking Flores.

"No, baby, it's fine. We only have a couple hours left; tell her I'm good. I will take this, though, thanks." Vera nabs the protein bar and turns back to the man in front of her table. I shift so I'm slightly hidden behind him and try to discreetly observe Peak.

She sits at the table for a minute, messing with the Sharpies and restocking some of the prints while Vera talks to the fan in front of her. She asks Vera again if she's sure, and Vera waves her off with a good-natured shove, telling her to quit hovering and go back to the vendor booth in case they need help. I watch their easy interaction, a little confused. Is Peak a con volunteer? An intern of Vera's?

I cut out of the line to follow her. Yes, I am missing my big opportunity to talk to Vera, but what do they say about never meeting your idols? Plus, this is important. I'll never stop obsessing if I don't get to the bottom of the mystery. It's not that I'm being a stalker by following her; I just want to see where she's going.

dontbecreepydontbecreepydontbecreepy

Maybe it is stalkery. I don't know. What does it matter, anyway? I'll be on a plane in six hours and never see her again. I just want to know how she fits. The peacock dress probably would have won the prom cosplay contest if she hadn't ditched with me. And I had assumed she was just a fan. But now.

But now?

She waves at a couple other artists as she walks by, and okay, weird, how does she know them? They're big artists too, Vera's level or higher, and they're waving at her like they're old friends. She's got to be an intern or something. Vera probably introduced her. Wait. What if she's not an intern—what if she's an apprentice who draws similarly kick-ass comics? Be still, my heart. Maybe she's beautiful *and* nice *and* talented. That should be illegal. It's not fair to the rest of us drudges. But Jesus.

I trail behind her until she walks into another booth, and then I freeze.

shitshitshitshitshitshitshitshitshitfuckshit

It's Verona Comics, the shop and publishing line that Vera owns. It's not unusual for artists—especially ones as big as Vera—to have a table in Artist Alley with everybody else and another one for their shop or publisher itself. This one appears to be carrying their old comics and toys and promoting their line.

Peak hands some change back to the woman running it, who looks so familiar. It takes me a minute to place her, and I wouldn't if I wasn't obsessed with Vera, but the woman Peak's talking to is Lillian Jones. The same Lillian Jones who supplied Vera Flores with her new and improved hyphenated last name a few years ago. She gives Peak a kiss on the cheek and Peak smiles, dropping into a chair in the corner. When I glance from Lillian to Peak, I realize that they definitely have the exact same eyes and nose.

No. I cannot be texting Vera's stepdaughter. I cannot be flirting with her. There has to be some other explanation. Maybe she's just an intern after all. An intern that Lillian . . . kisses on the cheek?

"You looking for something in particular?" I jump at the voice. It's Peak's friend with the awesome Shuri cosplay. She's in leggings and a T-shirt now, though, and looks to be around my age. Does everyone work here?

I shake my head and mumble, "Just looking," and she goes off to help the next customer. I pretend to be checking out a rack of comics but pull out my phone and google Vera instead. There are tons of pictures of her and Lillian, but I have to scroll forever to find one of their whole family. Maybe Peak's an outcast like me, which shouldn't make me feel reassured, but it does.

But then I find it, an old wedding picture that Vera posted on the Verona blog a few years ago. And there's Peak, smiling, walking them both down the aisle. The logical explanation is that Peak is . . . Vera's stepdaughter. Shit.

And I happen to know that Vera's shop isn't all that far from my dad's house. Which means Peak might not be that far from my dad's house. Which means . . . absolutely nothing. Because I'm flying back to the other side of the country tonight.

fuckfuckfuckfuckfuck

I'm still squinting at the wedding picture so hard, it's blurry from my eyelashes, when a text message scrolls down across my screen.

I don't recognize the number, but the response is unmistakable: **Hey! How goes it in the Batcave?**

I flick my eyes up, glancing at Peak, who is now staring down at her phone. I shouldn't respond. I should blend back into the crowd and forget any of this ever happened. Forget about everything but going back to grab my duffel bag and getting as far away from her as possible because this can't happen. It couldn't before, but it definitely can't now.

I look down at my phone. I mean to slide it into my pocket, I swear I do, but instead I find myself firing off another text: **Glad to see you didn't get eaten by any tigers last night, Peak.**

And as I turn to leave, my stomach in knots, I can see that she's smiling.

CHAPTER SEVEN

Jubilee

"PUT YOUR PHONE down," Jayla practically growls, swiping it out of my hand. Her car swerves a little when she leans over, and I glance behind us with a guilty look.

"Careful," I say.

We're driving back home from the con, just me and her. My parents are driving in the store van right behind us, definitely ready to scream if we so much as go a mile over the speed limit, but still, it's like being in a tiny little freedom bubble for the next hour. But if they think we're goofing off in here at all, I'm going to be back in the van, suffocating under a pile of comics, while Jayla drives alone in her little Civic.

"You're a terrible copilot. Who are you texting, anyway?"

"Nobody," I say, trying to swallow down the smile threatening to break across my face.

"You're talking to that guy again, aren't you?"

My cheeks get all warm. I hate being obvious. "Maybe." I scoop my phone up off the floor. We've been texting nonstop since he sent that endearingly formal *It was nice meeting you* text. Who even does that? It was six thousand shades of cute.

"What do you guys even talk about? The fact that he decided to go to the biggest cosplay event of the weekend dressed as Office Batman? Or the fact that it's weird people want to cosplay as a maladjusted man who dresses in a bat suit at all?"

"Close."

She glances at me out of the corner of her eye, one perfectly arched eyebrow reflected in the rearview mirror. "Really?"

"Well, close in the sense that he just texted me a picture of a baby-bat nursery."

"I'm lost."

"It's a long story."

"Try me," she snorts.

"You kind of had to be there?"

"I was across the hall, so I basically was." She sighs, messing with her septum piercing until the ball is centered. "Just tell me."

"Well, we were talking about bats having belly buttons last night—"

"As one does." She laughs.

"And then today he found a picture of an actual bat belly button, which then devolved into this whole weird sky puppy conversation and—"

"Sky puppy?"

"He didn't make up the term or anything. A lot of people call them that."

"He calls bats 'sky puppies'?" She grimaces.

"What's wrong with that?"

"I don't know. Instead of getting to know you, he's sending you bat pictures. That's weird. That's a weird thing to do, Jubilee."

I didn't think it was weird; I thought it was cute. What does she expect? I've known him for like twenty-four hours; it's not that deep. I roll my eyes. "Oh, what, is he supposed to be sending me dick pics on day one?"

She bursts out laughing, and I cross my arms. "What's so funny?"

"Nothing," she says, struggling to catch her breath. "Just that there's a whole world between baby-bat memes and dick pics, you know? Maybe you could find someone more in the middle."

"I don't really want to find anyone; this is strictly for the good of my music," I huff. "And hey, you encouraged this when I told you what this weekend was about."

Jayla messes with her stereo, plugging in her phone and pushing play. Loud music starts thumping through the speakers, making the world vibrate in her rearview mirror. I glance behind me; I can't help it.

"Relax, they veered off to get gas ten minutes ago."

"Thank god."

"You're gonna ghost this guy, though, right? The whole point of con crushes is that you leave them at the con. It doesn't really work if you don't."

"Yeah, probably," I say. "Besides, he texted me earlier that he lives in Seattle and is flying back there tonight, so it's not like we could ever be a thing anyway."

Jayla glances at me. "I thought you didn't have time for . . . things."

"I don't," I say, fumbling with my phone. "I'm just saying, even if I did—"

"Right." But then she peeks at me again, her eyebrows furrowing. "I'm starting to think you actually *like* like this boy."

"I don't even know him." I'd want to, I think, if there were enough hours in the day and he didn't live on the complete opposite side of the country. But there aren't and he does, and I have a cello to get home to.

Jayla goes back to staring at the highway. "Mm-hmm."

"I don't," I say again, not sure if I'm trying to convince her or myself.

CHAPTER EIGHT

Ridley

THE CON FINALLY ended at five, and an hour later, we're barely halfway through teardown. Dad's crew is currently boxing merchandise and running hand trucks full of comics out to the vans as fast as they can, probably hoping to escape a repeat of last year. I'm mostly standing around, chewing on my lip, trying not to combust. I'm so keyed up, I can't take it, between Peak—who I absolutely shouldn't still be texting but yet compulsively am—and trying to convince myself I don't actually care that I'm about to fly to Seattle by myself while Gray and my dad get to stay here.

I grab a box of leftover glow sticks and carry it out with the guys to the loading dock. Grayson's driving me to the airport soon, but she's still making the rounds, hugging pretty much every single person she knows—i.e., every single person still here. Most of the smaller vendors and artists are already done with teardown, just mingling with friends before they hit the road. Vera is already gone, and Peak along with her, but we've been texting nonstop since she hit the road.

My flight's not for three more hours, and I try not to think about the fact that our house is only forty-five minutes from here the way Gray drives, and I could conceivably go see it quick before hitting the airport. Not that seeing it would make it easier to leave. It would just be nice to be asked. There are so many things I want to know too, like is my room still the same, is the tree fort still there, does anybody notice I'm not around?

I slide the box into the van, frowning at my own neediness, and turn around only to be met with the sight of my dad stalking toward me, Allison in tow. His eyes are bloodshot, his forehead is creased, his mouth open and ready to yell, and this is not what I meant by wanting to be noticed. There's no way to escape without making a scene, so I just brace myself and try to remember to breathe.

I'm outside, the sun is setting, it's cold but not unbearably so, my dad is going to scream at me, and it will be okay, even if it is not okay. Radical acceptance, my ex-therapist said, is the key to life. Meet life on its terms, even if the terms are totally fucked up. I thought it was bullshit then, and I still do, but.

"If it isn't the prodigal son. Back to help now that everything's over," Dad slurs. He's drunk, probably courtesy of his pal "Chuckie." Judging by the way he keeps rubbing at his nose, probably more than drunk too.

"Hi, Dad," I say, standing a little bit taller. Hopefully this will prevent him from also yelling at me for slouching.

"Where the hell have you been? Allison told me you didn't come back until the con was over."

Of course she ratted me out. Of course. I look at the

ground to the right of him, hoping this will end quicker if I don't make eye contact.

"Did you think it didn't matter? You flip her off and disappear, and you think that's fine? After you left the goddamn prom last night too? What do you think I bring you here for? You're a brand ambassador, Ridley. I bring you here to work."

"I thought—"

"Thought what?" He takes a step closer. "You're on my time here, and I expect you to do as you're told." Each word he says is punctuated by the stab of his finger against my chest, and I flinch away from the smell of the alcohol on his breath.

itsokayevenifitsnotokayitsokayevenifitsnotokay

But that's not quite true, is it? Not when your dad is slurring insults in your ear. And it shouldn't sting when he calls me useless, and it shouldn't crack me in places I'd never say. And I'm not crying—I'm not—I'm just staring at the ground near his shoe, studying it because I want to and not because I'm scared.

imnotscared

"Look at me when I'm talking to you," he says, and I shoot my eyes to his, taking it in—the disheveled hair, the crumpled clothes, his skin wrinkled in places I've never noticed before. I don't think he's stood this close to me since I was little.

And I shouldn't still hope he'll catch himself, apologize, and hug me. I shouldn't. And even Allison—Allison, who is nearly the same age as my sister—is tugging at his shoulders and telling him to quit it now, and the guys at the loading dock have all walked away, some shooting sad glances behind them. But he doesn't stop, and I'm just standing there, pressed against the van with wide eyes, nodding while he calls me a piece of shit, like *yes, sir, you're correct.*

itsfineitsfineitsfineitsfineitsfine

Even Allison's looking at me with pity now, and good, because this is all her fault, and I rub my eyes with the palms of my hands, every word he spits a sliver shooting straight to my heart and—

icant

I want it to stop; I need it to stop. My phone buzzes in my pocket, the sensation overwhelming against my leg, and I slide it out without thinking, because, god, if ever I needed a lifeline, it's now. I hope it's Gray, but I don't even care who it is. And I realize too late that it's the exact wrong thing to do.

"Pay attention when I'm speaking to you," my father shouts, banging his hand on the side of the van, and even Allison is freaking out now, saying she'll call security if he doesn't stop. Allison, who feeds me to the wolves every chance she gets, and oh, this is bad, this is bad, and his hand is still slamming against the van, and his spit is flying in my face as he screams at me about respect and duties and obligation and how I am falling so, so short of it all. He knocks the phone out of my hand, and it skitters across the ground, and there it goes, my link to the outside world, lost and cracked. I dig my nails into my hands and scrunch my eyes shut, and I wait and wait and pray he stops.

"Allison saw you at the Verona booth, Ridley. What were you doing?" And here comes the paranoia; I should have known.

"You followed me?" I ask, and Allison looks away.

"Come on, Mark," Allison says softly. "Let's go back inside."

"What were you doing?" he asks again. "What did you tell her?"

"Nothing, I swear," I say, my voice a near whisper.

"Don't lie to me, Ridley." He leans closer, panting harsh, furious breaths, and all I see is the smudge of white powder still stuck in the corner of his nose and the hate in his eyes, and Jesus Christ. Jesus Christ, okay.

tapouttapouttapout

"I think I have an in at Verona. I was checking it out," I croak, my voice sounding tinny and garbled. Or maybe it's just that my brain feels so far removed from this situation, which is both happening to me and not, which is both okay and not. And I feel cold, so fucking cold and heavy, like my blood turned to lead, and I just need to lie down.

Dad's mouth opens and shuts, and he leans back a little. Enough that I can kinda slump down, that I can suck in air that doesn't smell like booze and fear.

"What do you mean?"

"I don't know," I say, losing my nerve. I skitter to grab my phone, but he grabs my arm, not hard enough to bruise but hard enough to hurt, and I freeze.

"What do you mean, you have an in?"

dontdontdont

But it's every man for himself in times like these, and I won't go down with this ship. Except.

Except.

Her feather burns in my pocket, and I press my lips

together in a tight line, one last-ditch effort to keep the words inside. But it's not like I'll ever see her again anyway. And she'll probably stop texting me once she's back home and busy with her real life. So if it's her or me—

He loosens his grip on my arm, rubbing it up and down, then letting it go completely and dragging his hand through his hair. He looks confused, surprised, and while his eyes are still bloodshot, he looks a little bit more like the guy I knew way back when. The guy who didn't drink so much, the guy who took me golfing that one time when I was seven and commissioned my own Venom comic for my eighth birthday. I've had enough people tell me everything happens for a reason. Maybe this is the reason. Maybe this is the way back.

itsnot

It could be, though. I flick my eyes to Allison, who's being quiet now. And my dad, he doesn't *smile* smile, but his lips turn up in the corners while he waits. "What do you mean, Ridley?"

I link my fingers behind my neck, staring at the asphalt as I say it. "I met Vera's stepdaughter at the prom. That's who I left with. We've been texting, and—"

My dad grabs my shoulders. "Does she like you?"

I shrug.

"Ridley. Ridley!" he shouts, like I just handed him the Holy Grail. "Think of how much intel you can collect for us to help with acquisitions." And he pulls me into a hug. A hug. And I can't remember the last time I had one of these, especially from him. "I could kiss you." He laughs, letting me go. And I think, *You used to once, every night before bed. What changed?* But I don't say it. I know what changed. I couldn't take the pressure, and he couldn't take the disappointment. Maybe this time I could make him proud. Maybe this time it could be different.

I wish I didn't like the way he walked me back to our booth with his arm around me. Or the way he raised my arm up in the air when we walked up to Gray, like I was some kind of champion, even though I felt ashamed and unsteady on my feet.

I wish I could say that I pushed him away and left with my integrity intact.

That I got on the plane instead of going out to dinner with him for the first time in years.

That I didn't feel a swell of pride when he asked me to sit next to him, while Grayson ended up at the other side of the table, where she couldn't hear anything.

That I didn't tear up when he asked me to stay in Connecticut with him, at the old house, in my old room, and said that Mom would have my stuff shipped out when she got back home.

Or when he promised to buy me a new phone to replace the one he just trashed.

Or when he said he had a place for me in the business, finally—on the recon team.

I wish the voice telling me that this was *wrong, bad, very terrible* was louder, and the voice weeping *finally, always, please* was quieter.

I wish.

CHAPTER NINE
Jubilee

I DRAG MY bow across the strings, glancing once at the piles of books around me—Bach's cello suites right on top—before shutting my eyes with a smile. After a weekend away, tonight I play for myself—no plan, no audition—just me and my instrument and the sounds that we make. The fingers on my left hand press and arch and slide, sending the notes curling and curving through the air until a song takes form.

It's a cover of a song from one of my favorite bands. I was still working out the notes before I abandoned it to focus on my audition, but after a few days away, "embracing and absorbing life," I'm just happy to be back.

I've been playing cello seriously since the third grade. I don't think anybody expected me to stick with it, but the first time I made it groan and squeal under the power of my inexperienced fingers, I was hooked. I was creating sound. Other people were making sounds, sure, but it wasn't *this* sound; this squeal and shriek were mine and mine alone, and only for that second.

I loved it.

I think that's my favorite part of music, the impermanence of it. A book or a painting, when it's finished, it's done. People admire it, but it's become its final form—it is what it is. But music is never finished. Every piece changes when you play it; the note has heavier vibrato in this performance or draws out every rallentando in that one. People cover it and change it and sing it with their own voices or, in my case, transcribe it to cello.

Music is different. It's alive. It's an action and a reaction all at once.

Somewhere along the line, though, that impermanence, that change, has become a source of pain instead of pride. Playing has become less about the joy of it and more about getting it exactly right: holding the notes for precisely the right amount of time, calculating it for maximum impact. I've been chained to this chair practicing my audition repertoire for months, and now, nine weeks out, instead of making it better, apparently my calculations have only made it worse.

But tonight, I don't know, I feel like playing for the joy of it. If I can figure out how to shove this feeling into my audition, then I should be set. Better than set, even. I sink back into the music with a smile. Maybe this whole pushing-the-boundaries thing worked. I play harder, feeling my acceptance to the summer program get closer with every note. But I know to really do that, I need to be perfect. Consistently.

The summer program is open to kids from all over the world, and I can't help that tiny nagging voice that sometimes creeps up in my head and says, I know I'm good, but am I good *enough*? Maybe I'm getting ahead of myself—I haven't even been formally invited to audition yet. There's a whole first round where you have to apply and send in a résumé of all your musical experience and get recommendations before they even invite you to audition. I turned it all in a few weeks ago, and now I wait.

Even if I do make the cut, the board gives out exactly one scholarship in the high school program each summer—and I need to be the one to get it. I don't know how we'll ever afford it otherwise. I've even heard my parents worrying about that late at night. So yeah, consistently perfect, that's the goal.

I don't even notice my mom is in my room until she pokes me in the shoulder. I jump, my eyes flinging open, nearly dropping my bow.

"Sorry, hon," she says, tucking some of her hair behind her ear. It's wet; it must have started raining.

"It's okay." I set my cello in its stand and stretch my arms out while I flex my fingers. "You're home early."

"Late, actually," she says. "It's almost eight. You hungry? Vera's bringing home takeout."

I'm about to say no, but then I realize I definitely am. I glance at my phone; I've been playing for four hours, a full hour longer than my usual school-night practices. "Starving, apparently."

My mom pulls her hair back with a yawn and gives my shoulder a squeeze. I know the feeling; coming home from the con last night and diving into school today wasn't fun, but it was probably worse for her, sitting in a real estate office, praying someone will wander in needing to buy a house just so she can get paid.

"I'm gonna go change," my mom says. "I'll shout when Vera gets home."

I nod and sit on my bed. My cat, HP—short for Harry Potter, don't judge me, I was eight—jumps up and starts rubbing her head against me. I scratch under her chin for a second, pulling away when she stops purring and bites me. My phone lights up with another message, and I drop onto my pillow to check everything I've missed. Jayla and Nikki have both texted me about a dozen times—both separately and on our group chat—but it's Bats's message that I click on first.

I've considered asking his real name about a hundred times in the last twenty-four hours, but he never asked mine—he just calls me Peak—and I kind of like the mystery now. He's everyone and no one, ever evolving, a living thing, like music. He is a pleasant program that lives in my phone, and I'm happy to have him.

A close-up of a baby bat's face appears on my screen, along with the caption *hello*.

I send him back two crying-laughing emojis and a heart-eye one, and I wait, a smile etched on my face, when the three dots appear.

BATS: Where ya been, Peak?

ME: Around

BATS: . . .

ME: School and stuff

BATS: School is overrated.

I snort—if only he knew he was talking to someone ranked second in her class academically (screw you, Ivy Pasternek; I'm coming for your rank next year)—and try to find the perfect meme to send back. I grin when I see it. It's a tiny bat being held down with a single finger, and the caption says, *No, stop touching me! I am the night!* I press send with a little squeal and add **you, probably**.

I wait for those three dots to come back . . . but they don't. The smile starts to slide off my face, and I wonder if I somehow actually offended him. And then I twist my lips into a full-on frown. I meant to ghost him, I did, but then I started thinking— if one weekend away from cello land could help me climb out of my musical rut this much, then imagine what text-flirting until my audition could do. Jayla didn't exactly believe me when I told her my theory; her response was something like "for the music, sure, I believe that," but still.

My phone buzzes in my hand and I grin.

BATS: More than you know.

ME: See, I'm onto you.

BATS: Let's hope not for both our sakes.

ME: You're such a dork. ☺

CHAPTER TEN

Ridley

I CLICK THROUGH the website, tallying the missing assignments as I go. Eleven. Eleven assignments will get me back on track for graduating. Less than I thought, honestly, but more than I feel like doing. Keeping up with my high school work—online only now—was one of the requirements my mom set before agreeing to let me stay here. She must not have realized I was way behind before I even left.

Which means I probably have a *very* tiny window before she calls my dad to flip out on him about the missing assignments. Which would suck. I've been tallying the good days (the mental equivalent of a chalkboard saying *It has been __ days since the last incident*) and we're at five now.

Five is a good number, actually. I'll take it, especially when it comes to my dad, who hasn't been able to decide whether to kill me or ignore me for as long as I can remember, especially since the whole Chandler McNally thing last year. I shut my laptop and head downstairs, the steps of the old Victorian creaking in a way I sort of remember. I try not to be bitter about the fact that it's been so long I don't know where to step to avoid it. It's fine.

Gray's coming over tonight to help me strategize my plan to get in good at Verona. She was shocked when Dad informed his entire team that I had an in. She doesn't know that it's Peak. Mainly because I'm pretending it's not. I can keep her separate. This is easy, this is Compartmentalizing 101, and I'm a seventeen-year-old pro at this, so yeah.

Peak is Peak. She lives in my phone. She exists in the land of memes and magical one-off nights. It's nice, and it's mine. For once, I have something that is. Especially since Mom hasn't even bothered to send me more clothes and stuff like she swore she would. She's been *busy with work*, which is whatever. So yeah, Peak. Lives in my phone. Is my secret. Is her own separate thing.

If she happens to *also* give me enough dirt to make the entirely separate person called Jubilee Jones (compartmentalizing! yay!) like me enough to share some info my dad can use, then fine. What he does with that information has nothing to do with me. At least that's what I tell myself between stomachaches. It's just business. I can have my cake and eat it too. I don't feel guilty. I don't feel anything at all. Promise.

I open up the kitchen cabinet, huffing out a breath. I asked Dad to get Fruity Pebbles and Lucky Charms at the store, but he just restocked his PowerBars and protein shakes and talked to me about how important nutrition is if I want to bulk up. Considering I'm not trying to bulk up and that my entire being consists of a combination of sugary cereal and anxiety, this does me no good.

It's fine.

Then today he ordered me a pizza before he left, which I love, but he got pepperoni, which I absolutely hate. I like extra cheese. Peppers and onions in a pinch. Pepperoni over my dead body. I try to focus on the fact that he tried and not the fact that he got it wrong. Soon Gray will be here anyway, hopefully with some actually good food.

The door slams open as if on cue, and she comes flying in, nearly tipping the drink tray. Her arms are full of greasy bags; she's even got one in her mouth. I take the drinks and reach for the bag in her teeth. She growls before letting go, and I roll my eyes.

"Don't think you're getting any of those cheese fries just because you helped carry them," she says.

I laugh and bring it all into the living room, flicking on the TV and dropping onto the giant couch. I'm not totally sure if we're allowed to eat in here—I mean, Dad never does—but the way Gray follows me without hesitating says it's probably okay. I bet they do this kind of thing a lot.

I pretend that thought doesn't sting.

"How are you settling in?" she asks, pulling out various plastic containers full of more food than we can possibly eat. There are burgers and onion rings and chicken wings and regular fries and, yes, cheese fries, which Gray immediately slides out of my reach.

I huff and grab one of the burgers; it's about the size of my head and oozing BBQ sauce. "Everything's great."

"And Dad?" She shoves a cheese fry in her mouth.

"Is great too. He seems glad I'm here." Gray is the queen

of seeing what she wants to see, has been forever, so I know she won't catch the lie. The truth is, I still can't really tell what he thinks, and I spend most of the time staring at my phone, waiting for Peak to text.

Gray wipes her hands on a napkin, her mouth pinching in thought. "I know it's been . . . complicated between you guys, but I'm glad it's going good. This could be a chance for you guys to reconnect. It's been a long time."

She says it like that's normal, like being seventeen and still not having a connection with your dad is a regular thing. Maybe it is. I don't know. But I know that she and Dad—and she and Mom, for that matter—are practically best friends, so it seems a little bit like bullshit to me. My parents used to joke that Gray and I were so far apart in age that they had two "only children." But that always just felt like a nicer way of saying all they had was a daughter and the accident that came after her.

"Hey." She pulls a small box out of her bag and tosses it into my lap. "I'm really glad you're here."

I pick it up, my fingers tracing over the silver letters stamped into the side of the black box. "What's this?"

"Open it." She shrugs, taking another bite.

I pull the box apart, my forehead crinkling when I realize it's a watch. A very nice, very expensive watch, to be exact. "Gray . . ."

"Consider it a good-luck gift."

I run my hands over the silver face. "This is too much."

"Nah," she says, grabbing a chicken wing. "You deserve it. I'm proud of you for stepping up for this job. It could be a fresh start for you, for all of us, really. Besides, I never get to do stuff like this with you hiding out in Washington, so consider this me making up for lost time."

I bite my lip, my eyes feeling a little watery as I slide the watch onto my wrist and mess with the band.

"Okay, that's enough sappy shit for one night, though," Gray says. "Since this is your first time on a street team, I thought we'd talk strategy."

I want to roll my eyes at her, because it's a little bit insulting that she doesn't think I can hang out at a shitty comic store and watch what's going on without screwing it up . . . but she's probably right.

The street team is basically a euphemism anyway. Usually when you call people a street team, they're, like, out there promoting your brand, spreading the word and talking it up, that kind of thing. My dad's street team is the opposite. They're lurking quietly in the shadows of the industry, trying to tear stuff down or make it their own. Sure, some of it is innocent, but anything having to do with Vera Flores probably won't be. He doesn't want to re-create what she's doing; he wants to own her and everything she makes, and he wants revenge for making him look like a fool. Suddenly, I feel a little warm, a little out of my league, a little—

whatthefuckiswrongwithme

"Rid, you okay?" And I hate when she asks me that because I know what she's really asking: *Are you going to fall apart again?*

"Yeah, I'm great." I shove an onion ring in my mouth whole and chew with it open. Gray gags and throws a cheese fry at me, which sticks to my shirt. "And you said you wouldn't share," I say, biting into it with a flourish. She laughs, and it feels like a victory.

Crisis averted. For now.

"There's my annoying baby brother," she says, pulling files out of her bag.

I shouldn't preen at the sight of my name on a file. It should absolutely not make me feel this good. But Dad had his people put this together—specifically for me to read—and then made Gray carry it over, and that's probably the most thoughtful thing he's done for me in a long time. Which, shut up.

"All right, so the basics are all in here," she says, sliding the file over to me. "I know you've been a fan of Vera's work pretty much from the womb, much to Dad's dismay, but I think that will pay off here. You can use that awkward fanboy energy to endear yourself to her. Just make sure her kid doesn't think you're using her to get to Vera."

"Even though technically I *am* using her to get to Vera," I blurt out, and shit, is that the sound of my conscience dying?

"You're okay with doing this, right?" Gray asks, her hand still pinning the file to the table so I can't open it.

"It's not a big deal," I lie. "I got it."

Gray looks at me for a second and then nods. "Okay, well, there's a lot of information in here. Study it, but don't memorize it. You don't want to accidentally say too much. Although you can probably pull that off better than most since you're such a Verona stan, but still, be aware of it."

"I got it, I got it. Read the file enough to have it down but not enough to come off as creepy."

"Right," she says, and she looks proud. "Generally, the people on the street team stop in and visit the store a couple times. Just grab some books, say you're new in town or whatever." She slides a paper out of the file. "Here's a list of titles to have them put on your pull list."

"I don't need a fake pull list." I cross my arms. It's insulting that they think I can't come up with one on my own. I've had a pull list—a list of comics the store preorders and holds for you—since I could talk. It used to consist completely of *DuckTales* and *Teen Titans*, but I'd like to think I've matured over the years.

"Ridley, come on, use the list. This is important. If you get Dad something he can use to make her sign on, you're going to be his hero."

His hero. That sounds nice. I would also settle for "person he vaguely likes."

I grab the paper out of her hand. "Let me see it." I scan it quickly; it's not bad—big enough to position me as someone the store wants to keep happy, but not so big that they get suspicious about where a kid like me would get all that money. There's a blend of indie stuff and titles from the big two, and . . . it isn't all that different from my actual list. I glance up at her. "How did you guys come up with these?"

"Dad brought in a bunch of market research people. They worked their magic and came up with a list that your average comic book consumer would have, I guess."

"Cool, cool, cool," I say, taking another bite of my burger

and frowning at the list because I am *not* average, not when it comes to picking books, and I resent the fact that some corporate suit developed some kind of algorithm that nearly figured me out. I've spent a lot of time curating my list, thank you very much.

"Anyway," Gray says, shooting me a weird look, "after that, just start hanging out around the shop more, work the daughter angle—which feels a little sleazy, not going to lie, but Dad said it was your idea, and I trust you."

"Yeah," I mumble into my burger.

She leans forward a little to catch my eye. "It was your idea, right, Ridley?"

"Yeah," I say, puffing out my chest. "Who else's could it have been?"

"Right." But it looks like she doesn't believe me. And now? Is now when she's going to look deeper? But then she goes back to eating and the look of concern slips away. "Enough work talk. How are things with Peak?"

And there it is, that little nagging feeling, subtle like having a piano dropped on my skull or stepping on a rusty nail.

imsuchanasshole

Deep breath. Compartmentalize. That's all.

"She's good," I say, which is true. She's been incredibly upbeat this whole week. It's a little unnerving.

"Just good?"

"What do you want me to say? She's great, I'm in love, we're going to get married?" I shake my head. "We text, Gray—that's it. She's funny, she's nice, but it's not like it's going anywhere."

"Why not?"

"Because it's not, Gray. Drop it."

I don't want to talk about her; Peak is mine, just for me, and even talking about it could dilute some of the magic. Or make things messier. I don't know. I'm compartmentalizing over here or whatever, and Gray needs to let me.

"Wow, okay." She crunches one of the boxes shut a little too hard. And oh no, I wanted tonight to be good.

"I'll let you pick any show you want if you drop it."

She freezes, looking at me out of the corner of her eye. "Even my werewolves?"

"Oh my god, Grayson, you are too old for that show."

"You're never too old for werewolves. That's a fact. Sorry, I don't make the rules."

"They're barely even werewolves! They're like Hollister models with five-o'clock shadows."

"Oh, so werewolves can't be hot? That's speciesist, Ridley. I'm disappointed."

"That's not what I said."

"Good—so you agree, then, werewolves are hot?"

"Oh my god," I groan, tossing her the remote.

"You'll watch it and you'll like it." She laughs. "Don't think I don't see the eyes you make at the alpha."

"Uh-huh," I say, trying to act like it's no big deal that she's joking about me crushing on a very hot, very male actor. She's the only person who didn't freak out about the "Chandler situation," as my parents refer to my brief and dramatic relationship with a state senator's son last year. I thought it was love; he thought it was something else—blackmail, mainly. It's whatever.

My mom yanked me from my private school when the pictures came to light, finally relenting and letting me attend classes online instead. She also immediately put me into counseling, which is hilarious because she didn't even do that after my dive off the roof at thirteen, the one that resulted in a broken leg, a sprained ankle, and too many bruises to count. To this day she insists I must have done it on a dare—even though I left a note.

So yeah, apparently liking girls *and* guys rates higher on the concern scale than . . . the other thing. I stopped going a couple months ago, though; I don't think my mom has even noticed.

I shift in my seat uncomfortably, but Gray has already started watching the show. I try to follow along, but I'm in a weird headspace now, so I mess with my phone to take my mind off things, relieved to see that Peak has texted me twice.

"Oh my god, why is this show so good?" Gray groans, actually groans, and I raise my eyebrows.

"Let's just agree to disagree on that," I snort. My phone buzzes again, and it's a picture of Peak's cat with its tongue sticking out a little. Only, Peak scribbled on the pic so it looks like the cat's wearing a Batman mask.

I smile and lean back in my seat. There are werewolves shoving people into high school lockers on my TV, and there's so much food, and my sister is smiling, and Peak is being cute, and for a second everything is not so bad. Given enough time, I could maybe get used to this.

CHAPTER ELEVEN

Jubilee

JAYLA SIGHS DRAMATICALLY and flips the page of her textbook. We're spending eighth period in the library for study hall, which means we have to be mostly quiet but can still talk a little. We have a history test in three days that we're both cramming for, though one of us is a bit more resentful about it. Jayla flips the page again, tapping her pencil until Nikki drops into the empty chair beside her and pulls it from her hand.

"Are you studying or trying to join Jubi in the music program?" Nikki asks a little too loud, which makes the librarian shush us. It also makes Ty Williams look up from the table next to us. She glances over to make sure he's looking and then pulls out her ponytail, letting her dark brown hair fall perfectly against her tan skin.

"Hey, Nikki," he says, sliding his chair back so he's closer to our table.

"Hey, Ty," she says, trying not to grin.

Jayla says Ty has been in not-so-secret love with Nikki

since the fourth grade and she's been in not-so-secret love with him right back, but since they both vaguely pretend otherwise, we just go along with it. Nikki flicks his hat off, and he makes a big show of scooping it up and dusting it off before shoving it back on his head.

"You're lucky you're cute, Hartley." And Nikki seems to swoon a little at the sound of her last name coming from his lips.

Jayla groans, ruining the moment. "This test is a third of our grade. How are you guys not freaking out?"

"It'll be fine." I sneak a peanut butter cup out of my bag and shove it into my mouth. "Relax."

"Easy for you to say—we can't all be musical prodigies destined to tour the world until we settle down to inherit publishing lines," Nikki says.

I shake my head. "If you think there's money in cellos or comics, you're nuts."

"Uh-huh, tell that to Marvel," Jayla says, casually holding up her Captain America folder and fanning herself with it.

I laugh as I flip to the next page of the study guide. "Verona Comics is hardly Marvel."

Sure, between Vera's freelance art jobs, the comic line she puts out, and the store, she does okay. Plus, my mom's real estate job has finally been picking up. But we're not Marvel level. We're not even Jayla level, where her parents can keep twenty dollars in a drawer for her at all times, replacing it whenever she takes it. We're just . . . okay. There's not really anything left over, but the bills are paid. Before Vera came along, though, we weren't on half as solid footing as we're starting to be on now. Like, there were a lot of postdated checks to my music teachers, and we pretty much lived off pasta and pancakes.

Nikki pulls out her notebook and starts studying too, and other than Ty asking to borrow a pencil—despite the fact that I saw him with one right before Nikki walked in—we settle into a comfortable silence while we read.

The bell doesn't work in the library; it's been broken since the end of last year. Even though I know the librarian will tell us when it's time to pack up, I grab my phone to check the time—and maybe my texts. But seriously, I have orchestra last period, and if I'm late, I'll spend the entire time dusting instruments instead of playing.

"Oh, you're pathetic," Jayla says, kicking my chair.

Nikki rests her head on my arm. "I think she's adorable."

"Who's adorable?" Ty asks, leaning back so far in his chair, he almost tips over. He flails around a little to regain his balance, and Nikki bites her lip to keep from giggling. "You know, forget it. I'm just gonna—" he says, pointing back at his homework sprawled all over the table in front of him.

"God, all you do is text with him now." Jayla slams her textbook shut, prompting another shushing from the librarian. "You barely even respond to my messages, but Bats friggin' texts you and the whole world stops."

I crinkle my forehead. "Why do I have to be texting you when you're one seat away?"

"I'm just saying, your response time has sucked since the con and it's annoying. You don't even know anything about this kid; he could be a catfish! You could be blowing me off for a catfish. I hope you're cool with that."

I roll my eyes. "How can he be a catfish when we've both met him?"

"I didn't meet him," she corrects. "I met his sister. At best, I glanced at him from across the hall."

"You shared an elevator with him," I say. "Plus, you thought his sister was cute."

"Irrelevant. It's been a week, and you still don't know his real name."

"So what? I know a lot of other stuff."

"Oh god." Nikki blushes. "I don't want to know."

I roll my eyes. "It's not even like that." And it's true—it's not like that at all, nothing even close to that.

"Then what is it like?" Jayla asks, arching an eyebrow.

I settle on "It's nice," which makes Nikki coo and get all dreamy-eyed again. "I like talking to him. He's funny."

"What if he's hideous under the mask? What if he's hiding some deep, dark secret?"

"I don't care," I snap. And I'm surprised by how true that feels, although I'm guessing by his absolute refusal to Face-Time that maybe there is something going on. Something he doesn't want to share.

Which is *fine*, because it's just harmless flirting, an attempt at getting the butterflies to last me through the audition. It's the texting equivalent of crossing my fingers or wishing on an eyelash—just a little extra insurance that may not make a difference but can't actually hurt. Jayla needs to relax.

"Are you coming to the soccer game tonight?" she asks,

changing the subject, and shit, I forgot about the game. I nod anyway, because unless I'm super sick, I always go when they play their rivals.

"I'll give you a ride after orchestra, then."

"Are you sure you want to wait?"

Jayla and Nikki both have early dismissal, and I don't. Jayla usually spends it getting in extra practice time, and Nikki usually walks home to check on her mom while she's waiting for us to finish up. I think it's awesome how dedicated Nikki is to her family, but Jayla says she wasn't like that before the accident.

I guess Nikki's dad does something in finance, and her mom used to be a pastry chef. They adopted her from Korea when she was two, and according to Nikki, they pretty much lived happily ever after until a drunk driver plowed through an intersection, hitting her mom's car and changing their lives forever. That was about a year before I moved here, though.

On her good days, her mom still bakes the most amazing desserts, which Nikki always brings in to share. On her bad days, Nikki says she can barely get out of bed. I can't imagine what it's like to have your whole life shift like that in the blink of an eye. It kind of makes me want to take this whole embrace-life thing a little more seriously.

"I can stay today; my dad is off," Nikki says, putting the cap back on her pen.

"You looking for something to do while you wait?" Ty shouts from the next table, but before she can respond, Mrs. Cavill, the librarian, is barking at him to quiet down and pack up.

"I'll see you guys in a little bit, then." I zip my book bag shut, and a picture of literally the cutest baby bat in all the world flashes across my phone screen.

"Gross," Jayla says, but I ignore her and text back a bunch of heart eyes.

As I walk into orchestra, I text my mom to let her know I'm going to the game, then click over to my conversation with Bats, ignoring the group chat with my string quartet. They think it's wild that I "waste my time" in a public school orchestra—their words, not mine—but I'll take any chance I can get to play.

"Phones off," Mrs. C says way too cheerfully. And even though I think that's a dumb rule, I hit the power button anyway. I suck in my lips and make a big show of dropping my phone into my bag. She's right; I have to focus. I have to get in the right headspace. I am infusing my music with passion. I am calculating exactly what it needs. I am exceeding expectations always. I am getting that scholarship.

CHAPTER TWELVE

BATS: Distract me. I'm begging you.

           PEAK: What's wrong?

BATS: I just gotta get outta my head for a minute and I think we've exhausted every bat meme in existence.

           PEAK: Want to talk about it?

BATS: No? Yes? I have to do something tomorrow. I can't tell if I'm dreading it or excited.

           PEAK: I get it. I feel like that before some performances.

BATS: Are you going to finally tell me what you're performing? Or are we sticking with "a thing"?

PEAK: Two guesses.

BATS: Tap dancing?

PEAK: No. It's an instrument.

BATS: Okay, I got it.

PEAK: Yeah?

BATS: It's the kazoo. It's definitely the kazoo. I can tell. The moment I saw you in the elevator, I said there's a girl that knows how to blow.

PEAK: Yeah . . . um.

BATS: That . . . came out wrong.

PEAK: Right.

BATS: I didn't mean it like that. I swear.

PEAK: Moving on . . . Cello.

BATS: Cello?

PEAK: The thing I perform.

BATS: Are you good?

PEAK: Yes.

BATS: How good?

PEAK: Principal in the all-state orchestra good.

BATS: I have no idea what that means.

PEAK: It means I beat all the other cellists in the state.

BATS: Holy shit, Peak.
Send me something.

PEAK: What???

BATS: Do you ever record yourself playing?

PEAK: Mostly just for auditions.

BATS: Can I see?

PEAK: I'm totally going to regret this.
MVMT 1 Final Final For Real
It's not a video, but . . .

BATS: Wait. Was part of that the ringtone from prom?

PEAK: ☺ ☺ ☺ ☺ Maybe. You like it?

BATS: I fucking love it.

PEAK: It's Beethoven.

BATS: I have to go.

PEAK: You do?

BATS: I'm intimidated by your amazingness, so.

PEAK: You're a huge dork, you know that?

BATS: I do, actually? And I'm sorry, but it's a chronic condition. So yeah. Get in or get out on that front. Except please do not get out.

PEAK: Here I was worried you were luring me in with your awkward dorkiness, only to later prove yourself a dashing trust fund playboy or something. ☺

BATS: Dashing trust fund playboys can be dorks.

                                        PEAK: Yeah?

BATS: I could be both.

                                        PEAK: Sure.

BATS: I could!

                                        PEAK: I said sure!

BATS: No you said "Sure." Totally different.

                                        PEAK: You caught me.

BATS: ☺ ☺ ☺ ☺

CHAPTER THIRTEEN

Ridley

I JUST HAVE to pretend that I'm skateboarding to a random shop, in a random place, for a random reason. I just have to get a grip, stop digging my nails into my palm, will my heart rate to slow down, and act normal. I just have to be the complete opposite of everything I am.

It's fine.

I take a deep breath and focus on the sound of my skateboard on the concrete, the steady rhythm of the cracks on the sidewalk. I prefer to ride in the street, but the number of ghost bikes in this town tells me the drivers here are not especially observant. Sidewalks it is.

Skateboarding is a multipurpose hobby for me. One, it's practical—other than a couple lessons from my well-meaning aunt Mary in Michigan, no one ever bothered to teach me to drive. Two, it burns off a lot of nervous energy—well, normally it does, but nothing's touching that today. And three, skating is basically my art form. I can't draw, I can't play an instrument, but I can do an ollie impossible *and* a 360 hardflip, so my life isn't complete shit.

This morning was kind of decent, all things considered. Dad's been sort of trying, and even "sort of trying" is a massive effort for him. Like, when I was leaving, he handed me a pack of Pokémon cards and said, "Good luck today." Positive reinforcement is always thrilling, but I still haven't worked out if the cards were a nod to the old days, when he would have my nanny give them to me if I did well at school, or if he actually thinks I still like Pokémon. Both scenarios are equally likely, and to be honest, I don't even know which one I'd prefer.

I slow down about a block away from the comic shop and hop off, flipping my board up into my hand and then strapping it to my backpack. I'm kind of surprised by how sweaty I got, even in this cold March weather. This is not the first impression I want to make. I run my fingers over the watch Gray gave me; I could use a little good luck right now.

Shoving down the hood of my sweatshirt, I start to walk, trying hard not to think about what I'm really doing.

Peak texted me until I fell asleep last night, sending me music clips and keeping me distracted. How shitty it was to have her comforting me when I was freaking out about spying on her own shop is another thing I'm trying not to think about.

As is the fact that Vera is apparently a human lie-detector test obsessed with honesty, which I learned when Peak gave me the play-by-play of their argument about her leaving con prom.

Oh, and don't forget the fact that I'm starting to really like

Peak, and that I'm probably torpedoing that relationship for the faint chance of building one with my father. So yeah, no pressure today or anything. Nope, none at all.

Bells ring when I step in the shop, heavy gold things that dangle over the door. So much for quietly slipping in and observing undetected. Vera—*the* Vera Flores—pokes her head out of the back room. "Hey, kid, I'll be with you in just a second."

"You don't have to be," I say, and she crinkles her forehead. "I mean, I'm looking here at stuff. I'm new. I don't—I'm good. You can do whatever."

"Hey, Margot?" she says, and I didn't realize she was holding a phone until just now. "Let me call you back."

"Oh no you don't," I mutter, but she's already hung up.

"I'm Vera." She walks toward me, extending her hand. "Welcome to Verona Comics."

"Ridley." I return her firm shake with my own limp one, feeling a little bit like the walls are closing in.

pretendpretendpretendpretendpretendthisisfine

"Nice to meet you, Ridley. What can I do for you?"

"I said nothing." And wow, rude, holy shit, abort, abort, abort. "Sorry, I'm . . . I don't know. I'm just—I was skating by and I saw your shop, and I just thought I'd stop in. I want to set up a pull list, though, since I'm here." I reach into my pocket for the piece of paper, wrinkled and soft from my hands worrying it all night, where I copied the list of comics my dad sent.

Vera stifles a smile and takes the paper from my hand. "You were just skating by, huh?"

pretendpretendpretendpretendpretend

She goes behind the desk and turns on her computer. She's still smirking, and I don't know why. It's starting to stress me out more, if that's even possible.

"Do you always skate around with a list of comics you want to buy in your pocket?"

Oh.

thinkthinkthinkthinkthink

"Yes?"

shitshitshitshitshitshitshit

"You're my kinda kid, then, Ridley." She laughs.

Crisis averted? Maybe? I let out a deep breath and run my hand along the long boxes on the table beside me. This is fine. I am fine. I am standing across the room from my comics hero, but this is fine.

Fine, fine, fine.

Oh god, I'm freaking out. I take another deep breath and blow it out. Vera looks up from her computer, and I spin around fast and start flipping through the comics in front of me, trying to calm down. If I blow this . . . I can't. I can't blow this.

getagripgetagripgetagrip

"Fuck," I whisper, trying to keep my hands from trembling.

"What was that?" Vera asks from behind the counter.

"Uh . . . nothing. I just, yeah." And I apparently lose the ability to speak in front of this woman. Awesome.

She laughs again, but it sounds warm, not mean, and I relax infinitesimally. "Did you just move here?"

"Yeah, a couple days ago."

"Well, welcome to town, then." She comes around the corner. "Your pull list is all set. I can't sell you any of the new releases until tomorrow, but a couple of them just came out last week. Did you need those?"

"No, I'm good."

"Normally, I would require a deposit for a pull list this big, but you have an honest face, so I'm gonna let it slide."

"Oh, uh, thanks," I say, and try to ignore the way that makes my stomach hurt. Also, I should have expected this; we always take deposits for pull lists at our comic shops too. I look around a little bit, taking it all in. "I like your shop."

"Thanks." Vera smiles. "I made it myself."

"I know; that's awesome." Because she really did. I read through all her old blog posts last night in a last-ditch effort to be prepared, including the ones about her making her own shelves by hand and personally sliding every book in place.

"Just skatin' by, eh?"

"Something like that," I say, realizing what I just said. I have definitely screwed this up, and there's no coming back. She probably thinks I'm a total weirdo. I'm probably making her uncomfortable. I'm probably—

"Well, my door's always open, Ridley. Come anytime the light's on."

"Seriously?" I sputter, because I've spent this whole time making an ass of myself, and still, she seems somehow completely unfazed.

"Are you going to school here? I have a daughter about

your age. I'm sure she'd be willing to show you around and introduce you to people."

Peak. She's talking about Peak.

dontthrowupdontthrowup

"No, I don't think so."

Vera's eyebrows draw together, but then she makes a little humming sound. "Well, maybe you two will cross paths some other way, then. In the meantime, why don't you come back soon. I'm inking a new book, and I'll let you take a look."

My eyes get huge at the idea of seeing a Vera original *in process*. Holy shit. This is amazing. This is impossible. Be cool. Be cool. I take a deep breath. "Yeah, that'd be great. I'll stop back."

"You do that," she says with the warmest smile I've ever seen.

"I have to go now." I start walking backward toward the door. "But thanks. It was nice meeting you."

"Nice meeting you too," she says as I hit the door and make the bells ring again.

I shove it open and step onto the sidewalk. I did it. It might have been awkward and messed up, and I wasn't like a James Bond–level superspy or anything, but I went, and I did it, and I'm going to go back. And that feels like a win. It feels good.

And then my phone buzzes in my pocket, and it's Peak checking in, wishing me good luck with whatever it is that I have to do today. And my heart sinks to the concrete, because every win comes with a loss for me. Everything good is also bad. Plus one with my dad means minus one with Peak.

CHAPTER FOURTEEN

Jubilee

HE'S BEEN IN the store for nearly five minutes, and other than getting startled by the bells—which Vera says he does every time—and then looking to see if I noticed, which I did, he hasn't acknowledged me at all. Well, technically, he did that ridiculous grunt-slash-nod combo thing boys do when I said hello. Hardly counts.

Vera mentioned he'd be in soon to get his holds, but it's weird he came in today, since the new books aren't out until tomorrow. I guess he's just into perpetually being a week behind or something—but I'm trying not to judge. She said to keep an eye out for the mop-headed guy in a hoodie, that he looked about my age and seemed like he needed a friend. Then she gave me a look, like it's my job to welcome him to the fold or something. No, thanks, I have enough on my plate.

Speaking of enough on my plate, I glance at my phone—and nothing. Well, there are a few texts from Jayla and Nikki, plus the two violinists from my quartet blowing up our group chat over which performance of the Haydn Quartets is the best and the violist trying to get them to chill, but . . . none from Bats, which is weird. Normally we talk nonstop when I'm at the shop. It's practically what gets me through the shift. This afternoon—silence. Granted, normally I don't work on Tuesdays—Mrs. G had to reschedule our usual lesson because she has the flu—but still.

I glance back up at the new kid, who is still standing awkwardly near the entrance. He's fairly unremarkable as far as new kids go, and I would know—I've met about a trillion in the three years we've lived with Vera. I swear to god, she collects wayward kids the way some people collect baseball cards. They come in and out of the shop, barely buying anything, but she lets them hang around anyway—feeding them, talking to them, giving them a safe space to be. My mom calls them strays, but Vera doesn't like that. I asked her about it once, and she said someone did that for her too when she was young and needed it, and she's just paying it forward. Which is great, honestly, but I don't see why I need to be a part of the welcome wagon.

I grab another snack out of the candy bowl on the counter—I take the peanut butter cups, always; Vera can keep the Skittles—while still keeping an eye on the new kid. He's cute-ish, I guess, with his little lost expression on his face, and he's rocking some bright white Vans that I don't hate. I guess cute-ish boys in rad sneakers is a theme now for me or something, not that I'm complaining.

I looked at his pull list before he got here, even though I

felt guilty about it because Vera says that's like looking into someone's soul. It was pretty good, maybe a little clinical, a little trying too hard. Objectively, they're all good titles, but collectively it doesn't *feel* cohesive. Pull lists have a style usually, a vibe. Like, even if it's a mix of indie and mainstream, and most of them are, you'll see themes and patterns emerge. If somebody shuffled all the comics in the pull boxes together, I'd probably still be able to easily sort out which ones belonged to our regulars. But this kid is all over the map. His pull list has taste but no heart.

It's like the difference between my audition rep and the music I'd put on a recital program. My audition requirements are strict: two excerpts, a Bach suite, a romantic concerto, and a twentieth-century solo work. It's curated to show off my technique, my musicality, and my range across all different periods—but it doesn't flow. If it were up to me, I'd just play all the Beethoven sonatas and call it a day.

I lean against the counter and sigh. He's moved from the door finally, but he's been staring at the wire rack near the new-release wall for too long now. I don't even think he sees it. I mean, it's the kids' rack. How long can one person really spend looking at the newest *DuckTales* cover?

He glances up at me, startling when we make eye contact, and then goes back to looking at the rack. I feel a pang of pity; obviously, I'm freaking him out. Comics are getting pretty mainstream, but we still get a lot of quiet, quirky folks in here too. Like James, one of our regulars, who's fine with Vera but can't talk to me with his eyes open. As in, he literally keeps them shut the entire time. It's totally fine, and we actually have a lot of great conversations . . . but it does make cashing him out a bit of an adventure.

And Macy, who's so shy she just hands us pieces of paper with the titles she wants added and practically runs from the shop when we give them to her. It's just part of working here. Besides, I'm not exactly the poster child for being a well-adjusted social butterfly either. If I were, then maybe I wouldn't have essentially been assigned "live a little" as a homework assignment.

I lean over the counter so I'm closer to Mr. Glaring-at-*DuckTales*—but not too close—and clear my throat. "Hey, if you're looking for Vera, she'll be back in a few. She just had to do a delivery."

He finally looks up at me and then nearly knocks over a stack of comics sitting on top of the dollar bin. I had been meaning to bag and board them—no point now. He scrambles to catch them, crinkling some covers in the process. Better than the new releases, but still.

"Help," he says, and I tilt my head as the blush creeps up his neck. "I mean, can I help you?"

"Uh, I think that's supposed to be my line, right? Since I'm the one who works here?"

"Right." He smooths the cover of one of the comics. "I can pay for these."

"It's fine." I wave him off. "We end up donating half of them to the children's hospital anyway. It's not a big deal if they're a little bit wrinkled on the corners."

"Oh."

"I'm Jubilee," I say, trying to look friendly because this guy looks like he's about to lose it. "You're the new str— Ridley, right?"

His eyes widen in response, and for half a second, I swear I know him. He must have one of those faces.

"How . . . ?"

"Vera said you'd be in to pick up your books. I've got a few holds over here whenever you're ready, but if you need anything else, let me know."

He scratches the back of his neck and does this half-cough thing, like he's got something stuck in his throat. "Thanks." I catch him grimace as he turns to the rack in front of him.

"There are other racks, you know, unless you're super into talking ducks," I tease, smirking at the way his ears pink up.

"Yeah," he says, moving on to stare at the actual new-release wall instead.

I pull out his holds, checking to make sure they're all there. I glance over when I see him pick up a comic. It's not one on his list, but it is one of my favorites. He flips through, looking at it like he wants to marry it, and then slides it back into the rack with a frown.

"That's a good one," I say. "And you're at a great jumping-on point. They're coming back from hiatus, and the first volume just came out. You grab that and the one in your hand, and you're all caught up."

"I have all of them except this one. I've been reading it from the start."

I crinkle my forehead, flipping through his books in front of me. "Oh really? Is it supposed to be in your pile?"

"No." He shakes his head. "I can't—I don't have—it's a thing."

I pull back, surprised. "Your parents monitor your pull list or something?"

He looks down, and holy shit, if there's one thing I hate most in this world, it's parents policing content. I can't help but notice that it's the very queer comic that they don't let him have; meanwhile, his pull list is loaded up with all the violent ones. Typical.

"That's so wrong." I come from behind the counter and pull the comic out of the rack. "Here, it's yours."

"I can't."

"Seriously, I read it on break earlier. I'll just replace it with my copy. It's fine." I push it closer until he takes it.

"Thanks." The corner of his lips turns up, and I feel a little swell of pride.

His eyes catch on my Green Lantern ring, sterling silver with an actual emerald in it. A gift from my mom on my sixteenth birthday. I'm about to show it to him when he opens his mouth.

"Did your boyfriend give you that?"

Cue record scratch.

"My boyfriend?" I roll my eyes. "I work in a comic shop. I don't need to rely on a boy to give me merch. I guarantee you my pull list is bigger than yours, and it was even before I started working here."

He shakes his head. "I didn't mean . . . I wasn't implying—"

I raise my eyebrows and cross my arms. "Uh-huh."

"I swear. I have a sister that's way more into this stuff than I'll ever be. If she even thought I implied—which I didn't, by the way—but if she even thought I did, she would kick my ass. It came out wrong. I didn't mean anything by it."

"Oh really?" I snort. "You didn't mean to ask if it was from my boyfriend, even though that's literally exactly what you said?"

His eyes go wide. "I was just making conversation!"

"By implying that I could only have this ring if it came from a guy?"

He rubs his hand over his face and frowns. "Listen, I really, truly did not mean it that way. I'm sorry."

At least he looks properly ashamed. "Fine. How did you mean it, then?"

"What?"

"How did you mean it? If you weren't asking out of some last-ditch misogynistic gatekeeping, why else would you ask if it was from my boyfr—wait, were you trying to see if I *had* a boyfriend?"

"I—" He blushes again and starts flipping through the books in the dollar bin. "No."

I sigh. "I don't know if that makes it better or worse."

"What?"

"Why are you all such clichés?"

"Comics fans?"

I roll my eyes. "No, boys. News flash, it's not okay to hit on every random person you meet."

"I don't, I swear. You're the exception, not the rule.

And technically, I didn't hit on you. I just asked if you had a boyfriend."

"I'm going to find out who your sister is and tell her everything."

His mouth pops open, and I swear to god, the boy looks terrified.

"Okay, now I want to find her even more. She seems fabulous, and I think I'm already in love."

"Does that mean I should have asked if you had a girlfriend too?" He chuckles and scratches the back of his neck.

"Probably, yeah," I say. "Also, congrats on making it even more awkward by questioning not only my relationship status but also my sexual orientation all within five minutes of meeting me."

He groans and drops his head down. "Can we just start over? Or else I could go over there with *DuckTales* until Vera comes back. I'd totally understand. I was trying to be funny, but I made it uncomfortable. That is . . . kind of my superpower." He grimaces.

"Ugh, now I feel bad. *DuckTales*? Really?" I huff. "Okay, fine, you get one last chance to turn this all around: tell me what book you'd recommend. You do a good job, you can stay. You don't, there's the door, come back later." I'm just messing with him. Of course I wouldn't really kick him out, but it turns out he's adorable when he gets flustered.

He crinkles his eyebrows, a little mischief in his eye. "I thought your pull list was bigger than mine?"

"I'm completely positive that it is, but I still want to know what you'd recommend, because obviously the pull list you made here isn't accurate. And I can tell a lot about a dude by what he reads."

He bites the inside of his cheek, looking from me to the wall and back to me again. He walks over to the third row and slides a glossy superhero book from the shelf. Ms. Marvel stares back at me from the cover.

"Explain your reasoning." I love it, but I want to know why he picked it. If he even tries to pull the teen-girl card . . .

"Eisner *and* Hugo Award–winning writer, fantastic art, amazing plot, compelling main character. I don't believe for a second it's not already on your pull list, but if you want to keep messing with me, fine. That's my first pick, and yes, I would recommend it to you even if you were a guy."

"Your *first* pick?"

"Give me two seconds; we're not done yet." He walks around the comic shop, pulling various trades and single issues. I already own most of them, which should maybe not impress me, but it does. When he pulls my favorite comic, a super-obscure indie book you pretty much have to be deep into the scene to have even heard of, my heart beats a little faster. Did it just get hot in here, or . . . ?

He walks back with a little smile, tapping his finger on it. "This one is a little out-there, but give it a chance. It's worth it."

"I own it. I love it. I have a signed copy." His face lights up as the smile turns into a full-on grin that stretches across his face, and oh my god, he has a dimple.

"Yeah? Not many people have even heard of it."

"I told you my—"

"Pull list is bigger than mine. Yeah, yeah, got it. So? How'd I do?"

"Okay, I guess." I laugh. "But now you have to put it all away before Vera gets back, and I need to finish organizing the books for tomorrow. I'd hurry if I were you; she hates when the store's a mess."

The little bell over the door jingles, and both our heads whip toward the entrance. Ridley darts to put the books away, and I swear he's still grinning, but it's hard to tell from the way he's hunched over by the racks.

"Ridley! You're just in time," Vera says as she bustles by us with bags of takeout. "You like Chinese food, right?"

Tuesday-night Chinese in the back room is a weekly tradition. Vera barters with the owner of the Chinese restaurant next door. We keep him in comics, and he hooks us up with dinner every time my stepmom delivers them. Usually I'm rushing here from my lesson to get some before it's gone, so I'm pumped to have first dibs tonight.

"I should go," Ridley says, sliding the last comic back in its place.

"Nonsense, come eat," Vera insists, and this, *this* is why she picks up so many strays. Vera and her stellar business sense. I mean, people love when they come to get their holds and find out they weren't sorted yet because everybody was too busy eating takeout, or that their sticky note with new requests was used as a makeshift napkin. I roll my eyes and follow my stepmom anyway, because Chinese food.

Ridley hesitates until I raise my eyebrows, and then he follows. He trips over the little half step between the back room and the store and then squeezes his eyes shut when I giggle. Okay, fine, it's definitely cute how easily he gets embarrassed. And if I had any extra time to "push the boundaries," maybe I would spend a little of it finding new and clever ways to make him blush.

But I don't. I can barely keep up with the boy that lives in my phone. Who still hasn't texted me since this morning, by the way.

"So?" Vera says, pulling cans of soda and white take-out boxes from the greasy paper bags. "Did our guest pass inspection?"

Ridley watches as I wave my hand in a *so-so* gesture. "It was touch and go for a minute, but he did all right in the end."

Vera shakes her head before looking at Ridley. "Jubi doesn't always trust my judgment when it comes to kids hanging out here. If she's giving you the all clear, you must be doing something right. Now sit, eat."

I kick a chair toward him with my foot, and he looks up when it bangs into his shin. "Sit." I shove my fork into a pile of white rice. "Unless you want me to change my mind about you."

Vera laughs, reaching for the box of crab rangoon. I smack her hand. "Not until he sits. It's rude."

Ridley stares at me for a second, watching the exchange with this sort of confused expression, and then he grabs the chair and slides it back to the table, sitting stiffly upright. His knee bumps into mine, and I feel it bounce up and down a little.

"So," I say, trying to get him to relax, "what brings your family to Silver Hills?"

Ridley coughs, choking on his egg roll, and I slap him on the back. "Easy, slick." He's sweet in an awkward-puppy way. It's familiar, and strangely comforting.

"Um," he says finally, when the coughing has subsided. "I'm staying with my dad for a while, so."

"Oh, is he here in town?"

"Outside of it. In Claremont. He's got a house there."

"Wow, fancy. Too bad your dad is such a tightwad about your pull list. I hoped maybe it was just a money thing."

"Jubilee!" Vera scolds, knocking the rice over in the process. The little bell over the door jingles, saving me from dying of embarrassment.

"I'll get that." I start to stand up, but Vera pushes me back down into my seat.

"Relax, it's probably just Rutherford picking up his holds," she says, disappearing into the store.

Vera says that all the time when the bell rings, that it's probably just Rutherford. It's become a running joke. Rutherford rarely picks up his holds. He'll come in once a year or so, slam down a few grand, and take everything home. The rest of the time they just sit, wasting space and money.

I clean up the rice she dumped and put it on a napkin. "Are you going to start at Silver Hills too, then?"

"Silver Hills what?" he asks.

"Silver Hills High School? We technically cover Claremont, although most of the kids there go to private schools."

"Oh," he says, looking down. "No."

"Private school?"

"Probably not."

I tilt my head. "Wait. How old are you?"

"Seventeen."

"So did you graduate early or drop out or what?"

"I don't really know," he says, shrugging like it's no big deal.

I take a sip of my Sprite, marinating on that thought. "I didn't think that it was possible to not know."

"It's just, it's a long story—"

"I've been texting you nonstop!" Jayla practically shouts, sliding back the curtain and stepping into the room. "This is getting ridiculous. You can't just—" She glances at Ridley and down at where our knees meet. "Am I interrupting something?"

"What? No!" I say, scooting my chair over closer to Vera's, which means the only place for Jayla to squeeze in is right between me and Ridley. She grabs a chair and sits, looking him up and down.

"Favorite Robin?" she asks.

"Uh, what?"

I roll my eyes. "She does this with everyone, sorry. Jayla, can we skip it this time?"

She flicks her eyes to mine. "Did you make him give you book recommendations?"

I bite my lip. "Maybe, but—"

"If you got to test him, I get to test him," she says, and turns back to Ridley. "Favorite Robin?"

"I don't know. I guess Dick Grayson."

She stares at him for a second before shifting so she only faces me. "Anyway, I've been texting you. I want to go—"

"Jayla," I say, arching my eyebrows.

"Ugh, fine," she says, turning her chair back to the table. "But he said Grayson, Jubi. Dick Grayson. Out of all the Robins, he's the worst."

"Well, my sister's named after—"

"Don't worry about it. She's just a Jason Todd fan," I say, hoping that explains everything. It should. There have been so many Robins standing by Batman's side over the years, but the Jason Todd fandom and the Dick Grayson fandom are especially precious about their guys each being the best of the best.

"Everyone should be a Jason Todd fan," Jayla says. "But seriously, how is the new guy already invited to takeout night? Shouldn't there be more of a vetting period? I mean, the kid likes Dick Grayson." She whispers the last part with an exaggerated cringe.

"I should go," he says.

"No, she's just being obnoxious," I say, widening my eyes at her. "She means it with love."

"No, I mean it with mild trepidation," Jayla says.

"Liking Dick Grayson doesn't make him problematic, Jay!"

"It means he's got poor judgment."

"I'm just gonna go," he says, standing up.

I lean around her to grab his sleeve and yank him back down. "Eat. She's kidding."

"Mostly," Jayla says, giving him the evil eye before laughing. "I'm Jayla, by the way."

"Ridley." He blows out another breath, looking uncomfortable.

"Welcome to the family, I guess. Try not to suck, okay?"

"I—" Ridley starts, but Jayla's already turned back toward me.

"Come on, Jubi—if we hurry, there's still enough time to hit up the thrift store before it closes."

"I'll catch up with you, okay?" I give her my most pleading look. "I'm still eating."

She rolls her eyes and slides her chair out. "Fine. Stay here with the Grayson-lover."

We sit for a while after she leaves, eating our Chinese food in silence. I fight the urge to break it with a random fact, because that's a me-and-Bats thing, and it feels like cheating to do it here with Ridley. He'd probably think it was weird anyway.

"So, she's great," he says finally. And I burst out laughing because he sounds so genuine that I can't even tell if he's being sarcastic.

"Her heart's in the right place. She's just very protective of me and my moms."

"Moms?"

"Oh, come on, you had to have known. That doesn't bother you, does it?"

"Nope," he says, shoving his chopsticks into one of the boxes in front of him.

I pull out my phone and check my texts. The quartet chat is still going bananas—something about Shostakovich now—but still nothing from Bats.

"Got someone better to talk to?" he asks, ducking his head a little.

"Apparently not." I sigh. "But I do have to catch up with Jayla. She'll kill me if I don't."

"Can't have that."

"Right?" I stand up, grabbing my coat. "And just so you know, since you're so curious, I'm not seeing anybody."

He chokes on his rice as I walk out with a smirk. Score one for pushing the boundaries.

CHAPTER FIFTEEN

Ridley

I FLICK OFF the bathroom light and turn the water to its hottest setting. Gray calls them my "sadbaths." But I kind of hate that. It's too close to *Sabbath*, and if I'm going to worship something, it's not going to be at the altar of depression and soap scum.

But there's just something about hot water and scorched skin and a quiet dark room that's . . . soothing. I squeeze my eyes shut and pretend it's my worries swirling around the drain instead of cheap hotel shampoo. Dad still hasn't bothered to stock my bathroom, so I'm relying on shit I stole from the casino. But still, it's fine.

I can't label what I'm feeling right now, but my head's been spinning since yesterday when Peak gave me that book, shoved it into my hands like it was no big deal. Like I deserved it just because I wanted it. Wait, no, not Peak, Jubilee. Jubilee Jones. I'm trying so hard to keep them separate.

It's harder than I thought.

I lean my head against the wall. I thought it would feel

different to be back in this house. I don't know what I expected. Like I would be better somehow if the water beating down on me was from pipes that run underneath the floor I learned to walk on instead of the floor of a new-construction house with no history and heating problems. And yet.

And yet.

I just feel more alone. If this isn't my home and that isn't my home, do I even have one?

I finish up, wrap myself in a towel, and pad across the floor. I wriggle my toes appreciatively when the cool tile of the bathroom gives way to the plush carpet of the hallway, leaving damp footsteps in my wake.

My ex-therapist suggested I keep a running list of good things to look at when all seems lost. I think she wanted me to actually write it down, but I never did. It's more of a running tally in my head. I add *plush carpeting* to the list, right after *dewy spiderwebs*, but before *baristas of any gender wearing sparkly nail polish*.

I grab a pair of boxers out of the duffel bag by the nightstand, shaking them out like anybody's going to care they're wrinkled, and then I flop back onto the bed with my phone. The urge to text Peak is strong, but I don't know. I kind of just want to think more about Jubilee right now. And I know, I KNOW they're the same.

But compartmentalization and all that.

I slide the comic out from where I hid it under my pillow, frowning at the silly sentimentality. It's not like it means anything; she didn't even have to pay for it. She probably doesn't even remember giving it to me.

It's fine.

I try to call my mom—I tell myself it's not because I'm lonely, it's just to remind her to send my stuff—but she doesn't pick up either way. I text her the reminder instead, and she responds surprisingly fast: **Can't talk, out with friends, will call later.** I'm not holding my breath, though. She has called exactly once since I've been here, and only because she couldn't find the remote. It's whatever.

I start to call my sister next but then cancel it. She's in Boston; she even sent me a snap earlier of her making fishy faces in the aquarium there. Boston's not too far from here, an hour or two at most, but I have no idea why she's there.

I pull up her Instagram and click through, anything to keep my mind busy tonight, and ah yes, it's a charity event sponsored by The Geekery. Makes sense. There she is, smiling with a bunch of sick kids at the New England Aquarium. There she is, posing with Spider-Man in front of a sign that reads SWING INTO ACTION WITH THE GEEKERY CHARITIES. There she is with a glass of champagne, laughing. There she is, visiting a hospital with Captain America earlier that day. I can't decide if I feel better that she's close if I need her, or worse that she's this close and not here.

Regardless, it's not her fault. I'm not her responsibility. A new picture appears right before I click off, a selfie of her pointing at the penguins in the enclosure behind her with an overdramatic "wow" face. I'm just about to leave a comment about what a massive nerd she is when a text pops up on my phone.

PEAK: Bats!

I stare down at the words on my screen like a deer in the headlights. And oh shit. This feels wrong somehow. Like sharing crab rangoon changed everything, and now it's all different and confusing.

donttextbackdontdontdont

ME: Peak!

imgoingtohell

PEAK: Oh good, so you're not
dead in a ditch somewhere.
You really did just abandon me. ☺

And okay, even with the emoji at the end, the idea that she felt remotely abandoned, kidding or not, just sucks. It sucks even more because I was right in front of her yesterday and couldn't say anything. And I kind of hate that. I don't want her to feel like that ever.

ME: I didn't abandon you

PEAK: You haven't texted me in forever

ME: I was working.

Okay, it's not technically a lie, but.

PEAK: Likely story. 😉

Be cool, Ridley. Steer this away from work. It's too fucked up.

ME: Cross my heart.

PEAK: Still doing promo for Satan's Comics? 😈

ME: No, something new. Just started.

shitshitshitshitshit
This is the opposite of steering things away from work. This is making work a priority. This is literally going into more detail about it. What if she figures it out? What if she already has? What if she's just messing with me, dragging me along? What if this is a setup?
whatifwhatifwhatifwhatifwhatif

PEAK: Funnnnn. Hope your coworkers were nice.

ME: They were exceptional.

fuckfuckfuckfuckfuck
WHAT IS THE ACTUAL MATTER WITH ME?

PEAK: Exceptional, eh? Should I be jealous?

ME: I can't even begin to tell you how not jealous you should be. Wait . . . Jealous?

PEAK: Can't go having some hot coworker stealing away my bat in shining armor.

ME: I don't have armor.

PEAK: Semantics. Bat in skinny jeans then. Same difference.

ME: The difference between jeans and armor is far greater than semantics. I don't even know where to begin.

PEAK: Nice subject change. 😊

ME: . . . ?

PEAK: Listen, you've been texting me nonstop for two weeks, and now radio silence. There's definitely a hottie.

Should I tell her? Oh god, I should. I should tell her everything, come completely clean. This is too stressful. I'm sure my dad will get over it, right? I mean, probably? Never mind.

ME: Would you really care?

ohgodohgodohgodohgodohgod

Am I really asking her if she's jealous of herself? What is the matter with me? Seriously. WHAT. IS. THE. MATTER. WITH. ME?

PEAK: Nope.

Annnnnd ouch. Well, okay, then.

PEAK: I mean, I would have.
But then maybe I met someone too.
Turnabout being fair play and all.

My stomach sinks to my toes. Fuck him, whoever he is. They probably met at the thrift shop after she left yesterday. He was probably donating all his very nice clothing while combing the racks for "authentic pieces." He probably has a nice house and a family that loves him. He probably is handsome and well-adjusted and plays sports and has hipster glasses or something. His laundry is probably always clean and good smelling. He probably has more clothes than he can handle because his mother didn't promise to ship them to him and then forget, and I bet his teeth sparkle in the sunlight. He probably doesn't even know how great his life is. He's probably the exact opposite of me in every way. She's probably already in love. She's probably never going to text me again after this. This is probably her way of cutting things off, since she seems too nice to ghost someone.

And I know I have to respond, that it's weird that I haven't, but the words keeping dying in my fingers.

> **ME:** I don't know what to say here.

PEAK: Really? That's it?

> **ME:** I hope you guys are happy?
> I don't know. What am I supposed
> to do with that? Good for you.
> Have fun. Etc. Etc. Etc.

And yeah, I'm pouting. And yeah, I know that's messed up. And yet. And yet.

PEAK: Oh god, I was just teasing you.

> **ME:** So . . . There is no "hottie"?

PEAK: Well, I mean, there is? But he's just
some rando who hangs out at my mom's store.
N E V E R going to happen.

I bolt up in bed, choking on my spit when I read the words on the screen, my mind whipping around itself, alternating between *holy shit, she's talking about me* and *wait, did I just cockblock . . . myself?*

Oh god. Seriously, no. I have to tell her. This is so messed up.

But I can't. I can't screw this up. My father is counting on me, Gray is counting on me, and even worse, what if telling her means I lose her on both fronts? Not that I have her on both fronts, but I could? Maybe? If we keep talking and hanging out.

No.

But now the silence is stretching on too long, and I have to get a grip. I have to write back. I have to handle this. Compartmentalize. Don't cross the streams. Figure it out.

thinkthinkthinkthinkthinkthinkthinkthinkthink

ME: Lucky me.

PEAK: Lucky you. 😉

God, this girl. This girl. She makes me feel like my brain is electric, in a good way for once. And I don't know. Maybe other people have felt like this before, but I haven't. Not like this. I don't know how anyone could? How do you go to the store, how do you eat, how do you buy toilet paper and brush your teeth and do anything other than sit inside your head with this feeling? I thought I had this before with Chandler, but this, this is next-level stuff, and I don't even know what to do with it.

I don't even know.

• • •

A knocking sound pulls me from my sleep, and I jolt up in bed. Suddenly, I am seven years old and I overslept again, and maybe it's my dad coming to wake me up for school. But he never would, not even then, and I'm a decade past seven, so.

The knocking continues, and it's not a hard knock, not a Dad knock, and not my sister's either.

"Ridley?"

Shit. If there was anything that would make me crash hard after getting high on Peak—or Jubilee, I don't even know how to keep that sorted or separated anymore—it would be the she-devil on the other side of my door. Satan's Comics indeed.

"Ridley?" Allison calls again, still knocking.

I glance at the time; it's nearly midnight. "What?" I groan, yanking open my door. I'm standing in boxers and no doubt have pillow creases on my cheek.

"Huh, and your dad said you never slept." Based on the way she crinkles her nose when she glances over my shoulder, she appears to find my room lacking. It's not my fault that the only thing my dad kept in here after I moved to Seattle was my old twin bed.

She walks over to where my duffel bag sits open on the floor and nudges it with her foot. "Is this all you have still?" Her tone changes then, pity lacing her words.

I cross one arm across my chest, grabbing my shoulder hard so I don't say something I'll regret. Yes, it's all I have. Yes, it's all that's mine. Yes. Yes. Yes. It's fine.

Allison shifts her weight. "We expected your first report tonight. Your dad wanted me to check on it, since he's held up at the aquarium thing."

Oh. Right. I was supposed to do that before I went to bed.

Oops. And then the rest of what she said hits me, and okay, sure, it doesn't bother me that both he and Gray did the charity event and neither of them invited me. It's whatever.

Allison lifts up one of my shirts strewn across the floor, frowning. "If you won't send it out with the wash, you should at least have our girl steam the wrinkles out before you wear it again."

"You don't steam T-shirts, Allison," I say, ripping it out of her hand and tossing it on top of my bag.

"Well, at least put them in the dresser, then," she grumbles. "We're all stuck together for a while. Might as well make the most of it."

"A while?"

"At least till the end of the month," she says.

nonononononono

I thought I'd have more time. I thought it would be different. I thought—

"That's not enough time," I blurt out, because two and a half more weeks sounds like nothing at all.

"Not enough time?" She turns back toward me. "Enough time for what? We already know what they're doing. We just need you to find us a new angle to approach a deal, and your dad will take it from there."

I swallow hard, switching gears. "Why is he so obsessed with Vera Flores?"

"It's a pride thing. You wouldn't understand."

I roll my eyes at her insult. "Don't you feel shitty, though?"

"About what? It's not like we're trying to put them out of business. Ultimately, we're looking for a partnership."

"Yeah, like when he *partnered* with Trinity Comics?"

"He learned a lot from that misstep, Ridley."

"Misstep? That's one word for it."

More like *all-out disaster*. Trinity Comics had three of the most successful comic stores in the Northeast, indie but big indie, with some serious scene cred. Then they had the misfortune of meeting my father.

He offered to bring them in to do a joint business venture, to become affiliates and go from there. We were supposed to stay separate. They were going to be our indie leg. Only they still repped The Geekery brand. And, shocker, Dad got obsessive about it. Pretty soon, he was bringing down rules and regulations "from corporate," but who are we kidding? He *is* corporate.

Then they weren't so much affiliates as something else entirely. A mash-up. A corporate store with an indie front. Artists stopped coming for signings, customers stopped coming in to buy, prices went up to cover costs, inventory went down. It became this weird, sad chimera, leaving everybody unsatisfied on both sides.

Finally, after Dad ran their business into the ground, he bought them out at a teeny tiny fraction of what they were once worth. Dad rebranded them as The Geekery mini-marts, selling mostly cheap merchandise and Funko Pops instead of comics. He even hired one of the old owners as the manager. Twenty-five years of comics history down the drain, and all they could do was watch.

The idea of him doing that to Vera . . .

"She'll never go for it. Ever."

"That's why we're counting on you to find a way for us to make an offer she can't refuse."

"You've been watching too much of *The Godfather*. Vera Flores is not a sellout."

"Grow up, Ridley. Everyone has a price."

"Whatever you say." I reach for my headphones, planning to tune her out completely, but then she says something I can't ignore.

"You did." She pulls my laptop off my desk and drops it onto the bed in front of me before slamming the door behind her. Fuck. She's actually right. Except.

Except.

Maybe I can still fix this. I open the report file on my computer and start filling it in, feeling lighter the more I write. And if it isn't *strictly* accurate, well, nobody has to know.

CHAPTER SIXTEEN

Jubilee

RIDLEY AND I are an hour deep into sorting and stocking books—he's been here so much this last week, I figure he's an honorary employee at this point anyway—when Jayla walks into the shop. She frowns when she sees him, and I sneak a glance at my phone and see she's been texting me this whole time. I dropped the ball. Again. I was working, though, sort of, so she can't really be mad.

I say *sort of* because, while I did help a customer, and we have gotten a bunch of stock out, we've mostly been talking. And laughing. And awkwardly bumping into each other accidentally on purpose. That's basically our MO here, and maybe, *possibly* the reason I've been picking up so many extra shifts.

I just like talking to him. Like today he was telling me all about how close he is with his sister, and I was telling him all about playing cello. I even almost told him about the audition but changed my mind at the last second. I'm weird about that. Superstitious. Like if I tell too many people, I won't be invited to the next round.

"Hey, Jay," I say, mustering up a big smile.

She glances at Ridley. "You work here now?"

"Just helping out."

Jayla hums and then checks the time. "My shift starts in a half hour, but I wanted to talk to you, Jubi. Alone?"

"Okay," I say, following her into the back room.

"You two sure are hanging out a lot," she says the second I'm behind the curtain.

"Is that what you dragged me back here to say?"

"No, I dragged you back here because I miss my best friend and you never answer my texts anymore."

My face falls. "I know—I'm sorry. I've just been busy. I've had to cram in practice around all these extra shifts. It doesn't leave a lot of time to—"

"Yeah, what's up with that? You never work extra shifts, because you don't get extra pay and it cuts into cello time."

"I'm just trying to help out more."

There's a shuffling sound on the other side of the curtain then, and I hear Ridley sliding comics into the rack right beside us.

"Yeah, seems like there's a lot of that going around lately."

I want to be mad, but I can see in her face that she's genuinely upset. And she's right; I haven't really been around lately. She's used to my hard-core musician schedule and constant studying, but this is different. Adding in Bats and Ridley lately has meant dropping the ball on other things, important things. And it's not cool.

"Listen, I'm out at eight tonight. Are you working till

123

nine still?" I ask, and she nods. "I'll ride my bike over when I'm done, and we can hang then. Okay?"

"What about cello?"

"I practiced before school. I knew I was meeting—I knew I was working late tonight. Seriously, I'll be there right after we close."

She smiles, but it looks forced. "Whatever you say, Jubi."

She pushes the curtain back, nearly tripping over Ridley on her way out. "Sorry, I have to go. I have to get to my actual job that pays me money to be there."

"We should all be so lucky," Ridley says, and I can't tell if that's a joke about us not paying him or something else. Jayla flashes him a look and then leaves. I slide the curtain into place, taking a second to regroup before stepping back out onto the floor.

● ● ●

"I don't know," I say, slouching in my favorite booth at the fro-yo shop. Jayla is supposed to be behind the counter, but she's commandeered the seat across from me to tackle her homework.

"Well, I can't answer you if I don't know all the variables!"

"Oh my god, fine, yes, they can get multiple flavors of yogurt and as many toppings as they want. Happy now?"

"Okay." Jayla sighs and flips the page over in her note-book. "Okay, this I can work with."

I laugh and slide out of my seat, going back behind the counter. Ten minutes to close means it's time to start wiping down the counters and pulling the toppings, and if she's too busy doing math homework, then I'm going to have to be the one to do it.

If the owner ever discovers that I help Jayla out sometimes, they will possibly kill me and definitely fire her. But it's March and it's dead here, which generally means that anybody wandering into this sad little fro-yo shop doesn't care who's doing the serving as long as the lights are on and the topping bar's filled.

There are fourteen flavors of frozen yogurt and seventeen toppings, and I suck at factorials, but Mr. Lucas is apparently giving extra credit to whoever can come up with the most complicated real-world math problem in his class. I guess figuring out how many combinations of yogurt and toppings exist counts as a "real-world" problem. I could be wrong, though; she's in a different math class than me.

I wipe down all the counters and hope Jayla doesn't go back to asking what I know she's dying to. I scrub the counter a little harder, frowning as I rub at a spot of hot fudge that probably dried on hours ago.

"So, real talk, what's the deal with you and the new kid?" she asks, glancing up from her notebook like she could hear my thoughts.

"No deal," I say, taking the tray of hot fudge and carrying it back to the fridge now that the lip is clean.

"Jubilee, come on. You're practically living at the shop now. And every time I walk in, you guys are making eyes at each other from across the store."

"We are not."

"You are! You're my best friend, and it's like you've fallen off the face of the earth."

"I'm not intentionally blowing you off, I swear." I wipe a few stray sprinkles off the counter and toss them in the garbage.

Jayla sighs. "You got like this with Dakota too. You crawl inside your little relationship bubble with your boyfriend, and it's like no one else matters."

"Ridley isn't my boyfriend."

"Are you sure? Because from the outside, it really seems like you both want him to be."

"We're friends," I say, sliding the lid over the maraschino cherries.

She puts the notebook down—I guess the factorials will have to wait—and comes over to help. Her pin-striped hat sits slightly askew on her curly black hair, and I resist the urge to fix it. "I don't think so," she says.

"And why's that?"

"Because I know you, and I know boys like him are your kryptonite."

"You were the one who said Mrs. G meant flirting and goofing off when she said to 'go find my passion' or whatever."

"No, actually, I said you had to try something new every day. And a con crush was *one* of them. And now you've warped it into, like, your main pastime and added in—I don't even know what to call it—a shop crush?" She pulls the pan of cherries out of my hands and starts walking back to the fridge. "You always fall for these tragic little antiheroes."

I huff, "Ridley isn't some tragic antihero. He's just a boy that likes the same comics as me. That's it."

"Is it?" she asks.

"I don't even have his number. It's a strictly in-shop relationship."

"And what about Office Batman?"

I roll my eyes. "Bats is on the other side of the country. There's nothing there with him either."

She drops her chin. "Jubi, you check your phone every five seconds to see if he texted you. That's not nothing."

"So what? Am I not allowed to have other friends? You've been texting Emily nonstop since you guys started hooking up!"

"No, you are, but Emily and I are different."

"How?"

"For one, I was actually looking for a relationship. And for two, I'm not ditching the whole rest of my life to fit her in."

"I'm not ditching my whole life."

"You are, though. You don't even know what's going on with Nikki or me or anyone."

I raise my arms up, utterly exasperated. "Then will you tell me what's up instead of wasting this whole night lecturing me?"

"I'm just worried about you."

"Why? Don't be."

"I don't know; I get a weird vibe from him sometimes. He shows up out of the blue, and now he's *always* around. Doesn't he have anything else to do?"

"I don't think he has anywhere to go or any money to go

there with. He made that comment to you about not having a job. I'm thinking of asking Vera if we can pay him. At least part-time." I can tell by the way she rolls her eyes she doesn't believe me.

"His watch could probably pay your mortgage for a year. Money is not the problem."

I tilt my head. "What watch?"

"That watch he wears all the time," she says. "He might walk in with a wrinkled Hulk shirt and jeans with holes in them, but that watch is straight off the yacht."

I bite the inside of my lip. I never noticed a watch, but then again, I wouldn't. Jayla's the one who spends her days buried in lookbooks and fashion magazines.

"It could be a hand-me-down," I say finally, and Jayla slams the lid on the strawberries hard enough to let me know exactly what she thinks about that hypothesis.

"That's this year's design. Nobody is handing down a ten-thousand-dollar watch they've barely even owned."

"Ten thousand?" I say, nearly choking on my gum. "It's gotta be a knockoff."

"It's not."

"How could you possibly be sure?"

"I know accessories," she says, and crap, she does. She really does. "The dude is hiding something."

"Come on." I groan. "He's not hiding anything, except maybe a rich uncle or something."

"Oh, you sweet summer child." Jayla laughs. "How about this, then: Do you know how much houses cost in Claremont?"

"What does it even matter?" I say, because I just want this conversation to end. "Even if he has money, it doesn't mean he can't love comics and hang out at the store."

"Look, you get three types of people hanging around at your mom's shop: the wannabe artists, the lookie-loo Vera Flores superfans, and the rare people who actually need her to, like, feed them or give them a job. Why is he acting like the third one when he's, at best, one of the first two or, at worst, something else entirely?"

"Like what?"

She shrugs. "You tell me."

"Maybe he's just lonely."

"Well, yeah," she snorts. "And obviously the dude's in love with you, but that still doesn't explain where he came from in the first place. Rich people don't slum it in our town just because they like comics. There's, like, three Geekerys on the other side of Claremont that are more his speed. And if he's not here for comics, and he hasn't been pitching his portfolio or gawking at your mom, then what is he doing here?"

"I love you, but you sound so paranoid." But even as I say it, I feel a tinge of concern. Jayla's planted a little seed of doubt, and it's unfurling across everything I thought I knew.

My phone buzzes and I pull it out, smiling when I see that it's Bats and texting back immediately. I don't even realize what I've done until I look up, coming face-to-face with Jayla's frown.

"Let me guess, Office Batman?"

I shove the phone into my pocket and go back to wiping down the counter. "Whatever."

"Yeah, well, just so you know," she says, wrapping up the last of the fruit, "if either of them hurts you, they die."

"They're friends," I say. "Though I *have* heard heartbreak is a good source of inspiration."

"Funny." She opens the cash drawer and shoves the day's take into a deposit bag, putting it into the safe's drop slot. She flicks the lights off. "So, Nikki and Ty have been hooking up."

"What?!" I shout. "Finally? Oh my god, this is amazing. Since when?"

"Since two days ago."

"Why didn't she text me?"

"We did; it's on the group chat. And she tried to tell you at lunch today, but you were too busy texting Bats."

And just like that, I feel like an ass. "Wow, I suck."

"Yeah, kinda."

"What else did I miss?"

"Nothing really, just, you know, Emily and me telling Coach that we're together because people wouldn't stop talking about it at practice."

"What?! When did that happen?"

"This afternoon. I texted you *and* called. That's what I came to talk to you about today, but then I saw Ridley and just—"

"How did it go?"

"About as well as you'd expect when a slightly conservative middle-aged man finds out that his two co-captains are together. We got a long, awkward lecture about making sure the team always comes first and no kissing on the field."

"Yikes," I say, feeling like crap. "I should've been there for you."

"Just promise you'll stop shutting us out, okay?"

"I promise. I'm sorry."

"Good." She smiles, and for the first time tonight, it seems real. "So dish, then."

"What?"

"You've got *two* boys in love with you. Are you telling me you don't need any girl time?"

And I know she doesn't mean it in any sort of way. I know by "girl time" she means "girl talk," but I can't help the knot that forms in my stomach. The "am I still queer if I date a guy?" knot. I hate it. It's a big part of why Dakota and I finally broke up too. I put up with a lot from him, too much, including the fact that he never understood something so fundamental about me. He actually once said, "How can you be bi if you're dating me?" Like dating him voided out every part of my queer identity or something.

"Let's just go," I say, because suddenly cold night air sounds incredible.

"What's wrong?" She locks the doors and follows me out to where our bikes are parked.

"Nothing."

"Yeah, that's not even remotely convincing."

"Is it weird that I like boys?" I ask, my breath coming out like fog in the night air.

"Well, I'm a lesbian. So yeah, I think it's weird anyone likes boys." She chuckles. "But like, in general, no, it's not weird that *you* like boys. Why?"

"Liking a guy doesn't make me straight."

"I know it doesn't." She looks legitimately horrified as we

get on our bikes and start to pedal home. "I don't care that you like boys. I just wish you had better taste in them."

"No, I know. I think I just needed to say that out loud." I take a deep breath. "Who I date doesn't change who I am."

"Right, and if anyone says different, they're going to have to deal with me. Personally. And I've been working out." She lets go of her handlebars and flexes her biceps.

I laugh. "Thank you for being so cool, even though I've sucked lately."

"It's my job as your best friend to both point out when you suck and tolerate a small amount of it, so you're good," she says. "But if I'm playing the supportive best friend role, then level with me—which of these two sad disasters you call crushes would you actually pick if you had to?"

"I have no idea," I say, shaking my head. "I feel this pull toward Bats, but he's on the other side of the country . . ."

"If Bats wanted you guys to date, like, hypothetically, if he wanted to be exclusive or whatever, would you do it?"

"I have no clue, because there's Ridley! And Ridley is right here, and also awesome."

Jayla laughs, pedaling faster. "So then what if Ridley asked you to stop talking to Bats? Would you be able to?"

"I really don't know." I spin the pedals backward and stare up at the moon. I wonder what Bats and Ridley are doing right now. I wonder if they're thinking of me. If they're wishing we could talk.

I wonder, if they had to choose, would they choose me?

CHAPTER SEVENTEEN

BATS: Hey, what are you up to?

> **PEAK:** Lying on my bedroom
> floor having an existential crisis.

BATS: Uh . . . I think that's my line?

> **PEAK:** Is there some kind of
> existential crisis timeshare we
> were supposed to negotiate
> ahead of time?

BATS: Yes.

> **PEAK:** I'm listening.

BATS: Wednesdays are reserved
for my angst only, so.

> **PEAK:** LOL

BATS: Oh good, you're laughing.
Now I don't have to sue you for
infringing on my official angst day.

PEAK: What days do I get?

BATS: 1am to 5am on Sundays,
3:30pm to 5pm on Tuesdays,
Thursdays from 6am to 7am.

PEAK: Those are all times I'm
sleeping . . . except for Tuesday,
which is when I have a lesson?

BATS: Yeah, that was the whole plan.
Sleep through your suffering or channel
it into music.

PEAK: Why don't you do that?

BATS: Because I have no self-control
and am needy as shit. And yet for
some reason you like talking to me.

PEAK: Stoooooop.
You're not needy.

BATS: . . . Have you met me?

PEAK: Once for a second, but I was distracted. You were v cute and nervous, and I didn't hate that.

BATS: I was trying for manly and strong, but.

PEAK: Have you met you?

BATS: Once for a second, but I was very nervous.

PEAK: 😂

BATS: Did you want to talk about it?

PEAK: ?

BATS: Whatever's got you lying on the floor creeping on my angst allotment.

PEAK: Yeah, but I don't think you would understand.

BATS: I'll try not to take that personally. (I'm totally going to take it personally, though. So thanks. I'll be needing that angst allotment back to deal with it. It might even

creep into your Sunday hours tbh,
but you brought this on yourself.)

PEAK: Ha. Okay fine. Do you
ever feel like you're not enough
of something? Or you're too
much of something else?

BATS: Every day.

PEAK: What do you do about it?

BATS: Nothing healthy.

PEAK: Helpful.

BATS: 🙁

PEAK: No, seriously. What do you do?

BATS: Obsess over ways I could make
myself more. Or less. Until I'm completely
spun out and don't know which way is up.
It is not a method I would recommend.

PEAK: Yeah. Sounds shitty.

BATS: Astute observation.

PEAK: I wish you were here.

BATS: Me too . . .

PEAK: I should probably get some sleep. It's late. Plus I don't want to take up too much of your angst allotment. It sounds like you need it.

BATS: I appreciate that. But Peak?

PEAK: Yeah?

BATS: Whatever it is, you're definitely enough. Like, exactly the right amount. I guarantee it.

PEAK: ☺

CHAPTER EIGHTEEN

Ridley

"I DON'T KNOW what you want me to tell you," I say, squeezing my hand around my phone so hard it hurts. I need to calm down; I can't get this worked up. I have to be at Verona in a half hour. Jubilee is working there after school, and I promised her I'd meet her—

"Ridley!"

If my dad will let me off the phone, that is. "What? I gotta go!"

"You know how important this is. Quit screwing around. Remember you're here for a reason," he says.

"Right, I'm here to get you what you need and stay out of the way."

My dad's barely even been home lately, and Allison stays locked in her room. Last night I even made dinner for all of us—I was feeling guilty about the whole fake-report thing.

My dad didn't even take a plate, because he was "full from a dinner meeting," and Allison just grabbed some and took it up to her room. It's whatever. At least I don't feel guilty anymore. I honestly didn't think it was possible to like a house *less* than the Seattle house, and yet.

And yet.

"You know that's not true, Ridley," he says, his voice softening just enough that I almost fall for it. Almost.

"Which part?"

He sighs. "Why do you insist on making everything so difficult?"

"Guess I learned from the best," I say, staring at the road below my window.

"Ridley, please. I'm happy you're here. I enjoy spending time with you, but I need you to find me something I can use. We're so close." He sounds so desperate, I almost feel bad.

I want to tell him there isn't anything, because so far there mostly isn't, but I know there's a huge chance he'll send me back to Seattle for that. And I can't. This house might blow to live in, but Verona feels like coming home. I'm not giving that up.

"I'll keep looking," I lie.

"There's always something," Dad says, which is my biggest fear. What if I do find something? What then?

There's a little thump at my door, probably Allison listening in, and I hate her so much, even though our eyes are matching in desperation these days. "Dad, I have to go. I'm meeting Jubilee soon, and I'm skating there, so."

"Why isn't Allison driving you?" he asks, like it never occurred to him that I might walk everywhere or take my board. That maybe Allison and I aren't even talking, let alone close enough for me to ask for a ride.

"I just want to skate."

I click my phone off while my dad is still talking and slide on my hoodie. It's cold enough for a full winter jacket, but I didn't pack one and Mom hasn't bothered to send it. Dad calls back but I let it go to voicemail.

He's got the same reports I do, which conveniently leave off the fact that I know Peak only works there because Vera can't really afford more help, and instead basically say Vera Flores is a comics icon and we're lucky to be alive at the same time as her and this buying-in thing is nonsense because it's never happening. Never.

As long as I don't do anything to fuck this up.

• • •

Warm air and the jingle of bells greet me when I push open the door to Verona. I breathe in deep, soaking in the scent of comics old and new. And this, this feels like home.

"Hey, Rid." I follow the sound of Vera's voice to the back room, where I find her buried in papers.

"Hey, Vera," I say, propping my skateboard against the wall. "What's all that?"

"Financial reports. I hate this side of things," she groans. "You any good with math?" She shoves a pencil behind her ear and pushes the paper a little way in my direction with a hopeful look in her eyes. I can't decide if I should look at them or if I should look away. Probably both, simultaneously.

"I suck at math," I say. Avoidance. Good.

"It was worth a shot."

My eye catches on her laptop, which is open to yet another article about my dad. I wonder what fresh way he's insulted her now, but then I make out the headline: "If You Can't Beat 'Em, Join 'Em: Everlasting Inc. Announces New Indie Line, Geekery Ink."

Shit.

Vera looks up, studying me. "You follow this stuff?"

"A little." I shrug, trying to play it cool despite the fact that my insides are churning.

"He's a piece of work, eh?" Vera says. "Starting a new indie line after what he did to Trinity? Mark Everlasting, and everyone who works for him, should be shot into the sun."

"Yeah, totally." I swallow hard, trying to ignore the voice in my head screaming to come clean or run or melt into the floor until everyone forgets I ever existed.

Vera tilts her head. "You okay, kid?"

"Great, excellent, why wouldn't I be? No reason." Nice, Ridley, smooth.

Vera raises an eyebrow. "Well, Jubilee should be here any second; she just got held up at—" The sound of bells and laughter cut her off. "Speak of the devil."

I trot out to see Jubilee and Jayla walking in, arms linked and laughing. I feel like I'm intruding somehow, so I hang back, just sort of standing awkwardly near the curtain, caught between two places I probably shouldn't be.

Jayla notices me before Jubilee does, and she raises an eyebrow. "I don't bite, you know. You don't have to lurk in the shadows when you see me."

"No, I know, I was just helping Vera in the back, and then

I didn't want to interrupt," I lie. Well, half lie. "You guys seem happy."

"You can come be happy with us," Jubilee says, shoving her backpack behind the counter.

I glance at Jayla and then at Jubilee. "I don't want to— you guys seem—it's fine. I can go back and see if Vera needs help still."

whyamisoawkwardfuckfuckfuckfuckFUCK

"Ridley, it's fine, come hang," Jayla says, and she's smiling, but I can't tell if it's sincere or not. Probably not. Very few people really mean it when it's pointed in my direction. But I go anyway. I'm willing to pretend if she is.

Jubilee nudges my shoulder as I walk by, and I drop onto the stool next to her. Jayla stays on the other side of the counter, leaning on one arm. She's looking around the store like there are customers in it, but there aren't. I try not to worry about that.

"So Jayla here just broke the pacer record for the third year in a row," Jubilee says.

"Pacer record?"

"It's a fitness-test thing in gym, tests speed and agility, kind of a big deal," Jayla answers, polishing her nails on her shirt and giving me a big showy wink.

I laugh. "Well, congratulations on both your speed and agility, then."

"Thank you." She bows. "I would be remiss to not point out that Jubilee also got news this afternoon. She was officially offered an—" Jubilee shakes her head, though, and Jayla's smile drops.

"Offered a what?" I ask, doubly curious now that Jubilee doesn't seem to want to share. I'm probably being an asshole for asking, but.

"Nothing," she says. "Just a music thing. Don't worry about it."

I look at her for an extra beat, but she just grabs a peanut butter cup out of the candy jar and looks away. I know that's not all, but whatever it is, she obviously doesn't want to share it with me. I paste on a smile and pretend that doesn't smart.

"Awesome," I say. I hope I sound genuine.

"What about you?" Jayla asks.

"Me?"

"You got some great accomplishment you're hiding up your sleeve?"

My brain starts to scramble. Let's see, I wrote a believable fake report, I convinced my father I was still spying for him, I had the willpower not to look at Vera's financial reports, I've been drinking enough water, I haven't tried to jump off the roof, and I responded to every one of Gray's texts this week so that she didn't worry about me. And I can say exactly none of that out loud. Every single one makes me sound guilty or worse.

"Uh . . . I made dinner last night?" I say, but it comes out like a question. And then I rub my hands over my face because I just made myself sound even more pathetic in my attempt to make myself sound cool.

"A man who cooks, not bad," Jayla says, but I notice the way she's looking at Jubilee.

She's probably thinking, *Seriously? I broke a record and*

Jubilee did whatever big thing she doesn't want to talk about and all you did was boil some pasta?

shitshitshitshitshitshitshitshit

"What'd you make?" Jubilee asks, and I can barely hear her over the sound of my heart pounding. She looks sincere, but.

holdittogetherholdittogetherholdittogether

"Spaghetti, asparagus, and bread," I choke out, and they both look at me. "I need some air." I hop off the stool and go outside, the cold wind burning against my skin.

I hear the bells tinkle again a minute later as the door pushes open, and Jayla comes out with her backpack on. "You okay?" she asks.

"Just needed some air," I say again, embarrassment painting my neck crimson. I tilt my head enough to see her out of the corner of my eye. She's watching me, but she doesn't look annoyed or mean like I expected, more like curious. Open, maybe. I don't know.

"Yeah, well, I have to get to work." She twists the strap of her backpack. "But if you ever want to come over when Jubi's hanging out, it'd be fine."

I look up at her, startled. "Seriously?"

She shrugs. "I gotta jet, though, and I'm sure Jubi is eager for you to get back inside."

I nod, because this feels like an olive branch, a peace offering, a genuine smile. And I don't know what to do with that.

CHAPTER NINETEEN

Jubilee

"YOUR ENERGY IS much better," Mrs. Garavuso says as I wipe down my cello and set it back into its case. "Whatever you're doing, it's working. Your interpretation in the sarabande was the best I've heard from you yet." She smiles. "I think you're nearly there for your audition."

"Don't jinx me," I say, heading for the door. I have tons of homework tonight, and it's already late, but I know Jayla and Nikki are waiting for me downstairs. I've been working on being a better friend since Jayla called me out on it, and tonight we're celebrating a major win for their soccer team.

"It's not a jinx if it's true," Mrs. G calls after me as I bound down her front steps.

Jayla's car is in the driveway, and both girls wave at Mrs. G when I come out. I slide my cello into the back seat and dive in after it, shivering even from the two seconds it took to walk to the car.

"Hot cocoa," Nikki says, handing me a cup. It's from Stacks, my all-time favorite coffee shop for reasons too numerous to count, and I smile when I taste the cinnamon.

"Awww," I say. "You guys remembered!"

"Like we could ever forget the cinnamon and live to tell about it."

"No Emily tonight?" I ask.

"I wanted it to be just us," Jayla says, messing with the radio.

"And Emily had to babysit her brother," Nikki adds.

"The truth comes out." Now that their coach knows, Jayla and Emily have been seriously inseparable at school. Jayla even started a new group chat with her in it, even though we mostly still use the old one with just the three of us.

"So where are we headed?" I spin the cup in my hand, letting it warm my fingers.

"Bowling," Nikki sings.

"Bowling? Why?"

Jayla sighs and I can tell this is a conversation they've already had. "Nikki suggested rock climbing, but since we have another game tomorrow and you have your audition coming up, I thought we should do something with a lower risk of hand and foot injuries."

"Good plan." I laugh. It feels good to be sitting here with my best friends, not stressing about school or summer programs or nerdy boys that live in my phone or my stepmom's shop. It's exactly what I need.

"Plus, it's black-light night at Bowl-A-Rama," Nikki says, and I want to question why she has the bowling schedule memorized, but I also don't want to know.

It takes a while to get there; the bowling alley is halfway

across town and we hit every red light on the way. I'm kind of grateful, though. By the time we slide into the parking lot, I've completely finished my hot cocoa and part of my history homework.

Nikki and I put our coats down while Jayla pays and gets our shoes. There are not many benefits to us all wearing the same shoe size (7 across the board) except that it's easy to remember and our footwear choices triple in a pinch.

Jayla drops our shoes on the ground, and we sit on the little set of steps separating the lanes from the snack area to shove our feet inside.

"Ready to lose, ladies?" Nikki laughs, standing up to grab her ball.

"Yes," I answer at the same time Jayla says, "Never."

• • •

"So when is the big tournament?" I ask. We're perched on stools at the Bowl-A-Rama snack bar, trying to ignore the overwhelming smell of beer and shoe polish while chowing down on hot wings. My lips are burning, but it's totally worth it. Bowl-A-Rama wings are undeniably the best in town, and—seeing as how I generally avoid the bowling alley at all costs—also a rare treat.

"The weekend after your audition," Nikki says, twisting slowly back and forth on her spinny bar stool.

The date of my audition has been hanging over us since I got the official invite last week. It's thrilling and terrifying all at once, a bright red X on the calendar that hopefully marks the beginning of the rest of my life.

"Great, so all of us will be anxious little stress balls for the next month," Jayla says, but the smirk on her face tells me she doesn't really mind.

"I've got it in the bag," Nikki says. *"Anxious little stress ball is not in my vocabulary."*

"Easy for you to say. You have a whole additional year of high school soccer to earn scholarships and make a name for yourself." I sigh. "I only have, like, five weeks to nail my repertoire, or it's game over."

"You will," Jayla says, squeezing my wrist. "You've been working toward this forever. You're going to make it happen."

Nikki grabs another wing. "It's not the end of the world if it doesn't work out, anyway."

I snap my head toward her. "Why would you even say that!"

"Because it's true. You're putting waaaay too much pressure on getting into this summer program. It's not like there aren't other ones out there. And it's not like you won't get into college without it. *You* have a whole other year left too."

"But this is my *only* chance to study with Aleksander Ilyashev before my college audition. I need this. I didn't even schedule auditions for any other summer programs."

She shrugs. "Maybe you should have."

"What the hell, Nikki?" Jayla says. She twists around so fast, I swear to god if these stools weren't bolted to the floor, she would have spun hers right over.

"What?" Nikki asks. "I think she'll get in! I'm not saying

she won't. But she's putting too much pressure on herself. There are way more important things in life. Things can happen outside of her control, and she—"

"*She's* right here," I say, hating the way they're talking over me. It reminds me too much of Vera and my mom. Like they know better than I do where I should be and what I should be doing. They don't understand; I wouldn't be putting this much pressure on myself if I didn't have to, if I didn't *need* that scholarship.

"Sorry," Nikki says, wiping her fingers. "I just want you to relax a little. Wasn't that Mrs. G's whole point? And you don't *have* to do the summer program with Aleksander what's-his-name to get into that school, do you?"

"Ilyashev. And no, but it would really help. Can you imagine his feedback? The edge it would give me when I audition with him for their college program next winter?"

"I know. Winning the Empire Classic would really help me too, give me a leg up going into my final year. Do you know how many college scouts are at that tournament?"

"I can guess," I say, hating that she knows more about my thing than I know about hers.

"I'm just saying, don't let one moment define you. Because there are going to be a lot of moments still to come, no matter which way things shake out."

Nobody says anything after that; we just eat our wings and listen to the sound of balls crashing into pins and people cheering or swearing. When the conversation does pick back up, we switch gears to safer topics—complaining about school, talking about how great Emily is, and joking about how Nikki and Ty are finally together but still aren't being super public about it.

But Nikki's words keep buzzing in my head, and I wonder if she's right. It doesn't feel like she is, though. For the first time, it feels like maybe she just doesn't get it. Like, at all. And it's weird to feel like that about Nikki, and maybe a little about Jayla too.

CHAPTER TWENTY

PEAK: I feel like an absolute alien
around my friends lately.

BATS: Really? What happened?

PEAK: So I don't want to jinx it
but . . . I'm trying to get into a really
intense summer program that would
let me study cello with my literal idol.
And tonight Nikki said it "won't be the
end of the world" if I don't get in.

BATS: And?

PEAK: I think I would die if that happened.

BATS: Do you mean that?
Peak, that's not okay.

PEAK: Not literally or anything.

BATS: Oh. Well, good.

PEAK: But I've been working toward
this for so long, and now the audition
is almost here and one of my best
friends in the whole world is just like
"oh, it's not a big deal." It is, though.
IT IS A VERY BIG DEAL.

> BATS: Yeah, that would suck
> to hear. Like they're minimizing
> your dream or whatever.

PEAK: Exactly! I can't believe she said that.

> BATS: I think some people don't
> understand what it's like to be so
> singularly driven. They're wired
> differently. You can't really get
> mad at that.

PEAK: Can't I get a little mad at that?

> BATS: Okay, a little.

PEAK: There is so much riding on this
audition. Like I can't just get in. I have to
get that scholarship, you know? And I can't
have Nikki acting like it doesn't matter.
I can't have that in my head.

BATS: It matters. Of course it matters.
It's a ton of pressure to be under.

PEAK: God, you just get it.
How do you just get it?

                             BATS: I have no idea.
                             I never get anything.

PEAK: You get me.

                             BATS: I hope so.

PEAK: I'm so glad you
were in that elevator.

                             BATS: Me too.

CHAPTER TWENTY-ONE

Ridley

IT'S NEW-COMIC day, same as every Wednesday, and I've been helping Jubilee out with a rare surplus of customers. Vera has offered to add me to the payroll more than once, since I'm here so much, but I declined. She makes me wear a sign around my neck that says INTERN whenever she sees me, to shame me into accepting pay—which I never will. I've noticed she gets around it by buying me extra food and giving me books. It feels good in a bad way.

A man named Rutherford came in a few minutes ago and picked up his gigantic stash of books, which had Jubilee laughing for some reason. But now it's just us again, back to restocking, and she's acting all jumpy and nervous.

"Sorry," she says the third time she walks into me.

"It's fine." I steady her with my hands, so starved for touch that even this little bit of contact makes my head spin. She smiles and I fight the urge to kiss her.

While Peak and Bats seem to be making a habit of baring their souls to each other, Ridley and Jubilee are much more tentative. We are stolen smiles and the occasional head resting on my shoulder. Peak and Bats are . . . more. And the closer they get, the shittier I feel about everything—especially since she handed me exactly the in my dad's looking for when she told me about needing that scholarship. God, I hate money.

She sighs. "I just have a lot on my mind today."

"Is this about the audition?"

"The what?" she asks, her face scrunching up. "How do you know about that?"

I should have known this would happen. I've been juggling too many balls at once, and that's never been my strong point.

"How do you know about my audition?" A little divot forms between her eyebrows when she asks, and I wish I could shrink down like Ant-Man and hide in it until she's less angry, or until she forgets about me completely. Whichever happens first.

"You told me," I say, but suddenly I'm not so sure. Did she tell me? Or did she just tell Bats? She must have told us both. She had to have. It's like *the* most important thing about her. She definitely would have told Ridley too—told *me* too, I mean.

"I didn't." She crosses her arms. "Conservatory prep and audition are inner circle only."

I wince at the implication that I'm not inner circle. But, of course, I'm not. I'm just the rando at her mom's store.

"Are you sure?"

"They only let in eight cellists, and I don't need anyone finding out I applied if I don't make the cut. Inner. Circle," she says, flicking me in the shoulder. "I wouldn't have told you. It's not the kind of thing I would let slip."

And okay, it is supremely fucked up, but a part of me is jealous that she told Bats all about it but wouldn't *let it slip* to me. I know.

I know.

But the bigger issue at the moment is that I know something I shouldn't, and she's standing in front of me, waiting for an explanation that I don't have. Here we go.

shitshitshitshitshitshitshitshit

I exhale slowly, fumbling with the rack we were just restocking. Maybe if I just stare straight ahead, another customer will come in, and Jubilee will forget all about this conversation we're having.

"Well," she says again, "I know I didn't tell you."

I chew on my lip, trying to buy myself more time. "Vera must have mentioned it?"

"She wouldn't. She knows how superstitious I am. There are, like, seven people in this entire world who know I'm going for the summer program, and I want to know how you make eight."

I turn around and walk back behind the counter, my heart pounding in my ears.

"Just spill it. I can tell you have something to say. I've known something was up for a while."

"You have?" I ask, because if she knows already, then maybe it's gonna be fine. Maybe there's still hope.

maybemaybemaybemaybemaybe

"Yeah, like I know you're not really broke, so whatever

you're hiding about your secret rich background or whatever, just tell me. I don't care. What, is your father, like, on the board of the conservatory or something? Are you going to break it to me gently that you've already seen my application?"

I laugh, hoarse and hard, and I hate it. But I can't believe this is what she thinks about, that I have money and she doesn't care. How big of her. When the fuck has anybody cared that somebody has money? Like, when has that been a detractor? As long as I'm the right kind of rich, everybody's in love. Jesus, why does everybody care so much about money?

She's not entirely wrong, though. I know for a fact that one of my dad's especially smarmy drinking buddies is on the board of the conservatory. If Dad told him about this, he probably *could* arrange for her to get the scholarship or make sure she never got it, depending on how Vera reacted. Which is exactly why he can never find out.

I clench my hands and shove them in my pockets. I don't want to do this anymore. I can't.

"Ridley, what's wrong?"

I glance up and meet her eyes. She looks worried, and I don't want to be the one to make her look like that.

icantdothisicant

Maybe I can leave. Maybe I can get away. Go back to Seattle. She'd still have Bats. And maybe Bats is better than nothing. Maybe. I don't know. I can't think here. There are too many books and not enough space.

gogogogogogogogogogo

"I have to leave," I say, and dart out the door.

It's pouring outside, because of course it would pour when

I have to skate three miles home. I'd call for an Uber, but I left my phone inside. Oh well, I'll just order another one.

And I know as soon as I get back to my dad's house, I'm going to lock myself behind a door nobody can get through and sit alone until the plane ticket processes and the Uber comes, until I can be a million miles away, where I can just be the boy that Peak texts when it's convenient for her, where I won't mess up her life just by being around.

I close my eyes and try to forget that, for a second, her leg was pressed against mine. For a second, I made her laugh, and she lit up my brain like the Fourth of July. For a second, she smiled at me. For a second, those were real things that happened to me, to her, and to us, but now I can't breathe.

I can't breathe.

I crouch down, not even caring that I'm in the middle of the sidewalk in the pouring rain, and it feels like hours but could be minutes before I hear the bells over the door clang behind her and then go silent.

"Ridley!" she shouts, and she's holding my phone. "You forgot this." Oh god, she's holding my phone; she's holding Bats and she doesn't even know.

Jubilee stands under the awning. Waiting. She's not chasing me, I realize; this isn't the end of some epic romance movie. She just wants an explanation, deserves one, even. "Tell me," she says, her eyes vacillating between concern and annoyance. "Tell me what's going on."

I stand, and finally, just to blow up the entire world—just to good and blow it up because of who I am and what I am and how I don't deserve good things anyway—I turn back to her with a grin that turns to a sneer that turns to a grimace as I feel all the fight fall out of me. This will definitely get me sent back to Seattle. This will probably ruin everything. But screw it. She deserves the truth.

She does.

"Hey, Peak," I say, my voice cracking.

She takes a step back, pressing her hand to the door. Her head tilts like she's trying to see more of me than what's in front of her, and then she raises her hand to her lips.

"Bats?" she says, like she can't really believe it, and honestly, I barely can either.

"Yeah."

"What?" There's a little smile on her lips then, and I shouldn't smile back but I do.

She pulls out her own phone and fires off a text, her mouth dropping open when my phone lights up in her hand. I shut my eyes.

"How are you here?"

I shrug, because I can't tell her that. I can't drop another bomb on her, especially not if there's a single chance that we can get through this conversation without her hating me. I didn't think there was, but that smile—that smile.

"Wait, are you stalking me?" she asks, crossing her arms around herself.

I hate that I did this.

"No," I say too loud. "No," I say a little softer, shivering slightly because of the cold rain and the March air and the mean look from the girl that I like. Shit. I do. I really like her.

I gulp the air because I can't breathe, I can't get a deep enough breath, and the world starts to spin, and I'm 200 percent positive that I'm going to suffocate in this moment, that this is the end, and if it is, I can't even care.

ideserveit

"Ridley," she says. "Bats." And I look up, because I didn't think that was going to be a word that I heard from her ever again. "Did you know that a cat's nose print is unique like our fingerprints?"

"No?" I choke out. The world seems to spin a little slower as I look in her eyes, but I can't quite trust it.

"Swear to god."

She looks at me from under the awning, and it feels like I can maybe inhale just a little. "Who tested that theory?" I ask.

And when she laughs, it feels like breaking through the surface of the water.

"Somebody really brave." She smiles, but then it fades. "I need you to tell me what's going on."

"I don't—" I huff and then look at the ground, shaking my head. I have no idea where to start.

"Why didn't you say anything?" she asks, the hint of annoyance back in her voice. "I've been texting you this whole time. I even told you about . . . you."

"I know."

"Is this a game?" Her tone changes again. Gets harder somehow.

"No, it's not."

"Okay? Then why did you let me keep thinking you were two different people?"

"I'm an asshole," I say, raising my arms and then dropping them. "I don't know what else to say. I was scared."

"Scared of me?"

"No, of not being able to text with you anymore. And—"

"And what?"

"I can't." I shake my head. "But there are reasons, okay? And I will tell you, but I can't right now. I can't do this. I'll—I'll text you."

"Uh-uh, you don't get to run away. Not after this. This is unbelievably screwed up."

"I know. I know! But what if you—"

"What if I what?" she asks, taking a step forward so she's as far out as she can be under the awning without getting wet.

"I'm not good at talking to people. I'm not good at a lot of things. But when I'm texting Peak—you," I correct myself. "When I text you, I don't get freaked out. I can relax. I can be there for you or be funny. And if I do get overwhelmed, I can just put the phone down and come back later. I didn't want to lose that. And I didn't want to know."

"Know what?"

I take a deep breath and drop my head. The rain is soaking into my sweatshirt and digging at my skin. "I didn't want to know if you liked that version of me better than the real me." I'm shaking now, but I can't tell if it's from the cold.

"I like both," she says, and looking back at her almost feels good. I can almost forget that there are more secrets lurking behind this one, that this is only the harmless tip of the iceberg destined to sink us.

"Ridley," she says, holding out her hand. "Come out of the rain."

"No."

"Why?"

"Because there's more. And if you knew, you wouldn't want me under that awning with you."

"So tell me, then!"

"I can't!" I shout, staring at the bricks on the wall.

icanticanticanticant

"Ridley, I just found out that the two boys I can't stop thinking about are the exact same boy, and I don't ever have to choose, so get over here," she pleads. "Whatever else there is, we'll figure it out."

Oh god, I want to, but.

"No," I say, so quiet I don't know how she hears me over the rain.

"How come?"

"Because if we pretend this is all okay, when you find out the truth and stop talking to me—and you will—I'll lose my fucking mind." I don't know if it's the rain or tears, but my face is wet, so I wipe it with my sleeve and hope she doesn't see. My hair is slicked down flat against my forehead, the longer strands slipping in front of my eyes. It's like I'm looking at her through bars. Fitting.

She takes a step toward me, and then another. My mouth has gone dry, and my clothes are soaked, and she's getting closer and closer, until we're both standing in the pouring rain. She wraps me in a hug that I want to melt into more than anything, but I don't. I just stand, straight and rigid, and wait for her to stop. It's everything I ever wanted, and nothing I deserve.

"You're shaking." She puts her hand over mine, lacing our fingers together, and the rain dripping down her face somehow makes her look even more beautiful. "Come on, let's go back inside. We can talk more while you dry off."

I almost give in. I almost think that I could belong in a warm, brightly lit room full of books with a girl that didn't run away. I almost let myself believe that the worst is over, that this is fine. That she never has to learn more than she knows now. That I can have my cake and eat it too. That I can keep her in the dark about who my dad is and keep my dad in the dark about what I found out. That I can make it all work somehow. But she looks at me, relief in her eyes because I'm following her, and I stop. This is wrong.

This is really wrong.

"Peak, wait," I say, and she turns around.

"What?" she asks, looking a little nervous behind her smile. The divot reappears on her forehead, and I want to smooth it away.

"My full name . . ."

"Is Ridley McDonough. I know, you told me."

"McDonough is my mom's last name. I use it when . . . sometimes," I say, taking a deep breath.

"Okay?" And the divot is bigger, her face more worried.

"My legal name is Ridley Oliver Everlasting."

She tilts her head. I can tell she's trying to figure out

where she's heard it before. "Everlasting?" she asks, and then her eyes get wide. "Everlasting, like Everlasting Inc.? Like the family that owns The Geekery?"

I swallow hard and nod.

"Are you messing with me right now?"

"No." It's not a lie, but I wish it was. I wish they weren't my family. I wish—

"What was all this, then?" she shouts. "A trick?"

"No. No! Please don't think that." I take a step toward her, but she pulls back.

"I thought people were paranoid after the Trinity Comics thing. But you guys really do have plants. And that's what you are, right? A plant, a spy for your company?"

I nod again, not breaking eye contact. "But I'm not spying. I'm not really doing it. I swear."

"Screw you," she says, "whoever you are."

CHAPTER TWENTY-TWO

BATS: I'm sorry, for whatever it's worth.

CHAPTER TWENTY-THREE

Jubilee

"I'M GOING TO kill him," Jayla says, and her screen gets blurry and starts cutting out just as she's miming a stabbing motion, leaving her stuck with big eyes and her fist in the air.

Nikki giggles. "You're freezing up, Jay."

We're in a group hangout on Skype. I texted everybody, begging for an emergency meet-up, but Jayla's mom wouldn't let her go out, because she missed curfew last night—thanks, Emily—and Nikki's mom's new home aide didn't show, so she can't leave either. Skype it is.

"I'll tell you who's about to freeze up," Jayla's voice cuts through, sounding at times like a stuttering robot. "Ridley, when I drag him out of his cozy little mansion in Claremont and dump him into the ocean right on his prep-school ass."

"I don't think he actually went to prep school," I say, not that it matters.

"Well, he—" Jayla says, and then she gets all pixelated, her voice turning into a series of weird-sounding vowels as her internet crashes. Her brother is probably live-streaming his video games again. It always messes with her Wi-Fi.

"What?" Nikki asks, leaning closer to her screen like it will help her to hear better. It won't. I shove another peanut butter cup in my mouth as Jayla's screen goes black and then just says CONNECTING.

"We lost her," Nikki says, looking sad. But Jayla will log off and back on, and if we get lucky, we might get a few more minutes with her before she has to do it all over again. The coffee shop would have made this so much easier.

"She'll be back," I say, more for me than for her. I need Jayla to come back on. She's my grounded friend; Nikki is the romantic. If she's not back soon, in all likelihood Nikki will have me forgiving him and picking out wedding flowers within the next two hours. And the worst part is, I almost want to.

Not the wedding flowers, but the forgiving-him thing. I know what Jayla will say, that I always do this, that I stayed with Dakota too long and forgave way too much, that I only see the good in people and people take advantage of that. But I don't know. Is it so bad to always look for the good?

"What are you going to do?" Nikki asks, tucking herself into the warmest-looking fleece blanket I've ever seen.

"I have no idea."

"What do you want to do?"

"I want to text Bats and tell him I've had a shitty day and let him make me feel better and pretend like none of this is happening."

"The hell you are," Jayla says, her face popping back onto the screen. "Do not listen to Nikki's star-crossed lovers BS. He lied to you. That's it. Game over."

I sigh and grab another piece of candy.

"It does seem a little like fate, though?" Nikki says, her voice lilting up at the end like a question.

"Screw that." Jayla leans closer to the camera on her phone. "It's not fate to manipulate somebody into caring about you so that you can spy on them. It's creepy and abusive, and we're going to tell the whole world what an absolute piece of trash he is and blast The Geekery all over the internet."

"No," I say firmly, "we're not."

"Why are you protecting him?"

"I just don't want to make it this big public thing. I'm not protecting him."

"Except you are," Nikki says, and okay, when even Ms. Optimist is calling you out on something, it's time to take a step back.

"How are you not more pissed?" Jayla asks.

I rub my finger over a smudge on my keyboard, avoiding eye contact. "I was furious earlier, but now I'm mostly just sad."

And lonely. I really miss them. Him? Both of him? This is so messed up.

Jayla sighs. I can tell she doesn't like my answer.

"I get it," Nikki says. "You lost two people you really cared about today."

"Yeah," I say, trying to ignore the ache in my chest. "I'm still processing it or whatever."

"That's it. I'm sneaking out," Jayla says.

"Don't!" Nikki shrieks. "Your mom will end you."

"Look at her face!" Jayla gestures toward her camera, and I can only assume she means me. "Jubilee called an emergency meeting, and she's getting one."

"Don't," I echo. "Seriously, I'm fine. I'm gonna crash soon anyway; there's no point."

"Okay," she says. "Here's what we're doing. Tonight, you mope. Tomorrow, you get angry. Friday night, we come up with a plan."

"Are we still watching *Captain Marvel?*" Nikki asks, and Jayla and I both roll our eyes.

"Yes," Jayla says. "Obviously. I need to scope out the costumes for our next con."

"Good, because I'm dying to—"

But I don't hear what else she says as I click my laptop shut. I can't think about this anymore. It's time to do what I do whenever I can't figure something out. It's time to play.

The bow is steady in my hand as I slide it across the strings, sending a long mournful note out into the atmosphere before changing tempo, making it more hectic, more agitated. I play until my arms are aching and my bow is fraying and sweat is dotting my face.

And when I can't play anymore, I collapse on my bed and pray for dreamless sleep.

CHAPTER TWENTY-FOUR

Ridley

I SLINK LOWER, the cold porcelain biting at my skin as I settle against the back of the tub. I bend my knees and dip even lower as the water rises—first to my chest, then to my chin, then to my nose. Sadbath central, but who cares. Allison has been screaming at me about my reports, and I just—I just need it to be quiet.

It's almost peaceful floating here, the water enveloping me, making me feel safe in a way I don't anywhere else. Somewhere in the back of my head, I know I should get out, need to get out, that I can't float here forever.

But there are bad things waiting on the other side of the bathroom door. Like the fact that Peak hates me, like I knew she would. She didn't even respond to the half-assed text apology I sent—not that I expected her to—or to the three I sent after it either. At the moment, exploring alternatives to living with what I've done seems pretty appealing.

I even tried calling my mom, telling her I was feeling down, that being here wasn't what I thought it would be. But she was rushing out to meet some friends and told me the standard "Tough it out, Rid. Tomorrow is a new day." Which, I guess, but.

The steam rises from the water and disappears into the air. I wonder what it's like to be like that, to fit so perfectly in the universe that you can disappear in it. I just want to *fit*. Somewhere. Anywhere. I don't know. I almost did for a minute. It felt like it anyway; goofing off at Verona with Jubilee was the closest I ever felt to home.

I slide down, all the way down this time, my hair floating up as my head hits the bottom of the tub. The water drifts up my nose and in my ears; it's a little uncomfortable but not bad, and everything is so quiet, just a hint of splashing and the sound of my heartbeat pounding in my ears. Somehow even that seems watery and far away, like it's someone else's heart in someone else's body. And it must be—it has to be—because it feels like Peak's got mine in her fist in the next town over.

I plant my feet against the front of the tub and shove up, breaking through the surface with a gasp as water splashes everywhere. The air feels good against my too-hot skin as I crawl out, grabbing a towel and leaving little wet footprints in my wake. I'll clean it up later. Or I won't. I suppose either way it doesn't actually matter.

I pull on some sweats and grab my phone, scrolling through to my sister's name. I promised Gray I would always call in an emergency, and I think maybe this is one. I know she's in Boston again, visiting friends, and I shouldn't be bothering her. But still, this is me keeping a promise for once in my life.

"Hey, Ridley," she says, picking up on the second ring, and I can hear her smile through the phone. It's loud wherever she is, and I glance at the time. It's barely nine o'clock; she's probably still out to dinner or something. Gray's like that—she's the kind of person who'll have dinner at eight, the kind of person other people want to be around.

"Hi." I try to sound cheerful. I am so not her problem, and I feel bad for calling now.

"Shit, hang on a second?"

"It's okay," I say, because truly I don't want to fuck up her night. I wouldn't have called if she hadn't made me swear.

"Can you hear me?" she asks half a minute later. Wherever she is now, it's quiet.

"Yeah, but don't worry about it."

"Shut up, Ridley. What's going on?"

"Nothing," I lie. "I was just bored."

"You sure?" She hesitates, and I know what's coming. "Are you safe?"

I roll onto my back and drop one arm over my eyes. I hate when she asks if I'm safe. It makes me feel like I'm two years old. "I'm fine. Don't worry about it. I was just calling to say hi."

"I'd rather talk to you than anybody in that room, and you know it. Whatever it is you're trying not to tell me, spill, or I'm driving over right now to make you say it face-to-face."

I scoff. "Boston's like ninety minutes away."

"Sixty in a rush," she says, her voice firm and worried. "Don't test me."

"Peak is Vera Flores's stepdaughter," I blurt out, because

Peak has been the subject of probably 60 percent of my texts with Gray lately, and she'll get exactly how bad that is.

"Holy shit," she says, and then goes quiet for a second. "How is that possible?" I don't answer, and there's a sharp intake of breath on the other end of the line. "You knew when you agreed to do this, didn't you?"

I roll onto my side, blinking hard. "Yeah."

"I can't believe I didn't put this together. Ridley, this is really . . ." She trails off like she doesn't know what else to say.

"I screwed up. I know."

"Peak was your in this whole time? I thought you liked her."

"I do like her! I really like her! But Dad was so happy, and it just snowballed. All of a sudden, I was back in my old room, and he was taking me out to dinner and making small talk, and he's never been like that with me."

"Ridley—"

"You know that's true! You and I might have the same last name, but we don't have the same parents. They aren't there for me the way they are for you. And when he dangled a chance to come *home*—"

"That's not home, Ridley. It's just a house we used to live in."

"You don't understand." My eyes burn, because she doesn't. She really doesn't.

"I'm trying," she says. "But you can't keep this up. It's not healthy for you, and it's not fair to her."

"I know. I told her today that I was Bats."

"Oh god, what did she say?"

"She seemed happy at first."

"At first?" Her voice sounds hesitant, and I squeeze my eyes shut because if I don't, I'm going to start bawling.

"Yeah." I sniff. "And then I told her my real last name, and she slammed the door in my face."

She sighs, and I count to five before she speaks again. "Okay, walk me through it."

I shrug, even though she can't see me. "There's nothing really to walk through. I told her everything, and now she hates me."

"All of it?"

"Well, she guessed a lot of it herself, but yeah."

"Oh, Ridley."

"I just couldn't do it anymore," I say, dragging a hand through my still-wet hair. "I care about her too much to lie."

"Do you love her?" Gray asks, and there's no judgment there, just a question.

"I don't know."

"That's a hell of a reveal for 'I don't know.'"

"Yeah. So how do I fix it?"

Gray's quiet again, and for the first time, I wonder if maybe she doesn't have the answer, but that's impossible. Gray has had the solution to everything since I was born.

"Grand sweeping gesture?" she says finally. "It works in the movies."

"Are you being serious?"

"No. Don't actually do that. Just try to talk to her, if she'll let you. And try to rebuild her trust. And stop spying on her store."

"About that. I'm actually not. It turns out I suck at screwing people over. No wonder I'm the black sheep of the family."

"Wow, thanks."

"I didn't mean it like that," I say, even though I kind of did. "But yeah, I've been sending fake reports too. I'd never tell Dad, but I did find out one thing that—"

"Don't tell me about it either."

I stare down at my feet, the reality of the situation washing over me again, making everything seem impossible. I swallow hard. "What do I do if she won't talk to me?"

"Then you back off and give her space," she says softly. "Either she comes around on her own, or you chalk it up to a lesson learned."

"That's it? You're telling me to give up?"

"It's not giving up; it's respecting what she wants, which you should have done in the first place by being honest with her. I want this to work out for you so bad, but what you did was beyond reprehensible, even if I get the reasons why you did it. Just be prepared, okay? Sometimes you can't fix things once they're broken. If she doesn't want to talk, then you need to back off."

"Yeah." I swallow hard and don't mention the fact that Peak's already been ignoring my texts.

Gray sighs again, and I swear I feel that shit in my soul. "Maybe tearing it all down wasn't the worst thing. Nothing good would ever come from the lies. So either you sped up the inevitable, or you have the chance to build something that's actually solid."

"Yeah, maybe," I say, even though I don't really believe it.

"I'm glad you called, Rid. Let's do something this weekend. Pick a cool spot to eat. We'll see a movie and go out to dinner after."

"Sure," I say, pretending not to notice that she's giving me something concrete to look forward to, a goal to reach. She read a bunch of self-help-type books a few years back—once she figured out what a mess I was—and decided I would benefit from concrete goals and plans. She's been not so subtle about doing it ever since.

"All right, let me know how it goes. I expect a text every day with an update."

"Yes, Grayson," I say, rolling my eyes at her and her goals.

It does weirdly help, though.

I set the phone down and then think better of it, scrolling to the last song Peak sent me. I put it on a loop and stay awake as long as I can, listening. And when I do fall asleep, I dream about butterflies.

CHAPTER TWENTY-FIVE
Jubilee

"YOU HAVE TO tell your parents," Jayla says. Nikki sits beside her, nodding in agreement.

I'm on my side on my bed, hugging my pillow and watching them paint their nails, while Captain Marvel saves the world on my TV. Nikki is going with pink; Jayla has gone for a brilliant yellow. I shut my eyes and try to forget about the fact that I basically broke up with both of my boyfriends this week, simultaneously. Not that I even realized I thought of them that way until after it was over, when I missed them so much I felt like I was losing it. *Him*—I missed *him*. I still can't get used to Ridley and Bats being one.

"Well, actually, maybe she doesn't have to tell them, unless he was really spying," Nikki says, and even though I declared it a state of emergency on our call the other day, I really wish we could talk about anything but this now. "He said he wasn't."

I shift the pillow to cover my face as I roll over onto my back. I hate this. I hate that he lied to me this whole time, and

I hate that I miss him so much I could scream. I should dislike him, like, as a person, probably forever. But I don't.

I'm more annoyed that all the times I said I wished he were here, he could have been. I wish he'd told me sooner. I wish there was more than a span of like three breaths between him saying "Hey, Peak" and me saying "Screw you." It isn't fair.

"Obviously he's spying," Jayla says, rolling her eyes. "He's an Everlasting; that's what they do."

Everlasting. It doesn't sound like a bad name, pretty cool actually, except for the family attached to it. Why does he have to be an Everlasting? Maybe he could get emancipated. That's a thing, right?

"Well," Jayla says. "What are you going to do?"

"I have time to figure it out," I say, flipping the pillow back behind my head. "I doubt I'll see him again anyway."

Jayla drops her chin. "No, you definitely will. What day do they have you working?"

"Sunday."

"With Vera or alone?"

"Alone."

"He'll be there," Jayla snorts. "I'd put money on it."

"He probably took the first private jet out of here," I say, all nonchalant, pretending like that thought doesn't hurt.

"He'll show," she says, going back to painting her nails, which makes my traitor heart twist in ways it shouldn't.

"Is he still texting you?" Nikki asks.

"Nope," I say, popping the *p* and scratching my eyebrow with my thumb. "Just the ones right after, and then nothing."

I climb off the bed and go over to my nail polish, picking out a wild shade of teal. I realize too late it's the same one I wore to FabCon prom.

"Don't you think this whole thing was one giant setup?" Jayla asks. "It's too convenient to not have been."

"Jay." Nikki waves her hand back and forth like that will make it dry faster. "You seriously think he rode the elevator up and down all night hoping you guys would get on? Doubtful."

Jayla shoots Nikki a look. "Not that part, obviously, but everything after that."

"It was fate, face it," Nikki says, like that's a totally normal, rational belief.

"Fate, right, that must be it." Jayla laughs, flipping over her buzzing phone to read an incoming text. "Crap."

"What?"

"Sorry, Jubi, but we gotta go. My mom needs me to pick up my brother, and I have to drop Nikki off first."

"It's fine. I'm okay," I say, even though I was hoping they could sleep over. But they have a super-early away game tomorrow anyway, so it's probably for the best.

"You sure?" Nikki asks.

"It was just a con crush, right? Who even cares?" I try to play it off, but those words hurt coming out.

Jayla narrows her eyes like she doesn't quite believe me. "Right," she says. "This is why we ghost them. Trust me next time."

• • •

"Jubi?" my mom says, peeking her head into my room.

"Yeah?" It's been an hour since the girls left, and I've been staring at my phone ever since, debating whether texting Bats back would be the worst thing in the world. Half of me has decided it would be. The other half has decided it wouldn't.

"I think HP got out."

I bolt upright. "What?"

"I just opened a can of her food, and she didn't come. I was hoping she was locked in here with you."

I flip off the covers and shove my feet into my unicorn slippers. "Nope. Vera was carrying in a ton of canvases earlier. I bet she snuck out. I'll go find her." This is bad; HP is *not* an outdoor cat.

"If she doesn't come running, we'll get her in the morning, okay?"

"Sure," I say, but there is no way I'm leaving my cat outside all night. One, it's cold; two, she's mean; and three, she has the common sense of a bag of rocks. Not a great combination.

My mom gives me a quick kiss on the cheek and says good night, and then, armed with stale cat treats, I head out to the back deck. The few times she's gotten out, that's where she's ended up.

"Harry!" I call, and . . . nothing. "HP!" I try, a little louder.

I walk to the edge and lean over the railing, shaking the treats as loud as I can. "Here, kitty, kitty, kitty."

There's a rustling sound, followed by some angry cat

noises. Shit. This is bad. What if she's fighting with that neighborhood stray?

"Harry?" I call, darting down the steps. My slippers are going to be ruined, but screw it. Some things are more important in life.

The angry cat sounds are getting louder, but now they're accompanied by someone shouting, "Dammit, stop. Ow— what's the matter with you?"

And that voice, it's a poison and an antidote all at once.

I pick up the pace, and we round the corner at the same time, nearly running into one another. We both stop at the last second, staring at each other with matching shocked faces, while HP hisses and tears at his arms.

"Ridley?"

"Peak, I—"

But HP swats him in the face—claws out—before he can finish. She goes flying as he jerks back, and I scoop her up before she gets too far. She struggles for a second but then seems to realize it's me and goes limp. I'd like to think it's because she's happy to see me, but I know it's more likely because she knows scratching and biting me won't work. I have a very high pain tolerance when it comes to her.

"Did you kidnap my cat?" I ask, utterly incredulous.

"No!" he says, his eyes huge. "I heard you calling her, and she ran by. I didn't want her to get away, so I tried to grab her, but, you know."

"Wait here," I say, walking back toward the deck. I deposit Miss Harry Potter inside the house, tossing her a handful of treats before walking back to the railing. Ridley has followed me, at least as far as the foot of the steps, his face illuminated by the motion-detecting light over the door. So much for following directions. I pull my hoodie tighter. "Why'd you come here tonight?"

"I missed you, and I couldn't take it anymore," he says.

I blink at his honesty, my breath escaping in a little huff.

He crosses his arms and then uncrosses them, opening and closing his mouth like he doesn't know what to say. "Peak," he says finally. "I majorly messed up; I know I did. But if you don't completely hate me yet, can we please talk? If you don't want to, I get it, and I'll go, but if you do—"

"How did you get my address?"

He looks down. "It was in the file my dad gave me about Vera."

"Right, of course. Every spy has a portfolio." I cross my arms. He's got a small plastic bag around his wrist; I didn't see it before in the chaos with HP. "What's in that? Are you here to bug my house? Maybe set up some spy cams?"

"Oh." He looks down like he forgot he even had it. "No—peanut butter cups. And Sprite. They're for you."

"Why?"

"You always pick the peanut butter cups out of the candy jar at the store, and Vera gets you Sprite from the Chinese food place, so I thought maybe they were your favorites." He drags a hand through his hair and then drops his head back. I almost don't hear his whispered F-bomb.

He's absolutely right—those are two of my favorite

things in the whole world, and when you combine them, it's next level. I can't believe he noticed, but it's really the F-bomb that seals the deal, or rather the little anguished exhale that follows it. It feels sincere in a way words never could, and I melt a little. Or maybe I'm just looking for a reason to forgive him. Probably a little of both.

"I know you probably can't forgive me," he says, his breath puffing out in the cold air. "But I wanted you to know that I never spied, and I never would. I made up all of the reports." He rubs at the cat scratch on his cheek, the little bag of Sprite and peanut butter cups smacking against his shoulder. "I like you too much to ever do that to you, which I know is messed up to say, because I shouldn't be spying on anyone regardless, but . . . Here, though—at least take these and I'll go." He walks closer to the rail and holds up the bag. "I just wanted you to know that."

"Why should I believe you?"

"You probably shouldn't, but it's the truth. I swear to you it's the truth. I have the reports, if you want to see them. I wouldn't . . . I wouldn't do that to you. You matter too much to me."

I should go back inside, go back to my room, hug my cat, and never talk to Ridley again. That's what Jayla would do. But he's standing here, looking wrecked, holding a bag of my favorite things, which I never told him about but he noticed anyway, telling me he didn't spy and wouldn't ever, and it's everything I've been wishing for since that day in the rain and more.

The motion light clicks off—we've been still for too long—and the moonlight is just enough to make this moment seem magical.

"Come here," I say, and I meant up the steps, but he jumps up and hangs from the railing instead, shoving his toes between the slats so we're face-to-face. The light clicks back on, and it's kind of perfect in a really strange way. I move my hand to pull him closer. He flinches, like I'd slap him, and my heart breaks. I would never.

"It would be so much easier if I hated you," I say when he finally dares to slide his hand against mine. His thumb is rubbing over the top of my fingers, and it feels so warm on this coldest of nights.

"Does that mean you don't?" he asks, and I don't miss the hope in his voice.

"It's actually annoying how much I don't hate you. I can't, not even a little bit, and I really tried."

He's trembling—from nerves or the cold, I don't know—as I cross those final inches and press my lips to his. It's nervous, tentative, but when his hand slides back to grip my neck, our breaths tangling like his fingers in my hair, we both smile.

CHAPTER TWENTY-SIX

Ridley

SHE LEANS FORWARD, resting her arm on the railing like she's manning a drive-through and not stitching my heart back together with every breath. She doesn't hate me, and I can't help but smile at that. It's not much really, not in the grand scheme of things, but it's a start. My toes are wedged under the railing, my free hand supporting nearly all my body weight, and this . . . does not feel great. But I'll dangle here all night if it means she'll kiss me again.

"Peak," I say, but that ends in a yelp when my hand starts to slip and I nearly lose my balance.

"Shhh." She giggles as she takes a step back and motions for me to follow her.

"Can I . . . ," I start, forgetting the words at the sound of her laugh. I clear my throat and try again. "Do you think we could go inside and talk a little?"

She nods and tiptoes back over to the sliding glass door. It's dark inside, but HP seems to be gone, or possibly just lying in wait somewhere in the shadows. I never did trust cats.

I climb over the railing, coming up behind her as she slips the door open. "Shhh," she says again as we step inside. "Take off your shoes."

"Jubi?" someone calls out, and I realize it's Vera. I have one shoe off and one shoe on and no idea what to do.

"Crap." Peak shoves me into the little alcove behind her table. I hop backward on one foot, nearly knocking over a rack of plants in the process.

"What's up, Vera?"

I hear feet pad across the linoleum to where Peak is standing. Three more steps and I'm busted. I hate sneaking around—it feels like more lying—but I also just really want to talk to Peak, so.

"How's HP?"

"Good, she came in without any trouble."

"I thought I heard her yowling out there."

"Oh, that. That was a stray."

"Okay," Vera says, but I can tell she doesn't totally believe her. Vera takes another step, leaning forward so I can see just a little of her head. I shove myself farther against the plants, wincing when they rustle.

"Um, Vera, if you and my mom aren't going to sleep after all, can I practice more?"

"It's not that I don't love it when you play . . . ," Vera says, heading back the way she came. She'd better love it. It's the most fantastic sound in existence.

"Right," Peak snorts.

"Good night, Jubi."

"Good night," Peak says, dragging out the last word.

I take a step forward, but she holds up her finger, standing completely still until Vera's door clicks shut down the hall.

I kick off my other shoe. I kind of love that they care enough to not wear their shoes inside. I always thought it was gross that we do, but my mom always says the housekeeper will clean the floors. Everything is someone else's problem in my family.

Peak slides the bag from my wrist after we dart into her room, slipping the door shut and locking it. She opens the bag of candy while I look around. Her room isn't a bad size, about half as big as mine but way more comfortable. Every square inch of her walls is covered with posters or pictures of her and her friends. A worn pink blanket covers her bed, but not like the trashed kind of worn—more like the soft and loved kind.

And then I see it. Peak's cello. And I can't breathe. It's like seeing the actual Mjolnir up close or something. Every word I had planned flies out of my head at the sight of her instrument.

"It's beautiful," I say, thinking of how those strings and that bow have gotten me through the roughest of nights since I came here.

"Well?" she asks, interrupting my thoughts.

I turn back to her, shoving my hands in my pockets and waiting to see if she says something else.

She raises her eyebrows. "That's it? Really?"

"There was a speech," I say, taking a step closer to her.

"There was?" she asks, not moving forward but not backing away either.

"It was a great speech," I say, desperately trying to remember it now that she's so close.

"Oh yeah?" And I think she's maybe getting a little annoyed again.

"I'm sorry." I hang my head. "Your lips seemed to have rewired my brain. I'm, uh, attempting a reboot."

She sighs and climbs into the center of her bed, taking the candy and soda with her. She grabs her pillow and hugs it tight to her chest. "I don't know what to do with you. Part of me is so amped that you're here and that you're Bats." I smile, but then her face falls, and I follow suit, trying to brace for whatever comes next. "The other part of me knows that this is extremely messed up. You were sent here as a spy, right? You completely lied to me this whole time?"

I swallow hard because accurate. Well, except the one thing. "Let me show you the reports. I never spied."

"Seeing *is* believing, I guess," she says, her voice flat.

For once, my anxiety making me overthink everything is useful. I pull off my backpack and unzip it, taking out the now-wrinkled papers I printed earlier. She looks them over. Her eyebrows draw together, but then rise as she lets out a breathy laugh.

"He actually believes this?"

"Yeah, why wouldn't he?"

"You make it sound like we're completely loaded and she's buried in offers."

I smirk. "It's a shame there's no room for my father to negotiate, considering how in demand she is, right? Best if he just backs off and cuts his losses."

"Smart." She tilts her head and smiles, but then her face gets serious again. "If I were to give you another chance—and I'm not saying I am, but if I did—would you screw it up?"

I take a deep breath—it feels like my soul is crawling up my throat—and shake my head. "Not if I could help it," I say, because we both know that's the best I can do.

"I need to know some more things before this can be okay."

"Anything," I say, because just the idea that a reality exists where we *could* be okay has me drunk on nerves and anticipation. This is all I ever wanted, Bats and Peak against the world, like two characters from Vera's books.

She scoots over on her bed, gesturing toward the empty spot. I sit on the very edge, not wanting to presume. I'm trying so hard to be still and quiet and patient and everything she would ever want, but my leg is bouncing a mile a minute, and I can't stop biting the skin around my thumbnail. I am fucking this up already.

She unwraps another peanut butter cup, eyeing me. "I still can't believe you're really an Everlasting."

"What, do you want to see my ID or something?" I joke.

"Kind of. Yeah."

"Seriously?"

"Show me."

I grab my wallet and slide out my Washington State ID. "I don't have a license; my mom never had time to teach me," I say, shame heating my cheeks because that's another normal-kid thing I never accomplished. "I went to visit my aunt Mary in Michigan once and she tried, but—"

"I don't have my license either; driving terrifies me," she says, snatching the ID from my hand. Her face falls as she stares down at it. "You're really an Everlasting."

I nod, wishing so hard my name was something I could peel off like dirty clothes and leave behind forever. I don't want it anymore, not if it means losing her.

"Did you know who I was at the dance?"

I shake my head.

"Are you lying?"

"No, I really didn't find out until later."

Her eyes burn into mine. "When you *did* find out who I was, why was your first reaction to sell me out?"

And that, that's a hard one. I rest my forehead in my hands, my knees—one still bouncing—propping up my elbows as I try to remember how to breathe. Her fingers graze my back, and I resist the urge to melt into them, scrunching my eyes tighter and shaking my head. I stand up and pace. This was a bad idea. I should go.

shitshitshitshitshitshitshitshit

"Did you know that dragonflies can zoom along at thirty-five miles per hour?"

"Peak, don't," I say, my voice shaking. I came here to make it better, but every time she tries to comfort me, I just feel a thousand times worse. "Why are you so nice?" I mean it in a bad way, but it comes out embarrassingly plaintive.

"I'm not that nice," she says.

I look at her and raise my eyebrows.

"I was planning to ghost you after the con."

"But you didn't."

"No, I didn't. I blame your dimple." She tosses me a pea-nut butter cup, which I miss and have to scoop off the carpet. There are still vacuum lines in some places, and it seems wrong to be tossing candy on it.

I take a step closer as she pops open the Sprite and sets it on the table beside her without even taking a sip. She reaches out her hand and pulls me down on the bed, so close our knees are touching, harsh denim against soft pajamas.

idontdeservethis

"Get out of your head, Ridley."

"How?"

"You can start by telling me everything I should know about you."

I huff out a laugh, dropping my head back and staring at the ceiling. "If I do that, then you'll definitely hate me."

"I might," she says. "But there's only one way to know. And I think I deserve to have all the information before I make up my mind."

My first instinct is to run, because nothing good will come of this. I've never shown anyone the truth of who I am, of what I am, of how much of a goddamn mess I am even on the best of days. But then I remember what Gray said, that it's not just my heart on the line. That I dragged her into this, and I owe her, so I take a deep breath and I start talking. I tell her about what happened at the end of the con, when she was already on her way home, and I hint about my relationship with my parents. And it's hard. When we were texting, I felt like I could tell her anything, but now I'm suffocating under the weight of her stare.

icantdothisicant

But she asked for everything. And this is a big part of everything, the biggest, maybe. I run my hands through my hair and try to choose my words carefully, which doesn't exactly work. But it's now or never.

"You have to understand how it was growing up. The only time my dad paid attention to me was when I fucked up—I was either invisible or getting yelled at, no in-between. And there was constant pressure from tutors and school and life, and Gray was so fucking *perfect* all the time, and I—I wasn't. Ever. I couldn't take it. Eventually I started thinking of exit strategies or whatever."

"Exit strategies?" she asks. "Like what? Running away?"

I look down, studying the little threads of her carpet. "A little more permanent than that, Peak." I hold my breath, waiting to see how she'll react. This is usually when people freak.

She just whispers "Jesus" and rubs her fingers over mine, wriggling them in until our hands are linked.

"Yeah, so, it's whatever," I say, feeling a little bit like throwing up. I'm a raw nerve, a full-body toothache, but she should know what she's getting into.

ishouldgoishould

She's still holding my hand tight, like she wants me to stay, and I can't figure out why.

"Do you still think like that? The exit-strategy thing," she asks.

I pull my hand back and bite my nail, trying to figure out what the right answer is. I said no more lies, and yet.

And yet.

"You don't have to answer—"

"I said I would tell you whatever you wanted to know." She opens her mouth to interrupt, but I just keep talking. "Sort of, I guess? It's different now; it's not urgent like it used to be. It's more like a habit, if that makes sense?" I glance at her face. "You know how some people go to movie theaters and have to find all the emergency exits, or they go out to eat and have to face the door no matter what, and half the time they don't even realize they're doing it?"

She nods, but kind of slowly, hesitant.

"That's how it is, just like a glitch in the comfort matrix or something. Something my brain tosses out there, and I'm like, 'Cool, thanks for the suggestion, but maybe we could just play a video game instead.' It's just crossed lines. It's fine." I'm downplaying it some, but whatever.

Peak crawls up behind me and wraps her arms around me hard, holding tight, like she's worried I'll float away if she lets go. I rub my cheek against her arm and sigh. "It's really not a big deal, so please don't worry. I shouldn't have said anything."

She doesn't answer me at first, just squeezes me tighter. I think for a half second that I'm going to cry, but this isn't the time, so I blink hard and open my eyes wide and try to suck the tears back into my eyeballs before she notices. She keeps hugging me, and I focus on the ceiling, which is full of brilliant green glowing stars, because it's easier than facing her.

I should feel relaxed, accepted, proud of myself for being

vulnerable, excited that I didn't scare her off. But I'm not. I'm antsy, freaked out, on edge, and the longer she doesn't talk, the worse it gets. My brain spins out in a thousand directions, each one worse than the last.

She's only being nice because she feels bad.

She wishes you would leave already.

She still hates you and can't figure out how to say it.

"I should probably go," I say, even though it kills me, even though I haven't told her half the things I'd planned to.

She slips down beside me and tilts my face toward hers, brushing some hair off my forehead. "You could stay."

Confusion etches lines across my forehead. "What?"

She takes a long, deep breath, watching me, appraising me, her eyes focused on mine. "I said you could stay. If you want."

I smile before I catch myself, and then my stomach sinks. I know what this is; this is Gray and concrete goals all over again. This is pity. I shake my head. "I'm fine, Peak, really. You don't have to babysit me."

"Good, because I'm not," she says, with just enough attitude that I sort of believe her.

"Why, then?"

She presses a kiss to my nose and pulls me closer. My heart is pounding, clawing at my skin to get to her. I wonder how she can stand it. "I like you, okay? That's why."

I bring my arm up around her, letting my fingers trail over her skin, trying to be cool, to be nonchalant, to act like my entire body isn't on fire right now. "I like you too."

CHAPTER TWENTY-SEVEN

Jubilee

MY PHONE IS buzzing somewhere in the background, and I chase the sound back to consciousness with a little sigh. I roll over, half expecting Ridley to still be there, warm and drowsy, with his arms tucked behind his head, just the way I left him. But there are only cold sheets.

We talked all night; he told me about his family, his sister, and about growing up in the shadow of The Geekery. We talked about the fake reports and his sister's reaction when he told her everything. We even talked a little about fate. He filled in all the blanks between Bats and Ridley, and somehow, around two a.m. or so, the two sides of him officially fused into one in my mind. And I really like it, maybe even more than like it, if I'm being honest.

There's a small part of me, though, a quiet part, that still feels weird about how everything went down, but I shake it off and grab my phone, smiling when I see that it's him telling me to

BATS: Wake up already!

                                              ME: You left!

BATS: I didn't want your moms
to see me! Now get up.

                                   ME: It's 8:30. On a Saturday.
The only people up now are
like athletes or masochists.

BATS: And people who have to work.

                                   ME: Of which we are none.

BATS: Also people who have dates. 😉

                                   ME: Oh my god. You are
a massive dork. 😊

BATS: Meet me at Malywick Park
in an hour?

                                   ME: An hour?!

BATS: Too soon?

                                   ME: I'll be there in 20.

BATS: Come on then, Peak.
I'm already here.

ME: ☺

I wiggle into some jeans, yank a sweatshirt over my head, pull my hair back into a ponytail, and toss my gloves onto my bed so I don't forget them. It's nearly April, but even spring-time in New England isn't so forgiving.

I am ready to go—teeth brushed, mascara applied, winter headband acquired—within ten minutes. I fire off a text to Nikki, because if there's one person who will have my back in this, it is definitely her. It's a short text, three words only: **We made up.**

She doesn't write back right away; I don't expect her to. She'll probably be tied up at the game for the next few hours. That's what Saturdays are like around here. I usually spend them practicing cello, but every other overachieving kid in town is either at a game or rehearsing for a play.

But today, today is different. Today is . . . fate. Today is meant to be. Today, we're going to test-drive this tentative more-than-truce we started last night and see how it flies in the daytime.

I slip out of my bedroom, tiptoeing down the hallway, but Vera's sitting at the kitchen counter already, her coffee steaming in front of her. She puts down her phone and looks up at me, her eyes still bleary. "Jubilee? You're heading out early. You going to a game?"

"No." I'm tempted to fib, but Ridley said no more lies. "I'm meeting a friend in Malywick," I say, lingering in the doorway. I know if I actually set foot on the linoleum, she'll start peppering me with questions I'm not ready to answer.

Even though Ridley is ready to be 100 percent transparent with his life, I'm not so sure I'm ready to do the same with mine. And I don't think Vera would be so forgiving either; you can't even mention The Geekery without her blood pressure rising.

"This wouldn't be the same friend who climbed our deck railing last night instead of using the stairs, would it?"

"Uh," I say, my face heating.

"They left muddy footprints everywhere."

"Maybe it was a raccoon?" I wince.

"A raccoon with size-eleven Vans that they left parked by the sliding glass door all night?"

"Maybe it was a very courteous raccoon?"

"I won't tell your mother, as long as it never happens again. Don't make me regret this."

"Deal."

She leans back in her seat, crossing her arms. "Will you tell me who it was?"

"Not yet, okay?" I say. "But I will."

Whatever Ridley and I have still feels tentative. Like a sudden gust of air could break us. I don't want to let anyone in who isn't going to be on board until it has time to grow. Until I know they can't scare it off. At least until I figure out a way to put a positive spin on the fact that he's an Everlasting.

Vera nods; she's always been the easier one when it comes to stuff like this. "It's cold out."

I point to my head. "The headband covers my ears."

"Bring your coat."

"I'm wearing a sweatshirt."

"A coat, Jubilee," Vera says, and then sips her coffee with a satisfied smirk.

• • •

The walk to Malywick takes way too long. Halfway there I curse myself for not riding my bike . . . but I didn't know what else Ridley had planned, and I didn't want to be pushing it around all day.

I turn down Southside Drive, grinning when I see the familiar sight of trees winding into the air. The park sits basically in the center of town, around the remains of some old settlers' houses. In the summer, the place is filled with tourists and buskers. Music and laughter—and the occasional argument—mix with the scent of the waffle cones from the fro-yo shop nearby, where Jayla works. This time of year, it's deserted, peaceful even, a place to sit and reflect in privacy.

The perfect place to meet the very cute boy who's currently sitting on top of a picnic table, bouncing his knee.

Ridley's hoodie is pulled down so low over his eyes, I can't even see them. He looks small, folded up like that, a little stress ball in a slightly too big sweatshirt. He glances up when he hears me, pulling back his hood, his eyes widening to match his smile. His hands are tucked into his pockets, but he jumps down without losing his balance.

"You came," he says, like he can't believe it.

"You knew I was coming!"

"I wasn't sure." He chews on his lip.

"I said I couldn't wait."

"I know, but."

I poke his shoulder, making him look up at me. "But what?"

"I'm kind of still waiting for the other shoe to drop, I guess."

"Well, it's not going to." I notice his skateboard tucked into his backpack beside the table, one wheel rolling lazily in the wind. He's had his board at the shop before, but I've never really gotten to see him skate. "Did you skate here?"

"Yeah," he says, a little shy, like I'll think that's dorky or something. I don't. I love it.

"I always wanted to learn. Show me?"

He pulls his board out and carries it over to a flat area away from the cobblestones, then changes his mind and walks down farther to the parking lot. "Have you ever skated before?"

"Once," I say, "but it doesn't count."

"Why not?"

"Because it wasn't with you." I meant it to be funny, but it comes out sounding sincere.

He blushes at my answer, ducking his head as I step onto the board. "Do you want to learn, or do you just want me to pull you along?"

"Both." I laugh.

"Okay, get your feet comfortable. Move them so they're kind of like this," he says, demonstrating on the ground.

I do as I'm told, marveling at how much warmer it feels when someone you like is giving you skateboarding lessons, even in an empty parking lot on the last day of March.

"Okay, push off," he says, reaching his arms out. I give it a shove, locking my arms on his when I start to lose my balance. "I won't let you fall."

I look up, startled, and he's smiling when our eyes meet, one dimple visible under the cold sun. We practice a few more times, until I start to figure it out, using his arms less and less as my confidence grows.

"What do you think?" he asks. "Should we give it a go?"

"Absolutely," I say, a little too enthusiastically. He chuckles, and then it's my turn to look down, embarrassed. "I mean, yeah. I think I've got this."

He drops his arms, and I kick off. The board slides forward; I'm a little wobbly but I keep it going, gliding faster and faster, shoving forward as fast as I can. I try to find a rhythm in the sound of the wheels on the asphalt, try to turn it into music so it makes more sense.

"Yes!" he shouts behind me, and I turn my head, almost losing my balance when I see him raising his arms up in victory. I hop off, running forward a few steps so I don't fall over, before I turn the board around to face him.

He grins, and it bolsters my confidence so much that I shove off a little faster than I mean to, careening toward him at a rate I'm not entirely comfortable with. He seems to sense the change in mood and races toward me, reaching me right as the board nicks the curb and sends me flailing in the other direction. I'm lost in the air, landing hard on top of him.

I cough into his elbow as I push myself up. He takes a deep breath and grunts beneath me, like I knocked all the air out of him.

"Oops," I say, sitting up and trying to give him space. "In fairness, though, you did say you'd never let me fall."

He raises his eyebrows and opens his mouth but then sighs in mock defeat. "Historically, I'm not good at keeping promises, so."

"Hey." I grab his chin. "None of that."

"Fine, half credit for catching you?"

"Half credit seems fair." I scoot forward, giving him the tiniest kiss on his cheek, not sure what the rules are in the daylight.

I slide beside him, looking up at the sky. I'd swear it was a summer sky if I didn't know any better. And god, summer with Ridley sounds perfect. Except how does that work? How do we keep our families from finding out that long? How do I figure out how to—

"Can I get another one of those?" he asks, catching me off guard.

"Another what?" He taps his cheek, and I twist my lips, trying to hold in a laugh. "You're shameless."

I lean in to give him an overexaggerated kiss on the cheek, but he turns his head at the last second, pressing his lips to mine with an innocence that make me giggle. He shuts his eyes then, and I shut mine, and the kiss turns into something different.

"Sneaky," I say when we break apart, before diving back in for another quick kiss. A cold gust of air rushes by, and I hunch down a little in my jacket. I'm glad Vera made me bring it.

He grabs my hands, and god, I wish I hadn't forgotten my gloves on my bed—they've gone numb from the cold, and I would've really liked to feel this.

"You're frozen!" he yelps, jumping off the curb and pulling me up. "Come on, let's get you inside somewhere." He does this little step move, and his board flips right up into his hands.

"So, that was awesome." I've never known anyone who really knew how to skate. A couple of my friends have longboards, sure, but that's just to get around, not really for fun.

He crinkles his forehead. "All I did was pick it up."

"Pretty sure you just worked some kind of skater magic and it flew into your hand. Do you do any other tricks?"

"Tricks?"

"Like, can you jump on stuff and slide across it?"

"Yes." He laughs. "I can jump on stuff and slide across it." He says it in a way that tells me these moves have actual names, but not in a way that makes me feel bad for not knowing them.

I tuck my jacket tighter around me. "Show me."

"You're freezing."

"I can be cold for another minute or two. Show me."

"Yeah?" he asks, like he's shocked I want to know more about something that so clearly matters to him.

"Yeah," I say, dropping onto one of the long marble ledges that run the length of the park. "Show me what you got."

He slides his board forward and runs after it, picking up speed when he hops on and shoves off harder and faster than I ever could. His wheels tear across the asphalt, dipping and racing with every thrust of his foot as he jumps and flips the board in the air. If my ride was music, then his is a symphony, and I don't want it to stop.

I clap—I can't help it—and he spins the board around to face me with a whizzing sound. He shakes his head like I'm ridiculous and sends the board forward again, racing toward me.

I tuck my feet up to avoid a collision, but he just sticks his tongue out and lands a jump on the marble wall beside me, the middle of the board skidding down its length like he's surfing. He flips the board off and lands on it without missing a beat, turning wide in the direction of the steps to slide down the rail onto the sidewalk below.

I stand up. I can just barely see the top of his head over the wall. He skates around and back up, doing the flippy thing again before coming to a stop right in front of me. He's a little bit out of breath, his cheeks pink from exertion and the cold, and he looks at me through his hair, waiting.

I want to be cool. But I also want to totally fangirl. I settle on "That was friggin' amazing."

And his face breaks into a grin so wide and beautiful that I want to turn it into a song and play it forever. He flips the board back into his hand, grabbing it with one and then reaching out with his other. "Come on, let's get out of here."

"Where are we going?"

His face falls a little, and I can tell he's thinking hard. "We could get coffee?" It comes out like a question, like I might say no. "If you'd rather just go back to your place or whatever, I understand that too." He looks nervous, like a rejection now would be a rejection always.

"Coffee shop sounds good. I could go for some hot cocoa and scones."

"Deal," he says, but then he's wrinkling his forehead as he looks up at the sky.

"What's wrong?"

"I know I skated by a Dunkin' Donuts, but I can't remember how to get there now."

"Why do we need a Dunkin' Donuts?"

"Your cocoa." He shrugs. "We could get an Uber maybe. I mean, if you still want to—"

"Oh my god, Ridley," I say, my eyes going wide. "There's no way we're going to Dunkin' Donuts when Stacks exists."

"Stacks?"

"It's only the best coffee shop on the planet. They have the best cocoa in town—they're, like, known for it. Well, I think technically they're known for their espresso, but the cocoa! They import it from someplace, and it's like a million dollars a cup."

"A million dollars a cup, eh?" He laughs. "Wow."

"My treat, by the way. I owe you for my skate lesson."

"I can't let you spend a million dollars on me," he says in mock horror.

"Okay, fine, they're four dollars, but when you think about it."

"I mean, yeah, I get it. It's so close, how could you not round up?"

I wait for him to pull on his backpack and readjust the board under his arm, and then I grab on to his hand again and drag him along behind me. "I don't know how you've been here for weeks already and never heard of Stacks."

"I literally know no one here except for you and your moms, so."

"Wait for it, Ridley. I'm going to blow your mind today."

We walk in silence for a few more beats, and then I hear him say it, so quietly I almost miss it. "You already have."

eads snap toward me like they forgot I was here.
comical if I wasn't so pissed off.

h god, I'm sorry, Ridley," Peak says.

at her blankly, not sure what to say. *"It's okay"*?
sn't. But I don't want to be rude. Especially since
n no position to be. I knew her forgiving me was
be true.

this is Frankie. Frankie, this is Ridley."

red that," I say, standing up to hold out my hand.
ke it sound funny, like I'm laughing it off, but the
eezes my hand hard while he shakes it suggests
come through.

meet you," Frankie says, not dropping eye con-
queezes a little harder.

ise." And okay, this handshake is going on way

" Peak says, swatting his hand. "Don't be an

force of habit." He lets go of my hand and crosses
's amazing they can even meet across his pecs. I
that's what Peak likes in a guy, someone all huge
nd loud. Someone the exact opposite of me. My
icks up, and it gets a little harder to breathe.

unrunrunrun

omes and stands by me, nudging my shoulder
our fingers together. The panic inside goes from
simmer, and when she smiles at me, it drops
rely anything at all. "Be nice, Frankie. This one's

CHAPTER TWENTY-EIGHT
Ridley

PEAK TAKES A seat while I get in line. The place is nice, a typical hipster coffee shop, and very busy. I insist on paying and order at the counter—two hot cocoas with cinnamon, exactly as Peak directed—and then drop into the seat across from her. "They said it would be up soon."

My knee is already bouncing. It was one thing when I had the skateboard to distract me, but it's another entirely to have only nerves and cocoa to get by with.

dontmessthisupdontmessthisupdont

"You're going to love it," she says, but her enthusiasm has waned a little. Like some of what we had was lost the moment our fingers disconnected. I bite the inside of my cheek and let the silence settle over us. Just getting her here seemed so impossible twenty-four hours ago, and now that she is here, I don't know what to do.

"Is this a place you hang out?" I ask, desperate to break the silence. She pulls her coat off, draping it over the back of her chair. Her giant chunky headband is still on, though, and it's kind of weirdly hot.

"Are you asking me if I come here often?" she asks, dropping her voice a few octaves at the end.

"Something like that."

She flicks a discarded straw wrapper back and forth between her fingers. "Pretty much. We're friends with the family who owns this place."

A waiter comes out of the kitchen and from behind the counter. Peak looks at him, her eyes going wide.

"Frankie!" she shouts, jumping up to pull the guy into a hug. He's huge, taller than my dad, and built like a linebacker. He's also carrying a tray with our hot cocoa on it, which he somehow has managed not to spill.

"JuJu!" he says, and he looks so happy I almost want to trip him. He's staring at not-quite-my-girlfriend-but-also-not-*not*-my-girlfriend like she's the best thing he's ever seen. Who is this guy? And then I know.

This is the other shoe, and it's ready to drop.

"Here, give me that." She reaches forward to take the tray, but he holds it back.

"It's hot, JuJu," he says, like his instinct is to protect her, to care for her, and how many nicknames does one girl get? One from everybody, probably.

The guy—Frankie, she said—lumbers closer to the table, and I slouch in my seat. He's not graceful; he just . . . is.

It's whatever. I'm not jealous.

He sets the tray down and then turns back, wrapping Peak in a hug so tight she coughs. "I'm so glad you're here!"

he says, his voice booming. So[r] doesn't have a quiet setting.

"I didn't even know you were

I slide my chair a little farther [a] ing on something private.

ishouldgothiswasstupidishouldg[o]

"I got back late last night. I over to your place in a bit. I thou[g]

Peak shakes her head. "You g[o] mom already put you to work? V have a word."

"Nah, I was just hanging out I said I'd take this one out. I was [b] the whole cinnamon thing."

"I'm touched you remember the sentiment sounds true enou[g]

"JuJu, you've drilled that int[o] years. How could I forget?"

I roll my eyes. Okay, so I've contend with here. Perfect.

"Oh my god," she says agai[n] at him. "I can't believe you're [r] jerk." She punches him in the [a] emailing me? I worry!"

"Do you know how hard it the boat?" He yawns and wip[e] What are you doing later? You that's not here?"

And okay, even I have my

I look at her when she says that, my eyes wide, but she's still looking at the beast across from us. His shoulders drop a little, not like he's disappointed, but as if he just completely relaxed. "Really?" he asks, tipping his head down while he looks at her. I expected something else, alpha male anger maybe, but instead, he looks kind of happy?

"Yeah," she says, giving my hand a gentle squeeze. "And I'd like it very much if you didn't scare him off."

"He couldn't," I say quietly, so only she can hear it, but the way Frankie laughs says otherwise.

"See?" Frankie says, raising his hands. "No harm done."

Peak rests her head on my shoulder. "Good."

"How do you two know each other?" I ask. I'm missing something. He's not a romantic rival, clearly, but he also seems like more than just a friendly neighborhood barista.

"My mom and her stepmom are best friends," Frankie says. "When Vera married JuJu's mom, she and I effectively became family."

"He's the big brother I never wanted and can't seem to get rid of." Peak laughs, and Frankie pretends to whack her on the head. I still feel that pang of jealousy, but now it's for a different reason. I'm homesick for a life I never had, where I had best friends and a loving family and bonds that don't break.

Peak seems to sense the shift in my mood and squeezes my hand again. "Ridley, Frankie just got back. He's in the navy."

"I was underway for a while," he says proudly, and I feel like I should know what that means. "How did you guys . . . ?" he trails off, gesturing between us.

"Ridley started hanging around Verona," she says, and I hate that she's covering for me. I just want to tell the truth, no more lies.

Frankie plants his hand over his forehead and pretends to swoon. "Love across the comic racks."

"We actually met—" I start to say, but then stop. Maybe Peak doesn't want people to know about our night at the con. Maybe she's not protecting me; maybe she's ashamed.

"At a prom at one of the cons we were at," she says, and I look up in confusion. "He had a Batman mask; I was dressed like a peacock."

"A peacock?"

"From *Fighting Flock*."

"It was a very intense outfit," I say before I catch myself. Peak blushes and Frankie shakes his head.

"Frankie?" a voice calls through the kitchen doors.

"I better get back there before my mom flips. But remember," he says, jabbing Peak in the chest, "don't do anything I would do."

I scrunch my forehead. "Isn't it 'wouldn't do'?"

"Trust me," Peak says. "He definitely means 'would.'"

Frankie snorts and gives me a fake stern look before pointing at his eyes and then pointing back at me. I give him a salute, and he shakes his head.

"That is not how you salute, my dude." He chuckles as he walks away.

Peak and I sit back down, and I slide a mug toward her. The air feels lighter, the mood happier, and she smiles when she takes a sip.

"Hey, so," I say, hesitating when she looks up at me. "Um, he's cool."

"Yeah, you guys would probably hit it off."

"He's not really my type," I say, and I don't mean it the way it comes out, but she tips her head toward me.

"Are guys sometimes your type?" she asks, like that's a normal question. Like it's fine.

I take a deep breath, deciding how best to answer. I've had this conversation enough times to know that admitting I'm bi doesn't always go well. Girls especially seem to be freaked out by it. Usually I just lie and try to pretend I'm straight or gay depending on the circumstances. It's less drama, even if it makes my stomach hurt and my chest feel like it's caving in all the time.

But. No more lying. Not to her.

She leans in closer. "You don't have to answer. But you don't have to not answer either."

I stare down at my cocoa. "I guess certain people are just my type?" I say it like it's a question, even though it's not.

"Same," she says.

"I figured from what you said that first day at the shop."

"Then why did you freak out when I asked about you?"

I spin my mug around in my hands. "I don't know. Bad past experiences, I guess."

"I almost don't want to ask, but—"

And my stomach drops, because here come the inevitable twenty questions: have you dated a guy, yes, did you bang him, yes, did he bang you, no, but he could have, are you sure this isn't a pit stop to gay town, also yes, are you sure you like girls, yes, have you dated a girl, yes, did you bang her, no, but I wanted to.

"—you don't already have someone, do you?"

Wait, huh? I snap my eyes up. "What?"

"We aren't going through all this drama just to find out you have somebody waiting for you back in Seattle, right? I don't want to just be an extended con crush."

The relief washes over me, and I laugh. I can't help it. "No, there is no one and nothing for me in Seattle anymore."

"What's so funny?"

"I thought you were going to ask me something else."

"Like what?"

"Girls don't always take it well when they find out I'm bi."

"Well, this girl doesn't care."

"Because you're also bi?"

"I'm still working out the whole label side of things," she says, kind of wincing in a really adorable way, before taking a sip from her mug. "I say bi or pan sometimes, but I don't know if it feels right. I've never dated a girl, but I've had serious crushes and almost girlfriends. And then last summer I did hook up a little with Nikki's cousin who's nonbinary. I guess I just like who I like."

"That's okay," I say, in case she feels weird, because she shouldn't. And also because I really don't want to hear any more about who she's hooked up with.

"It doesn't always feel okay, though," she says. "Like you and my mom are bi, and Vera calls herself gay, and Jayla's a lesbian, and Nikki is straight, and I'm just—"

"Jubilee," I say.

"Yeah." She takes another sip. "It doesn't feel like enough."

"It is."

"Can I ask you something else?"

"I told you, you can ask anything."

"You're seventeen, right? That's what you said in your texts."

"Mm-hmm," I say, not sure where she's going with this.

"How come you don't go to school?" And ah, okay, that's a fair question, but not one I really want to answer.

"I do. I go to an online one, but I'm way behind."

"Why don't you go to an actual school, I mean. How'd you get out of that? Teach me your ways, O wise one." She smiles. "Do you know how much more cello time I'd have if I didn't have to sit in school all day?"

"Nah, trust me, if you're doing good where you are, you don't want to follow my lead on this. But it *is* an actual school, like, it's still hard and a lot of work, but I get what you mean. I've been to pretty much every kind of school out there, but none of them worked out."

"How come?"

And here we go. I did not envision having this talk in the middle of a coffee shop with her military BFF watching from the back room, but. "Because it turns out that formal education and being crazy don't mix."

"You're not crazy."

"I told you last night—"

"That doesn't mean you're crazy. Stop it."

"I can literally give you the numbers of multiple doctors who will tell you otherwise."

"Stop saying *crazy*," she says, and she looks legitimately annoyed. We sit in silence for a minute, and I wait for her next question. I've learned already there will always be a next question with her. And I don't even mind.

"Do you have a diagnosis, then, or whatever? How does that work?"

I snort. "I don't have a diagnosis, Peak. I have a laundry list."

"Well, I don't care."

"Why not?"

"It's not a deal breaker."

"It probably should be."

"Don't say that."

"It . . . can complicate things."

"It doesn't matter to me, honestly. I'm glad we're here," she says, and I look up, startled. How can that be true? I think this is the first time in the history of my life that anyone has been glad I'm anywhere.

"Why?" I ask before I can stop myself.

"I just am," Peak says, smiling strong enough that I know she means it. She takes another gulp of her drink, and I want to kiss her so bad, to know what the chocolate tastes like against her skin, but I don't. I duck my head and shift in my seat and try really hard to think about anything else.

"Hey." She reaches her hand out and tips my chin back up. It feels like something. It feels important. "We're going to figure this out."

I swallow hard. "What does that mean?"

"It means my feelings haven't changed."

"You still want me to fuck off, then?" I say, just to break the tension.

She laughs. "No, my feelings after that. Or before that. Or before and after that, actually. Have yours?"

"No." I grab the seat of her chair and slide it closer to mine until our legs are slotted together. And this time, when she laughs, I go in for the kiss.

CHAPTER TWENTY-NINE

Jubilee

"YOU'RE JUST GOING to completely let him off the hook? So this is Dakota 2.0, then, another person stomping all over you while you stand there saying thanks?"

I slam my locker door, and Jayla's frowning face is waiting behind it. "It's not like that."

She starts walking to biology, and I follow behind. It's my least favorite subject but usually my most favorite class because it's the only one the three of us have together. I've been dreading it all day.

Yesterday, Jayla came into the store while I was working, took one look at Ridley helping me stack, and walked right out. She wouldn't answer my texts last night and didn't even come to lunch today. I saw her eating with Emily in the courtyard.

"Then what is it like?"

Nikki walks up, linking arms with each of us with a look that says she's deliberately ignoring the tension. "What are we talking about?"

"Jubilee and Ridley made up."

"I know. I totally called it, by the way." Nikki grins, fluttering her eyelashes and spinning around in a circle while clutching her chest.

"I can't believe you told Nikki first." Jayla rolls her eyes as Nikki sweeps herself dramatically down the hall. "Actually, I can."

"I love that you look out for me, I do, but this isn't like the last time."

She raises her eyebrows. "Jubi, come on."

"Hey," I say, because now she's taking it too far.

"Am I supposed to act happy that you're sleeping with the enemy?"

"He's not the enemy."

"Are you sure?"

"I am, actually," I say, pushing past her and walking into the room, but Jayla matches my pace. "I know what I'm doing."

"Do you?" Jayla asks, sliding into her seat beside me at the lab table. "Because from here it seems like you're totally wrapped up in another kid who's just taking advantage of you. It's like you're genetically programmed not to see when people are bad for you."

"That's not Ridley," I say, more firmly this time. "You don't understand."

"Help me understand, then," she says, pulling out her notebook. Nikki settles into the table behind us, leaning forward to hear my response.

"It's not my place to tell you," I say, but I know it's not

helping my case. "Look, he's not spying, and he had a reason for not coming clean."

Jayla uncaps her pen, shaking her head. "I'm sure. Just like Dakota had a good reason for hooking up with another girl while you were at your cello lesson."

"That's not fair. This isn't the same thing at all."

"You stayed with him for another month after that happened, Jubi!" she says just as the bell rings. Mr. Lillis is, thankfully, late as usual.

"She has a point," Nikki adds, biting her eraser, and I shoot her an incredulous look.

"Well," I say, turning back to Jayla, "you and Elissa were a total train wreck, and I still stood by you for all of it."

"Elissa didn't lie to me."

"No, she just lied to everyone else about you, so she didn't have to come out. And then you turned around and started seeing Emily even though you had to keep it a secret from your coach at first, so pot, meet kettle."

"It's not the same thing," Jayla says.

"It's exactly the same thing!"

"That's actually also a good point," Nikki chimes in again, and this time we both look at her. I would laugh if I wasn't so ridiculously frustrated right now.

"Will you just trust me?"

"No."

"Why?"

"Because I'm worried. Your summer-program audition is at the end of the month, and you don't even mention it anymore! You're barely ever around, and when you are, it's just been Ridley this and Bats that, and how perfect they are, and now we hate them, and now we like them again. It's annoying! Are you doing *anything* besides worrying about this boy?"

"Okay, that's probably the best point so far," Nikki says. "You really don't ever talk about music anymore."

"Forgive me for trying to get out and live a little—like everybody wanted me to do. And now that I'm doing it . . ." I grip my pencil so hard I nearly snap it. "I've got it under control, but thanks for your votes of confidence."

"Fine," Jayla says. "But I don't know how you see this all playing out. Eventually, your parents are going to find out, and then what? Did you even see the guest post your stepmom wrote on ComicsAlliance last week about how corporations are destroying this industry? She name-dropped Mark Everlasting and The Geekery specifically, saying they were this totally insidious force, not even realizing they were *already in her store!*"

"I don't care about our families' stupid fight!"

Mr. Lillis walks in the door then with a huge stack of books from the library, and oh god, not another research project, but at least it spares me from having to reply. I pour myself into the lesson, desperate to tamp down everything Jayla's stirred up in me. Maybe I haven't been practicing as much, or maybe I just found a better cello-life balance. And maybe I don't know how this will all come together yet, or what's going to happen, but I do know I love being around him, and that his arms feel warmer than any arms I've ever felt in the history of arms.

When the bell rings, I bolt from my desk before Jayla and

Nikki can stand up, running to the music room even though it's not my period. I need to play; I need to make music; I need to be in control for once. Mrs. Carmine nods when she sees me cut into a practice room and then turns back to the students gathering for their rehearsal.

I play so long that I miss my next class, but it's gym and Mrs. C will definitely write me a note to get out of it anyway, especially with the audition coming so soon. My phone vibrates on the music stand—it's a text from Ridley—and I finish the Bach, smiling the rest of the way through.

• • •

I'm currently propped up against Ridley, using him as a half pillow/half desk, doing my lit homework while he scrolls through his phone and plays with my hair. Now that my parents know we're together or whatever, they let him come over a lot—provided we keep the door open. It's perfect, or it would be if I could stop obsessing over my fight with Jayla and the bigger problem of Ridley's last name. I sigh and turn the page, and he gives my hair a little tug.

"You could just call her, you know?"

I roll to my side to look at him. "She should be the one calling me, right? She's the one who's pissed for no reason."

"It sounds more like she's just worried about you, which is kind of nice? And she's right about the long-term thing."

My stomach drops. "What do you mean?"

"I mean, how is this going to work? I'm tired of lying already. You know we have to tell Vera, and who knows how that will go."

I bolt up. "My parents will flip; you know how they feel about your family. They probably won't even let me hang out with you anymore, and they definitely won't let you in the store."

"It'd be okay," he says, running his hand up my arm. "We'd make it work. As long as I have you, I don't care."

"Ridley, think. If they don't let you in the store, and your dad finds out, he's going to send you back to Seattle. And then what? I have to stay here. You'd be out there alone, and . . ."

His face falls. "Shit, I wasn't thinking about Seattle."

"Yeah, shit. You can't go back there."

He shoves off the bed and starts pacing around my room. I try to pull him back down, but he shifts his arm away and bites his thumbnail, squeezing his eyes shut. "I'm so fucked."

"You're not. You're *not*," I say, trying to calm him down. "We'll figure it out."

"How?" He raises his arms and drops them before dragging his hands over his face. "I almost lost you because of lies, and now the only way to be with you is to lie even more? I am so sick of pretending to be something I'm not. I've been doing it my whole life!"

"Ridley," I say, and this time he lets me pull him down. He sits at the edge of my bed, shaking his head. "This is different. We're just buying ourselves some time. It's just temporary."

He shoves his fist against his thigh, hanging his head before looking back up at me. "You promise?"

I smooth out his hands and pull them into my lap. "In a couple months, it'll be fine. We can tell my parents the truth, and it'll be okay. And if it's not, it won't matter, because I'll be in Boston for the summer program, and you'll be eighteen and your dad can't make you go anywhere. We'll have the whole summer together. And by the time we get back, everything will have blown over. It'll work out."

He looks down at where our hands meet. "If you say so."

"It's the only way," I say, because I've thought through ten thousand options already, and this is the only one that didn't seem doomed from the start. My phone buzzes then, an incoming call.

"You should get that."

So I do, because I think he needs some space. It's Jayla calling to talk about what happened. She says it's coming from a place of love—and I know it is, but still—and we talk until we both feel better, until things are as resolved as they can be. She reluctantly agrees to support me and Ridley, even though it kills her, and I promise to go to her away game on Saturday and cheer the loudest.

And when I hang up, feeling better than I have all day, I realize that Ridley left.

CHAPTER THIRTY

PEAK: Can this week be over?
I feel like it's lasted foreverrrrrrr.

> **BATS:** Technically, after
> today it's the weekend, so.

PEAK: Still too long. Make it go faster.
I can't believe I won't see you until Sunday
because of "mandatory family time." 😳
Beam me up or whatever.

> **BATS:** Wait, is there a portal?
> Because if you've found a portal
> through time and space and have
> been holding out on me, I'm going
> to be pissed. And family time
> sounds nice.

PEAK: Family time is only nice when
they don't say "no outside visitors allowed."

Otherwise it's like being in jail with two
overly affectionate wardens. And no,
no portal here. I was hoping you had
one, Dr. Strange.

> BATS: Then we're screwed.

PEAK: Damn.

> BATS: Hey, you're the one going to the
> away game after your parole tomorrow
> instead of coming here, not me.

PEAK: I promised Jayla! And you
could come. I invited you!

> BATS: No, I'm good on that.

PEAK: Come on, it'd be so fun.

> BATS: Jayla hates me.

PEAK: She does not. She likes you.

> BATS: Liar.

PEAK: Come onnnnnnn.

BATS: I miss you, but no.

PEAK: Please?

BATS: No.

PEAK: *pouts forever*

CHAPTER THIRTY-ONE

Ridley

"I DON'T PAY you to not write the reports," Dad says, dropping down into a seat at the kitchen table, where I'm slurping up Frosted Flakes. Technically, this is the first time we've had breakfast together. In my life, probably, but definitely since I got here.

I'd give anything to already be skating over to Peak's house, but after her "family only" time last night, she's spending the day at Jayla and Nikki's away game, leaving me to fend for myself. I'm trying hard not to bother her, but trying not to text her just makes me want to text her more.

"Are you even listening to me?" he asks, the corner of his eye twitching.

I tug my hoodie lower over my head, shoveling in another bite of cereal. "There wasn't anything to put in it this week."

That's technically true, only because I didn't have the energy to make up any new lies to cover for the whole conservatory thing, so I just . . . didn't. I know I have to keep it up. I know I gave Peak my word, but I'm so exhausted. I've been lying for so long now, and to so many different people, I'm starting to doubt I even know the truth anymore.

"You barely even pay me anyway," I say, because I'm a masochist. Because I'm pouting. Because I just want to see Peak.

My father leans forward, jabbing his finger at me. "I pay for this house, I pay for this food, I pay for your ridiculous online classes. Everything you have, I pay for. And for what?"

"Cuz you're my dad?"

He leans back in his chair, glaring at me. I chew the inside of my lip. My brain—hopelessly hopeful as it can sometimes be about this family—thinks for half a second that maybe those words meant something to him, that maybe he's going to apologize and say it's great having me around. Follow it up with a "hey, kid, let's toss the ball around or get ice cream" or anything else those sitcom dads do.

He does not.

He's abandoned even the slightest performance of fatherly pride lately. I think I'd take him misremembering everything about me like he did in the beginning over the cold indifference that's settled back between us.

I stare down at my cereal until he slides his chair across the tile floor. "I should send you back to your mother."

And then he's gone.

I carry my bowl to the sink and pour the rest down the drain. I'm not hungry anymore.

• • •

I tried not to text her. I really did. I don't want to mess up her life or pull her from her friends or get in the way, but everything hurts, and I just don't want to be alone.

I should send you back.

I've been hyperventilating since he said that. I can't go back. I won't. I can't go from all of this to sitting alone again in that giant fucking house. My father left with Allison for the weekend right after our argument. I called Gray first—but she's on the West Coast with Mom—and then finally texted Peak. I've been pacing ever since.

I wasn't even sure she would actually come, but here she is, smiling on my doorstep, holding two hot cocoas and a bag of what I can only assume is some kind of breakfast food. I look behind her and wave to Vera, who was nice enough to give her a ride. I smile when she waves back, trying to do my best impression of someone holding it together. Inside, I feel like broken glass. She backs out of the driveway with a little honk, and I usher Peak into the house.

"Are you safe?" Gray asked when I called her.

Yes. Now.

I take everything from Peak, setting the drinks on the table, and she pulls her coat off, hanging it on one of the hooks near the door. She looks around, taking in the house— it's a lot, I know, too much—before looking at me, really looking at me, and sighing.

"I hate your father," she says, coming closer and running her hands through my hair.

"I don't," I say, shutting my eyes.

"That's more than half the problem."

It's barely scratching the surface, actually, but it's probably best not to say that out loud.

"I don't want to go."

"You're not." She takes the bag from my hand. "Can you eat? I brought bagels and butter and cream cheese. It always settles my stomach when I'm nerved up before a big performance or something. I thought it might—"

Her words cut off in a whoosh when I pull her into a hug and hold on too tight, shaking my head. The bag crinkles between us until it falls to the floor, a stray bagel rolling out, and I bury my forehead into her shoulder, breathing her in, letting her hold me together.

"Let's go lie down for a while," she says, and I nod against her neck before leading her up the stairs, the bagels abandoned on the floor where she dropped them.

I perch on my bed, watching her catalog the contents of my room. It only takes a minute; there's not much. My mom never got around to sending most of the things I asked for, and I threw out half of what she did send because of bad memories.

"Where's all your stuff?"

I shrug, suddenly feeling a little embarrassed. "I travel light," I say, because that's easier than explaining that nothing really feels like mine.

She glances in the empty closet, the doors wide open. "Really light, I guess."

I reach over the side of the bed and rummage through

my duffel bag, searching underneath the wrinkled clothes and the boxer briefs and about a dozen Sharpies that I somehow collected, until I feel the pointy plastic of the mask and curl my fingers around it.

"Still have this, though," I say, holding it up.

She takes a step closer, pulling the Batman mask out of my hand and running her fingers over it. "Awww, Bats."

"And this," I say as she watches me snap the back of the case off my phone and pull out her feather. It's a little wrinkled, sure, but still hanging in there.

"You kept that this whole time?"

She says it like it's been an eternity instead of a month and a half. It kind of does feel like that with everything we've been through, and are going through, and hopefully will keep going through, together.

"Is that weird?" I ask, twirling the feather. Because maybe holding on to it is a little stalkery or whatever, but it feels right.

"No, I think it's sweet," she says. "But—"

"But what?"

"But if you get to keep my feather, then I should get to keep the mask. Fair is fair."

I glance at the mask, wishing the idea of giving it away didn't come with such heavy regret.

"It was a joke," she says, trying to hand it back, but we both know it wasn't.

"No, no, keep it." I push it back toward her. "I want you to have it."

"You look like I broke all your crayons," she says, studying my face, "and then ran over your puppy."

"No, it's just—it's good memories. But maybe I don't need it anymore."

"Why?"

"Because you're here."

She smiles at me, genuine but cautious. She's smart to be like that—I know she is—but I wish that she wasn't. Because that's the truth under the lie. She can say it's going to be okay as much as she wants, but one phone call and my dad could have me on a flight back to Seattle. One slip-up and Vera could learn everything and keep us apart.

"I am," she says. It feels like she means more, but I don't want to think about real life for now. I just want to get lost in this girl, in this moment, and forget everything else.

I pull her closer, resting my forehead against her chest and running my arms up and down her sides. She laces her fingers through my hair, humming a song I don't know, and for a second, I let myself believe it's enough.

CHAPTER THIRTY-TWO

RIDLEY: I'm fucking everything up.

> **GRAYSON:** It sounds like you're doing the best you can with everything going on.

RIDLEY: I still think we should tell Vera.

> **GRAYSON:** Is it just that you feel bad, or?

RIDLEY: I feel bad all the time, Gray, so no. It's that it feels WRONG.

> **GRAYSON:** I hate when you say shit like that. It makes me want to like wrap you up in bubble wrap and feed you soup.

RIDLEY: Wtf?

> **GRAYSON:** I don't know, it just does. But yeah, there's no good answer here.

RIDLEY: But is there a right one?

GRAYSON: I just want you to be happy.

RIDLEY: Yeah about that . . . 🙁

GRAYSON: Okay, aside from all the drama with Dad and Verona, how are things with you and Peak?

RIDLEY: All her friends hate me, and her parents think I'm someone else. So good, I guess?

GRAYSON: Oh my god, Ridley. Why can't your life be easy?

RIDLEY: . . . right?

GRAYSON: Well, winning over her friends should be easy enough. Just go be your charming self.

RIDLEY: So funny.

GRAYSON: I'm being serious. Go hang out with them. Show them you're worth the trouble.

RIDLEY: I'm not though.

> **GRAYSON:** Ridley, don't make
> me come over there.

RIDLEY: That threat works better when
we're on the same side of the country.

> **GRAYSON:** I can be wheels up
> in an hour. Do not test me.

RIDLEY: Fine, fine, I'll hang out with them.
If only to spare some poor flight attendant
from having to deal with you.

CHAPTER THIRTY-THREE

Jubilee

I'M SITTING ON the bleachers, watching Jayla and Nikki wrap up soccer practice. They were running drills, but now they're scrimmaging and somehow they ended up on opposite teams, which means I don't even know who to cheer for. Yay, sports! It's their first outdoor practice, and it's unusually warm for April. The sunshine feels nice, relaxing even—or it would be if I wasn't sharing a bleacher with electricity personified.

Ridley sits beside me stiffly, the opposite of relaxed. He's chewing on his lip and bouncing his knee, which he's taken to doing whenever we leave the safety of our rooms or the store. I was shocked when he agreed to join me cheering on the girls today.

I slide our fingers together, wishing I could send him some serenity by osmosis or whatever, and he lets out a shaky breath. "Are you sure it's okay that I'm here?"

"Definitely," I say, and hope it's reassuring. I'm positive it's okay; they basically insisted on it. Even Nikki said it was time to break out of the relationship bubble, and she's all about romance. Not that this is romance lately—it's more like he's falling apart, and I'm putting him back together, and in between we kiss and I do homework. It's a lot . . . but I don't mind. And it's partially my fault for insisting he keep up the charade.

The scrimmage finally ends, 6–4 Jayla's team, and I head down to the edge of the field with Ridley. Jayla is leading a meeting, bringing the whole team back together and fulfilling her co-captain duties. Ridley shifts nervously beside me; we're supposed to be hanging out with everybody after this.

"Should we just go home?" I ask him.

"No," he says, a little too quick, and then squeezes my hand.

Nikki and Jayla grab their gear and jog over to us. Jayla's rubbing her side where she took an elbow at the end of the last half, but she's still smiling. "What's up, Batboy?"

Ridley nods but doesn't say anything. Nikki holds out her hand, and Ridley looks at it for a moment before shaking it, like he isn't sure exactly what to do. "I'm Nikki," she says, all out of breath.

"Nice to meet you," he says, so quietly that I squeeze his hand again. "I'm Ridley."

"I know," Nikki says.

"Right."

Jayla tilts her head but swallows whatever snarky thing she was about to say. I'll have to remember to thank her later.

"What's the plan now?" I ask.

Jayla picks up a giant mesh bag full of soccer balls. "I was thinking we'd head back to my house, hit the showers, get a pizza, and hang out, unless you guys want to actually go do something."

I glance at Ridley, not sure exactly how much socializing he's up for. "We could go back to your place for a little while and go from there." I told them I wanted this to be like a quick first visit to ease him in, but I guess they aren't going to let me get away with that.

"I'm gonna help Coach pack everything up," Jayla says, tossing me her keys. "You want to go meet me at the car?"

"I'll help Coach too," Nikki says, but not until Jayla elbows her.

The girls run off, and we head over to the parking lot, where I hit the unlock button over and over again until I finally hear the beep and find her car.

"Am I that obviously freaked out?"

"What? No," I say. I turn the car on long enough to put the windows down, and then pull Ridley into the back seat with me.

"They pretty blatantly just gave us time alone, so."

I nestle in, leaning my head on his shoulder. "This isn't a test, you know."

"I know," he says, but it doesn't sound like he believes me, and there goes his knee again.

I put my hand on it to stop it. "They just want to get to know you a little."

"Why again?"

"Because you're important to me." I chuckle. He's made me say this three times already today.

"I will never get tired of hearing that."

"Good, I hope you don't."

He leans in and kisses me . . . at the exact moment when Jayla and Nikki yank open their doors and drop into the front seats.

"Okay, lovebirds," Jayla says, "keep it PG back there or I'll split you up. If there are any suspicious stains, my dad is *not* gonna believe I didn't put them there."

"Oh my god, Jayla," I say, kicking the back of her seat.

"I'm just sayin'."

CHAPTER THIRTY-FOUR
Ridley

JAYLA'S HOUSE IS nice. It's big, not as big as my dad's, but more importantly, it's warm. Lived-in. A family stays here. A tiny dog greets us at the door, a teacup Yorkie named Cooper, Jayla says, and he continues hopping up and down around us as she leads us downstairs to a finished basement. This is obviously the hangout spot; couches and beanbag chairs take up most of the floor space, with an occasional textbook littering the floor. There's a giant TV against one wall, with every gaming system you could imagine underneath.

I wander around while everyone argues about pizza toppings and Nikki and Jayla fight over who gets the shower first, just taking it all in. Cooper follows me, sniffing at my pants. There are pictures everywhere: tiny Jayla missing her front teeth, middle-school Jayla in what looks to be some kind of play, all the way up to co-captain-of-the-soccer-team Jayla. Professional portraits of the whole family line the walls, probably done because they wanted them, not because they needed them for a press release. But it's the candid photos that really get me: Jayla and her brother, the kids and the puppy, Jayla racing her brother on a bike, Jayla—

"Hey, whatcha doing?" Peak asks, and I jump, lost in my own head.

"Oh, just . . ." I trail off, waving my hand around at all the pictures.

"Yeah, my mom is basically the paparazzi when it comes to me and my brother," Jayla says, walking by. "Embarrassing."

"It's cool," I say, and she looks at me like I just said the sky was green.

"Right, well, I'm gonna go hit the shower, so make yourselves at home. But not as at home as you did when Kai was here." Jayla narrows her eyes at Peak before disappearing up the stairs.

"What's that about?" I quirk up the side of my mouth with the dimple. I know how much she likes it, so maybe it will distract her from the super-invasive question I have no right to ask but also really fucking need the answer to. I know she said she hooked up with them; I just didn't think she meant like *hooked up* hooked up. It's fine.

This is fine.

"Jubilee got a little frisky down here once, and, um, they weren't discreet," Nikki pipes up.

I look back at Peak, who has turned bright red. "Shut up, Nikki!"

"Hey, he asked! And it's a thousand times worse for me than it ever could be for Ridley, because it was with *my* cousin."

I grab Peak's hand and try to give her a reassuring smile. "I did ask."

She huffs and rolls her eyes, tugging me over to the couch. "She didn't have to answer you." Part of me, the part of me that's . . . less good than I want to be . . . wonders if this is the couch where she—

"Bats," she says, and that word will always, always work. "Stop overthinking things." She ruffles my hair and settles in while Nikki flips through the channels.

Cooper trots up a set of tiny dog stairs at the other end of the enormous couch and curls up in Peak's lap with a big yawn.

"You guys are adorable," Nikki says before settling on some cheesy movie on cable.

I clear my throat to respond, but take too long, so everybody goes back to watching TV. It's fine.

pullittogether

We're just past the meet-cute and elbows deep into a commercial break when Jayla comes back in the room. She shoots me a look that kind of freaks me out, but I focus on the warmth of Peak's body pressed into mine and how steady her breathing is. Peak makes everything seem more . . . manageable.

"Your turn," Jayla says, scooting Nikki out of the chair and dropping into it in her place. She's wearing threadbare pajama pants with little llamas on them that say DRAMA LLAMA and a bright pink sweatshirt that hurts to look at. I admire how she doesn't give a shit about making a good impression on me.

She pours some lotion in her hands, rubbing it into her skin while glaring at the TV. "Did Nikki pick this?"

"Yeah, it's cute," Peak says, sitting forward a little. Cooper seems to take issue with the new position and jumps down off the couch with his nose in the air.

Jayla rolls her eyes and changes the channel to a cartoon. "Hey, Jubi, do you mind running him out for me? I'd do it, but I'm in my PJs," she says. "If Coop has an accident on this carpet, my mom will flip."

"Seriously?" Peak says. "Since when do you care? You've gone to school in your pajamas."

"Please, Jubi."

Peak glances back at me, looking worried. "Come with me?"

"He's fine," Jayla says. "I don't bite. You'll only be gone a second. I'm sure he can handle it."

"Do you mind?" she asks, and I don't miss the hope in her voice. It feels a little bit like my sister asking me if I'm safe, and it makes me bristle.

"It's fine. Walk the dog." I expected this, to be honest. Although, to be fair, I definitely did *not* expect the lecture would come from someone in drama-llama pants. And yet.

And yet.

Peak looks at me once more, and then a whine from Cooper seems to seal the deal. She hops up and slips his leash off the hook on the wall, clipping it onto him and stepping out the sliding glass door on the other side of the room.

"We don't have a fenced yard," Jayla says, like that matters. I feel like she would have found another way to send Peak outside even if they did.

I lean forward, resting my elbows on my knees, which I'm trying so hard not to bounce.

becoolbecoolbecoolbecoolbecool

"Is this where you give me the whole 'if you hurt her, I'll kill you' speech?"

She sets down the lotion and looks at me, really looks at me, and I squirm a little in my seat. "No."

"No?"

"No, I'm not going to give you the speech, because it doesn't matter."

"What do you mean?"

"It doesn't matter what I say. You're still going to hurt her." I start to protest, but she shakes her head. "It's not a knock against you. Everybody hurts everybody, even if they don't mean to. Especially if they don't mean to."

"Then why is she outside?"

She narrows her eyes. "I just hope you know what you're doing."

"I have no idea what I'm doing," I snort. "But I'm trying."

Her eyes flick down to my bouncing knee and then back to my face. "How messed up are you, exactly? Like very or just moderately?"

"Very," I say. I should be offended, but I'm not. I'm sure Jubilee has told her things; I'm glad she has someone to talk to.

Jayla nods, like she expected that answer. Peak said there wasn't a test, but there is, there always is.

"For whatever reason, Jubi is convinced that you're worth the drama. If she thinks you're this special, I doubt you totally

245

suck. I'd like it if we didn't hate being around each other, for Jubi's sake. That's all I wanted to say."

My ears get warm, and I stare down at my socks, wiggling my toes to distract myself. "Thanks?" I am profoundly uncomfortable now.

"I don't want to hug it out or anything, so don't look so excited. And this lying-to-Vera stuff . . . I know how she feels about your family, but—"

But then Peak bursts through the door, the dog rushing in and jumping up on me with damp paws. "Oh. Everything's okay?" She sounds surprised. I hate that.

I run my hand through Cooper's fur as he wiggles in my lap. "Yeah, we're just watching TV. What'd you expect?"

"I . . . don't know," she says, looking at Jayla and then back at me.

"All right." Jayla grabs her phone. "Pizza?"

"Yeah, definitely," I say. "I'm starving."

Peak waits for Jayla to go hunt down a menu and then squats in front of me. "You sure you're good?"

"Great," I say, kissing her forehead until she all-out grins. Another lie.

CHAPTER THIRTY-FIVE

PEAK: Are you ever going to tell me what Jayla said to you while I was out with Coop?

            BATS: No, probably not.

PEAK: Rude.

            BATS: I like your friends.

PEAK: I'm jealous. I want to meet yours!

            BATS: So, you want to meet yourself?

PEAK: Ha ha. Funny. No, I want to meet your friends back in Seattle.

            BATS: Awkward.

PEAK: ?

BATS: 😖

PEAK: You're so dramatic.

BATS: Yes. But you like it.

PEAK: Only very occasionally.

BATS: I'll take it!

PEAK: Seriously though,
tell me about them?

BATS: There's not much to tell.
I didn't have a lot of friends before
I left here, and I had even fewer in
Seattle. I wasn't ever in the same
school long enough. There were kids
who used me to get into Geekery
events, a few random hookups . . .
That's about it.

PEAK: Wasn't there anyone important?

BATS: One. But in retrospect, I don't
know if I'd say important. I thought
he was at the time, but now . . . ?

PEAK: Oooh, tell me everything.

BATS: Not much to tell. Rich boy with daddy issues. Trying to forget.

PEAK: I meant tell me about the other kid ☺

BATS: So funny, Peak. So funny.

PEAK: What happened?

BATS: Someone is always more into it than the other person.

PEAK: I'm sorry.

BATS: How do you know it wasn't him!

PEAK: I've met you?

BATS: ☹

PEAK: Am I wrong though?

BATS: Not telling.

PEAK: Uh-huh.

BATS: I'm trying to be
mysterious. Is it working?

PEAK: Nope.

BATS: Fine, it was me.

PEAK: I know.

BATS: You're a very rude person,
Peak. You're lucky I like you.

PEAK: I am.

BATS: A rude person?
Or lucky I like you.

PEAK: Not telling.
I'm trying to be mysterious.

BATS: It's working.

CHAPTER THIRTY-SIX

Ridley

I DON'T MEAN to overhear. I'm not even trying to eavesdrop, I swear. It's just that the store is so small, and Vera talks so loud, and with all the windows shut because of another cold snap, there's not even the sound of traffic to drown it out.

Which is why I'm awkwardly reorganizing the comics in the dollar bin and trying not to listen to Vera yelling at Peak for hanging out with me too much. She's shouting that it's distracting her from school, that she got a C-plus on a test for the first time in her life, that she never sees her other friends anymore, and that she doesn't spend enough time with her family. I hate knowing I'm a part of that. I hate that I'm dulling her shine—that instead of her pulling me up, I'm dragging her down—and now she's lying to her family the way I've been lying to mine.

Which, speaking of, her parents apparently also want to meet my parents, which can't happen for very obvious reasons, the biggest being that the second she sees my dad, she'll know exactly who he is, and who I am by default, and how I ended up in her shop. She's been grumbling about my dad more lately too—especially since he responded to her latest op-ed by going on a ten-tweet rant about the dangers of idolizing indie shops to the point where we ignore the "evolving landscape of our industry." Yesterday, Vera even made a joke that my dad probably has a whole team working on a plan to "evolve her right out of his way." Which made me feel like shit, because it's true.

I should tell her the truth, or I should go. Or maybe both.

Jubilee raises her voice at Vera then, shouting that she's going to college in a year, that this is her life, that there's more to it than textbooks. I want to go and break it up; I don't want them to fight because of me. I shouldn't even still be here, and I know it. We've been on borrowed time ever since I sent that first text.

And it's always the wrong thing, no matter what I do. It's lies on top of lies on top of lies, all of it, and god, Vera is the mom I wish I had, and Jubilee is the person I've always dreamed of meeting, but this is all a house of cards, trembling on a foundation made of sand, and I can't breathe.

I can't breathe, and Vera is still yelling at Jubilee about a missed lesson, how they don't have money to waste on lessons she can't be bothered to show up for, and about everything else that used to matter in her life, and should still, but doesn't because of me, and.

icanticanticanticanticanticanticant

The whole thing started because Peak asked her mom if she could cut out early to grab some dinner with me and

Frankie. And I told her not to; I knew this was coming. I told her Vera wasn't my biggest fan anymore. That she was giving me the look, the same one Jayla gives me when she thinks I can't see her, the look that says I'm ruining Peak's life. And you know what? I get it. I do.

If I had a kid, I wouldn't want them hanging around someone like me either, but that doesn't make it not hurt. That doesn't make my stomach not churn deep down, doesn't make it not grow from a spark to a full-fledged panic attack, so that by the time Peak storms out of the back room, I'm already outside, gasping for cold air with my back pressed hard against the bricks and my head between my knees.

"Ridley." She crouches down next to me, and I squeeze my eyes shut tighter. She combs her hand through my hair more gently than I deserve. "Want to hear something cool?"

I give her the tiniest nod, forcing my eyes open.

"Did you know that if you measured all the blood in a newborn, it would only equal about one cup?" she asks, her eyebrows raised as if I'm going to challenge her. I'm not. Mostly, I just want to know who decided to measure blood volume by baby. But then I start thinking of, like, freshly squeezed babies and all this other weird stuff, which kind of freaks me out more, and I put my head back down.

"Okay, wait," she says. "That was a bad one." She laces her fingers through mine, squeezing tight. "Let me think . . . um . . . did you know you're less likely to get bitten by a shark if you blow bubbles in its face?"

I sniffle hard and wipe at my nose, hating the way the cold makes it run, while I let my brain catch up to what she just said. "Wait," I say, my voice rasping out. "What kind of bubble mix can you use underwater?"

She wrinkles her forehead, and I drop my chin, realizing too late she doesn't mean the soap kind you buy in the store. "I . . . see my error now."

"Yeah, seriously." She laughs and sits down next to me. "Feel a little better?"

"Not really."

"It was just a panic attack. It's over."

I shake my head. "I shouldn't be the reason you're fighting with Vera."

"You're not!" She reaches for me again, but I slide back up the wall and shove my hands in my pockets.

"I heard you guys."

"She's just freaking out like she does every time she gets stressed. It's not even about us. She just put a new title on Kickstarter, and it way overfunded, and she's going nuts about distribution channels and finding a new offset printer. That's it. I promise. She always takes it out on everybody around her. Mom and I generally try to avoid her when she first launches for this exact reason."

"I just don't want to be the thing that stands between you and the rest of your life."

"You give yourself way too much credit."

I feel like I've stepped into some kind of a trap here, and I don't know how to get out of it. Because the truth is, I think her life would be better, easier, if I left, that it's the right thing to do—not just for her, but for her family *and* mine.

But I'm selfish.

"Seriously, Ridley," she says, dusting off her backside as she stands up. "If you think I'd give up my dreams for a relationship, you're out of your mind. I love you, but I love myself way more."

And my jaw drops, and I kind of huff out a breath, because we've never said it out loud before. Never, but that's what this is, isn't it? Love?

My sister used to say all the time, "You can't love anybody else until you love yourself," and I believed that for a little while. It made everything seem so much bleaker and more hopeless, but then I met Peak, and the thing is . . . I love her. I do.

And it has nothing to do with me loving myself, because I don't even know where to start with that. But she makes me want to be here, to kiss that spot behind her ear that makes her breath catch, to hear her laugh when I fall off my skateboard, to see the faces she makes when she's lost in her music. She makes me see possibilities that I didn't know existed. Like the capacity to love and be loved was not a thing that was on my radar before.

"What are you thinking about right now?" she asks.

"I'm thinking that you're pretty fucking amazing."

"It's true." She laughs, and the sound settles across my brain, calming me in ways even her endless facts never could.

"And that I love you too."

She grins and kisses me, because we said it. We finally said it. I wish it was all we had to say. I wish the biggest obstacle was "I like you—do you like me back?" But.

"And that I can't lie to your family about who I am

anymore, and you shouldn't be lying to protect me," I say, and she frowns.

Because that's the thing. Thinking about love is one thing, but saying it out loud comes with responsibility—the responsibility to do right by the other person, no matter what. And doing right isn't turning them into the person you're so desperately trying not to be yourself. We have to tell the truth now, to her parents and mine. We have to believe that our love could survive it. There's not a future any other way.

"Come on, let's walk," she says. We fall into an easy silence, our footsteps striking in perfect rhythm.

"Where are we going?"

"I told Frankie to grab pizza with us before I realized things were going to get so heavy. He's waiting at the shop across the street."

I shrug. "I think I'm just gonna head home. Allison's visiting her parents in New York, and my dad's not back from his work conference until tomorrow. Maybe you can come by later, if there's time?" And this is not how I thought things would go after my first declaration of love.

"I'd rather you come with me." She takes a half step away, and even though our arms are still linked, now we're walking off rhythm.

"I can't." Just thinking of walking into the pizza place with all the noise and smells is setting me on edge.

"Because of Vera or because of your little freak-out?"

And it feels like someone just shoved toothpicks under my nails and ripped out my heart. I can handle everybody else acting like I'm crazy, but not her.

I drop her arm, blinking hard. "Don't say it like that."

She hesitates before pulling her hands into her coat sleeves. "Sorry, I didn't—"

I walk a little faster, leaving her a few steps behind, and then hop on my board. "Tell Frankie I said hi."

"Ridley," she says, but I push off faster and don't stick around. I can't.

• • •

I'm lying in the tub, water only up to my chin this time because I'm being safer, more careful. The room is dark, another of my sadbaths, and it's not that I'm even depressed—well, not more than usual—it's just that I want to not think for a minute. I want my brain to be quiet. I want to sit in the dark and float and not worry about anything else.

Except now someone is ringing the doorbell, and it's so goddamn loud I could cry.

I towel off and throw on some shorts, and whoever it is has taken to knocking now too. I grumble down the stairs. Maybe it's Peak. I don't know. That would be nice. She didn't text, but.

I enter the alarm code and pull open the door, ready to apologize for torpedoing her perfectly good night. Except it's not Peak; it's Frankie, which is . . . weird.

"Took you long enough. Now invite me in," he says, holding up a pizza box.

"I'm gonna just grab a shirt," I say slowly, pointing upstairs. "What are you doing here?"

"JuJu was freaking out about everything that happened

tonight. I sent her home and told her I'd check up on you."

"Yeah, well, I don't need a babysitter, so." But my traitor stomach growls at the smell of food.

"Get your shirt," Frankie says, pushing past me. "Your kitchen this way?" He walks off, not even waiting for me to reply.

I make my way back downstairs a few minutes later, my damp skin sticking to the hoodie I found under my bed. He's already sitting at the table, the pizza box open in front of him. He's not even using a plate, but he did seem to find the good linen napkins. "Eat," he says, without looking up.

I grab a slice and sit down. "You didn't have to do this."

"Actually, I did," he says, pausing his chewing long enough to look at me. "For one, I would never hear the end of it if I didn't, and for two, I wanted an excuse to eat another pizza. It's more for my benefit than yours."

"Thanks."

"Listen. JuJu's really worried about you, you know. If you need someone to talk to, I'm all ears."

I take another bite of pizza, considering the offer. It has been a while since I dumped my shit on a stranger, and that was my primary coping method before meeting Peak, so.

"You'll just tell her whatever I say."

"Maybe." He shrugs. "Maybe not. Depends on what it is and if I think it's her business."

"How do you decide if it's her business or not?"

"I'll know when you say it."

And yeah, I probably shouldn't tell him anything, but

once I open my mouth, I can't stop. Peak has helped me so much, but one person can't carry it all. Not all the time.

So yeah, I tell him everything. I tell him how Peak and I met at the con. I tell him why I'm really in town. He stops me there and asks a lot of questions. I don't miss the way his hands curl into fists when I talk about my dad's plan for Verona Comics. And then I tell him how I want to come clean, even though she doesn't, because how much of a fresh start can I really get when I still have to report to my father every Tuesday and Thursday, just like the rest of his spies do, even if I *am* feeding him useless info.

And that's what I'm most bitter about, I realize—that I'm not even special. I don't even get to tell him directly, even when he's home. I just send my reports to the marketing email, just like all the other people he has working for him. There are probably twenty other people just the same as me, vying for his approval via form emails. And maybe I paw at my eyes while I'm talking, but I'm not sad, I'm upset, and it's just that sometimes my brain can't tell the difference.

And I tell him what even Peak doesn't know, that my dad has a good friend on the board of the conservatory that could complicate everything. If he ever found out, my dad would have all the ammunition he needed, and Vera would have every motivation in the world to go along with it. Frankie rubs his temples when I explain that part, and I know, *I know*, but I couldn't keep it to myself any longer.

When the words finally stop, when there's nothing else to confess, I feel ten pounds lighter and completely exhausted, like I could sleep for a year and still never wake up.

"Hey," Frankie says when he's sure that I'm finished. "Listen, I've found myself in some tough jams over the last couple years, and all I know is that if your gut is telling you something is wrong, it probably is."

"You think I should tell Vera, then?" I ask, leaning back in my chair and tucking my hands behind my head. "That's what you would do?"

Frankie blows out a breath so hard his cheeks puff out. "I don't know, kid. I really don't. I can see JuJu's point. You're not doing it anymore, it won't change anything, so why does Vera really need to know right now? Especially with the risk of you getting shipped off to the left coast. But I see your point too. You're holding in a big secret, and you're looking for a little redemption. And if Vera found out from someone else, it would be way worse."

"Yeah," I say, swallowing hard. "So what do I do?"

"I think you follow your gut."

"Okay. Next question: How can I tell if it's my gut talking or my myriad of anxiety disorders?"

Frankie chuckles. "Is there that much of a difference?"

I laugh too, and it's a bitter sort of laugh. Because I don't know. I sincerely do not know.

CHAPTER THIRTY-SEVEN

Jubilee

"COME ON." HE grins, holding his phone out. "Let me record it!"

"Why are you so obsessed with me?" I laugh, covering up my face, but I don't really mind.

It's just that Ridley's been taking so many videos lately. He says it's because he doesn't want to forget anything, but I'm worried it's something else. I can't shake the feeling that he thinks we're less than permanent now, which I guess, yeah, at almost seventeen and almost eighteen that's realistic or whatever, but it feels like he just got here and now he's getting ready to go.

"Because I love you," he says, and his words come so easily, even though his eyes are like storms.

"I love you too."

He backs up until he hits the bed and sits down to get the widest shot possible.

And it's hard to think straight with him looking at me like this—his lips slightly parted, his eyes sort of sleepy and inviting. This feels more intimate, fully clothed and twelve feet across the room, than it did a few nights ago, when our kissing got a little extra handsy.

I blush and look down, and then I glare at my open door. My mom has been pointedly walking down the hallway every fifteen minutes or so, being completely non-stealthy about checking in on us. It turns out that time Vera took me to his house alone was not officially Mom sanctioned, and the "two yeses or one no" rule has officially been reimplemented for all decision-making as a result. Same with the "open door at all times" rule, and the "Ridley can only stay until seven on school nights" rule.

"Play me that song for your audition. The one you're always talking about."

"The Bach? It's not a song. It's a suite and it's like a half hour long." I laugh.

"Then just play the first part."

"Why?" I don't want to think about that now. I don't want to think about the fact that even if everything goes right, I'm going to be spending the summer almost two hours away in a program so intense I'll be lucky to have time to text. And he'll be . . . I don't even know, on the other side of the country possibly. Or hiding in my dorm if I'm lucky.

Ridley cocks his head. "You need to practice. I'm happy to just be in the background."

"What if I don't want you just in the background?"

"I don't want to be a distraction. *Don't* let me be one."

"You're not," I say, because I want it so badly to be true.

"Come on." He sighs, hitting record on his phone. "Will you please play the Bach? I don't have it yet."

That's because I still haven't perfected it, I think but don't say. He's right; I really could use the extra practice. Even Mrs. G made a comment along the lines of "Okay, that's enough living life now, dear" at my last lesson, but I don't want him stressing about it. He stresses about too much as it is.

"What about our mutual improvement plan?" I smirk. "Don't you have more homework?"

And that's another rule, my mom's "mutual improvement plan." It was part of the deal to have him over on school nights *at all.* We both have to do our homework either here or at the shop, and she checks it now like I'm back in elementary school. You get one C-plus and—

"I'll do it after."

"Fiiiiine," I whine, but I've already turned to the page.

I pick up my bow and take a deep breath, looking right at him before I start. Just seeing him so expectant and calm settles the nerves inside me. He makes me feel like I can do anything.

He gives me a little nod that simultaneously melts my heart and steels my spine, and I slide the bow across my strings. For the first time, I don't miss a single note.

For the first time, it's perfect.

CHAPTER THIRTY-EIGHT

Ridley

I CAN TELL right away that Vera is pissed. I don't even know why I stopped by the shop today, other than I just needed to get out of my dad's way and had nowhere else to go. He's been working from home more and more—the number of days he stays home directly proportional to the amount he drinks.

I've been doing a decent job of avoiding Vera lately. Every time she's nice to me, it feels like a knife twisting in my belly. But it's Friday morning, which means Peak's in school, and it's just Vera and me in the shop. Peak and I have plans to hang out later—a quick hot cocoa, and then it's back to her house for homework and practice.

Which has actually been working, by the way. I'm three assignments ahead now, and my GPA is, well, passing. Peak is practicing more too. My phone is so full I have to keep deleting apps to make room for new recordings. I feel . . . not good exactly, but like the possibility of good. Like I've been tied in knots my whole life, and then Peak came along and undid one, and now I want to untangle all the rest of them.

I texted Frankie, which is a new thing that I definitely don't mind, and he said it's called hope.

But when Vera looks at me the way she's looking at me now, like she has something to say but doesn't know how to say it, all that hope goes right out the window. Because there's a storm brewing outside the little bubble Peak and I have made for ourselves, and there's only so long we can ignore it.

Vera opens her mouth a few times but then just sighs and hovers nearby while I pretend to reorganize the new-release rack. I count the times she clears her throat, and after the third time, I push up from where I'm crouching, because I'm almost positive I want to have this conversation standing up. "Vera, whatever it is, just say it."

She looks at me all surprised, like she thought she was being subtle or something. Which, maybe she was, but seventeen years of suffering through anxiety attacks while trying to act normal has gifted me with the ability to be oddly in tune with people. Also, it's possible she wasn't being subtle at all.

"It's nothing," she says, "none of my business." But I can tell she's not done, so I stand there, waiting, with my heart rattling around in my chest like a panicked bird.

"Actually," she says, shutting her laptop. "You know what? No, I'm sorry, but it is my business."

"Okay."

"What's your story?" Vera asks, narrowing her eyes, and I swear the floor drops right out from under me. "You're a sweet kid, but you came out of nowhere, and you don't seem to have parents, and you've got my daughter all—"

I knew this moment would come. But the words are dying in my throat, or I am, because I don't know what to do. I promised Peak one thing, but my gut says another, and I've been turning it over and over and over, because either way, I'm betraying someone. I need to sit down.

shitshitshitshitshitshitshitshitshitshitshitshit

"Ridley? Are you okay?"

"Mm-hmm," I force out, because if I open my mouth right now, I don't know what will come out: hysterical laughter, maybe, or vomit. I look at the window, praying for a customer to walk up or park out front, for anything to save me, for the world to intervene and get me out of this, but there's nothing.

"Did you know that a single cloud can weigh over a million pounds?"

I look at Vera, so shocked that I sort of see through the haze of panic and pull in a deep breath.

"Um, shit," Vera says, opening her laptop up. "That's the only one I remember."

"What?" I croak out. Where is Peak? I wish Peak were here. Why does school exist?

"Dammit. Hang on, the Wi-Fi's being slow again. Just . . . just take a deep breath. I'm almost there."

"I—I'm fine," I grumble out, and I feel tired, so tired, so I walk over to a pile of comics and kneel down beside it, hoping that it looks like I'm sorting through them, when really I'm using them for support.

"Bingo! It's up. Let's see, fun facts, fun facts, fuuuuuun facts."

"Vera," I say, but she doesn't look up from the screen.

"Did you know earthworms eat fourteen baby robins a day?"

"What?"

"Other way around. You know what I meant. Just, how many do you need?"

"How many of what?" I ask, my confusion distracting me enough to get to my feet.

Vera finally stops, looking up with a smile. "You scared the shit out of me." She walks over to the mini fridge she keeps behind the counter, and pulls out a bottle of water. She twists off the cap and hands it to me, and that's when I know for sure. It settles over me, all calm and shit, what a total head case I really am. My girlfriend gave her mom, like, a panic attack prevention plan for me. Fuck.

"Jubilee told me some facts just in case," Vera says, looking ridiculously proud of that. And now that it's confirmed, I want to crawl under a rack and melt into the floor. "She and Lil used to do that when she was little, too, you know."

"Wonderful." I know she did it out of kindness, but the fact that Peak and Vera definitely had a "my boyfriend is messed up and here's how to help him not lose it" talk just makes me feel worse. Dirty almost. Broken in a way I haven't felt in a little while. A very little while.

"She just wanted to make sure that if anything ever happened here, you would be okay."

"Right," I say, because still, it smarts, and I'm embarrassed, and also I get so tired after these things, I can't be bothered to say more.

"Ridley, I didn't mean to—it's just that, you're dating my daughter. My only daughter. And I care about you. You seem like a great kid . . ."

She pauses, and there's a *but* coming. I know because there's always a *but* coming, always an addendum, a reason why someone can love me but not unconditionally. When I die, my gravestone will probably say, *Here lies Ridley Oliver Everlasting. But . . .*

"But," she finally says, and I wince. "Jubilee is my priority. And I have concerns."

"Yeah," I say. "Makes sense."

"Ridley, look at it from my perspective. I don't know where you're from, or who your parents are, and Jubilee won't tell me anything. She's never shut us out like this. And maybe coming to you directly is a violation of her privacy, but she's put you at the center of her universe, and I just want to make sure that you deserve to be there."

"I don't," I say, biting hard on the inside of my cheek.

And she frowns.

I scratch the back of my neck. "But I'm trying to be someone who does."

She smiles at that, like it just assuaged all her fears or something. And I realize for the first time that this is someone who actually wants to be there, who wants to care about me. Who really wanted me to say the right thing. And I think I just did?

liar

"You're a good egg, Ridley." She comes up behind me, her hand burning into my skin when she places it on my shoulder. Because I think she just gave me her blessing, but also it's Friday, and I have to go write up another fake report for my dad.

I swallow hard, my skin crawling. I have to stop this. Today.

She squeezes my shoulder again. "I'm sorry for pushing. I just—I'm a mom. It's what we do."

I nod like I know what that means.

"I have to go." I grab my hoodie, push open the glass door, and walk the three miles back to my house, clutching my skateboard like a shield, trying to buy myself time to figure this out.

I want to say just the right thing when I get home, the thing to show that I'm mature, that I've thought this through, that I'm more than the inconvenience my mom thinks I am— she's barely called since I've been here—or the fuckup that my dad does.

That I've watched enough Captain America movies to know right from wrong, and this is wrong. That maybe if they let me, I could start a life here, maybe enroll in public school like a regular kid, even if I have to repeat my senior year. That it's not worth it to nibble on the scraps of their attention anymore, begging for it like a starving dog.

That I could have a life and friends and a future, and maybe that wasn't anybody's intention when I came here, but it could be the outcome.

But when I get home and I knock on the door to Dad's

study, he pulls it open like I'm bothering him somehow, and it all goes out the window. I stand there for a second, trying to steel my nerves—*What would Steve Rogers do?*—but he just raises his eyebrows and says, "I'm on a call, Ridley."

Like somehow that call is more important than finding out what I need. It's not. Not anymore. Because for this second, I have enough adrenaline coursing through my body to form words instead of excuses. For this second, I'm a Super-Soldier with a conscience, clutching his vibranium shield.

"Hi, Dad," I say, pushing into his office before I lose my nerve.

"I'll have to call you back," he says, and I didn't realize he had his Bluetooth thing in his ear. I hate those things; they make everybody look like sci-fi movie rejects. Nobody even uses them anymore except my dad and people like him, probably because they're also the only ones who even *make* phone calls anymore.

He pulls the device out and drops it onto the desk beside him. There are papers all spread across it, and he closes a file with a hard thud and then picks up his glass of scotch. "Okay, you have my attention." He leans against the desk a little bit, his legs angling out, taking up as much space as humanly possible. "What's so important that you had to interrupt me on a call to our German financiers?"

And I know I shouldn't be excited just by the thought of having his attention for once, his undivided attention, which I don't think I've had even once since I was born—stolen from German financiers, no less—but I am.

I am.

God, I am so screwed up.

"This is wrong," I say. And that wasn't how I meant to open, but it'll do. I tuck my hands behind my back and lean against the wall and hope my opening volley was a good one.

He blinks and then lets out a little sigh. "I wondered why you've been feeding us bogus reports. I should have anticipated this. You've always been the emotional one." He runs his hand over his chin. "It's just business, Ridley, glorified market research, nothing more."

"You knew?"

"I thought threatening to send you back to Seattle would bring you around."

Awesome, so his threat was actually a business strategy. He literally does not care. I swallow hard—I can't worry about that now—and steady my course.

"They're good people."

He turns around, shuffling some papers on his desk. "Why does that matter?"

"Screwing with good people is wrong." I can't believe I even have to explain this to him. This is like Being Human 101.

"Is that what you've been doing?"

"That's what you're making me do!"

"No, I brought you here, but everything else was your decision. All the nonsense you've been up to with Vera's stepdaughter—" He looks at my surprised face. "Did you really think I didn't know how much time you were spending together? I'd hoped you had learned from your last indiscretion not to get in bed with people we do business with. Your mother swore to me you wouldn't make this messy like—"

"Like what?" I shove off the wall and take a step closer.

He hesitates for a second, like he's trying to decide how far he wants to go, but then his eyes narrow and his cheeks kinda suck into this tight smile. "Like you're prone to do."

I nod, squeezing my eyes shut, trying to swallow down the anxiety coiling tight in the pit of my stomach. "Maybe if I had parents who—" But I stop myself. It's pointless. He's going to think what he thinks, and nothing I do will change that. "I've seen what a family is, Dad, and I know it's not this."

"Oh, that's rich coming from you," he says. "Do you know what you've cost us over the years?"

"Me?"

He pushes off his desk and takes a step closer. "We may not have had much time together, and I own that, but we gave you opportunities that most kids could never even dream of."

"I didn't want opportunities; I wanted parents!"

"We tried that, and you jumped off the roof, remember? This roof, actually. And then your mother made me buy her a whole new house across the country so you could have a fresh start. But you screwed that up by letting that boy take pictures of you. Do you know how much I had to pay that website to make them disappear?"

I shift uncomfortably. I didn't even know they existed until Chandler threatened to post them online, hoping it would derail his conservative father's political career. I guess queer kids hating their shitty dads is kind of par for the course.

"Who exactly do you think has been bankrolling all of your mistakes?"

I stare down at the carpet. "I just don't want to be a part of this anymore."

He scoffs. "A part of what?"

"Any of this." I gesture to the reports, to the room, to him.

He takes another step forward, and another, until my back is against the wall, and I wince from the smell of booze on his breath. Shit, it's barely afternoon.

"What would you do without any of this? You have no skills, no money, no education. You've been coddled to the point of uselessness." His voice changes, like he's letting loose years of pent-up frustration. "You are a black hole, Ridley. You always have been, sucking us all in with you. You want out? Nobody's stopping you. Not anymore."

I bounce my head against the wall a couple times, trying to ground myself, trying to put together the threat behind the words, to remember what's important, what matters, what I should do . . . but it's hard to remember when no one ever bothered to teach you.

"Yes," I say, and it comes out more like a plea. "I want to go."

He huffs out a breath like he doesn't believe me.

I spin off the wall and bolt to my room. I tear back the blankets to find my favorite pair of sweats and grab all the little notes that Peak left me whenever she came over, and the three hair ties she abandoned in my bathroom, and the little bit of money my dad has given me for my work. I shove it all in the black duffel bag at my feet, along with whatever clothes are within reach, and dart down the stairs.

My dad is standing in the doorway of his office, but he looks different. Resigned instead of mad. But if I think about that too long, I might stay to ask why, and I can't.

I can't.

"Ridley—" he says, but I don't look back.

CHAPTER THIRTY-NINE
Jubilee

RIDLEY IS LYING stone still on my bed, staring at the ceiling with his shoes still on. He never leaves his shoes on—he knows we don't allow it—and now they've left muddy smudges at the bottom of my comforter.

I'm too worried to care.

It has been exactly twenty-three minutes since Mom called me to the door with the tiniest bit of an edge to her voice. No one else would have noticed probably, but it's the closest I've ever heard her to panic. I didn't know what to expect when I ran down the hall, but it definitely wasn't Ridley standing on our doorstep with a black bag slung across his body and a haunted look on his face.

"I got this, Mom," I said, taking his hand and leading him back to my room.

She mouthed *Is he okay?* and all I could do was shrug because I didn't know. Our last texts had been about going to Stacks later today, and he'd seemed fine. Mom followed us to my room, lingering for a minute, and then shut the door behind us.

And now, with his heartbeat thumping in my ear like a metronome on speed, I know the answer is loudly and conclusively no, he is not.

I tried to talk to him at first. I tried to tell him some facts, to make him laugh, but he just lay down without a word, his eyes red and exhausted, his breath still hitching. I did the only thing I could think of: I curled up next to him, I told him I loved him, and I waited.

. . .

"I can't ever go back to that house," he says, and I startle a little. I thought he'd fallen asleep. I glance at the clock again; it's been two hours since he came to my door.

"What happened?"

"I got out."

I go back to stroking his hair, just relieved that he's talking. "What does that mean?"

He draws in a deep breath, holding it for a full beat before letting it out. "I told my father that I was done. He knew the reports were fake already. We got in a fight, and he said some stuff, and—it's fine." His breath hitches again as his words trail off.

I nuzzle in closer, kissing any part of him I can reach. "It's okay, Ridley. You're okay." When I stop, he looks down at me, frowning.

"He said I was a . . ." He's looking at me so intensely, it scares me. "Am I a black hole?"

"No," I say, sitting up. "I hate your father. I hate him. You are *not* a black hole."

He pinches the bridge of his nose with his thumbs and shuts his eyes. "But I am. I am. Look at what I've done to you."

"You haven't done anything to me."

"They're going to send me back to Washington, I bet. Back to that house, and it'll just be me and all those windows and a fucking housekeeper and nothing." He squeezes my arm tight. "I thought I could do the right thing for once, but it didn't matter anyway. I'll—"

"My parents will help us; we'll figure it out."

"No," he says, scrambling backward until he slams into my headboard. "Peak, if they find out who I am now, I'll have nothing. You were right; we can never tell them. I was stupid to think we could." He jumps up and starts pacing. I've never seen him this frantic. "What if my dad tells them now to screw with me? I can't—there's no—"

"It's going to be okay," I say in as calm a voice as I can muster.

"You don't understand. I can't go back. I'll—" And then, all at once, he goes completely still, and our eyes meet. "You could leave with me."

"What?"

"Leave with me, Peak. It's the only other option."

"Only other option than what?" I ask, the hairs on my arms standing up as I realize what he's talking about. I know exactly what he's doing: he's checking for emergency exits and coming up short.

"I won't go back to my mom's." He shakes his head. "And I can't stay here. Peak, if your parents—no, *when* your parents figure it out, it's all over for us anyway. Come with me."

"I have school. I have the audition for the summer program in, like, a week and a half! We can't go anywhere."

He scrunches his eyes shut, nodding in a way that feels more for him than for me. "You're right," he says, walking over to where I sit. "You're right. The audition. I'm so proud of you, Peak." He leans down and kisses me. It feels so right, so loving, that I almost don't realize what it is—a goodbye.

I grab on to his sleeve, but he shakes me off. "Ridley."

"It wasn't fair to ask. I'm not thinking straight."

"Ridley, stop. Seriously, you're scaring me. Stay here for tonight. It'll be okay."

He exhales, his nostrils flaring as he wipes at his eyes. "It will never be okay, Peak. That's the thing."

And then, before I even realize what's happening, he's shoved open my window and thrown his bag outside, putting his hands on the sill like he aims to follow.

"Wait." And I thought there'd be more time before it all came crashing down, that we'd get at least a few months of happiness. I thought if we could just make it to summer . . . I can't let him go out there alone, though, not like this.

"I'm coming with you." I glance at my cello; I can't help it, because leaving right now feels like losing it forever. Resentment rises up inside, choking me, but I swallow it down. There'll be time to be pissed—at his parents for failing him, at the world for putting us in this situation, at him too maybe—later. When he's safe.

He runs his hands through his hair, linking his fingers behind his head. "Peak," he says, letting out a hard breath. "This isn't—I'm trying to do the right thing here. I don't want to—I'm not going to be your black hole too."

And I swear to god, if I ever see his father again, I will claw his eyes out myself.

"I can decide for myself," I say, even though this is the definition of forcing my hand, but whatever. I grab my book bag off my chair and shove some clothes inside. I know this is a terrible idea, probably the worst I've ever had, but if I can get him through the night, then we can come back and fix it all when he's calmer and thinking straight. My parents are going to kill me, but I don't see any other choice.

I zip up my bag and turn to look at him, hoping I look more confident than I actually feel. Inside my stomach is churning. "Okay, let's go."

Ridley drops his arms and looks at me. "I'm not worth it."

"You are." I try to mask the annoyance in my voice. If he only realized that, we wouldn't be here in the first place. Why can't he realize that?

He turns around to hop out the window, but I pull his shoulder back. I nudge him out of the way, dropping my bag outside next to his. He looks at me, confused, as I walk to the bedroom door.

"Don't you think it would be a little suspicious if we jumped out of my bedroom window? We probably only have a few more minutes before they come open the door anyway."

"You're going to tell them you're leaving?"

"I won't tell them what we're really doing, but I'll say you're staying with Frankie for a few nights and I'm taking you to get settled."

"Get me settled?" He winces. "Like I'm a little kid."

"Ridley." I squeeze his hand. "I have to tell them something." And also, I'm kind of hoping I can convince him that Frankie is our best bet anyway, so it's not really a lie.

"Okay," he says, squeezing my hand back. "Okay."

CHAPTER FORTY

Ridley

IT WAS EASIER getting past her parents than I thought it would be, and somehow, even walking down this cold, dark street with the weight of both of our bags on my shoulder, I feel lighter than I ever have. I don't have to be a liar anymore; I don't have to pretend to be anything I'm not; I can just be a boy holding the hand of the person he loves and leaving everything else behind.

I look over at Peak, and she smiles, pushing some of her hair back and tucking it behind her ear. We've been walking in silence for a half hour, but if she's scared, she's not showing it. If I was one-tenth as brave as her, maybe—

"Where to?" she asks, her voice gentle, quieting all the noise in my head. Peak's magic like that.

"Just up here. I need to borrow something from my sister." Something flickers in her eyes, confusion maybe, or possibly relief, but I don't want to think about that too long.

"Oh, good idea. I was going to say we should go to

Frankie's for real, but your sister's is probably a better idea. Maybe she can help us figure it out."

I scrunch my eyebrows, shifting the bags up higher on my shoulder without letting go of her hand. Suddenly this seems so much more tenuous than I thought. If she thinks we're staying here, in town, that would explain why she's not freaking. Should I rip that Band-Aid off, or?

icantlosehericant

And shit. It feels so good walking here with her. So peaceful. Like in another life, it would be day instead of night, and our bags would have homework instead of clothes in them, and everything would be fine, and nothing would hurt. But that's a lie. And I'm done with lies, so.

"I'm not staying at my sister's, Peak."

"Okay," she says, and I almost believe her, until she says, "where should we go, then?" She pulls out her phone. "We could go to Frankie's or head to Jayla's basement for a few days. Her parents never go down there." I stop as we near the parking garage, and she looks up at me, confused. "What are you doing?"

"Borrowing something we need."

I cut across the street to where the valet parking is. I pull out a parking stub from my wallet and hand it to the attendant. Gray forgot it in Dad's car when he dropped her at the airport. I swiped it from him so it didn't get lost while she was gone.

"Normally, Ms. Everlasting has our driver deliver her car to her apartment," the valet says, frowning.

"She asked me to get it. She has a late flight tonight, and I have to get her." He looks me up and down, like he's not sure he should do what I'm asking, but then seems to decide I'm all right, or maybe that he doesn't care either way, and radios another attendant to bring the car around.

Gray's car appears a few minutes later, a shiny new Audi. The valet hops out, leaving the door open and even popping the trunk. He takes the bags from me and drops them in. Peak eyes me slowly before getting in the car.

I jump when the valet shuts the trunk.

"Is everything all right, sir?" he asks, coming around for his tip.

"Yeah." And god, I hope that's true. I really hope that's true.

I slide into the driver's seat, adjusting the rearview mirror and the blowers for the heat. Okay. I can do this. I had six hours of driver's ed last summer when I stayed with my aunt and cousin in Michigan because my mom needed a break from me. It was the best summer of my life. Best months of my life, really. And suddenly, I know just where we can go. She would definitely let me stay, probably Peak too. Maybe Peak could even fly back for her audition. Maybe it could be okay.

"What are you doing?" Peak asks, looking at me with wide eyes as she buckles up.

"Getting us out of here." I tap my fingers on the steering wheel. I can see the guys in the valet stand still watching me, and if I sit here for much longer, they will definitely know something is up. I try to shift into drive, but the gearshift doesn't move.

Peak stares at me, and as calm as she looked before, she seems really fucking concerned right now. "Sorry," I say, giving her a weak smile. "I forgot you had to be pressing on the brake. I remember that now." I push it into drive and ease off the brake, letting the car roll forward a bit.

"This is a bad idea. You don't even have a license." And she's right. It is a bad idea, but it's also the only other idea I have that ends with me still here.

"Do you want to get out?" I ask, my foot planted firmly on the brake again. And I mean it too. I might be running away from home, I might even be in the middle of grand theft auto as we speak, but. The valet guy knocks on my window; we've been sitting here a long time. But I can't go, not until she answers.

She hesitates and then shakes her head, and I could kiss her face—would be, actually, if the guy from the garage wasn't still knocking.

I lower the window. "Sorry, we were just trying to decide where to go eat. Am I in your way?"

I'm scared he's going to say something, like he realized something was up and called Gray or my dad, or that he could tell I didn't really know how to drive, or that the police were coming to arrest me for driving without a license. But he just says, "There's a great lobster bar down by the pier; it should be pretty quiet tonight."

"Thanks, we'll be sure to check it out." I flash him my

most winningest smile and hit the gas. The car jerks forward, and I ease it onto the road, tightening my grip on the wheel and saying a quick prayer that I can handle this.

"Ridley," Peak says, but when I look at her, she's turned toward her window. Whatever words she was planning to say dying on her lips.

CHAPTER FORTY-ONE
Jubilee

THIS IS BAD. I'm 99 percent sure that we just stole his sister's car, which is extremely illegal. Even more illegal when you don't have a driver's license, which neither of us do. I fight the urge to call my mom. She'd probably just call the police or something, not to be mean, but just to have them find me and give me a ride back home. But that would probably be worse in the end. The way Ridley is white-knuckling the steering wheel is already freaking me out. I don't know what he would do if we got pulled over. I don't want to find out.

Suddenly, I feel very small. Very small and unprepared. Running away seemed like a good idea when I thought it meant crashing in Jayla's basement for a day or two, or hiding out at Frankie's apartment and still texting my mom good night even though she was definitely going to ground me.

But this, this is completely different. This is so much bigger than me. Bigger than us. These are real problems, with real consequences, and I am not equipped to handle this. A few weeks ago, I thought if I didn't nail my audition, it would be the end of the world, but this night feels like it could actually *be* the end of my world, and that's scaring the crap out of me.

"Ridley," I say when I notice he's heading toward the freeway. He's been driving carefully until now, keeping to back roads and not going over thirty miles per hour. I can tell by the way he swerves and slows that we definitely shouldn't be going freeway fast. Not to mention it will have actual traffic, even late on a weeknight like this. I need to stop this; this is a mistake.

"What?" he asks.

"Watch the road," I say when he looks at me, but he stares at me for a beat too long anyway, and I feel like I'm going to throw up. "I was just going to say, don't get on the freeway."

"Why? It's the fastest."

Because we'll probably die, I think, but instead I say, "We can go the back way, take Route 9 all the way out. We'll see the coast and be low profile. What if your dad already called the police or something?" It bothers me, the ease with which I lie now. I've had a lot of practice since I met Ridley. I kind of hate that.

"Smart." He flicks on his turn signal and follows the Route 9 sign. I wait until we're a little farther out of town, driving through the woods on some back roads, to try again.

"Where are we going?" I'm trying to sound completely unfazed. I don't want to scare him again, not when he's driving, or whatever you want to call what we're doing. There's a reason people have to take tests to operate cars. I haven't even taken the test for my permit yet.

"I don't know." He takes one hand off the wheel and scratches the back of his neck. "Gray's on the other side of Canada, so I was thinking my aunt's?"

"Where does she live?"

"Michigan."

Okay, so that's not as close as Jayla's basement, but not as bad as driving to the other side of Canada. But still, I feel it settling over me, this feeling of doom, like it's all going off the rails and there's no way to stop it. I have to try, though.

"Have you talked to Gray about everything that's going on?"

"Uh, no, Peak, this was pretty spur of the moment. I came to you first."

I turn to face him, pulling one leg up on the seat. It's now or never. "Don't freak out, please. But this feels like a bad idea. I really think we should go back now."

He slams his head against his seat and looks at me, so hurt, so lost, and I wish I never said anything. "I told you not to come. And I gave you the chance to get out when we got the car. I can't stay. I thought you got that."

And he's so worked up, I need to adjust the timeline of my plan. I can't wait for him to calm down; cooler heads need to prevail now.

"I'm not asking you to go back to your dad's. We'll go to my house. I know my parents will let you spend the night." He makes a face like he doesn't believe me. "Just the night, and probably on the couch, but tomorrow we'll tell them everything. You've wanted to all along; you were right. Okay?"

"It's too late. I can't fix this. They'll hate me, especially now."

"They won't. They'll understand. Trust me, tragic origin stories are kind of their thing. Do you even read Vera's comics? And here I thought you were a superfan," I tease. I'm trying to break the tension; it doesn't work. "Fine, they'll be mad. But even if they're furious, they'll still help. I promise."

"You trust them way too much."

And oh, that breaks my heart. "You're supposed to be able to," I say. "Like, in a perfect world, everybody could trust their parents."

"Yeah, well."

"Bats." He looks at me quick and goes back to driving. "Please believe me. They might be pissed—they're definitely going to be pissed—but they'll help us. Tomorrow we'll call your aunt and your sister and figure everything out from there."

"I can't go back with my parents," he says, his eyes shining in the dashboard lights. He's slowed to twenty miles per hour, and if I can just keep talking to him, maybe I can get him to stop.

"You won't have to. I won't let that happen." He looks at me again, probably surprised by how intensely I said that. "Look, my mom will know what to do. Maybe she and Vera can even talk to your parents for you."

"They're mortal enemies," he deadpans, like this night hasn't been dramatic enough.

"Fine." I try to laugh, but it comes out more like a huff. "Then they'll call your aunt, and she can talk to your parents. Maybe you can even stay with her until you finish school?"

"You're here, though." He says it like it's the most important thing. And I thought it was too, I did, but this feels so much bigger than anything I've ever had to deal with. Somehow, I don't think grand theft auto with a boyfriend in crisis is what Mrs. Garavuso meant when she said I needed to live a little.

I tip my head toward him. "Michigan is a lot closer to Connecticut than Washington is."

The car slows to ten miles per hour, and then five, and then stops. "Why are you like this?"

"Like what?"

"Why are you so nice to me?" His voice sounds small and kind of far away, like his body's here but his head is not. "I cause you so much trouble."

"Not really," I say, acutely aware of the fact that we're now completely stopped in the middle of a dark road. "I mean, tonight sucks." I lace my fingers with his. "Which is why, right now, I need you to turn the car around. Please. You don't have to trust them, but please, trust *me*."

He stares out the windshield, out to where our headlights meet the darkness. The fingers of his other hand tap on the steering wheel. "I do."

He takes a deep breath, driving across the lane and then

shifting into reverse to do a three-point turn. For the first time tonight, I think things will be okay. Forty miles an hour toward home is a lot better than twenty miles per hour in the opposite direction, no matter what the outcome.

And that—that's the exact moment when everything goes to hell.

CHAPTER FORTY-TWO

Ridley

IT'S LIKE SLOW motion when the other car hits us, barreling in with its blinding headlights. There's no time to react. There's no time to do anything. There's no time at all.

Somewhere in the background Peak screams, or I do, and our car spins, and I think, *I always thought dying would be my choice.*

. . .

"Ridley!"

"Ridley, please, open your eyes."

"Yes, he's breathing. Okay. I'm putting you on speaker."

"Ridley."

I crack open my eyes, but it's hard. I'm tired, and something is making them burn. I reach up to wipe it away, and Peak grabs my hand and pushes it down.

"Ridley! Help is coming. Just stay still, okay?"

Help. Yes, Peak said we needed that. I'm glad. I turn my head a little bit, and everything hurts. Everything really hurts, but I need to see her. I need to know she's okay. She's clutching her shoulder with her left arm, her right arm gone totally limp. *That's not good,* I think, my eyelids drifting shut.

"Ridley, hold on."

Hold on to what? I wonder. But when I open my mouth to ask, nothing comes out.

"Shh, baby, shhh. You're okay. You're okay. They'll be here in a minute. They'll—"

She's still talking, probably. I think I can hear her voice somewhere in the distance, somewhere far away, somewhere I'm dreaming of, like if I listen hard enough, I can almost chase it back. I can almost get there. But I'm so tired.

She's crying now. I can hear that much, and I want to open my eyes. I want to tell her that everything is fine, probably. If only I could make everything less red.

We were going home. It was going to be okay. She promised.

I'm so tired.

I should sleep.

I should sleep now.

"Ridley, open your eyes."

"Ridley!"

CHAPTER FORTY-THREE

Jubilee

I'M STILL SOBBING when my parents burst in, pulling back the curtain as I'm trying not to hyperventilate while the doctor tells me that my shoulder's dislocated and I'll need surgery to fix the bones in my wrist. I don't even care, though—they can cut it off if they want—because Ridley wouldn't wake up and nobody will tell me what's going on.

A nurse told me he was okay when we first got here, but I've seen enough television to know that might not be the truth. They won't let me out of this bed, and the doctor is just droning on about how they need to stabilize the injury and I need to calm down, and I just want to scream at her to shut up, because WHAT DOES IT EVEN MATTER ANYMORE?

Ridley's hurt or worse, my audition is out the window, and I've been lying to my parents for weeks. I've lost everything that matters in one night. I'm hurt and I'm pissed and I'm scared, and I don't even know what to do with any of this.

"I'm sorry," I say when my mom and Vera wrap me tight

in a hug, uttering things like "oh thank god" and "you're okay." Their hot tears prick against my neck, and it reminds me of how warm his blood was on my hands, and I gag. My mom leans back and places her hand on my forehead like she did when I was little, and I just want to go home.

"What were you guys doing out there? Where did you even get a car? I thought you were going to Frankie's, and then the hospital calls!"

"He was turning around, Mom, I swear," I cry. "We were coming home."

"Jesus Christ, Jubilee. What were you thinking? And, Jubi, your arm! Your arm!"

"He wouldn't wake up," I choke out before dissolving into a fresh round of tears. The doctor stands in the corner, exasperated. "I was trying to help, Mom. I was trying to help! They won't tell me anything."

"Vera, go check on him," Mom says, sounding exhausted. Vera gives my leg one last squeeze and stands up.

The doctor—Dr. Philman, her name tag says—interjects, "The patient that came in with her is getting the care he needs. Only immediate family can see him right now, like I've already told her."

"He doesn't have a family," I sniffle. "He just has us."

The doctor's lips draw in a tight line. "I understand your concern for your friend, but I need to stabilize your arm and wrist before you injure it more."

"I'll go, honey," Vera says. "Even if they don't let me see him, I'll be there."

"Hurry," I say, but when she pulls back the curtain again

to step into the hallway, Ridley's father is standing there, looking down at his phone.

"Mark?"

"Vera," he sighs. "I don't suppose you know where my son is, do you? My wife is very upset. Apparently, she got a call he was here." He says it like it's no big deal, like it's a minor inconvenience, and if the doctor wasn't holding my arm in place, I swear to god I would slap him.

"Your son?" Vera asks, and I can't do this. Not now, when I just need to know he's okay.

Ridley's father glances up. "Don't play dumb, Vera. Do you know what room he's in?"

Vera and Mom turn back toward me, confusion covering their faces.

"I'm sorry," I say, and then it feels like the walls are closing in on me. The doctor gives me some oxygen and puts something in my IV, and everything gets kind of heavy and warm.

Somewhere, far away, people are shouting.

CHAPTER FORTY-FOUR

Ridley

I BLINK GROGGILY under too-bright lights, feeling pain in places I didn't know existed. Panic claws around my heart, sending its rhythm spiraling faster as I try to piece together where I am and how I got here. I turn my head, which, ouch, this is a headache like no other, and there's Gray sitting in the chair beside my bed. She sets her phone down, patting my arm with a sad smile.

"Hey, Rid," she says. "You're in the hospital, but you're okay."

"Peak?" I rasp. It hurts to talk, but I have to know.

"Peak's fine," Gray says. "She already went home."

"Fine?"

"Well, a couple broken bones, but nothing that can't be fixed." The relief mixes with whatever drugs they have me on, and I shut my eyes again, content to drift some more.

• • •

The next time I open my eyes, Gray's in different clothes and drinking coffee. I shift in bed, wincing.

"Hey," she says, scooting her chair closer and rubbing my leg. "Sleeping Beauty awakes."

"Am I . . . ?" I trail off, not sure what I'm asking. Alive? Okay? Still a part of your family?

"You're fine. Mostly. There are six staples keeping your brain from leaking out, and you have three cracked ribs, so nice work." She takes another sip of her coffee. "We're not even going to talk about what you did to my poor car. I just got that thing, Ridley."

I reach up and touch my head, wincing when my fingers ghost over the bandage. "How long was I out?" I ask, poking at all the holes in my memory. There was yelling, I think, and . . . Vera?

"You've been awake off and on for two days, but they doped you up really good, so I doubt you'll remember. I guess you were awake for part of World War Three the other night, but the nurses said you didn't make any sense. You just kept saying you were going home, but every time Dad said you would soon, you freaked out until they finally had to sedate you. They turned your meds down this morning. I think they're discharging you tomorrow."

"World War Three?" I rasp, and she finally hands me some water.

"Small sips," she says, and it's so automatic, I wonder how often she's been doing it.

"Tell me what happened." I focus on the feel of cold water sliding down my throat to stay awake.

"Apparently Dad was here, and so were Peak's parents."

"Vera." I huff out a deep breath.

"Yeah." Gray grimaces. "And from what I gather, it did *not* go well. The doctors ended up banning them all from your room."

"Vera must hate me."

"Actually, your night nurse said she was mostly ripping into Dad. I guess it got pretty vicious."

"Was Peak here?" I ask, because it doesn't make any sense that she isn't now.

Gray hesitates and then nods. "She stopped by when she was discharged. You were asleep."

"What aren't you telling me?"

"What matters is that you're here and you're okay. And we need to focus on getting you better right now. You—"

"Gray, just tell me. Whatever I'm imagining is probably so much worse." I'm so tired, but I can already feel the adrenaline kicking up.

tellmetellmetellme

"It's doesn't matter."

"What did she say?" The heart monitor starts beeping faster and faster; Gray stares at it, looking worried.

"All right." She shakes her head. "But you have to calm down."

"That's not how it works," I say through gritted teeth. "Just tell me."

Gray bites her lip, smoothing her skirt before looking back up at me. "She said she didn't know it was possible to love someone and hate them at the same time."

Oh.

I thought the staples in my head hurt, but this.

This.

"She was just upset, Ridley. People say weird things when they're in pain. Her arm—"

"Her arm?"

"I mean, I don't know the specifics or anything, but it was in a sling and her wrist was wrapped."

"Which arm?"

"I don't know. I wasn't paying attention."

"Think!" I shout. "Which arm? Right or left?"

"Left, I think." Gray closes her eyes, tilting her head back. "No. No, right. Definitely her right arm."

"Her audition is so soon." I'm going to be sick. Gray grabs the pan near my bed and shoves it under my face just in time. I've texted her so many clips of Peak playing, and we've had so many conversations about how important the audition is. She knows exactly what this means.

"Maybe they'll give her an extension," Gray says, rubbing my back while I try to get a grip. It turns out throwing up with broken ribs really fucking hurts.

"It's competitive," I groan when I can finally talk again. "Hundreds of applicants for eight spots. What do you think?"

"I think it sucks, but it could be worse. You guys could have been killed; you realize that, right?" She pauses, taking a deep breath. "Let's just all be glad it wasn't worse." She stares down at her coffee. "I think you're getting a ticket for driving without a license, but the other driver was speeding and had drugs in his car, so you got lucky."

I look at her and crinkle my forehead, which tugs at the bandage in an uncomfortable way, because seriously? Lucky?

"Well, not lucky," she says, but then she scrunches up her face. "No, it is lucky. You were both very, very lucky. What were you thinking, Ridley? Dammit." She stands up and slams her coffee on the tray hard enough that some of it splashes out. "Why didn't you call me? I would have done something. You promised me you always would. You swore!"

I clear my throat, and when she looks at me, her eyes are glassy. I hate that I keep hurting everyone I love. "I don't know. I didn't think you would understand."

"What?" she shouts.

"Dad's so different with you. I didn't want you to know how he really is, at least with me."

"I see a lot more than you give me credit for. I should have done something sooner. I just hoped . . . You're not dealing with this alone. We'll go back to Washington together. We'll—"

"I can't go back there, Grayson." I hesitate, searching for the words. "Whatever's wrong with me, Mom and Dad both make it so much worse."

"There's nothing wrong with you."

"There is."

She sits back down and grabs my hand. "It's different, harder maybe, I don't know. But it's not wrong, okay? So don't say that."

I shrug, because I want to believe her so much, but I don't.

"I was already looking at apartments in Boston. I'll get a two-bedroom; you can stay with me."

"You don't have to do that." I squeeze my eyes shut, because I know, I know that's not enough. And I don't want to screw up anybody else's life.

"I want to."

"I think I need help, Gray. Like more than you can give."

"Okay," she says, her voice sort of quiet and love soaked. "You'll get it, Ridley, whatever you need. We're going to work on this together, you and me. I don't even want to see Dad after some of the things he said, and Mom didn't even fly out."

"What did he—" I start to say, and then catch myself. "I don't want to know."

"Just, don't ever pull this again, okay? I'll—I'll teach you to drive myself. I'll buy us a car. Whatever you need. I'm gonna be there. Just don't make me see you banged up like this again."

"Promise?" I ask through my tears.

She grabs my hand and squeezes it. "Promise."

CHAPTER FORTY-FIVE

PEAK: I'm glad you're okay
and I love you, but I can't do
this anymore.

                                              BATS: I know.

CHAPTER FORTY-SIX
Jubilee

"CAN I TALK to her?"

Jayla is at the door, blocking the entrance, but his voice still cuts through me, making me ache in places that I wish it didn't.

I am sitting on the couch, staring at the TV, trying not to think. Jayla's parents let her stay home with me today since my parents reluctantly had to go to work and I'm only two days post-op. They both wanted to stay home, but they've missed so much already and will miss more with all the specialist visits. Ironically, instead of going out to audition Monday, I have a surgical follow-up.

I glance down at the bandage around my arm, wondering what it's going to look like after this is all done. And then I think about how it used to look playing cello, something I won't be able to do for weeks.

"You have serious balls," Jayla says, and I sigh. I could just sit here and let her handle it, but I know I need to see him. I need to talk to him. It's been almost a week since the accident, three days since I texted him, and it still feels like I can't breathe without him. We both know this doesn't work anymore, though. And if we don't, at least I do.

I know it was my decision to leave that night, and my decision to get in the car and stay there, but I didn't feel like I had a choice, and I think a part of me will always resent him for that. No matter how much I love him and want him, I just can't anymore.

"Let him in."

Jayla looks at me like I've lost my marbles but steps back and opens the door wider anyway. Ridley walks in and I look up, fighting the urge to hug him. I take an inventory instead. He looks smaller somehow, more jittery. He's all bruised up, and there's a bandage on his head. A large chunk of his hair is missing where they had to shave it. There are dark purple moons beneath his eyes that suggest he hasn't been sleeping. Maybe his pain meds aren't as good as mine.

He walks slowly, gingerly, to the chair across from me, and I don't miss the way he winces as he sits down. Jayla comes and sits next to me, and I give her a look that makes her roll her eyes.

"I'm gonna go make lunch," she says. I know how much she hates him for this, and I know how much effort it takes for her to give us space. Jayla has been my rock, through the tears for the audition and even the tears for Ridley. I don't know which I cried harder for, anyway.

It feels like the silence stretches forever, but we're not even back from the commercial break yet. Ridley hangs his head, and every molecule in my body is begging to touch him, to hug him, to kiss his lips. I want things to be okay, but they never will be, and it's just as much my fault as it is his. He squeezes his eyes shut and takes a breath.

"I know you need time and space," he says. "I know that the rest of our lives might not even be enough time and space for you. I am so sorry for putting you in this position, and I'm not going to make it worse by asking for your forgiveness. I just came by because I'm leaving tomorrow, and it didn't feel right to go without letting you know."

"Thanks," I say, taking a shuddering breath because why is this so hard? Why does it feel like I'm dying, or will die, or have died without him?

"Don't," he says. "But thank you for trying to help me. For trying to be there for me. I'm sorry that you got hurt because of it."

I don't know what else to say. I'm sorry too. Doesn't change anything.

"I love you, Peak," he says, and then holds up his hands when I open my mouth to speak. "You don't have to say anything. I know what I did. But I'm so glad that you exist, and that you're you. Because you showed me there's more to this life than I thought. That it's worth trying to figure out." He takes a deep breath, and I look away.

"Where are you going?" I ask, praying it's not back to Washington with that thing he calls a mother.

"I need help, Peak. I'm staying with Grayson in Boston for a while. She found this place that specializes in this kind of stuff, and there are horses," he says, and I can tell it's hard for him to spit it out.

"Horses?"

"I don't really know." He ducks his head. "I don't know why I led with horses. There's just—" He runs his hands over his face, letting them linger on his mouth, as he looks to the ceiling. "There are people there who can help me figure this stuff out. Because the way that you make me feel, I want to be able to feel it on my own too. I know it's selfish, but god, Peak, I am so fucking glad I met you."

"Ridley." My heart is breaking, and he's saying everything right, and it would be so easy for me to give in to this feeling, but so wrong of me to ask him to stay.

He looks up, his eyes piercing mine.

"I want that for you," I say, "so much." And he shuts his eyes and nods.

We sit there for a while, until his phone goes off. He pulls it out with a sigh. "Gray's outside. She got the rest of my stuff from my dad's. I didn't want to go back there, you know?" He stands up and walks over, brushing his thumb gently down my injured arm. This time when he kisses me goodbye, I don't try to stop him. I don't beg him to stay or ask to go with him.

"Bye, Peak. Thanks . . . for everything."

And when the door clicks shut, the tears come in earnest because I know that he changed me and I changed him. We'll never be the same, but maybe that's okay.

I bet the horses will be beautiful.

CHAPTER FORTY-SEVEN

Ridley

"YOU READY?" GRAY asks, leaning in the doorway of our new apartment. Dad threatened to cut her off, but Gray called his bluff and things are mostly fine. I think Gray's even getting glorified child support now too, but I don't ask.

It took a little while for a bed to open up at Greenwild Acres, the ridiculously bougie therapeutic equine facility my sister found that specializes in teens with clinical depression and anxiety disorders. They don't just load you up on medication there, but that is part of it, and they've already prescribed some in coordination with my new doctor. I was always really weird about having to take stuff, but it actually does seem to help.

Greenwild Acres is located on a sprawling horse farm just outside of Boston, which is where Gray and I live now, and I've been doing outpatient services there while I waited for a bed. Everybody is pretty cool so far. I'm nervous about going inpatient for the next six-plus weeks, but I feel hopeful somehow too.

Plus, they have a skate park there, and I can bring my board, which is awesome—except they'll keep it locked up at first because skate privileges need to be earned. I know I'm lucky to be able to go to a place like that; most people can't. I told Gray I didn't think I deserved all this special treatment, and she said it's not about deserving it and to shut up and pack. So I did. But I still feel a little weird about it.

I miss Peak, like, so much, but my therapists have got me pretty well convinced that if we're meant to be, we'll be, and that the best thing I can do is get myself in order before I go charging back. I really hope someday we're meant to be, but if not, I'm trying to just be grateful for the time we had.

I stare down at the words across the screen of my laptop. I'm on the admissions page for a community college near our apartment. If things go well, I might take a class this fall. My therapist said starting small was still a start, so.

I wait for the words APPLICATION RECEIVED to flash across the screen, and then I click it shut.

"I'm so ready."

Gray twirls her keys around her finger and then tosses them in my direction. "You're driving," she says, and I catch them.

Because yeah, for once I am.

CHAPTER FORTY-EIGHT
Jubilee

I WENT TO my first physical therapy session today, and it kind of sucked, so Jayla and Nikki are over trying to cheer me up. I'm a couple weeks post-op now, and everybody's extremely happy with the results. I am too, I guess, but this big rush to get me back to playing just seems pointless now that I've missed my audition. When we told the conservatory what happened, they offered to reschedule to the end of the decision period, but I had to decline. I knew I wouldn't be ready. Even if I was cleared, it would still take time to get back my technique.

Jayla shoves open my bedroom curtains and pushes up the window. The sounds of birds and traffic flood my room. The brightness is nice, but when it hits my cello case—highlighting a thin layer of dust—I swallow hard and go back to fiddling with the straps of my splint.

"Come on, Jubi, let's go do something," Jayla says, but I ignore her.

I don't really *do* anything these days besides go to school and hang out in my room, and Jayla knows it. I haven't been back to the shop since everything happened. Memories of Ridley cover every inch of it and I'm just not ready, and without that or my rehearsals and lessons, I find myself with a lot of free time. Too much, really.

Nikki flops down beside me while Jayla moves to open the second window. "Okay, no more moping. We can do anything you want, you name it."

"I want my cello to not be covered in dust, and I want to play it."

"No actual playing for at least two more weeks, doctor's orders." Jayla leans against the windowsill. "But we can definitely help with the first part. I wasn't going to say it, but this room is disgusting."

And so that's how we end up spending a perfectly good Saturday playing "keep or toss" while cleaning my room. We toss all the old painkillers and antibiotics and keep the get-well-soon cards. We toss the now deflated balloons and keep my hospital wristband. We take it item by item until it looks less like a recovery room and more like my own space.

Jayla is just sorting out my desk, and Nikki and I have been spending an inordinate amount of time cleaning my case and polishing my cello, when it happens.

"Keep or toss?" Jayla asks, her voice hesitant.

I stare at the Batman mask in her hand. They're both looking at me, waiting for me to answer, but I don't know what to say. I should say toss, right? The scar on the side of my wrist should be a permanent enough reminder of our doomed relationship . . . but it doesn't feel like it is.

"Keep," I finally say.

Jayla nods, setting it on my desk, and I go back to wiping down my cello and waiting for her to find the next emotional land mine. I know it's waiting over there amid the piles of clutter and empty glasses.

I can tell the moment she does. She freezes and holds up the wrinkled envelope, the word *Peak* scrawled on the front. I try not to react.

Grayson gave it to me the other day when she was in town. We met for coffee, and she convinced me to go to a CoDA—Co-Dependents Anonymous—meeting with her. She said she was too nervous to go alone, which, ironic, but I think she mainly just wanted to get me there. There were other teens there too, which was kind of surprising. It was interesting enough, and I saw a lot of me and Ridley in the stuff people were saying. I might keep going, I don't know.

Grayson gave me that envelope right before she left. There wasn't a letter in it, just a flash drive. Apparently, Ridley's therapists thought it would be a good move for him to delete all the videos he took of me playing cello off his phone. I don't know how I feel about that, and I *really* wonder how he felt about it. At any rate, Grayson told me he did remove them but couldn't bear to delete them. Instead he downloaded them all onto a flash drive and asked her to give it to me.

It's been sitting untouched on my desk ever since. Until now.

"Keep?" I say. I'm not sure.

"Is this from him? I can take it home and hide it, if you want it gone but not *gone* gone," Jayla says.

"It's videos he took of me playing. I have no idea what to do with them."

"Can I see one?" Nikki asks, helping me get my cello back into its case and setting it in the corner. It's rare that Nikki and Jayla get to hear me play. I always practice alone—well, before Ridley came along, anyway—and their soccer stuff often conflicts with my concerts and recitals.

"Knock yourself out. I play like shit in half of them anyway."

"Doubtful," Jayla says, firing up my laptop.

I flop down onto my bed, dropping my hands over my eyes as the music floods my room.

"Look at you," Nikki says after the second one.

"Jubi, these are incredible, seriously incredible," Jayla says after the third piece.

"I missed a note on that last one. Delete it."

"Are you kidding me? These are awesome."

I start to protest, but movement in my doorway catches my eye. My mom is there, a wistful look in her eyes, listening to the music. "I miss that sound," she says when she notices me watching her.

"Pretty soon, Mrs. J," Jayla says, "she'll be back to playing so much, you'll be sick of it."

My mom smiles, but her eyes still look sad. I know this has been rough on her too. She's cheered me on at every competition since the third grade, carted me to every lesson, spent money on my music even when there was barely any money to spend. She's been almost as much a part of this process as I have.

I know this isn't the end of the world—it's one summer program—but I can't help feeling like it is. I've worked toward this for so long. And now—

"Will you please play the Bach? I don't have it yet."

Hearing his voice again, even through my computer speakers, cuts deep. I try to play it off but don't do a very good job.

"I'll stop it," Jayla says, rushing to shut my laptop.

"No, leave it," I say. "I want to hear."

• • •

Hours later, when Nikki and Jayla are both asleep on an air mattress and my parents have long shut their door, I open an email and I write.

CHAPTER FORTY-NINE

Ridley

THERE ARE TWO kids on boards when I get to the skate park, if
you want to call it that—it was maybe slightly oversold in the
brochure. It's more like a small area of concrete with a few rails
and some wooden ramps, but it'll do. Earning board privileges
at Greenwild feels like a huge accomplishment, and I've been
chomping at the bit—pardon the horse pun, but—to finish my
journaling work this afternoon and actually get out here.

I push off, picking up speed to slide a rail to shake off the
day. It was a tough one, even with the horses serving as a
distraction. My therapist met me at the barn for my morning
session, and we talked a lot about my relationship with my
father while I brushed Westley and Buttercup and cleaned
out their stalls. I think she knew that wasn't a conversation I
could handle sitting still.

I didn't have group today, so afterward I went to my room
to do a journaling exercise, which was when my peer coun-
selor surprised me by awarding me my board back and said
I was making "exceptional progress." It was awesome, and

now I'm here, the board dipping and swaying as I cut around the course, leaving it all behind.

I don't know what I expected inpatient therapy would be like, but it's not awful. Some of that is definitely related to the fact that Gray insisted I go inpatient at a place that feels more like a country club than a hospital, but still. It's more exhausting than I expected. Like sometimes I feel more tired from journaling and group than I do from spending a day mucking out all the stalls.

I haven't really made any friends, though. Not that that's the point, but we talk a lot about support networks and stuff for when we're back on the outside, and right now that list consists only of Grayson and the people she pays to care about my mental health—like the staff here. I've seen some of the other kids hanging out and making connections, but it's whatever.

I push harder, skating over to the ramps and doing a few kickflips on my way. The two other kids hop off their boards and walk over.

"You're pretty good," the first kid says. "You new?"

"Ish? I just got my board back today."

"Congrats, man, that's good. That's big. Where you from?"

"Boston," I say. "It's like twenty minutes from here."

"Yeah, I think I've heard of it," the second kid says, feigning surprise. He flashes me an easy smile, and it feels less like he's making fun of me and more like he's having fun.

"Right, yeah," I say, flipping my board into my hand. "What's your story?" I ask, wondering where they've been hiding. I'd think they just got here, but the fact that they already have skate privileges says otherwise.

"I'm Hector, and this is Quinn," the first kid says, holding out his hand. "I'm from Boston too, but Quinn's from here."

Quinn nods. "My mom's one of the doctors; she lets me skate sometimes when she's working, depending on who's here."

Hector thwaps his hat. "He's also an alumnus, which he should have mentioned because that's the real reason he gets to use the skate park. But that was before his mom came here. Now he's sort of an unofficial mascot."

"I'm the official mascot, asshole." Quinn laughs. "Me and Buttercup are on the front of the brochure. But yeah, he basically covered everything. My mom fell in love with the place when I was here for treatment. She started working here after, and I kinda became a fixture. My mom actually helped me petition to have this built."

"Well, thanks, because I was losing it without my board." I suck my lips over my teeth and shake my head, realizing what I just said. "I guess technically I was losing it before that, but."

Quinn smiles. "Hey, if we can have horse therapy, we can have skate therapy too, right?"

"Yeah."

"Why are we just standing around, then?" Hector asks, dropping his board and aiming for the ramp.

"Hey, what's your name?" Quinn shouts, barreling after him.

"It's Ridley."

"Okay, Ridley, let's see what you got."

CHAPTER FIFTY
Jubilee

"JUBILEE!" MOM CALLS from the kitchen, and I set down my bow, flexing my fingers.

I still get stiff, but the physical therapy is really helping and my playing is getting close to where it was before. I love my PT team, but I can't wait to be done.

"Jubilee, come here."

I hate when she interrupts me, but the urgency in her voice has got me curious. I slide my splint back on—I'm still supposed to wear it when I'm not playing—and head down the hall.

Mom and Vera are both sitting at the kitchen table, and they look way too excited for this early on a Saturday morning.

"What's up?" I ask, glancing between them.

"There's a letter," Mom says, pushing an unopened envelope toward me. "From the conservatory."

"Oh yeah?" My voice cracks from nerves, and Vera tilts her head, watching me.

"It's thick," Vera says. "Open it."

I snatch it out of her hand, tearing open the envelope and scanning the words on the letter as fast as I can.

"What does it say?" Mom asks, her eyes going huge.

"Dear Jubilee—" I clear my throat.

We would like to cordially invite you to attend the Junior Summer Orchestra Program at the Carnegie Conservatory.

While taped auditions are generally reserved for our international students, we were willing to consider your application, in light of your extenuating circumstances.

We hope you will be sufficiently healed to join us in this program next month, as the selecting committee was deeply moved by your performance.

Please review the tuition and fees breakdown and acceptance information provided in the enclosed packet. We look forward to a wonderful summer filled with music.

"Holy crap," I say, tears flooding my eyes. "I got in."

"You got in!" Mom shrieks. "How, though? I thought you withdrew!"

"Remember that day when Jayla and Nikki were watching those videos Ridley made?"

My mom's face falls; she still gets nervous when I talk about him. "Yes, but what does that have to do with anything?"

"He had my whole repertoire on that flash drive. I figured I didn't really have anything to lose, so I emailed it to them last minute and asked to be considered after all. I didn't tell you because I didn't want to get your hopes up. The application fee was nonrefundable anyway—I thought we may as well make them work for it."

"Oh my god, baby." Vera laughs. "You did it; you're going to the conservatory!"

And then I realize what the letter doesn't say, and my stomach drops to the floor.

"What's wrong?" my mom asks.

I flip the paper over and look in the envelope, but there's nothing else besides a brochure. I swallow hard. "I didn't . . . I didn't get the scholarship, though."

"Let us worry about that," Vera says. "You got in. You're going."

"It's too much."

"We've been setting aside little bits for this whenever we could, just in case." My mom gets up and kisses my head. "And Vera's been having a *very* good year on Kickstarter."

"Wipe that worried look off your face." Vera smiles. "Because you're going to the summer program, Jubi. You did it. You did it!"

"Oh my god. I'm going to Carnegie!" I squeal as they smother me in hugs.

CHAPTER FIFTY-ONE

PEAK: Are you still in Boston?

CHAPTER FIFTY-TWO
Ridley

IT'S SUNNY OUT, borderline too hot, but not too humid for mid-August, and I'm sitting on a picnic table, waiting. She's late. A part of me thinks she's not coming, but I am prepared to sit here all day.

I pull out my phone and make a note of that in the app. I should probably mention that in group, just to be sure. I think it's probably okay, though. I think some people are worth the wait. But what do I know? As my therapist says, I'm still "recalibrating my normal meter." I've graduated back to outpatient, but there's still a lot of work to be done.

It turns out I have a whole host of issues, which I knew going in, but there are also a lot of ways to manage them, which I definitely did *not* know. Apparently when you're the child of narcissists *and* not the golden child *and* predisposed to mental health problems, it kind of fucks you up extra. But we're working on it, and it's mostly okay.

My therapists know I'm here, and what I'm doing, and they don't think it's the worst thing, so that's cool. We talked a lot about boundaries and expectations, and I think I'm sort of prepared for whatever happens. And if I'm not, I've got all their numbers programmed into my phone. Plus Gray's. And Hector's. And Quinn's.

I'm still living with Gray and will be for the foreseeable future, my parents effectively cut off. We tried some family therapy with them, and it didn't work. Like, at all. So now it's just me and Gray mostly. It's a small family, but a good one. She still works for The Geekery, though, and managed to convince—okay, blackmail—my dad into calling a truce between him and Verona, which was pretty damn cool. She travels a lot less for work now too, and when she has to go, one of my friends stays over or my aunt Mary comes. It used to bother me that I needed a babysitter, but now I know what it really is: a solid support system, which is something that I never had before.

It's kind of nice.

I feel healthier than I ever have. Hector, Quinn, and I even started recording ourselves skating, and our YouTube channel is getting tons of hits. We plan to turn it into an actual web show once the new camera we ordered comes in. Who knows if anything will ever come of it, but it's nice to have goals and dreams of my own for once.

There are still a lot of dark times; there's no fix for that. But for the first time it feels like surviving them is an option—an option I really want, no matter what happens with Peak today, or anybody else for that matter. So that's new.

I run my hands through my hair and sit up a little straighter. I don't know how it will go when she gets here, but I miss her. Now that I'm sure I'm not just trying to fill up my empty spaces with her love, we all—meaning my therapists and me—thought it was probably okay to respond to the text she sent me the other day. We even had a plan for if she didn't text again after my response, which would have sucked but also been okay.

But I'm so glad that she did.

She's been in Boston all summer, and it's been hard knowing that she's been so close and still so far. We emailed a couple times in the beginning—she wanted to tell me she got into the summer program, and since I was still inpatient, I didn't have my phone. I was open about where I was and what I was doing. She said she was glad, because she worried all the time that I was dead. I said there was something really wrong about that, and I was sorry for what I had put her through. And then I didn't hear from her again. Until the text.

It's been hard not texting her—I know she still sometimes talks to Gray—but I wanted it to be her decision to reach out . . . Well, more like my therapists wanted it to be her decision, if I'm being honest. But they helped me see that I really didn't want to force my way back into her life; I wanted her to want me there. And if she didn't, that was fair and fine and valid, and I would work through it in my counseling sessions.

"Ridley?" she says, putting her hand on my shoulder, and I jump, because I was expecting her to come from the path in front of me and she snuck up from behind.

God, she looks so beautiful. Her hair is longer, and she's

got a bit of a tan. I notice a small scar on her wrist and fore-arm from the surgery and frown, but only for a second before it moves out of sight as she pulls me into a hug. And maybe I breathe in a little too deep, trying to memorize the scent of her shampoo. I had forgotten what it smelled like until right now, and I don't want to forget again.

"It's so good to see you," she says, stepping back and tucking some of her hair behind her ear.

"You too."

We both sort of laugh a little awkwardly, and she looks down, toeing designs in the sand with her white tennis shoe.

"I missed you," I say, and then clap my hand to my fore-head, because I didn't mean to be this obvious.

"I missed you too," she says with a little laugh.

"Yeah?"

She raises her eyebrows and nods, like I'm ridiculous for even asking that.

"Do you want to . . . ?" I trail off, not sure how to finish. Start again? Get lunch? Be my girlfriend? And shit, I wasn't going to be this eager; I wasn't supposed to push.

"Ridley," she says sadly.

"Right." I mean, she knows I've been working on myself, but she hasn't seen it, and that's fair. "I'm getting ahead of myself. It's really good to see you. I want you to know I get that we can't pick up where we left off. I've done a lot of work around understanding that."

"That's good to hear. I've actually been working on that too."

"Really?"

"Yeah." She takes a deep breath and unzips her messenger bag. "And I decided that I don't want to pick up where we left off. That was . . . bad."

"Right, no," I say, jumping down off the table, and I hope my voice doesn't sound like she just drop-kicked my heart into next week, even though it feels like she kind of did. "I talked about this in my session this morning. We made a list of outcomes, and you meeting me for closure was one that we put in the positive-outcome column. Although, I don't remember why. I did at the time, it made sense, but right now I—" I look down and shake my head. "I took notes, and I can email them to you if you want. They're actually right in the car. I could go grab them now. You know what? I'm rambling. Sorry."

"Wow."

"I'm really nervous," I say, because Dr. Gabriella says labeling my feelings is an important tool to help control my anxiety. If I address what's at the root of it, too, sometimes I can stop it from spiraling out. I suck at figuring that part out, but I'm working on it.

"Let me finish." She pulls the Batman mask out of her messenger bag and slides it onto my head. She stops short of pulling it over my face, and okay, I was not expecting this. "I don't want to pick up where we left off. I'd rather rewind farther than that."

"You want to—"

"Have a redo maybe and see where it goes," she says. "Slowly. Extremely slowly. Like glacial."

"I can do glacial."

"Like occasional cups of coffee as friends with several days in between."

"I love coffee," I say, a little too eager. "Are you sure, though?"

"No, but I want to try. I miss you a lot, and if you think— if you're in a good place, I thought maybe we could start talking again. Just talking."

"I would like that." I grin; I can't help it. "Hang on." I grab my phone off the table and pull the tattered feather out from the case, twirling it in my fingers.

"You've carried it the whole time?"

"Whole time."

She smiles so big it's blinding, and maybe my eyes water a little, but who's really checking, anyway.

• • •

Later, when she's back at her dorm and I'm cooking dinner with Gray, I text her a picture of a baby bat, and she texts me a picture of a ridiculous peacock, and . . .

I don't know where this is going. Maybe nowhere. Maybe somewhere. Life is an unpredictable and strange thing like that, but.

But.

It's also kind of amazing.

And I'm so glad I'm here.

RESOURCES

If you or someone you know is struggling, there is help available. Please reach out. The world is better with you in it.

National Suicide Prevention Lifeline:
1-800-273-8255 | suicidepreventionlifeline.org
The Trevor Project Lifeline:
1-866-488-7386 | thetrevorproject.org
Trans Lifeline:
1-877-565-8860 | translifeline.org
Crisis Text Line:
text HOME to 741741 | crisistextline.org

For more information on Co-Dependents Anonymous, the support group Jubilee visits to learn more about healthy relationships and setting personal boundaries, please visit CoDA.org

ACKNOWLEDGMENTS

I am so lucky to be surrounded by so many talented and hard-working people. This book would not exist without them.

A massive thank-you to:

My agent, Brooks Sherman, and my editor, Stephanie Pitts, who once again made this entire process a blast from start to finish. I am a better writer because of you both. Jen Klonsky for your support and insight, Lizzie Goodell for being my publicist extraordinaire, and Christina Colangelo, Bri Lockhart, Felicity Vallence, James Akinaka, Friya Bankwalla, and everyone at Penguin Teen and Putnam—*Verona Comics* truly could not have asked for a better home.

Jeff Östberg for once again bringing my characters to life with an amazing cover illustration. I am forever in your debt.

My writer coven, Karen Strong and Isabel Sterling—I would be lost without you two and definitely not still chasing that licorice candy. Becky Albertalli, my brain twin, for too many things to count, but you know. Roselle for just getting it. And Kelsey Rodkey for her eternal patience, advice, and beyond excellent friend and critique partner skills. Can you believe it's a whole book later and you're still reminding me to drink water?

Hannah Capin for her music expertise—anything I got right is because of her; anything I got wrong is on me. Sarah Grimes, even though Bucky is still mine, and the many writer friends who have been there for me this year—especially Erin, Meredith, Sophie, and my DVSquad pals.

And especially Shannon, my eternal BFF, and Jeff, who lets me steal her near weekly for horrible TV dates and laughter but is also a most excellent friend in his own right. My big brother and best friend, Dennis, for always, always being there—but stop saying we're twins when I'm four years and 364 days younger. My mom and family for their unwavering support, and Brody, Olivia, and Joe for loving me even when I'm cranky and on deadline.

And also all of my readers—your support means the world. Thank you.

ABOUT THE AUTHOR

Jennifer Dugan is a writer, a geek, and a romantic who writes the kinds of stories she wishes she'd had growing up. Her debut young adult novel, *Hot Dog Girl*, was called "a great, fizzy rom-com" by *Entertainment Weekly* and "one of the best reads of the year, hands down" by *Paste* magazine. She is also the writer/creator of two indie comics. She lives in upstate New York with her family, her dogs, her beloved bearded dragon, and an evil cat that is no doubt planning to take over the world.

Learn more at JLDugan.com
Or follow her on Twitter and Instagram @JL_Dugan

The Future
as an Academic Discipline

Ciba Foundation Symposium 36 (new series)

1975

Elsevier · Excerpta Medica · North-Holland
Amsterdam · Oxford · New York

ISBN Excerpta Medica 90 219 4040 x
ISBN American Elsevier 0444-15184-2

Published in September 1975 by Elsevier/Excerpta Medica/North-Holland, P.O. Box 211, Amsterdam, and American Elsevier, 53 Vanderbilt Avenue, New York, N.Y. 10017.

Suggested series entry for library catalogues: Ciba Foundation Symposia.
Suggested publisher's entry for library catalogues: Elsevier/Excerpta Medica/North-Holland

Ciba Foundation Symposium 36 (new series)

Printed in The Netherlands by Mouton & Co, The Hague

Contents

C. H. WADDINGTON Introduction 1

H. WENTWORTH ELDREDGE The Mark III survey of university-level futures courses 5
Discussion 15

KARL-ERIK ERIKSSON & ANDERS LUNDBERG A university experiment in Sweden 19
Discussion 29

ALEXANDER KING The future as a discipline and the future of the disciplines 35
Discussion 47

F. R. JEVONS A dragon or a pussy cat? Two views of human knowledge 53
Discussion 62

HAROLD G. SHANE Social decisions prerequisite to educational change 1975–1985 73
Discussion 81

JOHN M. FRANCIS From academic hothouse to professional dugout: a mean free path 89
Discussion 97

J. N. BLACK Sclerotic structures and the future of academic organization 107
Discussion 114

KIMON VALASKAKIS Eclectics: elements of a transdisciplinary methodology for futures studies 121
Discussion 136

YEHEZKEL DROR Some fundamental philosophical, psychological and intellectual assumptions of futures studies 145
Discussion 154

JOHN PLATT Universities as nerve centres of society 167
Discussion 183

SIR WALTER PERRY Patterns of education for the future 191
Discussion 199

General Discussion 207

C. H. WADDINGTON Concluding remarks 217

Biographies of the participants 221

Index of contributors 225

Subject index 227

Participants

Symposium on *The Future as an Academic Discipline* held at the Ciba Foundation, London, 6–8 February 1975

C. H. WADDINGTON (*Chairman*)   Institute of Animal Genetics, West Mains Road, Edinburgh EH9 3JN

Lord ASHBY   Clare College, Cambridge, CB2 1TL

J. N. BLACK   Bedford College, Regent's Park, London NW1 4NS

Y. DROR   Department of Political Science, Hebrew University of Jerusalem, Israel

H. W. ELDREDGE   Department of Sociology, Dartmouth College, Hanover, New Hampshire 03755, USA

J. M. FRANCIS   Heriot-Watt University, Research Park, Riccarton, Currie, Edinburgh EH14 4AS

F. R. JEVONS   Department of Liberal Studies in Science, The University, Manchester M13 9PL

A. KING   The International Federation of Institutes for Advanced Study, 168 rue de Grenelle, 75007 Paris, France

I. F. KLIMES   *Futures*, IPC House, 32 High Street, Guildford, Surrey GU1 3EW

K. KUMAR   Keynes College, University of Kent at Canterbury, Kent CT2 7NP

A. LUNDBERG   Department of Physiology, University of Göteborg, Göteborg, Sweden

F. OLDFIELD   School of Independent Studies, University of Lancaster, Fylde College, Bailrigg, Lancaster LA1 4YF

Sir WALTER PERRY   The Open University, Walton Hall, Milton Keynes
MK7 6AA

J. R. PLATT   Mental Health Research Institute, The University of Michigan,
Ann Arbor, Mich. 48104, USA

Sir HUGH ROBSON   Old College, University of Edinburgh, South Bridge,
Edinburgh EH8 9YL

H. G. SHANE   School of Education, Indiana University, Education Building,
Room 328, Bloomington, Indiana 47401, USA

Sir FREDERICK STEWART   Grant Institute of Geology, University of Edinburgh,
West Mains Road, Edinburgh EH9 3JW

R. D. UNDERWOOD   School of the Man Made Future, University of Edinburgh,
15 Buccleuch Place, Edinburgh EH8 9LN

K. VALASKAKIS   Département des Sciences Economiques, Université de
Montréal, Case postale 6128, Montréal 3, PQ, Canada

M. H. F. WILKINS   Department of Biophysics, University of London King's
College, 26–29 Drury Lane, London WC2R 2LS

Sir ERNEST WOODROOFE   The Crest, Berry Lane, Worplesdon, Guildford,
Surrey GU3 3QF

J. M. ZIMAN   University of Bristol, H. H. Wills Physics Laboratory, Royal
Fort, Tyndall Avenue, Bristol BS8 1TL

Editors: G. E. W. WOLSTENHOLME (*Organizer*) and MAEVE O'CONNOR

Introduction

C. H. WADDINGTON

Institute of Animal Genetics, University of Edinburgh

We are here to discuss whether universities in general and British universities in particular should take account of the problems that mankind is obviously going to face in the next few decades, and, if universities are to do this, how should they do it? It is only because the situation in the next few decades is clearly going to be unlike what it was in our grandfathers' days that I think the question arises so seriously now. We all recognize that we are facing a series of crises which can't be completely separated from one another. Each one of them—atomic warfare or the population problem or the environment problem or the energy problem or what have you—is a considerable threat. The whole set together form what the Club of Rome has called the *problèmatique*.

How far should universities do anything specifically in connection with this? It seems to me there are two aspects to this. One is the question of incorporating into the universities any of the pure scholarship that is going on in these fields. That is relatively simple for universities to do, even if the scholarship doesn't fall into any previously well-defined disciplines. A great deal of profound thinking of an academic kind is going on in these fields now, at the highest levels of academic scholarship. There is some high-level thinking about the methodology of dealing with complex systems—things like the stability theory, the catastrophe theories of Thom and derivatives of this. Many of these developments can, if you like, be regarded simply as mathematics, but they are a type of mathematics that applies specifically to dealing with complex systems such as confront us historically in the social sphere. They are not only mathematics in the abstract.

There are also scholarly studies on the precise and detailed economic, political and industrial questions. For instance, the economist Jan Tinbergen is working on a project for the Club of Rome which he originally called 'Renewing the world system', and which he has now given the slightly more modest

1

title 'Reviewing the world system'. In it he is considering how all the economic, industrial and natural resources with which the world is working at present should or could be made to work in a more equitable manner. This is a major work of imaginative scholarship.

Most of these things are at present being done outside the universities and I think universities should make a bigger effort to bring in some of these studies, or at any rate be closely connected with them. They constitute one of the most significant types of academic scholarship in the world today. It is not too difficult for universities to bring them into their existing structure, which is always rather flexible in relation to research and postgraduate aspects. But we need to think seriously about the undergraduate aspect of this problem. Until a short time ago universities were basically there to provide a general education. It is less than a hundred years since a man had to be in Holy Orders before he could be a Fellow at Oxford or Cambridge. And about a hundred years ago the basic purpose of the universities was to produce either clerics or well-educated generalists. The idea that the universities are there to turn out highly-specialized professionals is a recent change in their purpose. I think many university people have found it upsetting. I read the other day that a questionnaire sent to some physicists asked them whether they were high energy particle physicists, and if so were they working on hadrons or kleptons or something else. Not only that, but were they working on positive or negative hadrons? The physicists were not really allowed by this questionnaire to take an interest in anything more than one hypothetical subnuclear particle, and some of them complained about this.

Universities are in some danger of finding themselves fossilized into these sorts of divisions. There are a lot of young men who badly need to understand how the world is working and who realize that they don't really do so. So far as they get taught anything about the processes of thinking, they get taught about linear sequences of cause and effect: A causes B, B causes C, C causes D, and so on. It is quite clear that that is not the way the world works now. In the past, when man's industrial resources were such that he could only scratch at the surface of the world, any particular scratch could probably be considered relatively independently of any other, and one could maybe get away with thinking of everything as happening in isolated linear cause–effect sequences. Now that we are dealing with the world in a more profound manner, going much deeper, where everything we do runs into everything else we do, we can't escape from a whole lot of feedback circuits, interactions and non-linear effects. Thinking in terms purely of cause and effect in the old-fashioned way is totally inadequate in our present situation. I think most young people realize this and know that they are not being taught any of the newer ways of dealing with the problems. The methods don't fit into any standard curriculum. Possibly engineers have to learn a bit on one side, and possibly economists will learn another bit, but nobody in general knows all the different types of thinking of this kind, and most people go through university never having heard of them. I think possibly something should be done about that.

Secondly, in this great complex of problems any single problem is itself complex. We may think that the food problem is easy enough, but nobody actually knows how much of any sort of food we really need, or when food starts doing more harm than it does good, and so on. The population problem also sounds simple until, again, we look into it and find that it is extremely complex, depending on the age structure of a population, how fast it is going to reproduce, the social aims, the rate of material progress that is likely if the size of the family is limited, whether it is economically better to have six sons on the basis that at least one will be left alive when his parents are old and unable to work, and so on. In any one of these problems we find that we are hitting against the fringes of the others. We don't try at present in ordinary universities to give anybody a general overall picture, and it is my belief that we ought to do this.

I have been trying to introduce this type of undergraduate teaching in Edinburgh, on a voluntary basis, for a year, and I hope that we shall soon be able to turn it into one of the options in various courses. I thought that the only way of convincing people that this was an academically respectable course for undergraduates was to write the textbooks and thus explain what I think ought to be in the course. I have written two textbooks for half-year courses. They are at second-year level; that is to say they really are going to skim over everything, with nothing gone into in any depth, but the aim is that if you take the course you can't avoid rubbing your nose in everything: you won't know much about it but at least you'll know it is there. One book is called *Tools of Thought about Complex Systems*. It could also be called 'A Child's Guide to the Fashionable Jargon'. It aims to show what methods people are developing about how to think in more subtle terms than linear sequences of cause and effect. Then I have a more factual book called *The Sources of the Man Made Future*, on the components of the world's *problèmatique*, under twelve headings. Both books will be published by Cape and Paladin Books in 1975. This is just an approach to what I think is a genuine gap in the education we are at present providing for our young people. I have some experience of the way they react to being offered such a course, and I think they feel they need this. There are very few places they can get it from. It can be, and is, an academic discipline in the sense of being a scholarly pursuit. It can or should be—and is, in a few places— part of the educational opportunities which we offer to students.

Professor Eldredge has for some years been making surveys of what courses are being offered and he should be able to tell us what other countries and universities are doing about the future.

The Mark III survey of university-level futures courses

H. WENTWORTH ELDREDGE

Dartmouth College, Hanover, New Hampshire

Abstract Six years of information-gathering and three reports on some 500 university-level futures courses give rise to the following generalizations. Most academic disciplines and fields are to some degree alerted to the future implications of their research and teaching. The numbers of future-oriented courses in many varying forms have increased; but individuals seem to come and go in the field. There appears to be a somewhat negative intellectual image of futurism and futures studies today; the need to define the field, upgrade methodology and recruit wisely is clear. Societal forecasting (especially values forecasting) based on valid sociocultural change theory is the weakest aspect in the futures complex, along with fumbling attempts at creativity training. 'Futurizing' existing courses appears the most valid operational ploy for introducing future dimensions into university curricula at this point. Technological forecasting joined to technology assessment offers the most promising methodology (excepting perhaps cross-impact matrices), especially if joined to modelling, and it is certainly backed by powerful government and private forces. Informal educational systems may be extremely efficacious in futures studies. The delivery of insights and knowledge (such as it is) about the future in a cybernetic policy-studies fashion is the most pressing next step.

After collecting information (primarily by questionnaire) for six years and writing three critical analytical reports [1,2,3] on university-level futures courses, with information now in hand on about 500, I venture to say that futures studies, as a quasi-discipline at least, are tolerated on the academic scene. The enormous shock to western society of the 'surprising' energy crisis (although more or less precisely forecast in physical terms for at least a decade), coming after the generally heightened public consciousness on environmental questions, has had its overspill in academia. The rapidity with which the underdeveloped Muslim nations internalized political compact-making and cartel-design (societal technology) of the western type convinced even the most obtuse that the world was on the move at an accelerating pace and that we might be

5

witnessing one of the major revolutionary breaks in history.

Triage—whom do you allow to die by starvation? [4,5]—and 'the lifeboat theory'—whom do you throw overboard to save the others?[6]—are the questions that now face the affluent societies, and especially the United States. Has our vaunted humanitarianism merely been the result of a once teeming plenty or are we Americans as 'selfish' as Europe and Asia—not to mention the developing areas and the communist bloc—have of necessity always been?[7] Trapped by the Marshall Plan and our own 'bleeding hearts' are we doomed to feed the foolish globe to its own Malthusian destruction? It would seem that all systems may be 'no go'.[8,9] In fact Frank Davidson of early Chunnel fame gives a course on 'failure' with the System Dynamics Group at MIT's Alfred P. Sloan School of Management. All this has now been sharply punctuated by India's detonation of a 'peaceful' nuclear device as well as Israel's frank admission of military nuclear capability. In the late 1960s, the youth revolt and ethnic unrest dramatized the smouldering discontent of large segments of the populations of western civilization with the lack of human depth in our life patterns. This upheaval certainly forced the young clients of North American universities to wonder about what their future had in store for them. Could they anticipate long and drab lives or fiery extinction? And, on a more optimistic level, could they have some say in creating possible alternative futures of quality? In view of all this turmoil it is hardly surprising that an increasing number of university researchers/teachers have attempted to forecast the future for their students in university-level courses.

This attack on the future has come from a number of directions and is of varying quality. *Demography*, long interested in extrapolation (initially egged on by profit-minded insurance companies), continues to plod ever more wisely into the future. *Utopianists* (literary or design-oriented) reach back through a long tradition linked to the legends of primitive man and spin possible futures which criticize the present or prefigure a better world. This latter group are joined by the *science fiction* enthusiasts who seem to feel that all global ills can be solved by a 'technological fix', although increasingly they prefigure far-out psychological and behavioural technologies. Big business and big government, immensely serious, have inspired assiduous *technological forecasting* in the business administration schools; and latterly, brought up short by shifting social values (for example, environmental concern led to the cut-off in the supersonic transport programme and the near-stoppage of nuclear power plant construction in the United States), business and government have become increasingly involved with *technology assessment*—still in its infancy. *Educationalists*, who fancy that they hold the future in trust through their manipulations of the young, show spots of inventive futures techniques in education (as do others), in addition to 'futurizing' their course contents. *Sociologists* are among the strongest supporters of futures studies, at least among the younger social change/operational types intrigued or horrified by the *Brave New World* cleverly glimpsed by Huxley.[10] *Political scientists* are getting into the act increasingly and if all the members of the future-oriented Policy Studies Organization (80 programmes are run by members) were added to the political scientists offering futures courses, they would possibly be by far the most numerous social science group. I do not pretend that Table 1 which lists by discipline those giving futures courses who reported to the Mark III Survey, is a valid sampling of discipline/field interest—here are recorded merely those course-givers who fell into my net—but it may be instructive as to interest.

The techniques for learning/teaching futures studies rest quite obviously on what exists to learn/teach. It would appear that there is little that is excitingly fresh to be discovered (*a*) in reliable knowledge in the futures field, except in technological forecasting/technology assessment, systems dynamics and the policy sciences, (*b*) in new teaching techniques, or (*c*) in people-oriented experiential learning (except Syncon, a highly complex form of group dynamics). It should be noted that technological forecasting/technology assessment, systems

TABLE 1
Future course-givers, by discipline, reporting to the Mark III Survey

	1973–1974 Reports	Cumulative 1969–1974
Anthropology	4	9
Business administration	32	57
Computer science (modelling, etc.)	24	27
Demography	2	2
Economics	7	10
Education	28	40
English	5	10
Engineering	17	26
Geography	7	10
History	5	8
Humanities (overlap with English)	16	19
Law	3	4
Natural sciences	13	25
Political science	19	33
Psychology	3	3
Sociology	50	77
Theology	5	10
Urbanists (including architecture)	15	28
Miscellaneous	58	78
	313	476

Note: Science fiction, policy studies, peace studies are not included in these totals.

dynamics, and policy studies in general tend to eschew the label of 'futurism'. The standard methodological ploys that I explored in my 1970 and 1973 surveys are still with us, adding little to the twelve that Daniel Bell staked out a decade ago.[11] These standard methods may be conveniently grouped under five headings:

Type A: Intuitive methods ('genius forecasting') and codified intuition or Delphi; now enriched by cross-impact matrices;

Type B: Trend extrapolation;

Type C: Ideal state and/or alternative possible futures and scenarios;

Type D: Dynamic models;

Type E: Social (societal) indicators and Quality of Life (QOL) indices, which constitute an adjunct methodology crucial to the delivery of futures research.

The total evidence in hand indicates that in late 1974 all the standard futures research and teaching methodologies (conventional wisdom?) were still in use, with little firm evidence at hand to verify the reliability or heuristic value of any! The *validity gap* faces all futures study, it would seem. In five general directions, however, there appears to be some purposeful activity in the development of research/teaching methodology, at least in these significant areas: (*a*) technological forecasting/technological assessment; (*b*) general systems theory and systems analysis/dynamics, (*c*) Delphi/cross-impact analysis, (*d*) creativity and experiential learning, (*e*) policy studies. I shall examine the first four of these in turn.

(a) Technological forecasting (TF) and technology assessment (TA)

Long firmly based in advanced military hardware planning, TF is making increasing inroads into both governmental and corporate planning. No nation wants to be caught short by an enemy's gadget or by resource depletion (or resource cornering), although almost everyone seems to be caught sooner or later. No private corporation wishes to be lapped by a competitor's *nouvelle vague* product or crushed by a value shift (as supersonic transport was). The penalties for sleeping at the switch are national extinction and corporate bankruptcy. Inadequacies are painfully evident and painfully penalized. Thus the unemotional vigorous schools of business administration with their generally highly motivated students appear to be testing both the concrete and the general outlines of the future. A leading sage of technological forecasting berates all sociologists (through me) unceasingly and probably quite correctly: 'The important point to convey to the sociologists is that we are receiving continual pressure from industrialists to get them some help on predicting the interaction of social change with technological change. In other words, give them some insight on social forecasting' (private communication).

The brilliant paper by Richard L. Henshel and Leslie W. Kennedy[12] has shown that as our skills increase in these directions so will the complications resulting from self-defeating or self-fulfilling prophecies.

The rapid recent growth of interest in TA all over the globe and in trans-economic social (or societal) indicators, with sensitive Quality of Life indices being developed in Japan, Germany, England, and the USA, to cite but a few involved nations, bodes well for an eventual humanistic weighing of TF on a professionalized scale. The key node of this activity is the International Society for Technological Assessment in Washington, D.C.

There is in this whole TF/TA complex the seed of excellent futures research. With TF stemming from the graduate schools of business administration (originally from Harvard), it is hardly surprising that, in addition to some precise theorizing, the store of *case studies* of both TF and TA in operation is increasing. The finest way to test a method is to examine the results of using it in real-world situations (often neglected by social scientists, who serve usually as mere analysts, *not* operational planners). Actually TF/TA in my estimation will fall far short in practical results unless they are married to systems analysis/systems dynamics and general systems theory.

(b) General systems theory and systems analysis/systems dynamics/modelling, etc.

While not necessarily so, basic systems analysis tends to be increasingly mathematical. Systems dynamics is clearly dependent on computer storage and manipulation. These rigorous, highly intellectual technologies seem to be at the very roots of the alternative futures game, and they seem of considerable interest to America's mathematical youth. Are we spawning an intellectual technocratic élite as guardians of esoteric processes? In any case, the game must be played; all teacher/scholars are increasingly involved with the computer—like it or not. The variables are too complex for anyone to test out mentally unaided by the planning–forcing techniques of systems analysis—generally computer based—and the game is too changeable in process for us not to include a continuing cybernetic feedback on the values, resources and organizational structure, in an endless chain reaction. Even *intuitive futurists* use mental models. Whether the sophisticated mathematical crutches already available will ever cope adequately with the infinite complexity of future reality is doubtful, but they are already better than the sages' guess-estimates. It is more than likely that all futurists will need to master this difficult bundle of technologies if they wish to produce more than 'hot air'. From the University of Pennsylvania's Wharton School of Business Administration came this nugget: 'I teach a seminar on forecasting methods. It's called "Long-Range Forecasting: From Crystal Ball to Computer".'

(c) Delphi techniques/cross-impact analysis

Based on lumps of 'genius forecasting', Delphi projection techniques in mini or maxi form edge into a great majority of courses in all fields. A clear externality of the use of students as 'experts' in Delphi operations is experiential learning through participation. But Delphi is more than that and the time is now ripe to evaluate its successes and failures after more than a decade of use in increasingly varied fields. The handy time span of a decade is available for testing the validity of its projections and reshaping the format of use so that it can do better in precise prognostication. The development of cross-impact analysis, into which leading Delphi practitioners have moved, indicates a formal awareness that 'everything is related to everything else'. One is reminded of the Kahn/Wiener fifteen-fold interlocking trends from the 1960s and of total environmental planning/holistic planning on the urban/regional/national scene, now almost two decades old. Obviously straight-line and complex extra-polation curves do fit into this cross-impact method. Since both Delphi and cross-impact analysis have clear (formal organizational, too) relations with TF/TA and with general systems theory, systems analysis, and systems dyna-mics, this complex of research thinking is forming a veritable powerhouse of methodology. The Rand Graduate Institute (RGI) had in 1973–1974 some twenty persons in a doctoral programme—each working in an area tied to a real-world current or past Rand project in policy studies—clearly a new depar-ture in sophisticated extra-university future-oriented education. All futurists should learn to manage mathematical modelling with their left hand as they cleave ahead (hopefully) with their right guided by 'creative intellect' under a holistic systems theory. Clearly there is also a useful and fascinating teaching device in this bundle of skills.

(d) Experiential learning/creativity/scenarios

These enormously varied and vital activities, both in research and in teaching, can hardly be classed as 'hard' technology. But who can gainsay the basic importance of fresh creative insights—'more of the same' promises little. It would appear that a most unusual collection of tricks is available (essential?)

for the well-equipped futurist teacher. Mod and trendy instructors do not 'tell' students anything but serve hopefully as exciting resources, even models, for the neophyte to use in expanding up to his presumably ample God-given potential. Assuredly the educational structure is in ferment, as should be amply evident to readers of the ubiquitous newspaper (not averse in capitalist countries to inflating and to exploiting the spectacular over the drab norm), and quite unlike the pattern in 'socialist' lands where teaching is a solemn authoritative business. 'Doing something sticks in the consciousness better than reading about it' goes the new wisdom. Just how do you 'live' in the 5th century B.C. of Athens or 2000 A.D.? A mock-up could be fashioned, of course, and museums of the future growing in both Denmark and Minnesota are early attempts in the direction of 'living in the future'.

In a rough way, there appear to be two innovative poles of activity in futures studies, one at the hard or 'right' pole: TF/TA, policy sciences, corporate cramming courses of a high excellence and precision in non-standard time formats. In the middle, there are free educational structures marrying futures orientation with 'futurist' educational restructuring and open course management. At the 'left' or soft pole are the intentional communities and the full gamut of often curious experiential learning experiences, as well as attempts at fostering intellectual creativity.

There is a hodge-podge of new directions in this last rubric, many left of centre, difficult to conceptualize in any adequate fashion. Futurist teachers tend to be innovative and iconoclastic, interdisciplinary, and by definition probers of the unknown—not always in any way that could be called planned by any stretch of the imagination. Consciously or unconsciously they do covertly or overtly push for systems breaks. The gamut of educational 'gimmicks' used to stir up client students, presumably to foster creativity as well as culture/future shock, seems endless: simulations; telephone interviews; movies; TV scripts; participatory planning; poetry readings; formation of a collective; expressive dancing; technological cum group-think jamborees such as Syncon and the World Game; a voodoo experience; scenario building/intentional communes for future living; 'happenings'; confrontation/encounter sessions; role-playing; modelling; brain-storming; free-form courses; nature worship; a futures fair; a personal life history projection; visits to 'futuristic' locations such as California; videotapes; survival training and solos; individual obituaries. In my ongoing survey I shall continue to record, often with amazement, the things people do in attempting to make other people think! If such an assault did not unsettle the recipient, it would be surprising, but what does this *ersatz* and slanted experience actually add up to? Obviously all courses do not employ all techniques. But is 'creativity' also a product of such bustle? Do glorious and valuable thoughts emerge—thoughts which are so much needed before rigorous testing and experimentation if viable alternative human futures are to be created for man? In my surveys, no answer has as yet been revealed. In short, there is little or no evidence of any sophisticated controlled development of creativity—a serious gap. An interesting people-involving Open University (England) course, 'Art and Environment', planned to start in 1976, exemplifies neatly the neo-populist faith in the untapped abilities of the common man and exemplifies also certain participatory futures-teaching techniques as well as content.

The impact of futures studies on two important professional graduate fields in the United States can be seen in two courses. The first example is the attempt, at Syracuse University's respected Maxwell Graduate School of Citizenship and Public Affairs in 1973-1974, to link administrative techniques with insight into the future in a course on 'Post-industrial administration and social change'; the second is a similar venture made in a seminar on 'Planning for alternative possible urban futures' offered at Harvard's Graduate School of Design, Department of City and Regional Planning, in the autumn of 1974. Both courses seem to indicate that, although a reasonable *tour d'horizon* can be made in which futures studies are related to existing professional training, little more than that can be expected within the short span of a few months. It proved heartening in the Harvard case to have pre-professionals—with so much operant knowledge to digest in so short a time—still eager for mind-stretching in a futures direction. The urbanists have finally come to future life, heralded by William Ewald's massive editorial job[13,14,15] for the American Institute of Planners—an organization curiously long dormant in the face of the rather obvious fact that at least the physical works of urban planners live long into the future (see the Roman colosseum). BART, San Francisco's Bay Area Rapid Transport System, will undoubtedly be around in 2075, barring a MIRV barrage. Portions of London's Underground were laid out for steam trains in the 1840s! *The California Plan Tomorrow: The Future is Now*[16] offers a California One scenario in which the quality of life becomes seriously impaired before 2000, and a California Two 'which makes possible person fulfillment within an amenable environment'—one hopes! *Hawaii 2000*[17] chronicles the wide participatory planning 'five-ring,' multi-media drive of that state towards human futures, backed heavily by the State Government and the State University, offering at least six 'alternative Hawaiis'. *Inventing the Future Memphis*, a lively effort by Southwestern University's Center for Alternative Futures in that city, has struggled ahead and is now getting ever-better results in public education and realization. Joining *Tomorrow's London* are *Washington 2000*, *Seattle 2000*, and *Atlanta 2000*; the latter city, largely influenced by the private sector, is rapidly building a spectacular and commercially outstanding central city. Is the Quality of Life (QOL) quotient quite so highly served as the profit motive in this spectacular central business district with 'futuristic' glassed construction of high rise and high-cost commercial and transient hotel recreational facilities?

A significant development is the application of Forrester's urban dynamics to the real city of Lowell, Massachusetts, a decaying manufacturing city from the early nineteenth century, buffeted by technology shifts and the movement of the textile industry first to the South and latterly out of the United States.[18] A team from the MIT System Dynamics Center for the past three years has worked closely with the city officialdom and people and, using a computer-ized mathematical dynamics model as a heuristic device, has upgraded com-munity decision-making in four key directions: (a) values for the future city, (b) final land use (c) property tax and (d) housing policy.

What are the results of this third iteration of my survey of futures courses? Specifically, analysis of the 300 courses collected by the standard questionnaire in 1973–1974 revealed, among other things, these five salient conclusions:

(1) Futures studies *per se* have grown steadily but not spectacularly as university-level courses both at the undergraduate and graduate levels. Other fields, not labelled 'futurism', but with a clear future-orientation (such as: environment/ecology; TF/TA; long-range planning; policy sciences; peace studies; general systems theory; systems analysis and dynamics; even science fiction; black studies and women's studies) appear to have increased more rapidly than futures studies in North America.

(2) The population of course-givers in 'pure' futures studies seems to fall into a sieve from which some old hands drop out each year, to be replenished by a fresh stream of generally young recruits. This suggests the somewhat negative present intellectual image of futurism (an identity crisis?)—an image perhaps derived from its 'pop' manifestations or from disillusionment with its success at reliable forecasting and immediate delivery. It also indicates clearly the necessity of defining the futures field, of upgrading training in the relatively slight corpus of reliable knowledge (including embryonic theory) of futures study, and of stepping up the enlistment and development of fresh young minds *already grounded solidly in some recognized discipline or field*. European universities appear, from inadequate evidence at hand and with the possible exception of technological forecasting and general systems analysis/ mathematical modelling, to have approached futures studies much more gingerly.

(3) Societal forecasting, and especially values forecasting based on valid sociocultural change theory, is the weakest aspect of the entire futures com-

plex. It is to be hoped that experienced anthropological and sociological researchers will contribute here eventually.

(4) Futurizing the content and point of view of existing solid courses in recognized fields and disciplines seems the most valid operational strategy for extending futures studies for the moment. Many physical scientists burned by the now revealed diseconomies of atomic skills do this. Increasingly alert researchers/teachers in varied fields glance 'over their shoulder at the on-rushing future', as do many of their rather pessimistic young clients. This is especially true for those dealing with new medical technologies.

(5) In my personal estimation, technological forecasting for big business and big government is the most highly motivated and successful research-oriented complex on the American and Canadian scene—and has the best methodologists apart from the modellers and the users of cross-impact matrices. Brought up short by value shifts, the TF fraternity is flailing about (with some new environmentalist recruits) in technology assessment. Many of these people tend to see 'technology' much too narrowly, failing to grasp that there are also (feeble, admittedly) societal and behavioural technologies based on the social and behavioural sciences. And that all basic science and the resultant technologies subsist on a burgeoning intellectual technology resting heavily on the 'gadget' assistance of the computer.

Finally, are there further tentative insights that can be drawn from my six years of research in futures' teaching? Here are three:

(1) The folders on 500 course-givers, filling six file drawers, are now too numerous to be handled adequately by a one-person 'team'; a much more rigorous delving is needed into the realities of what actually goes on, rather than what respondents state happens. Questionnaires have clear limitations; follow-up is most necessary. The coverage of the non-North American experience is much too feeble. Data storage and retrieval is inadequate and the detailed interrelationships and interconnections must be subjected to a much more rigorous analysis than one individual's resources in time, energy and expertise permit. Futurism and futurists do seem stuck on a developmental plateau. To these ends a search has been instituted for a powerful research group, public or private, profit or non-profit, who could build on my shoulders.

(2) The future, hanging ominously or looming in an excitingly challenging fashion ahead, is too crucial to be left to amateurs, part-time 'genius forecasters', woolly-headed visionaries (however well meaning), and publicity seekers. The uses made of futures studies by the national governments of France,[19] Sweden[20] and the Netherlands,[21] and the location of these futures bureaus (at least as early warning systems or look-out stations) close to central decision-making, are facts emphasizing that alternative national futures can

possibly be removed from control by the 'hand of God' or conversely from control by capitalism's beloved invisible hand.

(3) Futures studies must link up as a subset with convoluted policy studies or advanced delivery systems[22] if human civilization is to survive or possibly even continue to flourish. If there is to be a systems break in the next decades, no doubt futures studies could serve as a helpful bridge over that chasm. The universities and other types of less traditional learning/teaching centres (with or without walls) have a central role in training societies and their leaders for these alternative *futuribles* (possible futures). It is unimportant whether future-oriented learning is entitled 'futures studies' or not, so long as a man-centred, holistic, operational, long-range, flexible planning effort is forwarded.

Discussion

Waddington: One of the great questions facing us at this meeting is whether we should be teaching about the future as a whole, with everything brought into it, or whether specialists should give specialist courses that look a bit into the future of a particular specialty. For instance, until two years ago the energy experts in the United States were forecasting that the US would consume four times the current amount of petroleum by the year 2000. That doesn't look very convincing if we take into account considerations other than those concerned only with the use of energy. In the whole subject of looking into the future within a specialty, how far can we get without bumping into the future in other specialties? Can we find a way of looking at the futures of all of them together?

Platt: The question is illustrated by the fact that until a year or so ago, demographers and United Nations forecasters repeatedly based their forecasts for world population on expected numbers of children, or on expected dates for the 'demographic transition' to fewer births, totally ignoring factors such as food and resources. But it is only when food and resources are put into the equations formally, or into the thinking, that we begin to see certain limits which have no historical precedents. Instead of forecasts of 7000 million or 12 000 million people after the year 2000, we then suddenly come up with numbers like 5000 or 5500 million people by the turn of the century, with perhaps 1000 million people dying of starvation between now and then. The *Limits to Growth* forecast by Meadows and others in 1972 showed, I think for the first time, that the population would necessarily be a substantially lower number; and this was because they took into account the interaction of these other factors.[23]

Dror: Professor Eldredge's work is one of the most hopeful signs of futures studies. Someone is trying to do some self-evaluation, which is unusual.

Futures-studies teaching faces six main problems or choices. First, many futures classes are based not on any research but only on transferring ideas and on intellectual resources which themselves are still underdeveloped. The relationship between teaching and research is a symptom of the main dilemma of where the dividing lines lie in futures studies. Second, there is too much emphasis on utopian or anti-utopian images of the future, and too little on feasibility and on lines of continuity—on how past and present evolve into one of several alternative futures. Third, in many programmes we do not know how value sensitivity should be handled—that is, how we can achieve clinical detachment towards a subject with which we feel highly emotionally involved. This causes great difficulties, especially with young students who feel very agitated about problems which nevertheless have to be treated on an intellectual level. Fourth, how can we convey a real sense of the complexity of things in a short undergraduate course lasting one year? The danger is that we may sell an over-simple view of reality hidden behind some complexity of words. Fifth, the need for a real interdisciplinary basis for futures studies has to be balanced against the ease of basing a university course on single teachers. Sixth, how can we sensitize students to the problems of the future when they are concentrating on working in depth in their specific fields of study? And how can we, at the same time, prepare futures studies professionals? Also—and this is a fundamental fault which sums up some of my main points—a large number of the futures courses represented in Professor Eldredge's excellent surveys suffer from a serious disease which I call 'well-intentioned naiveté'. What is really needed is a strong dose of sophistication.

Valaskakis: Professor Eldredge's surveys are perhaps too inclusive. It could be argued that all science is really involved with some kind of prediction or other. The distinction I would make between futures studies *per se* and science in general is the long-term versus short-term orientation. This is not just a question of time but also one of approach. The 'long term' is a period long enough to provide for structural change, and this structural change can only be perceived in an interdisciplinary fashion. That is why I disagree with Eldredge's point that futures studies should be considered as part of policy studies. I would say that policy studies should be part of futures studies, the latter being a much larger concept which includes value reorientations, value forecasting and definitions of utopias (in the non-pejorative sense of utopia). A specialized monodisciplinary approach would not be suitable for futures studies *per se*. It may be marginally suitable to have a futures orientation in existing disciplines but this does not go very far.

Eldredge: I probably didn't manage to make myself as clear as I should have in the time available for my presentation. In fact, I am a holistic planner. I do not think that there is just one road into the future, or that there is only one discipline that knows it. I was one of those in the US who played a part in switching urban planning away from physical planning into societal planning as well. Almost all the main American urban planning schools are run now by social scientists, not by physical designers. Futures studies have developed in a haphazard way in most universities, where they now exist with originators and recruits from a great variety of backgrounds. I am quite aware that as a long-term strategy a highly sophisticated and holistic futures operation should be organized in various centres. A number of excellent schools of public adminis-tration, at Syracuse, Berkeley, Harvard and to a certain extent MIT, are keenly interested in the longer-term futures orientation.

Of course, being a good academic, I could nitpick with Dr Valaskakis im-mediately and say that it is not just a matter of long term and short term, but that there is also a medium term. He is implying that we are in a systems break; in my paper I said that almost all futurists are aware that we may be at one of the great watersheds of history. My whole background has been inter-disciplinary and I see that in futures studies the question is whether we should turn a natural scientist into a futurist or a futurist into a natural scientist. Should we turn a social scientist into a futurist, or vice versa? Should we make a philosopher into a futurist, or vice versa? I rather lean towards 'futurizing' an existing scientist, physical or social. I used to say, simplistically, in urban studies, that any 'damn fool' can make a plan, but that then one has to put the plan into operation in a cybernetic way. The old planning formula is: goals, resources, alternative plans, the plan, operations. Then cybernetically goals change, resources change, the plan changes and so on. I am not thinking of policy studies as a tool but as part of the cybernetic system, with values and futures all part of it and with policy studies/'wise' decision-making as the important end to which futures studies could truly contribute.

References cited

1 ELDREDGE, H. WENTWORTH (1970) Education for futurism in the United States. *Technological Forecasting and Social Change*, 2, 133–148
2 ELDREDGE, H. WENTWORTH (1972) A Mark II Survey and critique of future research teaching in North America. *Technological Forecasting and Social Change*, 4, 387–407
3 ELDREDGE, H. WENTWORTH (1974) A Mark III report on university education in futures study. *Fields Within Fields*, December
4 PADDOCK, W. & PADDOCK, P. (1967) *Famine, 1975*, Little, Brown, Boston, Mass.
5 EHRLICH, PAUL R. (1968) *The Population Bomb*, Ballantine Books, New York

[6] HARDIN, GARRETT (1968) The tragedy of the commons. *Science (Wash. D.C.) 162*, 1243–48

[7] GREENE, WADE (1975) Triage: who shall be fed? Who shall starve? *The New York Times Magazine*, January 5

[8] VACCA, ROBERTO (1973) *The Coming Dark Age*, Doubleday, New York

[9] HEILBRONER, ROBERT L. (1974) *An Inquiry into the Human Prospect*. Norton, New York

[10] HUXLEY, ALDOUS (1932) *Brave New World*, Doubleday, Doran, Garden City, N.Y.

[11] BELL, DANIEL (1964) Twelve modes of prediction—a preliminary sorting of approaches in the social sciences. *Daedalus 93* (Summer), 845–880

[12] HENSHEL, R. L. & KENNEDY, L. W. (1973) Self-altering prophecies: consequences for the feasibility of social prediction. *General Systems, 18*, 119–126

[13] EWALD, WILLIAM R. (ed.) (1967) *Environment for Man: The Next Fifty Years*, Indiana University Press, Bloomington, Indiana

[14] EWALD, WILLIAM R. (1968) *Environment and Policy: The Next Fifty Years*, Indiana University Press, Bloomington, Indiana

[15] EWALD, WILLIAM R. (1968) *Environment and Change: The Next Fifty Years*, Indiana University Press, Bloomington, Indiana

[16] HELLER, ALFRED (ed.) (1972) *The California Plan Tomorrow*, William Kaufmann, Los Altos, California

[17] CHAPLIN, G. & PAIGE, G. D. (1973) *Hawaii 2000*, University Press of Hawaii, Honolulu

[18] SCHROEDER, WALTER W., III (1974) *Urban Dynamics in Lowell*, MIT Urban Dynamics Group, Cambridge, Mass.

[19] CAZES, BERNARD (1974) L'utilisation des études à long terme dans la planification française. *Consommation—Annales De Crédoc*, No. 2, 63–71

[20] ROYAL MINISTRY FOR FOREIGN AFFAIRS AND THE SECRETARIAT FOR FUTURE STUDIES (1974) *To Choose a Future*, Norstedt, Stockholm

[21] NETHERLANDS PARLIAMENT (1973) Law of October 26, 1973 establishing the Scientific Council for Government Policy in the Netherlands. An informal translation. Session 1973–1974–12668 Netherlands Parliament Royal Message No. 1 Bill No. 2

[22] DROR, YEHEZKEL (1971) *Design for Policy Sciences*, American Elsevier, New York

[23] MEADOWS, DONELLA H., MEADOWS, DENNIS L., RANDERS, JØRGEN & BEHRENS, WILLIAM W., III (1972) *The Limits to Growth*, Universe, New York; Earth Island, London

A university experiment in Sweden

KARL-ERIK ERIKSSON and ANDERS LUNDBERG

Centre for Interdisciplinary Studies of the Human Condition, and Institute of Theoretical Physics and Department of Physiology, University of Göteborg, Sweden

Abstract   The Centre for Interdisciplinary Studies of the Human Condition in Göteborg, Sweden, is an official university institution which has existed for almost three years. It functions as a forum for interdisciplinary contacts within the university, mainly in relation to serious problems of a global nature. Membership is open to research workers, teachers and graduate students, and a total of 400 people have joined. Lectures and seminars are sponsored on topics of interest to many disciplines, and the Centre has arranged a number of interdisciplinary undergraduate and graduate training courses which are recognized by the university. Members of the Centre participate in problem-oriented interdisciplinary study groups and the results are usually summarized in reports which are distributed to all members of the Centre. One of the aims of the Centre is to contribute to the factual basis for the process of public opinion formation and for decision-making at different levels in the society. For this purpose many members engage in *external* activity, often utilizing material from the reports from study groups.

This external activity has grown rapidly and its present scale has revealed a desire in society for contact with the universities which previously has not been fully recognized in our country. According to our experience the internal inter-disciplinary work provides a good platform for the external activity.

The Centre depends almost entirely on the voluntary spare-time work of people employed in teaching and research in specialized disciplines.

We must accept that in recent decades there has been a major shift in the public view of science. Many people, particularly the young, are becoming increasingly disillusioned with it. It seems to have lost some of its prestige, and the confidence entrusted in it as a tool for ensuring the progress of mankind seems to be on the wane. This may appear rather surprising to many members of the scientific community, since our time has witnessed so much important progress in science, including a large number of advances of great benefit to man. Nevertheless, there seems to be a spreading public view that science is almost powerless in relation to the major problems facing society. Some even feel that these prob-

19

lems have their origin in scientific and technological advances. This lack of trust in science is in striking contrast to the confidence it enjoyed during the post-war period only twenty-five years ago. At that time few had any doubt that it was a major tool for ensuring progress in western countries ravaged by the war, as well as in underdeveloped countries. Now we are witnessing a spreading disenchantment with what many consider a runaway technology, and even a growing concern for the long-range survival of the human species. Inequality between the rich and poor halves of the world, overpopulation and mass starvation, depletion of natural resources, interference with the balance of the biosphere, and destruction of the environment are some of the components in what is now described as the global crisis.

Since the crisis is at least in part a result of scientific progress, the reaction against science is not surprising. Yet we believe that this reaction is both irrational and temporary. The realization that science has given enormous power to man has created a shock, but if we have any rationality left we shall soon realize that science is of the foremost importance if we are to achieve a solution to man's problems. Science has indeed already played an important role in identifying and measuring the threats which man is facing.

But how can science contribute when the main problem is not science itself but the utilization of scientific results, over which the scientists can exert little influence? The main problem seems to be that society does not have the ethics and the politics to match science and technology. Neither nationally nor internationally do we have governing agencies, political or administrative, which are equipped to face the serious long-term problems. Governments have their hands full, staggering from one crisis to another. Unemployment, social unrest, economic difficulties, etc., are familiar issues requiring remedies which at best—if provided—are only temporary. There is little energy and time left for the fundamental long-term problems, and in any case our political systems—whether parliamentarian or authoritarian—are fit to cope mainly with short-term problems.

If the presentation of global problems given above is correct, it follows that 'the innocence of academic science cannot be regained'.[1] The social responsibility of the scientist—which so tormented the atomic physicists after the Hiroshima bomb—has now become a major concern for a growing number of the scientific community. It concerns above all the academic scientist, since he enjoys a relatively high degree of independence. Chomsky[2] has formulated his views in this respect as follows:

'The university should be a center for radical social inquiry, as it is already a center for what might be called "radical inquiry" in the pure sciences.

It should loosen its "institutional forms" even further, to permit a richer variety of work and study and experimentation and should provide a home for the free intellectual, for the social critic, for the irreverent and radical thinking that is desperately needed if we are to escape from the dismal reality that threatens to overwhelm us'.

The present structure of our universities makes it hard to imagine how the task envisaged by Chomsky should be carried out. The main difficulty is probably the increasing degree of specialization which has been, is and will remain necessary for the production of new knowledge. Although there are some notable examples of individual scientists who applied their knowledge to man's situation,[3,4,5] the scientist's specialization makes it difficult for him to function socially. There is the danger that his outlook is too narrow, so that his attention becomes focused on only one issue of a complex problem. Unfortunately narrowness is sometimes also coupled with specialist arrogance. It is almost a truism to state that virtually all problems facing man and society have many facets and require contributions from many sciences for their solution. And yet who is trying today to make a synthesis of the contributions from the different disciplines? Precious few attempts are being made in the scientific communities themselves. Hence the executive branches of government and industry are left to find their own way in the bewildering stream of information flowing from the scientific institutions. It seems to us that the synthesis of knowledge must become the responsibility of the universities to a much larger extent than is the case at present. Such a synthesis requires close interdisciplinary contacts which may widen the outlook of the scientist by forcing him to view his own field and results in the perspective of knowledge contributed by other disciplines.

If research results are digested in this way they will become more accessible to society than at present. An even more important effect of such interdisciplinary contacts may be to catalyse individual concerned scientists into action. By himself the scientist may be powerless and frustrated, but the combined knowledge of many disciplines may give him a platform from which social action will be more meaningful.

In recent years, there have been many demands for increased interdisciplinary contacts and research and even recommendations for new institutional forms.[6] At the University of Göteborg we have a forum for interdisciplinary contact called the Centre for Interdisciplinary Studies of the Human Condition. Since the Centre has now been in action for almost three years an account of how it came into being and how it operates may be of interest here.

In October 1971, seriously concerned by the increasingly negative effects of specialization, some members of the Faculty of Mathematics and Natural

Science at the University of Göteborg started an integrative science course for their graduate students. The graduate level was chosen for two reasons. First, there is considerably more freedom to introduce new contents in the curriculum at the graduate level than at the undergraduate level. Second, graduate students are more experienced and can contribute relevant information from their own fields.

The course was called 'The humanistic–scientific picture of the world'. The term 'humanistic' was chosen to emphasize an outlook paying due respect to man and human society. This course met with an unexpectedly vivid interest. About ninety students entered the course when it began. Very soon thirty graduate students of medicine also entered the course. With its 120 students this was probably the biggest graduate course ever given in Sweden.

Outside the lecture hours the students met in smaller interdisciplinary groups for studies centred around topics freely chosen by themselves. The written reports produced by these groups turned out to be of high quality. Almost all of them dealt with serious problems of a global nature. When the course ended, in February 1972, a statement based on the group reports was agreed upon and signed by a large majority of the participants. A few days later this statement was published in *Dagens Nyheter*, the largest daily newspaper in Sweden.

A few weeks later a small conference was held to which all faculties and all graduate students of the university were invited. At this conference the idea of an interdisciplinary centre* was put forward. During the spring of 1972 the Centre for Interdisciplinary Studies of the Human Condition was established. According to its charter *the aims of the Centre* are

- to promote interdisciplinary research and training as well as debate and exchange of information;
- to cooperate with different disciplines in the search for new knowledge and in restructuring knowledge already gained;
- to provide a better factual basis for the process of opinion formation and for decision-making at different levels in society.

In order to realize these aims the work of the Centre will be directed towards

- studies of the historical development of the sciences and their theoretical foundations;
- a continuous effort to build a scientifically founded picture of the world;
- analyses of the global situation of man on the basis of humanistic values.

* In Swedish university terminology 'Centre' is used to denote an organization for collaboration between departments.

The number of members joining the Centre soon reached 300, mainly from the University of Göteborg and the Chalmers Institute of Technology in Göteborg, but also scholars from other universities, as well as writers, journalists, librarians and administrators. The number of members now exceeds 400. The university has accepted the Centre as a university institution and provides adequate premises and an annual budget, including the salary for one secretary. The Centre is directly responsible to the university council. So far the Centre has arranged a fair number of public lectures. Series of seminars on different topics have been held for members. Members also meet in small study groups or project groups which present their results in seminars and written reports.

The Board of the Centre has appointed several committees to decentralize its many functions. There are committees for planning futures courses, for contacts with the mass media, for library matters, for editorial work, etc. *Ad hoc* committees are often formed to handle specific problems or recommend proper action.

One basic activity of the Centre has continued to be graduate courses of general interest. The courses are recognized by the university and are financed through special university grants. During this academic year (1974–1975) three graduate courses are being given: first, a new version of the 'world picture' course open to students from all faculties; second, a course on 'Malnutrition in developing countries—social, economic, political and medical aspects'; third, a course on the 'Popularization of scientific knowledge'. Since the 'world picture' course this time does not have to meet an accumulated need, as it did in the first course, the number of students is now considerably lower. However, the general interest in the Centre's interdisciplinary courses still remains quite large. During autumn 1974 a course in *human ecology*, open to undergraduate students, was introduced and has met with a lively interest. This course includes not only topics from the natural and social sciences but also a substantial contribution from the humanities.

Starting this academic year, Georg Borgström, professor of food technology and economic geography at the University of Michigan, is attached to the Centre on a part-time basis. Professor Borgström is an internationally renowned expert on the global food problem who has written a number of widely-read popular books in this field. In March 1975 he is to give a series of lectures on the three recent (1974) United Nations conferences in Caracas, Bucharest and Rome.

The Centre has not yet had any capacity for research in the usual sense of this word. However, the constant ambition in the Centre to combine and to restructure available knowledge has influenced the work of some university institutions and has led to definite plans for interdisciplinary research projects.

Two projects concern the planning of a housing area according to ecologically and socially sound principles, using available scientific, technical and practical knowledge. From such studies we hope to be able to assess human needs for land, energy, water, and various materials in a well-planned technically advanced community.

Work in study groups and project groups has led to conferences. So far the Centre has organized five conferences:

(1) In September 1972 a conference was held with journalists on the selection and presentation of scientific information to the general public.

(2) A conference with members of the Swedish parliament in June 1973 discussed economic growth from an interdisciplinary perspective. This conference constituted a first and very valuable contact with national politicians.

(3) In January 1974 artists and writers were invited to a conference on 'Life quality and cultural patterns'. Ways of obtaining contacts and collaboration between scientists and artists were discussed at this conference. Such collaboration may become a source of inspiration for both categories and lead to new forms of cultural activities.

(4) In March 1974 a second conference was held with members of parliament, this time devoted to energy and arranged in collaboration with the Swedish Society of Members of Parliament and Scientists. The resulting report was called 'Energy—not only a technical issue', which illustrates the wish of the Centre to broaden a debate that runs the risk of becoming dangerously narrow.

(5) Our latest conference, in August 1974, dealt with research policies and was arranged by the Centre in collaboration with the Secretariat for Future Studies under the Prime Minister's office. Representatives from the universities and research councils as well as from government and higher administration participated. The title of the conference was 'The planning of research in the face of an uncertain future'. Several problems of vital importance to the role of the university in the society were subject to lively—and at times quite penetrating—discussion.

Sweden prepares for reforms through officially appointed commissions of inquiry. We have the unique system of circulating the reports of such commissions to various bodies in society for their opinion and comment *before* they are brought to parliament. On a number of occasions the Board of the Centre has submitted its comments on such reports. Many members have been active in preparatory work for such comments.

As the Centre is the only institution in the university—and in some sense in the whole country—with truly interdisciplinary ambitions and with the ambition of being available to society at large, the Centre has been overwhelmed by an enormous demand for seminars and lectures, for articles in newspapers and journals, for participation in public debates and for expert opinions. Our most important external activity is directed to school teachers. We provide lecturers for meetings lasting one to three days, which are scheduled in the regional teachers' training programmes. The Centre has also planned and participated in study groups within the previously mentioned society for collaboration between scientists and members of parliament. Some local study groups in different parts of the country are working in constant contact with the Centre and can be assisted when needed.

Our capacity is not sufficient to satisfy all the demands made on the Centre. Yet a large number of members are active, not only in the internal work of the Centre but also in the external services for society at large.

In the general discussion concerning the country's future energy policy, members of the Centre have participated actively. One conference on energy has been mentioned already. Some ten members of the Centre have contributed to hearings arranged by the government's Energy Council, which has the Prime Minister as its chairman.

To keep members informed about the various internal and external activities of the Centre a monthly bulletin is issued. Besides announcing forthcoming events it also includes progress reports from study groups, travel reports, bibliographical notes and sometimes short papers on topics of common interest. It is possible for people outside the Centre to subscribe to the bulletin and the number of such subscribers is rising. The total circulation is now 1100.

Summarizing the experience from almost three years of activity in the Centre for Interdisciplinary Studies, we may state that it has contributed towards a change in our university environment. The possibility for easy contact with colleagues from other fields represents a break with specialization which has increasingly isolated representatives of different fields from each other. We do not know whether this lack of contact is more marked in Sweden than in other countries, but it has certainly been very marked here. The competition for meagre resources within a tight budget may even create some animosity between disciplines: many scientists certainly have a rather childish feeling of prestige regarding their own subject. To meet colleagues from entirely different fields for discussion of common problems, and to share teaching duties in problem-oriented interdisciplinary courses, has been a useful and intellectually stimulating experience for many of us. Joint appearances in external activities and conferences with politicians and administrators have contributed to a feeling of unity amongst us. We do not know whether it has made us more humble but two other effects are clearly evident. First, we have been forced to abandon our specialist jargon which is a great barrier to the exchange of thoughts, and one that is difficult to overcome. Second, it has given us an op-portunity to view our own special field from a new angle. Consciously or unconsciously, we are all bound by internal scientific traditions, often specific to each field. It is useful to reflect from another perspective on the criteria which guide us in the daily routine of research and teaching, and to view them in the light of their possible impact on society. It is as yet difficult to know what effect, if any, these interdisciplinary contacts will have on research in special-ized fields. We wish to make it clear that so far most members of the Centre do not participate in interdisciplinary research. For all except a few of those who have shared in the limited research referred to above, it has been a part-time activity.

The most significant impact of the Centre has probably been its function as a platform for external contacts. As an almost automatic result of the internal problem-oriented interdisciplinary work there were contacts with individuals and organizations outside the university who were interested in the same problems. As a result we have today an extensive network of contacts which is unique in our country. When word spread about the existence of our organization, we were approached from different quarters with requests for information, advice, assistance or collaboration. These requests revealed that society had a need for contact with the universities—a need which had not previously been paid due attention. Through our organization we can now easily channel a request to an appropriate addressee or call on a group of members if the issue, as is usually the case, has interdisciplinary aspects. If this work has had some suc-cess it is probably due to the preparatory work in seminars and study groups which has trained the members to use everyday language, and which has per-haps broadened them by counteracting some of the negative effects of special-ization.

Members who participate in this external activity do so because of their belief that the universities should be of more direct use to society, and in most cases also because they have a strong belief that present society needs radical long-term changes which cannot be brought about without an enlightened public opinion. When participating in the public debate with articles in news-papers, or in television or radio broadcasts, each member expresses his own views. The Centre as such has no opinion of its own. However, members are usually introduced as belonging to the Centre for Interdisciplinary Studies and since most members who appear in public hold similar opinions on serious global problems the public may have got the erroneous impression that opinion within the organization is unanimous. However, the Centre should function as a forum for debate and naturally there are considerable differences of opinion among members. For example, while many members are very concerned about Sweden's nuclear power programme—which, measured by expenditure per head of population, is the most ambitious in the world—there are some strong proponents of nuclear energy. On some topics the Centre has issued statements as an organization. The decision is then taken by the Board. The plenary meeting has sometimes exercised its power of criticizing the Board. Our policy in this matter is currently under discussion.

Our activity during the last three years has been an interesting university experiment. It is now time to raise two questions. Should such an activity as ours become an integrated part of life in the university? If so, how can it be maintained? Let us consider the second question first. Opposing forces may be *external*, coming from those bodies on which the universities ultimately depend for funds and for the maintenance of their relatively independent status, but they may also be *internal*, coming from within the university and the scientific community itself. On festival occasions politicians and administrators may talk about the freedom of the universities and urge them to use this freedom for 'radical social inquiry'. But how will they react if such an inquiry yields results contrary to their own convictions and recommends lines of action quite contrary to their own plans? It would be presumptuous to claim that the impact of the Centre for Interdisciplinary Studies of the Human Condition has been so strong in our society that this problem has become a reality. Nevertheless we must keep it in mind. So far, we have met with benevolence and been encouraged by higher authorities in charge of university affairs. Special requests from the Centre for (modest) grants to arrange conferences or to meet occasional emergencies have been promptly satisfied outside the regular budget of the universities. On the whole our work has also been favourably viewed by the mass media: the press, radio and television have all been attentive.

It is interesting to note that our activity is rather in line with some of the recommendations in a report from a government committee. Some years ago the government appointed a committee (or perhaps rather a working party) to enquire into questions related to 'Studies in the future' in Sweden. Their report (abbreviated version in English: 'To choose a future')[7] deals partly with technical questions related to planning but a major part is devoted to the impact of the serious global situation on long-range planning in Sweden. They emphasize the long-range significance of basic research and they contrast 'the precarious state of university research with the buoyant growth that has infused certain investigative and planning functions among government agencies as well as manufacturing firms and trade associations'.

The authors of the report recommend that special support should be given to three new types of research activities:

(*1*) *Critical research*, implying research that challenges or denies the values and priorities that actually govern the direction of planning. In this connection we quote from the report: 'A free society is obliged to ensure that critical research stands a fair chance of working, and it stands to reason that universities make the forum where such research is most readily accommodated'.

(*2*) *Alternative planning*, implying an elaboration of Sweden's investigation-by-commission system. Although the reports by the government commissions are ambitious and often extremely thorough and detailed, they rarely give more than one concretely worked-out proposal. Accordingly they are often unsatisfactory when the issues involved are long-range and they 'afford a pretty frail foundation on which to nurture debate of real long-term alternatives'. The authors of 'To choose a future' propose that when a 'heavy' government commission is appointed, funds should be set aside to finance a small number of critical enquiries into the same problem at the same time.

(*3*) *Long-term motivated basic research*, coming close to autonomous basic research but related to the future according to certain criteria.

The government has adopted the last of the three proposals and parliament has now given funds for 'long-term motivated basic research'. A portion of these funds is at the disposal of the Secretariat for Future Studies directly under the Prime Minister's office; another portion is administered by a more independent committee.

So far our government has not taken any decision with regard to funds for 'critical research' or 'alternative planning'. But the very fact that they were recommended in an official report may have contributed to legitimizing the activities of the Centre for Interdisciplinary Studies. In the report 'To choose a future' the authors also call for external university activity. They write: 'Scientists and scholars the world over, acting as enlighteners, warners and enthusiasts, have been highly instrumental in the moulding of public opinion... this vital critical function must prevail'.[7] They recommend more active contact with the mass media and with the system of voluntary public adult education. Clearly the work in our Centre is well in line with these recommendations.

Let us now consider internal opposition from within the university. Chomsky ends his essay on 'The role of the university in a time of crisis' by stating that one barrier to serious reform and innovation will be 'the fear of the faculty that its security and authority, its guild structure, will be threatened'.[2] So far our activity has been strongly supported by the council of our university. There is little doubt that some faculty members dislike it and find it incompatible with academic dignity and the status of science. So far they have not found the time opportune for voicing their criticism openly—it appears as a general reluctance, perhaps tinged with some contempt. Since the opposition is silent we do not know its extent. In this connection it is relevant to point out that so far we have drawn very little on the monetary resources of the university. All members have their main obligation to teaching and research in their specialized disciplines. A core of highly motivated members has been the driving force, but the results achieved depend mainly on the spare-time work of a large number of members. Nevertheless it is clear that in many cases these activities have 'interfered' with research in the specialized disciplines, because devoted scientists have no spare time. However, a conflict may appear if we request a larger share of the funds available to the university. For different motives powerful specialist interests may then react,[8] and this is not difficult to understand at a time when many departments are desperately short of funds for staff appointments and when resources for basic research generally are shrinking.

It is strange that the reaction against science to which we referred at the beginning of this paper has hit mainly the universities, while other research bodies continue to flourish. Those research bodies, created for direct service to society, government or industry, are often highly specialized. They may be well suited to dealing with short-term problems arising in each sector of society, but hardly to dealing with the incredibly complex long-term problems related to man's future.

The university has not only an important educational function. It is also society's *focal point of learning*. Through both these functions, and through the discovery of new knowledge, it fills a crucial role in society. If the university does not respond to the present crisis, then society will have to develop other institutions to carry out these functions.

Discussion

Waddington: The Centre for Interdisciplinary Studies at Göteborg is a most remarkable development, showing just what a university can do in these fields. At postgraduate level, the Centre is looking at the whole human future, and it has this remarkable series of external contacts with the government on one side, artists and writers on another, and schoolteachers on a third side. But how far have you been able to get an undergraduate programme going, Professor Lundberg? The undergraduate parts of the university are the ones most tied up by legislation and full curricula.

Lundberg: We only started the undergraduate course in human ecology this academic year (1974–1975). Also, in our country more formalities are required at the undergraduate than at the graduate level. We did submit a plan of the curriculum last year, and establishment of this course actually required a special decision by the government. However, our proposal for such a course passed through the higher administration with lightning speed and was approved at all levels. I believe the higher authorities, including the Department of Education, were genuinely interested in the proposals but in any case a refusal was hardly possible in view of the anticipated reaction from an alert public.

Jevons: It seems to me that we are in danger, through insufficiently careful use of the word 'interdisciplinary', of overestimating the novelty of interdisciplinarity. Nearly always when the problems of the real world are being attacked, we have to call on a range of academic disciplines as defined by academic criteria. Engineering, forestry, business management, architecture and so on are all in some real sense interdisciplinary. Do you see your venture in Göteborg as a transitional stage before more permanently institutionalized forms come into being for dealing with problems such as malnutrition in the third world, human ecology, and so on? Or do you see the Centre as a mechanism for continuously injecting novelty into a system which would otherwise be in danger of ossifying?

Lundberg: Rather the latter. It is quite true that problems of the 'real world' require an interdisciplinary approach. But my very point is that many university scientists have become so specialized that they are almost inaccessible to a non-expert. It is our hope that interdisciplinary contacts within the university will bring about a changed situation, making us more ready to apply our knowledge to society at large. I believe this is vital at a time when man's future is at stake.

Dror: I have no doubt about the importance of the work of the Centre, but isn't its usefulness going to be partly a question of critical mass, in the sense that if really solid suggestions are to be provided on complex matters, a group of people working on a full-time basis will be needed? In other words, to provide studies in depth, wouldn't you need permanent staff from different disciplines who would slowly evolve into some kind of full-time 'think tank'?

Lundberg: We cannot sit and wait for such an institute but will have to try our best within the existing framework. If we all seem to agree on the necessity for interdisciplinary work, why not make a start by establishing interdisciplinary contacts? Research projects may grow out of such contacts. Meanwhile let us not forget that we can be useful by making existing knowledge available to society.

Dror: How do you handle the value problems? Do you recommend alternatives so that others make the value judgements, or are your own value judgements expressed in your recommendations?

Lundberg: The value problem is a difficult one but mainly in relation to the internal work. There have been some clashes between Marxist and non-Marxist views but we have learned to live with that. When the organization as such acts externally it has certainly never recommended alternatives to suit different value judgements. However, most external appearances are by individual members who express their own views.

Perry: In the Open University, when we tried to produce multidisciplinary or interdisciplinary courses our experience was that the time and money spent was far greater than that spent on single-disciplinary courses. A striking development at the Open University is that people who came from single-disciplinary studies to work in interdisciplinary ones have already, in a relatively short time, significantly changed their research interests in the direction of the interdisciplinary. Have you seen this in Göteborg?

Lundberg: It is also our experience that interdisciplinary teaching requires considerable effort—in both planning and execution. In our special case the monetary cost is small because we depend largely on voluntary spare-time efforts. A large number of members have now been quite active on a voluntary basis for some years but more financial support will certainly be required in the long run. A few members have switched their research interests but I believe it is still too early to assess the impact of the Centre on research activity.

Woodroofe: Are the universities themselves going to become flexible organizations, with their currently well-defined disciplines less water-tight than they used to be, or will they remain the inflexible organizations that they are now? Here you are already arguing about the discipline of policy studies as against that of 'futures studies'—in other words there is evidence of the beginnings of some ossification even in studies for the future. The idea of study of the future is that it will enable us to take decisions now which will be better for mankind, but it has not been ordained that the problems of the world will be defined in terms of the faculties or disciplines of the universities. To solve those problems we shall need a variety of disciplines. Different problems will require different mixes of disciplines, and different proportions of effort from those disciplines. As we move along the stages of looking at those problems we may need additional disciplines, and others may have to drop out. Could there be some sort of department within a university, an initial central core, which would give continuity and have the ability to draw in teams, loosely structured, which would deal with the problems? Then as the problems changed the teams could alter too.

Waddington: Present financial restrictions may conceivably lead to a situation where the universities can no longer completely man the rigid hierarchies in which they are now arranged. And conceivably these financial restrictions may act as a loosening-up situation, simply because the universities can't man the hierarchies.

Eldredge: Although the US is a completely chaotic country compared to Sweden, which has been very disciplined indeed, some of the situations are quite similar. Having had a lot of experience in problem-oriented work in universities, through urban studies, I see futures studies as a similar sort of opportunity for bringing people together, with all the results that you have suggested and perhaps others, Professor Lundberg.

It is interesting that it is apparently a characteristic of futures studies everywhere that they are started up by lively individuals who use their own free time to talk to others in other universities and in other continents. In the United States, we have 2300 institutions of higher learning, at least 500 of which, someone remarked, 'should be hit on the head'. Nevertheless, with a disorganized situation like that, one can be quite innovative. One doesn't have to go to the Minister of Education for permission to start a course—no one would quite know who to go to. One has to get a little money of course, and though everybody is perfectly willing to have innovation, nobody wants to pay for it. So what happens is that starting a futures course going comes out of some instructor's hide, or free time. I would think that the Cabinet or politicians at a similar level would be the people who should lean on you, work with you, and perhaps make a higher synthesis for application in the real world than the university would. This is a national research opportunity to which the university can contribute greatly.

Francis: Part of my experience has been in teaching a technology foundation course within the Open University. This course leans very much on the approach to futures studies down a perfectly respectable academic path, although it certainly isn't directly described under that heading.

The Open University differs from most other universities in having undergraduates over a wide age distribution. In courses where people with a wide range of industrial experience join others who have had entirely different experiences outside the university, the fusion of ideas takes place much more easily than in undergraduate classes of a more conventional kind. Have you attempted to create a course in Sweden which allows people with a varied cross-section of professional and other backgrounds to come in from outside the university and make their contribution in the 'teaching and learning' situation? This seems to work effectively in the Open University courses. There is a critical mass and many of the groups quickly evolve a self-help capability, with the tutor/counsellor in a position to prevent misinterpretation or misdirection of effort.

Lundberg: Our experience is exactly the same as yours. About half the students taking the undergraduate course in human ecology are from outside the university, some of them with rather long professional experience. They have mixed well with the 'regular' undergraduates and certainly made important contributions to the course. The facilitating effect from the external students was a new experience to the teachers.

Waddington: In the School of the Man Made Future in Edinburgh quite a lot of people have come in from outside the university. They certainly liven up proceedings quite a lot.

Wilkins: We all seem to agree that we are faced with some fundamental difficulties. We have heard about the need for serious work and joining disciplines together, but presumably most of us would accept that we seek some fundamental innovation of approach. Professor Lundberg, you quoted what Chomsky[2] said about the universities possibly being centres for radical enquiry —which of course, except for the presence of some outstanding individuals, the universities never have been. You also referred to the fact that your Centre had connections with 'alternative' groups. Did these groups include political groups other than those represented by the government? To what extent can one usefully feed in not only the thinking but also the general attitude of all the radical and alternative groups? What use does the Club of Rome make of contacts of that nature? How can one feed these contacts into the universities? I agree it is most desirable that universities should try to break out of their institutional strait jackets and make contact with the community outside.

Lundberg: We have connections with 'alternative groups' as part of our contacts with the community outside the university. Like other countries we have groups of individuals trying out low-energy technology, subsistence economy and new types of social relationships. Established political forces tend to view such groups with suspicion and they cannot get any economic support. But it is important that these groups should get whatever advice they need and that their experiences should be evaluated. Within a fairly short time society may need large-scale experiments which will try out radically different technological, economic and social conditions. Meanwhile we can prepare ourselves with theoretical studies of how a low-energy society might function but it is certainly also important to incorporate whatever practical experiences are available.

References cited

[1] RAVETZ, J. R. (1971) *Scientific Knowledge and its Social Problems.* Oxford University Press, London

[2] CHOMSKY, N. (1969) The role of the university in a time of crisis, in *The Great Ideas Today*, Encyclopedia Britannica, Chicago, Ill. (Reprinted in *For Reasons of State*, 1970. American Book-Stratford Press, New York)

[3] CHOMSKY, N. (1971) *Problems of Knowledge and Freedom: The Russell Lectures*, Pantheon Books, New York

[4] MONOD, J. (1971) *Chance and Necessity*, Collins, Glasgow

[5] SACHAROV, A. (1968) *Progress, Coexistence, and Intellectual Freedom* [Translated by *New York Times*, New York]

[6] CELLARIUS, R. A. & PLATT, J. (1972) Councils of urgent studies. *Science (Wash. D.C.)* 177, 670–676

[7] ROYAL MINISTRY FOR FOREIGN AFFAIRS AND THE SECRETARIAT FOR FUTURE STUDIES (1974) *To Choose a Future*, Norstedt, Stockholm [Abridged English translation of *Att välja framtid*, SOU (official state report) 1972:59]

[8] STRAUS, R. (1973) Departments and disciplines: stasis and change. *Science (Wash. D.C.)* 182, 895–898

The future as a discipline and the future of the disciplines

ALEXANDER KING

International Federation of Institutes of Advanced Study, Paris

Abstract With the approach of the end of the millennium there has been a recent proliferation of studies of the future. This has been stimulated by the present rapid rate of change—political, economic, social and technological—which necessitates a prospective approach to policy planning. Mere extrapolation of sectoral trends is no longer sufficient in view of the importance of factors external to each sector, producing discontinuities. The situation is particularly difficult in technology, owing to the long lead time of research and development, which necessitates early decisions on projects which will be effective decades ahead and can no longer be left exclusively to the market forces.

There is a need on both national and international levels to encourage and make known the results of futures studies to the public and to decision makers, and for the encouragement of academic research, both on methodology and on particular issues and situations (including model-making). Many countries are considering how to do this. Within the university the location of such teaching and research, which is essentially transdisciplinary, is somewhat uncertain and has hitherto arisen in various departments as a result of individual enthusiasms.

Futures studies, as those on policy research and other transdisciplinary matters, are unlikely to constitute a discrete discipline. Indeed the growing number of such fields throws doubt on the continuing validity of static disciplines, and a more dynamic approach to the classification of knowledge is outlined.

In recent years there has been a rapid upsurge of interest in forecasting the trends in human affairs, of predicting future situations and of presenting scenarios of various possible or probable societies, desirable or undesirable, which may be pressed upon us, or towards which the authors of the studies would have us strive. Many of these are speculative—good or bad literature— and often deliberately provocative; some are patently false, while others are painstaking attempts to indicate the consequences of continuing with our present life styles and national policies, made in the hope that early warnings may result in corrective measures being taken in time.

35

Of course there is nothing new in this preoccupation with the future. Even the Delphic Oracle and the Old Testament prophets must have had ancient precedents. Our preoccupation reflects the distinguishing feature of *Homo sapiens*: that he is capable of thinking ahead, at least to some minor degree. What is new is the present recognition of the need to probe more systematically and rationally into the trends of present events, to foresee as far as possible the consequences of such trends, to see difficulties ahead, and to make a deliberate attempt to shape the future in accordance with evolving human needs.

As a result of this recognition, future-oriented activities and institutions which undertake these have recently proliferated, as have forecasting techniques and attempts to evolve a systematic and scientific approach to such studies. The present meeting is therefore to be welcomed as an attempt to place these new activities in an intellectual perspective and to see how far they are appropriate within the academic system and whether they are, in fact, the embryo of a new scientific discipline.

REASONS FOR THE NEW INTEREST IN THE FUTURE

The most elemental cause of the present interest in the future is the mystical significance of the approach to the end of a millennium and the reassessment of the human condition and destiny which this encourages. This is reinforced by the intuitive feelings of many, that change and impending change in the world is ominous and that we are at an important point of inflection in the evolution of society, if not at the brink of disruption. This is no mere *fin de siècle* flurry, but is, appropriately, an order of magnitude more serious. This situation has many similarities to that which existed during the decades preceding the end of the first Christian millennium when the end of the world was predicted. It gave rise to much uncertainty and restlessness, a sense of futility and unwillingness to take decisions, which quickly dissipated when the fateful day passed without disaster. It may well be that the year 2000 will likewise lead to calmer times, but preoccupation with the future is likely to persist.

This situation gave rise, a few years ago, to a rash of studies of the year 2000, some merely speculative but others useful as systematic assessments of present trends and taking account of various possible discontinuities.

A much more important reason for the present concern with futures studies arises from the rapid rate of change in the world, caused basically, perhaps, by technological change arising from scientific discovery, but manifested also in economic, political and social terms and through the rapid and uncertain modification of human values. In general, governments find it very difficult to look ahead in their legislation and to adjust policies in the face of external change.

The democratic system, with its average electoral cycle of less than four years, encourages an almost exclusive preoccupation with immediate issues, on the part of both governments and oppositions. This mattered little in earlier days of slower change, but today with the increasing importance of forces external to a nation and beyond its control, such as monetary difficulties, contagious inflation, scarcity and high costs of imported raw materials and energy, a period of five to seven years can see a fundamental transformation of the situation; hence the immediate issues on which a government was elected and which were of closest concern to the electorate can become quite marginal in relation to the somewhat longer-term developments.

Of course, governments have for many years attempted to project and to forecast. Medium-term forecasts are made, for example of economic development and growth, employment and demography, agricultural production, etc., and these can be important inputs in the formulation of national plans, where such exist. Such forecasts are, however, almost always strictly sectoral and pay little attention to cross-impacts from other sectors. Likewise national plans, whether dirigist or indicative, have up to now been strictly economic and have taken only marginal notice of social or technological development. Concern with the environment, the consequence of population increase and urban growth, recognition that economic growth is not an end in itself but the means to provide for social, educational and other development—these and many other factors in modern society are suggesting more and more the need for a new type of integrated and integrating planning which will require the development of reliable social indicators and many new types of forecasting and assessment of future trends.

These considerations suggest that futures studies cannot be developed and used in isolation, at least as far as their influence on policy-making and the public acceptance of change are concerned. They are to be seen as part of the approach to the problem of the management of complexity. In a world whose dimensions have been shrunk by science and invention, problems of scale compound with those of rapid change to generate a momentum and complexity which existing policies and institutions will find it hard to manage. Although strictly outside the scope of this meeting, the problems of complexity are so intimately linked to the need for futures research that it may be useful to enumerate a few of the elements of this complexity. These are:

— recognition in a starkly practical sense of the interdependence of the nations and of the vulnerability of energy and raw material supplies and price levels to political as well as market forces;

— recognition of the interdependence of both problems and solutions and

the need to foresee the interaction of solutions to sectoral problems with those in other areas;
— the fact that world population is increasing very quickly and will double in just over thirty years;
— increase in the scale of world activity and hence of the demand for raw materials, energy, products and services, arising from both population increase and faster economic growth;
— rapid rate of change;
— generalization of expectations within the industrialized countries and between the rich and the poor countries of the world.

The situation has been likened by Dennis Meadows to that of a large ocean liner which, owing to its momentum, requires many miles before it is able to change course and hence needs early warnings from radar to avoid rocks ahead. It is, of course, essential that the radar—or future forecasts—should be adequate and it is doubtful that futures techniques have yet reached such a state of reliability.

CATEGORIES OF FUTURES STUDIES

The future is inherently unknowable and forecasts based on the projection of present trends are rarely realized because of discontinuities, uncertainties as to the time of levelling-off of exponential curves, and the inruption of external forces. Nevertheless much can be done. The central issue is whether the world and its constituent nations can build in time a capacity and an initiative with regard to future events and prepare contingency plans and policies to meet them, rather than acting *post facto* when problems arise. It is a matter of decreasing the degree of uncertainty with regard to the future rather than a matter of crisis government. This new approach is not merely a matter of forecasting by the extrapolation of past and present trends which can easily collapse under the pressure of forces external to each nation. It is rather a matter of exploring the unknown by probing where chinks appear, of analysing the trends and potentialities of the present and of assessing the relative significance of each trend, of examining choices and options and the probable consequences of various combinations of these, of foreseeing incompatibilities, physical road blocks and inter-goal conflicts, of constructing possible and desirable microfutures. It will have to be a continuous process, kept under constant review as events and deeper insights render modifications necessary. It is a concept of dynamic rather than of static planning.

Regarded in this light the prospective approach is an essential and inherent part of the new policy science, and futures studies are an important part of policy research.

The degree of uncertainty about forecasts of the future varies greatly from field to field. For example, technological forecasting, which was fashionable a few years ago, should be inherently possible since most technology arises from scientific discoveries which have already been made, but even here the uncertainties are very great.

Such futures studies as have already been accomplished vary greatly in method of approach and relevance. They can be categorized in many different ways, but it may be useful to suggest a few basic types and their characteristics.

— Firstly there is the purely *speculative approach*, generally literary rather than scientific, but at its best comprising many useful intuitive and imaginative elements; most of the utopias, Brave New Worlds, the 1984s, and much of science fiction fall into this category, which has little policy significance but which can greatly influence general thinking.

— Related to the above, but often more scientifically based, are *direct projections of existing situations* and trends, ranging from the not always irrational forecasts of Old Moore's Almanack to the reasoned scenarios of Herman Kahn.

— *Prophylactic futurology* projects and interrelates present trends to indicate the probable consequences of their continuation, not as prophesy but in order to draw public and political attention to future dangers so that deliberate changes may be introduced to ensure that the consequences are avoided and the curve of projection bent. The Forrester-Meadows limits to growth was of this type.[1] Technology assessment has a similar objective.

— *Prospective planning*, whether political, economic, technological or social, has important futures inputs as a necessity and is capable of using a wide diversity of techniques. It takes into account present trends and their interactions, includes the working out of the probable consequences of different possible decisions and the creation of alternative policies and strategies to meet the more likely contingencies.

— The *construction of utopias* or designing of desirable futures is a further approach which endeavours to suggest in detail general, sectoral or microfutures regarded as desirable, as goals towards which society should move and which may be taken as policy targets by society or its decision makers. Naturally such constructions are value-loaded and reflect essentially the values of their creators, who may, however, have been given their general specifications by particular political or ideological groups.

THE FUTURES APPROACH IN SCIENCE AND TECHNOLOGY

The time factor is particularly important in science and technology. The time scales of the world of science are widely different from those of the world of politics, a fundamental factor of national development which is insufficiently appreciated in political thinking and, indeed, in that of the economist, who habitually assumes that new scientific discovery and appropriate technological development are conjured up in response to economic forces. Much of the economists' hope of solving the longer-term problems depends on an implicit reliance on the 'technological fix'—without, however, giving sufficient importance to the time constraints.

Research and development are inherently long-term processes. From the first creation of a basic new concept in the mind of the scientist until its generalized application in the form of a new product or process or new type of institution takes upwards of thirty years. Of course there are innumerable smaller innovations which can be accomplished much more quickly, while major developments can be greatly speeded up by the massive efforts of crash programmes of the type which the United States used for getting men to the moon. But crash programmes are extremely expensive and are bound to remain the exception. In general, therefore, the research–development–production chain is very long and, for energy, for example, it threatens to be much longer than political exigencies will permit. Even when no fundamentally novel features are involved the process is slow. For example, in the French nuclear power programme—not a pacemaker in technological development—a quarter of a century elapsed between the first experimental pile going critical and the first nuclear power station going into service. When the rate of political, economic and social change is great, i.e. when the interval between successive, distinct sets of circumstances is shorter than the normal lead time of research and development, there is the fear that their results will come too late to have a fundamental economic and hence political impact. In periods of slower change, new technological developments did indeed evolve mainly in response to the forces of the market and helped to create the wealth and prosperity which we have enjoyed. In planned economies, likewise, technological developments are pursued mainly in support of a slowly evolving economic expansion.

These circumstances indicate the need to give special attention to futures studies in science and technology, and to relate such work to the political and economic process. It is a matter for partnership of a quite new kind between science, industry and government.

THE INSTITUTION OF FUTURES STUDIES

Viewed thus, from the point of view of the necessity of generating and refining futures research for the benefit of a nation or of the world, it is clear that such work will have to be developed in close cooperation with the user—the government, the international organizations or industrial enterprises—if they are to be fully effective. There is probably a need for two distinctive types of institution, the first an essentially policy-oriented unit close to the decision makers, which generates, stimulates and selects the necessary inputs of a prospective type and ensures that they are taken account of. The second type of institution is that for research, both of a long-term character, including the development of new techniques and the refinement of existing ones, and applied research which explores particular trends or constructs particular futures, micro or macro. The two types of institution would, ideally, be in symbiotic relationship and the futures policy units would no doubt stimulate research and, at times, have it undertaken in the futures research bodies by contract.

It may be useful to look at a few of the existing or projected institutional arrangements in this field. The pattern suggested above is, for example, being discussed at the moment in Canada where a conference of the interested parties has been called jointly by the Senate of Canada and the Economic Council; the proposal is to create (a) a national look-out centre on future trends and forecasts for the use of governments (federal and provincial), industry and the public, and (b) a futures research centre within the Economic Council to stimulate such research and act as the centre of a network of research activity in the universities and independent research institutions.

On the policy and applicational aspects, much is already being done by industry, where the trend of events which followed the petroleum crisis has given a new impulse to longer-term thinking and planning. Several large, progressive firms now have important units, generally working close to the president or managing director on long-term corporate policy, taking account of world political and economic trends, and looking for new opportunities and often, it should be added, for a new image. In some cases the director of research and development is given this role, which is an important move since it brings research planning much closer to overall corporate strategy than is normally the case.

On the governmental level, countries are taking a variety of measures. In the United States futures studies, like other activities, are approached in a pluralistic sense with little attempt to centralize or coordinate. Government departments have for many years been interested in such an approach, particularly with regard to defence strategy and technology, relying mainly on quasi-independent bodies such as the Rand and Mitre Corporations to undertake it by contract. Now however a number of major projects are in progress within the executive branch, for example in the Departments of Labor and of Commerce. There are said to be about eight separate governmental and non-governmental short-term forecasts of economic trends. A new body of some significance has been set up by the legislature to advise Congress on the physical, biological, environmental, social and political consequences of technological development. This Office of Technology Assessment has no counterpart as yet in other parliaments. Also in the United States, there are many non-profit bodies devoted to futures studies, such as the Institute for the Future in California, Forecasting International, and the Hudson Institute, while a large number of academic centres are devoted to such work, including the Center for Futures Studies at Portland, and the System Dynamics group at MIT and at Case Western Reserve University which houses the American end of the elaborate Mesarovic–Pestel World Model.[2] Significant also is the Commission for Critical Choices set up by Governor (now Vice-President) Rockefeller.

Another country with a plethora of futures activities is Japan, where the government's Economic Planning Agency is attempting to include social as well as economic factors and is working out social, inflation and welfare indicators. Large numbers of specific, regional and global studies are being carried out in government departments, private organizations such as the Japan Techno-Economics Society, and in the universities. The Netherlands also has a wide variety of forecasting and futures activities, ranging from the sophisticated work of the Central Planning Bureau, through the new and interesting Scientific Council for Government Policy, which is an experimental body responsible to the Cabinet as a whole and required to formulate long-term problems and policy directions for the country as a whole, to a number of interesting university studies and model building. Sweden likewise is taking a systematic approach. As mentioned by Professors Eldredge and Lundberg (this volume), the Prime Minister set up, in 1971, a commission to advise on this area of interest and to review needs and possibilities. As a result of its report 'To choose a future',[3] a Secretariat for Futures Studies has been set up in Sweden with strong financial backing from the government to promote research in the universities, to undertake technology assessment studies and to plan university courses on forecasting and futures. Similar activities are arising in many other countries.

The international organizations have been much slower in entering this field, although the Organization for Economic Cooperation and Development (OECD) has done a good deal of economic forecasting and is now engaged in looking at the long-term and medium-term supply-and-demand aspects of energy as well as at the concomitant technological and research needs. The United Nations was given a strong lead in this direction by U Thant before his retirement, and has recently set up, within UNITAR (United Nations Institute for Training and Research), its own commission for the future. The European Economic Commission has also entered the field of long-term assessment and forecasting and has set up its group, Europe plus Thirty, to advise on whether a comprehensive and continuing activity should be mounted.

Finally, an increasing number of private organizations on an international or national level, such as the Club of Rome, while not strictly futures study groups, are concerned with establishing a prospective approach. The Club of Rome was formed essentially through the conviction of its members that governmental and intergovernmental organizations with their archaic structures and weight of bureaucracy were too slow and too traditional to solve the complex, interactive problems of our quickly changing world and that a new impulse must be given. This has resulted in a significant stimulus to future-oriented research. Simultaneously and in informal relation to the Club of Rome two new international institutions have been created. The International Institute for Applied Systems Analysis in Vienna, with a competent international staff, should contribute greatly to the development of new techniques for probing the future and should be able to maintain high academic standards. The International Federation of Institutes of Advanced Study, with its twenty-three constituent institutes, each of which has great competence in its specialized field, is endeavouring to promote multidisciplinary contact between its member institutes and to organize common projects between them and other interested institutes and individual scientists. Its existing projects are all strongly future-orientated.

IS FUTURES RESEARCH A SUITABLE SUBJECT FOR ACADEMIA?

I shall not attempt in this brief paper to give a survey of the state of the art with regard to futures studies or to comment in detail on their validity and scientific level. It will be realized from what has already been said, however, that the subject has already penetrated deeply into the universities of certain countries and that the now recognized need for the results of such work is likely to attract more and more academic attention.

The answer to the question, therefore, seems to me to be very simple. If, as I believe is true, the universities are essential innovators in society through the development of new concepts and methods of thought, they can hardly avoid taking up the challenge of exploration of the future which is being forced upon us by the exigencies of our times, and which in many ways is a consequence of scientific discovery as well as of the technology which has been built upon it, stemming from earlier innovations of academia.

Certainly the quality of existing studies of the future varies greatly. Much of it is scientifically very weak, superficial and subjective, but not noticeably much more so than in many researches in the behavioural sciences which are already well embedded in the universities. Furthermore we are already seeing great advances in technique and sophistication and it is probably only in the universities and a few independent research institutions that the necessary interdisciplinary contact and deep competence in elements of the subject exist which will enable this process of refinement and development to progress on a sound intellectual basis.

This brings us to the point of discussing how such activities can find their place in the university system. Studies of the future are essentially multidisciplinary or transdisciplinary. They have a need for a basic statistical and mathematical competence; they require a sound input from economics, sociology and psychology; at times they require the help of the computer; they have elements of cybernetics and systems analysis; they require deep political insights. It has been mentioned already that from the point of view of their application, futures studies can be regarded as a branch of policy research, itself a new, horizontal and multidisciplinary field. In fact the problem of futures research and the universities is part of the larger question of how university structures and attitudes can be modified to allow for an increasing extent of interdisciplinary contact and of multidisciplinary team formation. This need is widely recognized and receives a great deal of lip service, but in fact the results, especially in many of the older and more traditional universities, are far from convincing. Amongst other obstacles, career lines in a particular specialization are clear and good work leads to promotion; so time spent in multidisciplinary work is all too often regarded as a diversion from 'serious' research and teaching and detracts from career prospects. The result is often that, while a few devoted and adventurous people are willing to take such career risks, many brilliant people who might contribute greatly to the new horizontal fields are dissuaded from entering them. The fundamental need, then, is for innovation in the structure and attitudes of the universities if they, by the cultivation of the new, multidisciplinary fields, are to remain the chief innovators of society. This is a subject to which we shall return in the next section.

To my mind there are two essential requirements for the proper cultivation of futures thinking in the universities. Firstly there is a quite general need to encourage a more prospective approach in many subjects and faculties, in law and in education, in technology and in social studies. Too often it is assumed that tomorrow will be a slight modification of today and that tomorrow's teaching will be only marginally different from the present. In most subjects this is simply no longer true. The change to a more prospective approach is bound to be slow, but it will be forced into being by external events, public opinion and the demands of new cohorts of students. It could also be accelerated greatly in universities where there are lively centres for futures research which involve in their work colleagues from many departments and disciplines on an *ad hoc* basis.

The second and more difficult requirement is for the creation of centres that will undertake serious research on the future, developing methodology, bringing in all the necessary disciplines, and having intimate contact with the users of its work—decision makers in industry and politics. It is not possible to give any generalized opinion as to where in present university structures such a unit should be placed. This will be different in different cases and will often be determined by the vision and enthusiasm of individuals drawn to the field, from whatever department. At times the futures unit will be associated with policy research or international affairs; often already they are offshoots of an economics department; they may develop within science policy units—another multidisciplinary subject—or, if the impulse is essentially social, they may be under the dean of social sciences; again, they may well be found within new groups for systems studies, or arise from computer science. The location matters little, as does the diversity of titles which such units may invent. What is essential is that they be broadly based, genuinely multidisciplinary, and with relations throughout the relevant departments of the university.

ARE DISCIPLINES REALLY NECESSARY?

The present structures of education and of research, into which the new multidisciplinary subjects fit with difficulty, were historically determined by the classification of knowledge which crystallized in the middle of the last century when, especially through the gaining of new knowledge by experiment, specialization became inevitable and the scholar could no longer claim familiarity and authority across the whole field of learning. In the universities and elsewhere, science is still taught in terms of the disciplines laid down then—neat little boxes marked chemistry, physics, geology, botany, etc., which long appeared to be self-contained and practical, although the relationships between the disciplines were always appreciated. As the content of each of these boxes filled up, sub-classifications had to be devised, such as physical, organic and inorganic chemistry, which through specialization tended to become isolated from each other. Later, interface subjects such as biochemistry and geophysics began to appear and to find their importance, both intellectually and through their applications. In some cases the lines of demarcation became very diffuse. I still find it difficult to distinguish between physical chemistry and chemical physics, for example, and this tinge of sectarianism is still more marked in the social sciences where, for example, social anthropology, social psychology and sociology appear, at least from outside, to be distinguished more in the sense of orientation than of fundamental discipline.

With the expansion of research and the fine-structuring of specialization, still more complicated intersectional subjects began to appear in both pure and applied science, such as molecular biology or cybernetics and also fields essentially based on a particular methodology or set of techniques such as systems analysis. Finally, and more recently, less clearly defined fields of growth have been emerging, including futures research, policy research and other topics of a high degree of transdisciplinarity and no longer at the well-defined interfaces of a static two-dimensional or three-dimensional model. One such case with which I have recently had some concern is the study of brain and behaviour which lies at the point of convergence of a number of non-contiguous disciplines including molecular biology, neurophysiology, biochemistry, psychiatry, etc. Another such field is the intellectual background behind computer and information science, with its mix of mathematics, logic, information theory and linguistics.

With such new fields of investigation, the simple box classification of knowledge seems as irrelevant as the early Bohr models of the atom in an age of wave mechanics. Yet, as already stated, our university and research structures still operate on the early simplicist model which makes the exploration of the newer multidisciplinary fields difficult.

I therefore take the opportunity of this discussion of futures research as a discipline to raise the question of whether the time is now ripe for the classification of the sciences to be reassessed, with the structural and conceptual consequences which this would entail. The growing understanding of the linkages and interactions of the problems facing society, as well as of the linkages and interactions between the diverse fields of learning and approaches to the discovery of new knowledge, suggests the need to adopt a holistic and dynamic approach: in some sense a return to the reality of the unity of all knowledge. The newer interdisciplinary subjects such as that of our present concern should be regarded, perhaps, not as new and discrete disciplines but as foci of advancing knowledge, temporary subjects which can be consolidated only by contributions from many other fields and many techniques. They will later extend, by mergers with other approaches from equally transient points in the advancement of knowledge, to create new and probably equally temporary outposts on the frontiers of understanding, within which the forces of science will assemble for still deeper penetration into the unknown, including the unknown future. How can the institutions of research and learning be restructured in terms of the unity of knowledge and the dynamic nature of the evolution of science? Such restructuring is not merely a conceptual but a practical necessity.

Discussion

Valaskakis: The prophylactic approach that you are talking about, Dr King, is a useful one as long as it is not the only approach used. What it implies—and this is apparent in the first two reports to the Club of Rome[1,2]—is a sort of pathological model of society where we identify the bottlenecks and the negative aspects of society when the system actually breaks down. This pathological model is useful but in future Club of Rome activities (if not in the fourth or the fifth report then in subsequent reports to the Club of Rome) I would suggest that a positive reformulation of the world *problèmatique* should be attempted, where *opportunities* would be identified instead of bottlenecks. In other words what I am advocating is an eventual definition of *health* in society. This definition should precede the pathological findings. To achieve this I think a page could be borrowed from the French '*Prospective*' movement which distinguishes between two types of scenario. (The French 'Prospective' movement is concerned with the scientific investigation of the future and uses the scenario approach to define alternative contrasting futures.) One kind is the *projective* scenario which starts from the present situation and develops into the future. The other is a completely different type called the *horizon* scenario which starts with a future situation and returns to the present. If the return to the present is impossible, we still have a horizon scenario that is desirable but not feasible. The intellectual exercise at least provides us with a model of what we want and cannot have. What concerns me is that futures studies, almost everywhere, tend to be too overwhelmed by feasibility, and therefore too constrained by the present. What we end up studying, implicitly or explicitly—and I think this is true of the first and second reports to the Club of Rome[1,2]—is the 'future of the present' or in other words the future of the *status quo*, whether the *status quo* has lasted twenty years, fifty years or two hundred years. My plea then is for more *horizon* scenarios to reformulate problems and situations in a new light. The dominance of the projective scenario must be resisted.

King: I am in full agreement. The second Club of Rome report has already gone a little in that direction. Mesarovic and Pestel[2] are not considering the faults in the present system; they are providing scenarios, to indicate which alternative decision might represent the most desirable situation.

Waddington: Horizon scenarios, or normative scenarios, in which one tries to formulate the ends one wants to reach, really make better sense when certain value systems in the present can be identified which could define those required ends. But if one starts by being totally disconnected from the present, which has nothing to do with the projection, then I think one gets pretty unrealistic. If we connect ourselves, not to present circumstances but to some present value system, we may make a projection which has more realism.

Ziman: Dr King and Professor Lundberg quite rightly want to put inter-disciplinarity into the university, but the word 'discipline' suggests a serious scholarly approach—something that is not done in one's spare time. Of course such work is also done in people's spare time; but the term really implies a completeness of attention and professionalism that will produce valuable results. Anything less is scarcely worth the effort. Our experience in science, overall, is that we must do things thoroughly and wholeheartedly: scientific problems are difficult and are not solved by good intentions.

Now why do people work at their disciplines? What makes them serious? There are really two reasons. One reason, in the context of the discipline, is that people are exercising their scholarship in public. They are putting something before their colleagues, who are going to be so critical that they have to be exactly right. This is the German scholarly tradition, and an excellent technique for getting first-class work. But I am quite sure that it is not the way you want futures studies to go. That approach leads in the end to *academicism* directed towards the solution of artificial problems, within the paradigm of a particular group of scholars but lacking external reference. It is important to emphasize the other incentive towards getting it right, which is to have to solve a real problem. That is the *practical* reason for doing good work. For example, the radar development that was needed in the 1939–1945 war forced people to give of their best: they had to get it right for quite different reasons from scholarly ones. I don't see how you can get the universities involved and active in futures studies unless that very strong practical aspect is given adequate weight. Without it these studies will inevitably degenerate into yet another manifestation of scholasticism.

King: We do not need a lot of isolated scholasticism but we do need serious studies, for example on the elaboration of new methodologies for what I would call probing the future rather than forecasting it. Very few institutions outside the universities are capable of doing this. On the other hand the coupling of futures studies with real-life problems, with policy-making, decision-making and so on, is difficult to achieve, and possibly it cannot be done directly between the average university, particularly those in the Latin countries, and the decision makers. It is not a black and white picture. We need both approaches.

Ziman: What would be the criteria of success, in a particular study, in a particular university, by a particular group or scholar?

Waddington: In operational research during the war we were modelling systems, and advising executives to issue certain orders on the basis of the model. Then we really had to find some facts very quickly, by observing what the results of those orders were. It was P. M. S. Blackett who really invented the whole operational research idea, and he emphasized that it had to be a short-term alternation, between model-making, and observation with empirical factual data. This is what we so far lack in futures study. The Club of Rome has no feedback on what actually happens when action is taken on the basis of its analysis, and it is difficult to see how the Club can get that feedback.

Ziman: In wartime operational research, you could take action—try something out, see what happened. We carried on with our model just long enough, or far enough ahead, to get something from which we could get a factual feedback.

Oldfield: My thinking at the outset is impeded by what I suppose is an elementary worry. When we look at the past, we see that all our research is ultimately academic, and the only thing we can alter directly is our perception of what happened. When we look at the future, study and research is in a fundamental sense non-academic, because we can in theory alter both perception and experience. This shift of mode, if I can call it that, often seems to be disguised, in writing and in speaking, by an illusion of the continuity and comparability of positive evaluation as we move from past to present to future. Has everybody else grown beyond this rather naive worry, and does it matter?

Waddington: I think this is one way of seeing the same problem. It is so difficult to get any factual feedback. In considering the future only fifty years ahead, we ought to be able to consider a gradual passage into the future, and we ought to be able to get some feedback from this. But it is difficult to see how to do it in many of these contexts.

Dror: There is an intellectual difference. Operational research is mainly oriented towards concrete decisions, while part of futures research is oriented towards what Sir Geoffrey Vickers calls 'educating the appreciative systems of the decision makers'.[4] So, broad educational effects should also be among the main targets of futures studies.

King: That is true. In the Club of Rome context our main approach is to talk to the decision makers and probe their concepts.

Platt: There is an area here which I think needs a new disciplinary base, a new theoretical base. That area is the nature of scientific inference when one is dealing with a complex ongoing flow system, where one cannot test to destruction—that is, one cannot cut off the child's protein if one wants to find the effects of protein on the brain. What we need is what I call 'green-thumb inference', the kind of inference that the woman taking care of her plants makes when she moves the plant into the sun. She does not make a physicist's measurements, by cutting off all the water, but instead she looks for a few little signals that show her whether there is too much sun or too little sun, or she puts a little water or plant food on it, and then watches for small indicators in the ongoing flow system.

In operations research, the anti-submarine warfare in World War II[5] was one of the best formal examples so far of this kind of ongoing process. We cannot stop the submarine chase that is going on, using the old methods, in order to test our theories about new methods. We have to continue with the old methods but make use of small fluctuations and small test operations if we want to infer the important variables underneath. I think we need to formalize this green-thumb inference method, or step-by-step bootstrap method of knowledge and control, if we are to understand or have any cybernetic guidance of society. The cybernetic ongoing understanding of the future is collecting as we go, and this cumulative process needs a formal theoretical analysis that has not been done yet.

Woodroofe: Is this really a new concept? Isn't economics based on observations of systems whose conditions the economists cannot control? Many so-called laws of economics have been postulated but lots of these laws have now been shown to be wrong. Conditions have changed.

Platt: That is why I think economics is a bad example of a way of acquiring futures-controlled knowledge. Economists have never learned from their failures.

Waddington: The balance sheet was useful in the past as a flow check-up but it is beginning to be inadequate, and anyway it only covers certain aspects of what happens.

Lundberg: In my opinion Dr King took a too pessimistic view with regard to the universities. We cannot destroy the present system with specialized disciplines, since they are needed in both teaching and research. But the universities may not be so inflexible as some of you seem to believe. We have to find ways of supporting forces within the university which can contribute to a renewal and this is better done with the carrot than with the stick. One of the problems is the present career structure. At present young research workers who move outside the central line of accepted disciplines are almost excluded from a future academic career. We must find ways of encouraging and supporting young research workers who want to devote themselves to the urgent problems of mankind. Financial support from special research councils devoted to future problems is one possibility.

Shane: Among the things that we rarely confront when we think about the roles of such organizations as the Club of Rome are some of the problems of multinational corporations. For example, until two or three years ago American oil companies were doing what the Arabs have been doing more recently—although without having it as widely known. When oil cost 16 cents a barrel, oil companies maintained the price at $1.75, and it cost American taxpayers nearly $5000 million in depletion allowances and about $3500 million in profits, sums that many would consider far too high. We also have the problem that many of the socioeconomically privileged in developing countries, the owners and rulers at the top of the pyramid, have more in common with the élite groups in other countries than they have with their own people. This has led to serious abuses. For instance, cash crops have been preferred in developing countries to food crops, with the present disastrous results in a period of famine. One cannot but wonder whether groups like the Club of Rome should endeavour to turn our universities into arenas for the debate of such problems rather than let them remain the cloisters for debate that many are now.

Waddington: We had better discuss this again later. This comes back to the question of should the universities teach their students something about these matters.

King: I was of course exaggerating in my remarks about university disciplines. I would not want to stop teaching of chemistry or pathology or any other discipline. But I think that fairly radical changes are required even to get the minimal necessary amount of transdisciplinary development.

References cited

1 MEADOWS, DONELLA H., MEADOWS, DENNIS L., RANDERS, JØRGEN & BEHRENS, WILLIAM W., III (1972) *The Limits to Growth*, Universe, New York; Earth Island, London
2 MESAROVIC, MIHAJLO & PESTEL, EDUARD (1974) *Mankind at the Turning Point*, Dutton/ Reader's Digest, New York; Hutchinson, London
3 ROYAL MINISTRY FOR FOREIGN AFFAIRS AND THE SECRETARIAT FOR FUTURE STUDIES (1974) *To Choose a Future*, Norstedt, Stockholm
4 VICKERS, SIR GEOFFREY (1965) *Art of Judgment*, Chapman & Hall, London
5 WADDINGTON, C. H. (1974) *Operational Research in World War II*, Elek, London

A dragon or a pussy cat? Two views of human knowledge

F. R. JEVONS

Department of Liberal Studies in Science, University of Manchester

Abstract Knowledge-handling institutions should be organized in a way that takes due account of the nature of knowledge. The basic question concerns the limits within which knowledge might change as societies change. Is it adaptable to our collective will? Or is it objective and impervious to human actions and wishes?

The writings of Popper and Kuhn help to throw some light on this question. With them as background, two current debates are examined. It is concluded that new knowledge systems will be alternatives within science rather than alternatives to science; and that technology is not completely socially determined but has a measure of autonomy.

It is important not to underrate the importance of the constraints set by what is externally 'given'. A dogmatic element in education seems to be an epistemological necessity. The implications for the organization and power structures of universities are not as conservative as they seem at first sight. 'Cliff effects' in the social distribution of expertise should be avoided.

I am not very ashamed to admit that I get very confused by those bits of the literature on the future which I have read. Quite apart from the undeniable possibility that literally anything *might* happen, there are such diverse views of where we *want* to go, and authors are not always careful to consider critically the basic aims of the societies they envisage.

Thus William Leiss[1] takes Bacon to task for implicitly equating scientific with social progress. Certainly I agree that the desirability of 'the effecting of all things possible' (Bacon[2]) is not self-evident. But Leiss's own criterion of social progress seems to be 'the abatement of social conflict', and although that sounds fine, it is not self-evident to me that it will automatically lead to, or is even compatible with, some other aims which also sound fine, such as the enlarging of consciousness, or human achievement in various other directions. The argument of *Report from Iron Mountain*[3] about the non-military functions of war and threat of war cannot be dismissed out of hand.

Then again, some people want technology to supply material goods and services in such copious abundance that we can use them with careless abandon and concentrate our efforts on higher things; while others, struck with the finiteness of the earth's resources, regard that attitude as like that of a man falling from the top of the Empire State Building and saying 'all right so far'. To David Dickson, in his book on *Alternative Technology*,[4] it seems to come as a matter for pained surprise that liberty and equality might not necessarily go hand in hand; whereas in practice, I usually see those two sitting on *opposite* sides of the negotiating table, and the formulas that finally emerge containing trade-offs between them.

It is against the background of such radical uncertainty about the direction of change that I want to consider the nature of that powerful agent of change, knowledge; and I do this with a very pragmatic purpose in mind. It seems important for knowledge-handling institutions to consider what kind of commodity it is they deal with, for on this depends the appropriate mode of operation and organizational style for them to adopt. Just as a cut-price grocery store is not likely to flourish if it adopts the same mode and style as a public electricity undertaking, so universities and other educational institutions are most likely to succeed if they structure themselves to take due account of the nature of the knowledge they handle. The theory of knowledge thus takes on a direct practical relevance; epistemology becomes too important to be left to philosophers.

LIMITS TO CHANGE IN KNOWLEDGE

Perhaps the most basic question to ask is: how far is knowledge adaptable to our collective will? Within what limits can it change as society changes? This is the question posed in picturesque terms by Feyerabend[5] in a passage from which I take the title of this article. Feyerabend says he prefers 'an enterprise whose human character can be seen by all... to one that looks "objective", and impervious to human actions and wishes. The sciences, after all, are our own creation...' Adopting this view, he says, 'changes science from a stern and demanding mistress into an attractive and yielding courtesan who tries to anticipate every wish of her lover. Of course, it is up to us to choose either a dragon or a pussy cat for our company. I do not think I need to explain my own preferences'.*

Pussy cat knowledge, in other words, is relativist: it is formed according to circumstances, which vary from place to place, and from time to time, and from

---

* In asserting that it is up to us, Feyerabend begs the question and, as I hope to show in this article, falls into his own trap.

society to society; it is not dictated by what is 'given' externally to human beings or societies. It is socially constructed, not imposed by outside authority. What an attractive view this seems! We are promised the kind of knowledge system we want. We are offered the opportunity to change it at will. Whatever kind of society we may in the future decide we want, we can have a knowledge system to fit it.

The modern relativist movement derives sustenance from the charismatic book by Kuhn on *The Structure of Scientific Revolutions*,[6] which in a mere thirteen years since it was first published in 1962 has become remarkably influential. Kuhn emphasizes that we cannot see uninterpreted facts of nature; we can only see nature through the spectacles of one paradigm or another.* Different paradigms or conceptual frameworks represent different commitments and, in the extreme interpretation, they are incommensurable, so that there are no standards by which we can say that one is better than another, except for standards based on our tastes and preferences.

I think this won't quite do. True, we can't know truth as such, or at least we can't be certain we know truth as such: all scientific knowledge is conjectural. But this does not mean that objective truth does not exist or that it has no bearing on our knowledge systems. Objective truth is the ideal we aim at, even though it is impossible to achieve, or at least impossible to be certain that it has been achieved. This view of truth is one of the deceptively simple, brilliant insights which can be retrieved from the exasperating thornbush of Popper's writings. Popper asks us to realize that 'all of us may and often do err, singly and collectively, but that this very idea of error and human fallibility involves another—the idea of objective truth: the standard which we may fall short of'.[9]

There is here a severe and salutary limitation on knowledge. Without having to fall back on a simplistically sharp distinction between facts and values, it offers a solution to the problem of the place of facts in a world of values, which seems a more pressing problem than that of the place of values in a world of facts.[10] Knowledge is seen not to be a *totally* human creation.† I take the scientific enterprise to be essentially the invention of regularities which more or less fit nature. Scientific knowledge is therefore bilaterally determined: the invention must be a human act but the fit depends also on what is 'given' externally to us in nature.

With this as background, let me now turn to somewhat less abstract matters

---

* For brief treatments of Kuhn and the Popper-Kuhn controversy, see Sklair[7] and Jevons.[8]
† I cannot therefore agree with Johnston,[11] whose reading of Kuhn enables him to see a 'bright gleam of hope' in the recognition that knowledge is 'a totally human product'. Cf. p. 59n†.

by tackling two questions which have cropped up in the literature recently. They are more closely related than may at first sight appear. One concerns the possibility of new and alternative knowledge systems; the other concerns the autonomy of technology.

ALTERNATIVE KNOWLEDGE SYSTEMS

It has been suggested that the urge to conquer and exploit nature extends itself to the urge to conquer and exploit man:[1] that the Baconian urge, if you like, inevitably turns into the Faustian. How far the link between the two kinds of exploitation is an essential one, and how far it is only a contingent combination, seems to me to be an open question: surely the wage slaves of industrial society are not more grossly exploited than were the domestic slaves of the ancient civilizations. But be that as it may, there are those who believe there is a connection and, being anxious to see an end to the domination of man by man, look for less domineering knowledge systems to go with less oppressive social patterns. Anti-science is once again quite fashionable. Blame for defects in modern societies should be attached, it is suggested, not to misuse of science but to the nature of the science itself.* Western science has, after all, been practised for a mere three or four centuries; perhaps mankind has not tried hard enough to test alternatives such as might be found, for instance, in Taoism or Zen.

I remain somewhat sceptical of these efforts. Those who complain of the domineering ways of the western scientific–technological mode are upset, I suspect, not so much by the fact of domination as by the crudity and messiness of the means of domination that have been used up to now. It is all very well to talk of living in harmony with nature instead of trying to dominate it, but do we really want that to extend to a policy of non-interference with the typhoid and cholera organisms? We should not confuse the wish for subtler and less obtrusive means of control with the suggestion that helplessness might be a virtue in itself. Persuasion may be a subtler means of control than command, but it is a means of control nevertheless.

The conquest of our physical environment does not inevitably lead to a better society, but better societies do surely depend on having power to control nature. The idea that technology is intrinsically bad is, I think, intrinsically absurd. What is bad is bad technology. *Absence* of technology would mean that we were evincing an incomprehending, blind helplessness in our material environment, and that cannot be better than wise use based on understanding.

Alternative knowledge systems will be evaluated according to the same ul-

* Calls for an 'African chemistry'[12] or a 'truly Indian science'[13] rest on analogous, though less extreme, assumptions.

timate criterion as scientific theories: do they work?* It is not a defence of science's current repertoire of theories and effects, which is indubitably imperfect and incomplete, to claim that science, regarded as the invention of regularities which fit nature, is a uniquely successful knowledge system. Its monopolistic position seems unchallengeable. Knowledge that works must be based on regularities, and regularities give power to control.† If some practice from African witchcraft turns out to work in alleviating disease—perhaps because, as Horton suggests,[15] it rests on analysis of social stresses instead of mechanical use of drugs—then it does not replace science but is incorporated into it. It becomes, not an alternative, but an addition to science. We have alternatives *within* science—for instance, different sources of energy and different ways of controlling insect pests—but new alternatives do not become alternatives *to* science as long as the current corpus of science does not become totally impermeable to novelty. And although science is assuredly not an entirely open-minded enterprise, neither are the paradigmatic blinkers completely effective in keeping out new viewpoints; not even the most ardent follower of Kuhn has been able to draw *that* interpretation out of history.

THE AUTONOMY OF TECHNOLOGY

It has recently become fashionable to insist that technology is not autonomous or neutral but that it is socially or politically determined. Thus Seymour Melman[16] criticises 'the myth of autonomous technology' and Dickson[4] makes a similar attack on 'the myth of the political neutrality of technology'.

Of course it is true that a society's technology to a substantial extent reflects its preferences and priorities. If, as Melman says,[16] more than half the research and development engineers and scientists of the United States functioned on behalf of defence, space and atomic energy agencies during the 1950s and 1960s, it is no wonder that American technology matches the needs of those agencies. But the match is never complete or perfect. If it were, technology would be the ideal slave: one that does exactly what his master (society) desires, and does nothing else at all. Such an ideal slave does not, unfortunately, exist. Melman says that each machine has built into it 'the particular requirement of whoever decides its characteristics and the uses it must serve'. That is so, but the characteristics are not *exhaustively* described by user specifications. Melman calls it

---

* There may be a wide variety of aims. If Zen works in producing certain states of consciousness, it can be regarded as a sophisticated behavioural technology. Moreover, theories need not work in the sense that a simple causal theory works; structure and process theories, for instance also 'work' in their own ways.[14]

† Not unlimited power, of course. Knowledge of the regularities of planetary motions does not enable us to control the motions.

'a distortion of understanding' to make technology 'appear as though independent of man's will'. But it is equally a distortion of understanding to deny that
technology is *partly* independent of man's will.

The social determinist view of technology is a misleading half-truth because
it fails to take due account of two things. First, it ignores those effects of technology which are either not foreseen or not desired or both. Such effects cannot be determined by any individual or group, except in some stretched sense.
The effects of DDT on bird populations can hardly have been politically determined; nor, I imagine, was it part of the social function—whether manifest
or latent—of the development of transistors to force pop music on those who
dislike it.

Second, the social determinist view is based on inadequate appreciation of
technology as a range of capabilities which goes beyond those which are actually
used in any period of time.* One of the examples Dickson[4] uses to show the
non-neutrality of technology is the telephone system. The system as we have
it, he says, reflects the 'individualistic' nature of our society because it is designed for communication between two individuals rather than for group discussions. But to adapt the system for group use is easy: the technology is almost
identical. The way we use the technology is of course determined by social
preferences, but the range of capabilities is not.

Let me take another example: the stabilized world envisaged in *The Limits
to Growth* by Meadows *et al.*[19] It is a world full of technology: stability was
achieved in the computer runs only with a lot of resource recycling, pollution
control and restoration of eroded and infertile soil. The argument in the book
is not that technology is dispensable but that technology by itself is not enough.
What kind of technology would be needed to help to stabilize the world?
Many of the particular devices would doubtless differ from those now in use,
but they would unavoidably rely on largely the same principles and components
and skills. Much the same underlying know-how and hardware can serve both
the god of growth and the fad for zero growth.

I conclude that technology does have a substantial measure of autonomy
from the kind of society which uses it. In an important sense it is politically

---

* Ambiguities inevitably arise from different definitions of technology. Some definitions see
it as a capability; for instance, Schon defines it as 'any tool or technique, any product or
process, any physical equipment or method of doing or making, by which human capability
is extended'.[17] Others see it as a process in action; for instance, Galbraith defines it as 'the
systematic application of scientific or other organised knowledge to practical tasks'.[18] Both
etymology and current usage favour the first type of meaning: etymology because *logos* means
discourse, so that technology means knowledge about technique, not the act of applying it;
and usage because we talk about technological capabilities—about technologies being available—irrespective of whether they are actually being used.

neutral and culture-independent. In so far as it is based on regularities in the physical world, in which we all have to live, it transcends social change. By its use of the most rigid inflexibilities of nature—those revealed by physical science—technology gives the greatest flexibility for social action.*

The fundamental issue is the degree of malleability or plasticity of knowledge. To take a totally social determinist view of technology would be 'relativist'; it would extend to the material world the implications of a relativist view of knowledge for the intellectual world.† I have argued that such a view of technology is misleading because technology is not determined entirely by society but has some life of its own, some properties which are not voluntarily put into it. We cannot pretend that it is created entirely according to our wishes; although we can try to change it in the long run, we must for the time being accept it for what it is.‡

COMING TO TERMS WITH THE DRAGONS

The common feature I have tried to draw out of the two issues—alternative knowledge systems and the autonomy of technology—is the importance, as a constraint on knowledge, of what is 'given' externally to us and stops us from moulding our knowledge systems to our taste.§ Knowledge, in other words, has a dragon element as well as a pussy cat element. Personally, I am not too unhappy about that conclusion. Unlike Feyerabend,[5] apparently, I am not too fond of cats, and I think dragons could be rather useful if we can get them on

---

* The separation between a capability and the decision to use it has another important consequence, which is obscured by failure to recognize the separation. Abuse-proof technology is a chimera. The appeal of sun and wind as energy sources is enhanced for Clarke[20] by the apparent difficulty of using them for military purposes: 'it is not easy to envisage what a solar bomb or a wind-powered missile would be like'. But Archimedes, according to the story, set fire to the enemy ships with burning mirrors. Man's inhumanity to man is not dependent on high technology; one can kill, maim and torture with the simplest technical means. However specifically a pitch-fork is designed to pitch hay, it can also be used to attack a neighbour; and ordinary workmen's tools will do to pull out toenails or to cut out tongues. This illustrates once again that technology is at the disposal of alternative political arrangements and value systems. It follows that technology is an inadequate moral scapegoat for the shortcomings of modern societies. As a converse of the fact that technology is partly independent of man's will, man's actions also remain partly independent of the technology he uses. Social choices about developing technology do not eliminate options for further choices about using it.
† Melman says 'only man, in fact, designs and shapes every particular technology'.[16] I cannot accept the 'only', for the same reason that I do not accept the 'totally' on p. 55n†.
‡ If you fail to recognize this, you must prefer Lysenko's genetics, which promises to develop new cereal varieties with preplanned characteristics in $2\frac{1}{2}$ years, to Vavilov's genetics, according to which it will take much longer.[21]
§ Even human creations, once they have been created, become part of the 'given'; short of complete collective amnesia, an item of knowledge is 'there' and cannot be wished away any more than can the Atlantic Ocean.

our side. The problem is how to make sure that they are on our side—remembering that, being to a degree autonomous, they will not automatically side with us, as they would if they were entirely creatures of our will.

Dragon-like knowledge to some extent dictates to us how it is to be handled. That is one of the things about it which is 'given' and independent of our wishes. The most important implication, as I see it, is that students are well advised to put up with a certain amount of dogmatism from their teachers because there is accumulated experience to learn from which will help to give expertise.

The notion of accumulated experience is contained in the epistemologies of both Popper and Kuhn, though in different forms and in each case in a somewhat backhanded way. In the Popperian scheme, although the supreme commandment is to be critical and to try to overthrow theories, it is nevertheless the case that the current corpus of knowledge is the result of a long process of evolution by trial-and-error and by learning from mistakes. The sub-title of Popper's book *Objective Knowledge* is 'an evolutionary approach'.[22] Modern knowledge contains the fruits of much hard-won experience, in the same way that modern living organisms embody the results of learning from a long series of evolutionary mistakes.

In Kuhn's view, although it is questionable whether the succession of paradigms is cumulative, the power to solve problems which an established paradigm gives is acquired by *accepting* the ground rules which the paradigm defines and the mode of approach which it dictates. 'A more efficient mode of scientific practice begins' says Kuhn, when a group of workers 'take the foundations of their field for granted'.[6] Education therefore must have something of the character of an initiation into problem-solving traditions. A dogmatic element in education seems to be an epistemological necessity. The epistemological price students have to pay is to recognize that their active participation cannot extend to the creation and criticism of all the theories and conceptual frameworks to be used.[23]

The consequences for university practice are that student-centredness has to be tempered with subject-centredness, and participatory learning–teaching styles with the recognition that there are some things about which teachers do on average know more than students. If we ask what it is about universities that makes us feel that, if they did not exist, we would have to invent them, the answer must surely include making the experience of the past available to the present for the sake of the future. The function of education, it is said, is to let the young learn from the mistakes of others instead of, more painfully, from their own; and that is just what Popper's evolutionary theory of knowledge amounts to, in much-enriched form.

There are implications also for power structures and patterns of control in universities. Sociologists of education are only half right when they say that what counts as valid educational knowledge is socially defined by those who hold power in the educational system—by the 'politics of the curriculum', in short.[24, 25] The reverse also holds: the appropriate distribution of power and social control reflects the nature of the knowledge being handled. Simple vice versa fantasies* about student control should therefore be resisted on epistemological grounds.

This sounds like a very conservative position. Is my appeal to accumulated experience just the time-honoured reactionary cry of those who resist innovation? Far from it, for two reasons. First, the argument is emphatically not an argument for no change. Rather, it concerns the type of change needed—which should be thought of, I suggest, as being a process of redirecting knowledge that already exists as much as it is a process of finding substitutes for it. Those are two very different matters; the strategy and tactics appropriate for redeployment are different to those required for replacement. Over-emphasis on replacement, which could be implied by calls for new knowledge systems, would reduce what is available for redeployment.

Second, I am not suggesting that all knowledge is of the dragon type. I have chosen here to emphasize the dragons,† but that does not entail forgetting about the pussy cats. There are aspects of knowledge where continual re-creation is as important as drawing on accumulated experience. Here the knowledge of the young compares favourably with that of their elders, and students can learn as much from each other as from their teachers; one of the best things a teacher can do is to adopt a fellow-student role and periodically to admit defeat in an argument.‡

For understandable reasons, this kind of educational experience is becoming more popular with students. Pussy cats have a more immediate appeal for many people than dragons. It would therefore be all too easy, in the expansion of educational provision, to leave things increasingly to the pussy cats. Society, it might be argued, does not need dragon-handlers in large numbers; a few engineers and technocrats are enough to keep the wheels turning, leaving

---

* The allusion is to the novel by Anstey[26] in which father and son swap roles.

† I have argued here for the dragon-like element in science and technology, where it is easiest to show, but there is such an element in most areas. For painting, Gombrich explicitly compares 'the rhythm of schema and correction' in the processes of perception and representation with Popper's philosophy of science.[27] Nevertheless, differences between subjects should not be obscured. The epistemological egalitarianism of Young[28] is ill-founded, as I have argued elsewhere.[23]

‡ He should also try unobtrusively to raise the level of discussion. The formation of value systems and the definition of social goals is not *only* a matter of taste and commitment beyond the reach of critical discussion. There are often inconsistencies and incompatibilities which can be exposed.

the rest of the population free to cultivate aesthetics or athletics or whatever takes their fancy.

Far be it from me to suggest that all students should be funnelled into the technocratic rat-race; but I would like to suggest that, unless we are careful, we might end up with an undesirable distribution of expertise through society. We should try to avoid what I would like to call 'cliff effects'—abrupt discontinuities in the level of expertise.* For experts isolated in their little islands of expertise it is all too easy to convince themselves and even others that choices are technologically dictated. It is not surprising if nuclear engineers regard the desirability of nuclear power stations as obvious. What should be options become disguised as imperatives, and that leads to the one-dimensionality that Marcuse[30] complains of.†

So I would like to see the contours of expertise widely spaced, and dragon-handling capacities diffused through society. I don't see how we can otherwise get the networks of overlapping competences necessary for pluralistic interests to be genuinely represented in the setting of social goals, and for expertise to be made or kept genuinely accountable to the wider public. For that reason, among others, I hope that the dragons will not be forgotten as education expands.

ACKNOWLEDGEMENTS

I owe much to stimulating discussions with Dr R. D. Johnston and other colleagues in the Department of Liberal Studies in Science.

Discussion

Black: There seems increasing reluctance to learn the factual basis of a subject, and we often forget that until we have this information we can't talk about it or make any useful progress. However, disciplines and subjects are man-made groupings, for the convenience of study, and if their existence creates intellectual blinkers they must have a marked effect on the ability of universities to accept innovation. From an epistemological point of view I think they may be basically irrelevant.

---

* An extreme discontinuity is that between the Morlocks and the Eloi in Wells' novel *The Time Machine*.[29]

† To accept the justification for this complaint is not to fall for Marcuse's confidence trick about 'true' and 'false' consciousness. All consciousnesses are influenced by social environment; it is difficult to see how one could judge what 'true' consciousness would result from the 'free development of human needs and faculties', because no consciousness uninfluenced by a social environment is available for questioning.

Eldredge: Professor Jevons, why don't you think that pure science leads technology? The results of pure science can be spun off in technologies but the 'engine' is pure science. $E=mc^2$!

Jevons: The notion of technology as just science which has been applied is much over-simplified. We have done a fair bit of work on this in Manchester. The metaphor that I think best represents the contribution made by science to technology is that science is not the mother of technology but nursemaid to it. It helps innovation to grow. It doesn't usually generate it, it is rarely the first impetus for industrial innovation, but it does help to overcome the difficulties that arise during the development of that innovation. When one tries to identify science inputs into industrial innovations, that is the kind of relationship that one finds.

Stewart: The progress of science and technology is an immensely complicated network in which pure science, applied science, development and exploitation each contribute to advance in the others. All parts of the system are essential.

Eldredge: Do you admit behavioural or societal technology as valid technologies, and if so what do you think of them?

Jevons: That seems too large a question to go into here.

Francis: How do you assess the comparatively recent tendency of people in the scientific community to become self-critical about the social dimensions of technology, Professor Jevons? This movement has achieved some significance in the United States. Barry Commoner, for example, has established a school of 'critical science', and he and people like him are closely linked with decisions of political and economic significance, such as the factors governing the introduction of supersonic transport. How much of this do you think is due to scientists waking up to the renewed possibility of being more directly involved in political processes? It is a dimension that even in our system of government in this country has been under-explored and under-exploited. In fact the scientist has traditionally been under-represented within the organs of government. The House of Commons Select Committee on Science and Technology has become the only open forum on questions of national science policy. Do you think that some movement in the UK will develop which is likely to correct that situation, even though these matters currently fall outside the framework of an orthodox training in science and engineering?

Dror: Before you answer that let me say something in the opposite direction to give you some more choice, Professor Jevons. Part of your dragon is in fact a paper dragon, but there may be a real or meta-dragon around. Most scientists are unable to handle policy questions because they are rather unsophisticated about policy matters. I would perhaps agree that the not too many scientists who are 'policy-sophisticated' don't play a sufficient role, but if the question is whether scientists as a whole are under-represented, I would say, rather, that they are sometimes over-influential. Many scientists are just not sufficiently in tune with the content, methods and climate of policy-making, and frequently they do more harm than good. So to move all of them into a different kind of symbiosis with knowledge and power requires, first of all, the re-education of scientists in policy-making. From this point of view I think that a lot of the scientists still need to meet the real dragon.

Jevons: I would half agree that scientists have been under-represented in policy-making but, bearing in mind your reservation about the different kinds of skills that are involved in the natural sciences, Dr Dror, I would re-emphasize the point I made at the end of my paper about the overlapping of areas of expertise. The 'dragon' kind of knowledge is by its nature more powerful than some other kinds of knowledge. It is knowledge that has proved its effectiveness in certain contexts and therefore carries certain kinds of power. These were emphasized in the 1960s when the science policy movement was at its height.

It almost seems sacrilege to say it in this company, but I sometimes wonder how much worse our current crisis is than crises that people have faced in the past. We heard earlier about the present 'crisis of crises'. As I look back in history, though, I am led to ask, when was the last period that did not have people who considered themselves to be going through a crisis?

Wilkins: In those previous situations, we weren't able to destroy practically all life.

Jevons: It would have needed more people to destroy nearly all the rest, certainly. Nuclear weapons have undoubtedly changed the situation drastically. But when has it been possible to take the future of mankind as guaranteed?

Woodroofe: In my experience, most scientists are not interested in policy areas. They are interested in their own specialization, and the cobbler wants to stick to his last.

Dror: I am not sure that we should always be sorry about this. Being a specialized scientist is often bad preparation for policy.

Valaskakis: You imply that technology is possibly a dragon because of the unanticipated consequences of technological decisions, Professor Jevons. I will take this argument further and imply that every human action has un-anticipated consequences. As the old Greek (or was it Chinese?) saying puts it, we should never call a man happy until he is dead, because all sorts of things may happen between now and his death to cancel previous evaluations. I am suggesting that in any kind of decision theory, in any kind of decision-making process, there is always a perpetual gamble. If you take this gamble too seriously you probably end up not making any decisions at all. An example may illustrate this idea: a friend of mine overslept one day and thereby missed a plane which was supposed to take him to an important business meeting. He subsequently felt very guilty and lazy until he found out the plane he was supposed to be on had crashed! This was an unanticipated consequence which righted what would hitherto have been a wrong move: oversleeping. What I am suggesting is that, if we accept the idea that whatever we do is a perpetual gamble, then why not forge ahead anyway? Of course we need a technology assessment, and prudence is a high virtue, but I am a little concerned about completely freezing technology because of its unanticipated consequences.

Jevons: I agree.

Valaskakis: So you agree that the dragon elements do not actually belong to technology alone but to almost any field of human endeavour, in different degrees of intensity?

Jevons: Yes, in the sense that in almost any field of human endeavour there are consequences which are unintended or unpredicted. The argument that technology has no autonomy seems to me to be very misleading because it suggests there are no consequences of technology other than those which are anticipated.

Valaskakis: What would your position be, for instance, if a wonder-drug was marketed to cure cancer if insufficient research had been done to assess its second and *n*-order consequences? Would you recommend forging ahead or would you recommend long and painful research for years? This is the sort of dilemma that a decision maker has to face every day. The dilemma in fact is as follows: if the wonder-drug is marketed, at best it will cure cancer; at worst it will both fail to cure cancer and at the same time generate unpleasant second-order consequences (as for instance in the thalidomide scandal where the drug caused the birth of deformed babies). If the wonder-drug is not used, a good twenty years may pass before the medical association or government declares it free of noxious second-order consequences. In the meantime many terminal patients who could have been saved have been left to die.

Jevons: There are already mechanisms for ensuring that a good deal of research is done on possible side-effects. But the dangers can never be reduced to zero.

Dror: This is not a scientific question but one about lottery values, a question about the evaluation of risks, or one value issue against another value issue.

Valaskakis: Risk can be mathematically computed. Uncertainty is a state of ignorance so great, in the technical sense, that no odds can be computed.

Dror: Whether you define the risks or not, choosing between alternative risks, including certainties, is a value issue.

Platt: I think Professor Jevons was saying that there are some subjects where teachers do know better than students. I am sure this is so, but you mustn't interpret teachers in this context as always being university professors or the ones at the front of the classroom. Increasingly, in a world of rapid change, we have found that it is the young assistant professor who knows the new biology and the old biologist who does not. Or it is the graduate student who does the top line research that informs the assistant professor. And frequently it is the first-year graduate student who has read the latest edition of the basic book who knows his subject better and hasn't mislearned or made the same mistakes that the older graduate student has.

In the last ten years, in the universities in the United States, it has been the students who insisted on environment and ecology courses, not the teachers. And it was the students who insisted on more black representation on the faculties, on more women's courses, and on a whole range of studies which had been neglected by the disciplinary professors. If I might go further, today a teenager knows more about how to repair a Suzuki than I do, and I need to go to him humbly as a student when I want to repair my motorbike. The eight-year-old girl may know more about hopscotch, and even the two- or three-year-old child may know more about laughter than I have forgotten, and I need to relearn it by sitting as a student beside that child.

In a healthy society, we all have our areas of expertise and we need to be mutually open to learning from each other. The old are learning from the young, and part of the meaning of the revolt today against the disciplinary professors is that the rest of society has its own expertise, its own values and its own knowledge which must be mixed in.

Jevons: You have given some splendid examples of overlapping fields of competence.

Ziman: I want to be a dragon's advocate here and breathe a little bit of fire and smoke over some futurology. The future only exists as a mental construct, an intellectual extrapolation of the present. This extrapolation is made uncertain by unpredicted or unpredictable events and these uncertainties multiply uncontrollably as time goes on, until the future becomes vague beyond comprehension. Even if, in some sphere of activity, we had a 'calculus of extrapolation' it could not model the whole future of the human race. The best calculus can model only one small aspect of the future and, therefore, can only make a prediction subject to the assumption that adjacent and related aspects do not change.

Yet we know that every aspect of life—natural, technical and social—has its characteristic 'transformation time', which I have tried to set out in this table of characteristic transformation times. For example, if you don't have food

Table 1 (Ziman)
Characteristic transformation times of various aspects of human affairs.

	"Natural"	Technical	Social
1 minute	Respiration	Accident Fire Traffic jam	Nuclear War Murder
1 hour	Cell Division Digestion	Cooking Flight	Riot Theft Repose Meeting
1 day	Storm Flood Illness	Food Garbage Voyage	Battle Revolution Foreign Exchange Conference
1 month	Starvation Epidemic Gestation	Manufacture	War Stock Exchange Commodity Market
1 year	Crop Infancy Bird Mammal	clothes Apparatus Car	Political Power Employment Education
10 years	Childhood Generation Human	Machine Factory Railway Furniture	Economic Growth Marriage Corporation Party
100 years	Tree Population Forest	House Canal Road City	National 　　Development Dynasty Church
1000 years	Landscape Climate	Irrigation 　　System Tomb	Language Culture
10,000 years	↓ Species		

for a month, you starve; you are *transformed*, in that length of time. A modern war takes from a few days to a month to resolve itself, so the situation has changed in that interval. A nuclear war takes a few minutes, so they say. The Stock Exchange changes over a period of months to the extent that one loses the feel for a 'trend'. The values suggested here are sheer guesswork, and we could argue about all sorts of details; but I think that most of them are within a factor of 10, one way or the other, of what anyone would write down about the characteristic time scale of actual events—the way we see the world, the rate at which things do change.

Mathematically speaking, it is impossible to make a reliable extrapolation for any *particular* aspect of the future over a time that is much longer than the transformation times of the *other* aspects to which it is connected. I am not saying here that you couldn't try to do it and make plausible-looking predictions. You might have a perfectly good calculus for discussing how the Stock Exchange is going to behave over a long time, in terms of Stock Exchange forces. But you are bound to bring into that calculus other features in the diagram—political decisions, changes of government, commodity prices, and various other economic and social factors—which would be beyond the predictive scope of the calculus. The unpredictable events or changes in these other aspects would introduce uncontrollable uncertainty into the attempt at extrapolation. You might think that you have a perfectly sound formula for the factors that you are explicitly predicting, but the statistical fluctuations in 'external' elements connected with your chosen aspect are going to force it into uncertainty. In the absence of a complete Laplacian prediction machine this is the fundamental limitation to all attempts at studying the future. The fire and smoke of the dragon are not to be sneezed at; these are the realities that one learns as a 'hard scientist' in the prediction game.

Dror: What are the possibilities for changing some of the longer time cycles through the social applications of modern technology, such as genetic engineering or climatological changes? Isn't it one of the problems that technology will change some of the nature-given time cycles?

Ziman: I am talking about a different problem. I am not talking about possible interactions between various 'aspects' or 'factors'; whatever we may achieve by conscious effort those events are eventually going to be dominated by other events beyond our control. If the climate cycle is changed by human intervention in, say, atmospheric circulation, does that mean that the sunspot cycle can be changed?

Dror: A 2 per cent change may be critical for human survival but not significant in the cosmic scale. We must put a subjective time interval into the calibration of times, as a focusing or prismatic device for seeing how a policy perspective differs from the point of view of some pure scientific interest.

Ziman: The technology for climate control will assume, for example, some sort of political stability for the whole of the earth, to maintain the enormous devices that would be needed to make it work over long periods. This is one of the great problems about nuclear power. As we look at history, we learn that a dynasty or a power system, a type of society, may only last a few hundred years.

Dror: That is more than enough for present policy purposes.

Ziman: Yes, but that is the limit. When you say you are going to predict something, and drive it through, you are going to have to overcome what might be called the inherent climatological correlation time, whether it is fifty or one hundred or five hundred years, by technical power and prediction. I insist that that is a purely intellectual construct, because there is inherent in your argument an assumption about stability in other factors which is not justified by any of the evidence that we have at the moment.

Platt: This is why *limit* calculations, as in *The Limits to Growth*,[19] can be so important. They may be absurd in terms of a small-scale structure, or extrapolation from the present; but if you see what you believe to be physical or biological limits, these give an overall shape, an overall size, to the bottle within which the other reactions and changes must take place. It is important to know where those limits are.

Shane: In 1973 I published a study of trends amongst futurists.[31] In the early 1960s much of the thinking that was being done was done on a linear basis. By the middle 1960s, the future had begun to be thought of as a fan-shaped phenomenon, with a number of alternative, probabilistic futures of the kind that we now anticipate. By the late 1960s students of the future had reached a point where they accepted the concept of cross-impact: the concept that what was going on in one field (e.g. holography or mood-influencing drugs) would, in the long run, have a substantial impact on, say, the methodology and the content of instruction in secondary schools. These trends are cumulative, of course: linear projections were not discarded. They all became tools for futures research. At present the emphasis, it seems to me, is on value decisions which have to do with how we cope with the different alternative futures that loom before us. Most futurists, in the United States at least, have become extremely chary of making any projections of the kinds that Kahn and Wiener made in the late 1960s,[32] because they have been inaccurate so many times.

Eldredge: You seem to think that the bottle of the universe has already been built, Dr Platt, but the bottle might conceivably be rebuilt if we interfered, at a sophisticated level, with reality. You also say that these things happen in time-sequences. If anybody happens to believe, as I do, that there may be a useful societal and behavioural technology, then that would change the whole framework of how decisions are made and speeded up. As a very soft scientist, I think you are mistaken in assuming that the bottle of natural things is completely fixed. I think we can 'mess about' with almost everything in the universe.

Platt: Let me give you an example of what I meant. American television sets are now turned on for six hours a day on the average—but if the human race lasts for a thousand or a million years people will not watch television, or any other representation of an external world, for sixty hours a day because there are limits—there aren't that many hours in the day. Similarly with such things as exploration of the globe—in the last forty years people have gone to the top of the highest mountain, the bottom of the deepest ocean, and lived at the North and South Pole with hot and cold running water and helicopter service. Today, satellites go around the globe every two hours, photographing things down to the size of a football. This means that the exploration of the globe is finished. We have come to the end of that particular bottle.

Eldredge: Who is left at the bottom of the great Atlantic trench? Do we know all about that?

Platt: No, but it is very different from the age in which Burton spent three years searching for the source of the Nile with a hundred porters and then didn't find it. The speed of light has limits, the earth has limits, sunlight has limits, life has limits; and it is useful to know approximately where these limits are before we reach them. The kinds of optimists who always say 'But we will invent new things beyond the limits!' are like people in a bus heading towards a cliff who do not try to turn the steering wheel but instead discuss how some day they can invent buses with wings. It may be true that they could do this, but it shows a lack of perception of the real-time, real-world operational limits.

References

1 LEISS, W. (1974) Utopia and technology: reflections on the conquest of nature, in *Man-Made Futures* (Cross, N., Elliott, D. & Roy, R., eds.) pp. 20–30, Hutchinson Educational, London

2 BACON, F. (1627) *New Atlantis*. Reprinted in Johnston, A. (ed.) (1965) *Francis Bacon*, pp. 161–181, Batsford, London

3 LEWIN, L. C. (introduced by) (1968) *Report from Iron Mountain on the Possibility and Desirability of Peace*, Penguin Books, Harmondsworth

4 DICKSON, D. (1974) *Alternative Technology and the Politics of Technical Change*, pp. 146, 178, 183, Fontana/Collins, Glasgow

5 FEYERABEND, P. K. (1970) Consolations for the specialist, in *Criticism and the Growth of Knowledge* (Lakatos, I. & Musgrave, A., eds.) pp. 197–230, Cambridge University Press, London

6 KUHN, T. S. (1970) *The Structure of Scientific Revolutions*, 2nd edition, p.178, Chicago University Press, Chicago

7 SKLAIR, L. (1973) *Organised Knowledge*, Hart-Davis, MacGibbon, London

8 JEVONS, F. R. (1973) *Science Observed: Science as a Social and Intellectual Activity*, Allen & Unwin, London

9 POPPER, K. R. (1965) *Conjectures and Refutations*, 2nd edition, p.16, Routledge and Kegan Paul, London

10 TISELIUS, A. & NILSSON, S. (eds.) (1971) *The Place of Value in a World of Facts (Nobel Symposium 14)*, Halsted Press/Wiley, Chichester

11 JOHNSTON, R. D. (1974) On scientific knowledge. *Times Higher Education Supplement*, 26 July, London

12 JEVONS, F. R. (1972) Chemistry in Africa. *Nature (London)*, 236, 92

13 REDDY, A. K. N. (1974) Is Indian science truly Indian? *Science Today*, pp. 13–24, January

14 ELIAS, N. (1974) The sciences: towards a theory, in *Social Processes of Scientific Development* (Whitley, R., ed.), pp. 21–42, Routledge & Kegan Paul, London

15 HORTON, R. (1971) African traditional thought and Western science, in *Knowledge and Control* (Young, M. F. D., ed.), pp. 208–266, Collier-Macmillan, London

16 MELMAN, S. (1974) The myth of autonomous technology, in *Man-Made Futures* (Cross, N., Elliott, D. & Roy, R., eds.), pp. 56–61, Heinemann Educational, London

17 SCHON, D. (1967) *Technology and Change*, p. 1, Pergamon Press, Oxford

18 GALBRAITH, J. K. (1969) *The New Industrial State*, p. 23, Penguin Books, Harmondsworth

19 MEADOWS, D. H., MEADOWS, D. L., RANDERS, J. & BEHRENS, W. W., III (1972) *The Limits to Growth*, Earth Island, London

20 CLARKE, R. (1974) Alternative technology, in *Man-Made Futures* (Cross, N., Elliott, D. & Roy, R., eds.), pp. 333–339, Hutchinson Educational, London

21 MEDVEDEV, Z. (1969) *The Rise and Fall of T. D. Lysenko*, translated by Lerner, I. M., p. 19, Columbia University Press, New York

22 POPPER, K. R. (1972) *Objective Knowledge: an Evolutionary Approach*, Clarendon Press, Oxford

23 JEVONS, F. R. (1975) But some kinds of knowledge are more equal than others. *Studies in Science Education 2* (in the press)

24 YOUNG, M. F. D. (1971) An approach to the study of curricula as socially organised knowledge, in *Knowledge and Control* (Young, M. F. D., ed.), pp. 19–46, Collier-Macmillan, London

25 BERNSTEIN, B. (1971) On the classification and framing of educational knowledge, in *Knowledge and Control* (Young, M. F. D., ed.), pp. 47–69, Collier-Macmillan, London

26 ANSTEY, F. (pseudonym of Guthrie, T. A.) (1882) *Vice Versa*, Smith and Elder, London

27 GOMBRICH, E. (1960) *Art and Illusion*, p. 271, Phaidon Press, London

28 YOUNG, M. F. D. (1974) Notes for a sociology of science education. *Studies in Science Education 1*, 51–60

29 WELLS, H. G. (1895) *The Time Machine*, Heinemann, London

30 MARCUSE, H. (1968) *One Dimensional Man*, Sphere Books, London

31 SHANE, H. G. (1973) *The Educational Significance of the Future*, Phi Delta Kappa, Bloomington, Indiana

32 KAHN, H. & WIENER, A. J. (1967) *The Year 2000: A Framework for Speculation for the Next Thirty Three Years*, Macmillan, New York

Social decision prerequisite to educational change, 1975–1985

HAROLD G. SHANE

School of Education, Indiana University, Bloomington

Abstract   It is a common premise on the part of persons who are less than thought-ful that schools should provide leadership as humankind moves from the present to the future. This paper takes the position that the schools have not performed, and in all probability never can perform, any yeasty leadership function in social change.

If, like a highly polished speculum, schools can merely reflect the society in which they have their being, then certain social decisions are prerequisite to any new basic educational change. The success with which social change occurs depends on the image or images of the future which a given human sub-set accepts and the way this group chooses to approach the future.

Points developed include: (1) some premises which may be helpful in contempla-ting the future, (2) probable developments of the next decade which are likely to have a bearing on cultural change, and (3) a roster of important decisions which must be made if schools are to have clear guidelines as they seek to serve the society that supports them.

The paper concludes with speculations on the probable nature of educationally portentous decisions that are emerging, and with a timetable for educational change between 1975 and 1985.

During 1972–1973 I had the privilege of studying certain aspects of the status and current directions of futures research (sometimes called policies research) in the United States.* The project, funded by the US Office of Education (USOE), was based on 82 personal interviews in more than twenty futures study centres such as Rand, the Hudson Institute, and the USOE Educational Policy Research Centers at the Stanford and Syracuse Research Institutes.

During these months of inquiry, and in the past year of study with specialists

---

* The futures research study was reported to the U.S. Commissioner of Education in mimeo-graphed form early in 1973, then rewritten and published as *The Educational Significance of the Future*.[1]

in a number of disciplines* it has become apparent that education has a critical, important role to play during the closing decades of the present century. By 'education' I mean to include the many sources of instruction to which traditional 'schooling' is rapidly losing its monopoly: the mass media, federally supported programmes such as the Job Corps, self-instructional materials, 'teaching packages', and the like.

Even as I became more and more deeply aware of the importance of education during the 'crisis of transition' and the 'crisis of crises'[2] through which the world has been passing, I became increasingly aware of the fact that faith in the power of education *per se* to solve many of humankind's problems was not only naive but a potentially dangerous misconception.

THE PARADOX OF WEAKNESS AND STRENGTH IN EDUCATION

Education has never been an effective ingredient in changing society. For example, while there were many significant developments in the culture during the 1960s in the US, they were neither stimulated nor initiated by the schools and education-related agencies. It was pressure from blacks in the US that led to the development of black studies, for instance, and it was demands from students goaded to the point of rioting that led to curriculum change and to the 'greater relevance' now presumably found in the curricula of secondary and higher education. It was *not* pioneering by educational leaders that led to the drive for improved women's rights. Pollution, resource depletion, and the tragic wars in which our age specializes were assailed for the most part in scholarly and political arenas that were remote from the classroom, and usually by people who were not professional educators.

While the schools, like a highly burnished speculum, tend to *mirror* rather than to *initiate* social change, they are nonetheless important elements in the processes of cultural change that are underway. How does one explain this paradox of education's combined weakness and strength: weakness as a change agent and strength as an agency for reinforcing change?

For one thing, it is the men and women exposed to the mass media and educated in the public and in the independent schools of the developed world who have, since 1900, removed ten-year-olds from our coal mines, revolutionized worldwide concepts of human rights and human dignity, broken genetic codes, experimented with behaviour modification, smashed the atom, and devised 'Green

* My work during 1973 was funded predominantly by the Danforth Foundation in St Louis, Missouri. This organization provided substantial support, including money for three 1974 symposia that I planned. Participants included Kenneth Boulding, Lester R. Brown, Theodore Gordon, John Platt, Robert Heilbroner, Willard Wirtz, Jonas Salk, and William Irwin Thompson.

Revolutions' (cf. deRopp[3]). To phrase it succinctly, the schools and other educational media might be likened to intellectual launching pads for the careers and contributions of men and women whose ideas and whose influence would one day change the earth. Through the established processes of education they transmitted both the cultural heritage and a large measure of substantive content.*

Second, since we recycle our school population every twelve to fifteen years, education—broadly conceived—is an indispensable means of introducing children and youth to emergent social decisions and to their role in the world of the future. Third, education effectively can be used to attack certain specific social and environmental problems ranging from illiteracy to the need to borrow from rather than to consume the world's resource pools. Finally, education often can help the learner to develop a talent for identifying and implementing or discarding new alternatives in the light of their consequences. It is contributions such as these that probably will continue in the future to motivate us to give support to schools which, in the US, consume more tax money at present than anything except expenditure for armaments and for the cost of past wars.

SOCIAL DECISIONS PREREQUISITE TO EDUCATIONAL CHANGE

While education, including traditional concepts of schooling, is an enormous potential asset as our society moves into the emerging futures that lie ahead of us, its full value cannot be realized until certain antecedent decisions are made by society.†

More explicitly, in the contemporary crisis of transition, education very much needs to regain its wonted sense of direction. This, I think, can be acquired only from a societal matrix which has once again developed a body of accepted values that can serve as a gyroscope whirling to keep the society on the course it has laid out for itself. As noted earlier, the effectiveness of our educational agencies will reflect—admittedly with some distortions—the social setting of either a healthy or a sick society. They can supplement, implement and reinforce change, but they cannot create it.

We can only hope that the decisions that society makes, either purposefully or by default, will be moral ones. By 'moral' I mean choices that are *just* and

---

* There are those who argue that the schools are deteriorating because, judging by some indicators, median achievement scores have declined. I would contend that *youth of top ability* continue to perform as well or better than a generation ago. However, lower median scores, in an era of universal compulsory education, tend to draw attention away from the *range* of performance which continues to reflect the work of a number of first-rate young scholars.

† Throughout this paper, unless otherwise noted, the term *society* refers to the US. While I believe that all or most of my generalizations apply to other developed nations, it would be difficult for me to defend the transferability of these generalizations.

equitable. I will not look too carefully at this hope, even though I am convinced that present threats to the biosphere will serve to heighten our consciousness and help us to find the wit and wisdom, the character and compassion, needed to move us from our present evolutionary stage as creatures who are 'the missing link between animals and human beings' as Loren Eisley once phrased it.

Whether our social decisions ultimately prove to be equitable ones is a matter for speculation beyond the scope of this brief paper. Let me turn instead to some of the actual problems and issues which confront humankind. The decisions they demand promise to extend our intellectual stature by several cubits in the quest for viable solutions.

The problems which I have singled out as being particularly in need of attack were not selected arbitrarily on the capricious basis of subjective judgement. They were compiled—as already noted—from the 82 conversations with futurists that I recorded in 1972–1973 (Ref. 1, pp. 42–49). These problems were confirmed and some additional ones imperilling the human prospect were identified in 1973 and 1974 through four projects for which I obtained funding.*

So much for background information. Let us now look at a roster of important decisions that need to be made if education is to regain the sense of direction it has lost since 1950. These include:

(1) Decisions regarding our future use of technology: continuation of present exploitative policies versus more prudent evolution or even sophisticated devolution (dynamic contraction) of present practices.

(2) Conclusions regarding the prudent use and sharing of transnational resources such as air and water and regarding the equitable sharing of national products such as wheat, soybeans, oil, tin, lead, coal, copper, and so forth.

(3) Choices regarding the use of electrical, chemical, and psychological behaviour modification techniques—a grievous problem which is further complicated by the question of whether we have the wisdom that should be exercised as a prerequisite to decisions about the raising or lowering of levels of such qualities or behaviours as aggressiveness, violence, memory, docility, or withdrawal.

(4) Selection of policies that can restore and maintain in the future the

---

* The Association for Supervision and Curriculum Development funded a small by-invitation conference in Washington, D.C. during August, 1973 for purposes of identifying problems of the near future and the decisions they required. Among the 14 participants were Alvin Toffler, John Platt, Lester R. Brown, Elise Boulding, Arthur Okun, and Thomas Green. The Danforth Foundation in 1974 (see p. 74 *n*) funded conferences in St Louis in January and February of approximately 300 persons each and also sponsored in October a three-day Washington D.C. dialogue treating the moral aspects of imminent social decisions.

integrity of our economic–industrial and political–military systems.

(5) Decisions regarding what we consider the 'good life' to be in a world becoming less and less able to have wrenched from it the raw materials that are needed to maintain the life styles developed in the West since 1900.

(6) Conclusions regarding the use of finite and dwindling financial resources* to provide for the needs and wants of wide-ranging human sub-sets: the old, the very young, the poor, the advanced student, occupational groups, ethnic and religious minorities, youth, dependent children, the handicapped, and so on.

(7) Choices as to whether the gap between the 'have-nots' and the 'haves' can and should be decreased and, if so, by what variety of means.†

(8) Selection of policies and practices which can minimize some of the shortcomings of mass media and maximize their value—especially the value of television—without resorting to imposed controls, including censorship.

(9) Decisions regarding what the developed world is willing to give up (if anything), and in what order, so that a more equitable distribution of food and other resources can be ensured for the world's poor.

(10) Choice of what honourable compromises shall be made in the processes of reaching decisions such as the nine exemplars listed above. Patently, many diverse opinions will need to be reconciled as such compromises are reached.

The importance to education, and more explicitly to schooling, of the decisions facing society can scarcely be underestimated. The content of instruction and the attitudes that education presumably should strive to foster are at present the objects of uncertainty and disagreement, at least in the US. This is a relatively recent development. For most of the past two hundred years American educational institutions have shown great viability. As Tyler wrote recently,[5] '...during these two centuries the illiterate learned to read, immigrants from many diverse cultures were assimilated in an increasingly pluralistic society, and social mobility and gains in individual economic status have been phenomenal since 1875. The labour force has been educated for both a technological and a post-industrial society. Furthermore, socialization of students in the spirit of the

---

* From the early years of the Kennedy Administration (1962) to the last full year of the Nixon Administration (1973) Medicare, housing and student subsidies, federal welfare costs, etc., grew from a few billion to over $41 000 million (cf. Glazer[4]).

† As reported in the *Washington Post*, August 8, 1974, the idea of a ceiling on all earnings has been seriously proposed in Sweden by Professor Gunnar Adler-Karlsson.

"new education" (as advocated by John Dewey, William H. Kilpatrick, George S. Counts and others of their persuasion) has not inhibited the development of either individuality or of unique talents.'

The educational achievements to which Tyler refers, however, were made possible by an era of certainty. The Englishman or American of 1910 or 1915— and in all social classes—*knew* what was 'right' and 'wrong', what was black and what was white. There were few if any of today's infinite shadings of grey to impede decisive action. Education helped to preserve yesterday's behavioural maps even after it began to be recognized that these maps no longer matched the changing terrain of 1930 or 1960.

Patently, the schools and other educational agencies now go begging for the want of a society that has developed new certainties that are congruent with new and still-emergent survival patterns for the planet as a whole.

PROBABLE DEVELOPMENTS OF THE NEXT DECADE WITH A BEARING ON EDUCATION

It is always comfortable to speculate with respect to what Stuart Chase labelled 'the most probable world',[6] since no one has completely reliable information about the future. That which has yet to occur can't be organized for study—we can only select and project possible developments that our enquiries suggest will take place, keep a tight rein on our prejudices, and perhaps avoid creating self-fulfilling or self-defeating prophecies. Therefore the paragraphs below attempt to avoid presenting propaganda for the sort of world which personal bias might motivate me to describe. There seems to be no way, however, completely to control my selection of the scholars on whose ideas I have drawn.* I seem to remember best the ideas of thinkers whose reasoning I find to be most stimulating.

First, if we are to have a workable and individually satisfying society in the future, it seems almost certain that a maturing humanity will need to be appreciably more self-disciplined than the one which developed in the US between 1950 and 1975. What does greater self-discipline imply for education? While I do not see us returning to an arid, didactic, rote-memory type of education, the elementary school seems likely to place more stress on basic skills in an 'open' setting.

At the secondary level, programmes seem likely to become less permissive, to emphasize greater self-discipline and self-direction, and to provide more

---

* While not a comprehensive guide, the references suggest the range of writers whose views I found stimulating.

'action-learning' and 'service learning' in the world of work. There probably will, in a more disciplining educational environment, be more exits from and re-entries to secondary and postsecondary schooling. Content doubtless will be modified further to stress consideration of the biosphere. That is, in a school of engineering one may learn not only *how* to build a commercial airstrip, but *whether* the proposed site is ecologically a sound one.

A *second* development that probably can be anticipated, as Seaborg has suggested, is that in the developed world we will begin rather soon to think in terms of being *users* rather than *consumers* of basic resources.[7] All educational agencies, and the mass media in particular, will be placed on their mettle to put this concept across if Professor Seaborg's idea proves to be one whose time has come.

A *third* possibility—a likelihood, rather—is that we are in the twilight phase of extravagant, self-indulgent living. Tomorrow's society may well prove to be a post-affluent as well as a post-industrial one! How well we learn to be 'users' rather than 'consumers' will be a challenge to education—a challenge to carry us quickly from the twilight of conspicuous consumption into a new day in which, in Gabor's apt phrases, we will achieve '...a mature society, stable in numbers and in material production, in ecological equilibrium with the resources of the earth'.[8]

Space permits mention of no more than a *fourth* opportunity for education, although a dozen could be listed. This is the probability that the intellectual and technological capacity of humans will, respectively, improve and increase. Laboratory research reviewed by psychologist Krech[9] indicates that we may be on the threshold of learning a great deal about behaviour modification as well as about its concomitant problems! Extension of technological skills and accomplishments and their almost inevitable increase in sophistication need no documentation.

How educational agencies actually will interpret and respond to probabilistic futures such as the four sketched above it is difficult to say. But two points—perhaps rather obvious ones—can be made with considerable confidence: (1) The clarity and forcefulness with which pressing social decisions are made and implemented by adequate funding surely will weaken or strengthen our educational agencies accordingly; and (2) as a tested vehicle for fostering the views supported by their supporting society, the schools and other instructional media remain one of our best bases for attacking basic problems and for creating a suitable psychological climate for promoting wise choices among alternatives by persons of all ages: the very young, youth, mature students, and senior learners.

FIVE PREMISES FOR THE PRUDENT GUIDANCE OF FUTURE EDUCATIONAL CHANGE

Once society has made up its mind about the future for which it is willing to strive, educators and citizens have the interesting task of deciding what posture to assume as they confront the coming decade. The following advice with a bearing on educational change is offered:

(1) Recognize that the future is analogous to an edifice of infinite size: its structure takes form one brick or block at a time, but its general architecture must be planned in advance, just as lunar landings in the past decade took years to consummate. Good education is built day by day, but also must have a constantly expanded horizon.

(2) Be prepared to be surprised. An unanticipated system break of some kind is forever around the corner. Keep educational agencies flexible.

(3) Keep in mind that the future is not what it once was thought to be: it has been 'contaminated' by our spectacular success in, say, lengthening life spans, improving material comforts, speeding up transportation and communication (although the *means* of communication have outraced *intelligibility*), and in mediating the environment. Our very success has betrayed our 1950 or 1960 visions of what 1980 or 1990 would bring.

(4) Avoid populating the future with projections of today's accepted guidelines for conduct; they will almost certainly be inadequate as we work to bring about the educational change which tomorrow will require.

(5) Remember that facts can be the enemy of truth. Much of what we believed in the past—even in the hard sciences, and certainly in the soft ones—has been discredited or modified. Today's 'facts' may well be yesterday's fables when tomorrow comes.

The social decisions of which our schools and related instruction agencies stand in need should be made as quickly as possible. Among other reasons, it is essential that these decisions be reached to relieve the pressures of present uncertainties.

If we in education are fortunate enough to achieve from society a renewed sense of purpose and direction, we can hope to move through three stages of educational evolution in the years immediately ahead. I would speculate that from 1975 to 1980 we will find ourselves in *Stage I*, an interval which I shall call the 'preintervention period'. Here our route is clear: we need to begin to understand 'what we must do'* but curricular and instructional intervention will be difficult to achieve overnight because of the inertia of large educational agencies.

Stage II might be thought of as an 'alternative approach' interval, one which I speculate could extend from, say, 1980 to 1990. During this decade the ideas generated in Stage I could be methodically phased into the workings of the educational community. Our route is less clear, but the opportunity for change is greater because of the lead time provided by Stage I.

After 1990 or 1995, we should be crossing the threshold of *Stage III* which is one of 'crucial uncertainty'. *Uncertain* because it is difficult to envision world dynamics fifteen or more years hence; *crucial* because humankind has relatively few years to put itself in order. And by Stage III we should begin to know whether or not the sequence of social decisions→educational change→goal achievement has begun to improve our chances for attaining better techno-futures, sociofutures, biofutures, and human futures for the people on our planet.

Discussion

Waddington: Our discussion is about what the universities can or should do about the problems of the future, rather than about whose estimate of the probabilities of the future is best. Professor Shane has given us a splendid summary of the major problem areas which are very much in everybody's mind at present. He mentioned that there are several ways of approaching each problem area, with nobody's answers likely to be 100 per cent correct. This of course is what biological life in general is about. Success in evolution depends on ability to deal with the unexpected. The problems facing man today are already thoroughly in the minds of many students, and it is quite time that the universities started doing something about them.

Ziman: Professor Shane's list of decisions that need to be made is a splendid list of standard and familiar liberal aspirations, reforms, programmes, worries, extrapolations, etc., of our time. But I would be very worried if teaching about the future or about its possibilities were left just to those rather bland categories. The future may be much harsher than Professor Shane implied, and people need to be armed by their education to meet graver eventualities than those we have been talking about. Nuclear war is one of the harsh possibilities which were not mentioned. This seems to be the terrible problem of our time but strangely it is not one of the things people teach about.

* I refer to the education dimension implicit in John Platt's article.[2]

Waddington: It is discussed in my futures textbook.[10]

Ziman: It is one of the central problems for peace research. Then there is revolution. Revolution is not just about the social contract between haves and the have-nots. What Professor Shane refers to as 'The poor and so on' may be what it looks like in the US, but it doesn't look like that in Africa or Brazil. The possibility that the whole social structure of the world may be rearranged by these forces has to be taken into account. We should not necessarily support such forces but we should try and see what they are about. Yet they are not on that list either. Another problem, a more difficult one to talk about, is the possibility, not merely of the corruption of the politicians but of their psycho-pathologies—the Amins of this world. Some of us here calculated that one per cent of the human race at any one time has always lived under a political monster. This is part of the human condition and it is one of the possibilities. Not to teach that seems to me again a failure to arm people for the future.

Valaskakis: Once again I would like to point to the very real danger that exists when we are too constrained by the present. Professor Shane mentioned that universities can, or should be, a mirror of society. I think the danger lies in the universities being *rear-view* mirrors of society. I see the ideal function of the university both as a *distant early warning system* for the future, and as a mirror or rear-view mirror of society. And for this I would like again to make a plea that we should have more normative forecasting and horizon scenarios. I have a suspicion that some of your suggestions in the list may be mutually incompatible, Professor Shane. I would take the fifth item, the definition of the good life, as my starting point for defining all the others. The others seem to me very much a reflection of present problems and present perceptions, in the same way that Charlton Heston is now seen by us as both the definitive Ben Hur and the definitive Omega Man. If we moved from projective forecasting to horizon forecasting we would achieve a salutary divorce from the present. The most useful forecasting so far has been done, in the opinion of many, by science fiction authors: they have separated themselves from their present, and have created scenarios of the future, and they have not been bogged down by present circumstances, present viewpoints, present paradigms.

Waddington: Universities of course have several different functions. Undoubtedly the early warning system is one important function. Universities also have to handle young people, aged from 18 to 21 or so. The items in general surveys such as Professor Shane has given us are all around us, in the atmosphere as it were; but it will take students some time to put all these things together if they are left to themselves, and if they are all under pressure to get a degree in some specialist subject. Once they have caught up with where thought is at present, we can start thinking about helping them to look into the future. But we must not forget the down-to-earth function of bringing them up to date with current thinking.

Jevons: Professor Shane and Professor Platt have both referred to students as the originators of women's studies, black studies, and so on. Sociologists say that innovations tend to arise not from the middle of the hierarchy of seniority but from the top or the bottom. Does that apply to innovations in universities? Professor Shane, as a professional educationalist, have you any evidence about the sources of innovation in education?

Shane: Until the 1960s much leadership input tended to come from persons at the top, from established educational thinkers. But from the 1960s onwards there was much more pressure from students in the drive for women's liberation and the various 'student liberation movements'. It was pressure from these groups, ethnic groups, and the like that brought about many changes in the content of instruction on our campuses in the US.

Waddington: Have women's liberation and the student movements really contributed anything new to the world's wisdom, or to professional education? Did women's lib. add to our understanding of how society works, and of women's position in it?

Shane: My own insights were appreciably deepened in the 1960s with regard to the under-the-skin feelings of an appreciable number of blacks, women, undergraduates and so on. I was insensitive at first, say, to women's rejection of male-oriented language. I tended, for example, to think of *man*kind rather than *human*kind, simply because it was the usage I learned in childhood. It was many years too, before I realized the nature of the inner seethings in the hearts of many blacks. But we were able to communicate more effectively by the late 1960s. The passing years have heightened my consciousness of the inner feelings of other people.

Waddington: I think the question is partly local.

Platt: I think we are facing not a gradualist future, but a decade of disasters. Nuclear escalation is a probability with the superpowers. At a lower level, Professor Shane did mention nuclear terrorism. It is highly likely that within the next few years there will be a Hiroshima-type bomb on Tel Aviv, or New York City, which is somewhat easier to get into and has a larger Jewish population than Tel Aviv. Economic disaster is possible. Maoist revolutions may happen in South Asia, in Africa, in South America—not that they are necessarily disasters for the rest of the world. They may in fact be considerable gains, somewhat like the Chinese gains in bootstrapping people off the bottom of poverty. But the response to such revolutions by the CIA and by Russian world politics could trigger some of the larger nuclear disasters.

I could go down a considerable list of such potential disasters in the next decade. I think it will be very different from the last decade or two, where in a certain sense the alarms and developments in the high information society, becoming aware of its large problems, have been relatively peaceful. Today we have moved into the international arena with this high information and with these new global problems, and we have all the problems that come with multiple actors in non-zero-sum game theory, problems of conflict, cooperation, game-playing and so on, where large numbers of administrations are forced increasingly into situations that no one wants yet everybody gets into. I think we are in a pre-revolutionary situation in which it is essentially impossible to predict the year 2000—just as it would have been almost impossible in 1775 to predict the year 1800, with the French and American democratic experiments still ahead. Even seventy years ago, in 1905, with the Russian revolution ahead, with one-fifth of the human race going communist, the destruction of all the aristocracies and kings of Europe, the flapper era, and so on, it would have been impossible to predict the year 1930. The future will depend, in a quite unexpected step-function way, it seems to me, on accidents of constructive leadership or accidents of assassination or accidents of collision of two crises at a crucial moment, with somewhat unpredictable public and international responses. The possibility of forecasting the year 2000, and the kind of global structure we shall have at that time, depends on the way in which we make use of these crises, and the way in which we do our homework now to prepare to make use of them. The alternatives are very hard to predict, but I think that in this kind of quantum-jump situation, all extrapolations, Delphi forecasts, or gradualist or incrementalist forecasts, are almost certain to be wrong.

Perry: Does the fundamental dilemma for the universities spring from the enormous growth of communication at all levels in the world? What the universities may have to decide is whether they go on teaching about futurology to an intellectual élite who will then make their mark as leaders in the world, or whether they should try to turn their attention to a much larger segment of the population. In other words, should they reach down to a lower level and to larger numbers? The response of leaders is eventually going to be determined by what they judge their followers will accept. Maybe that is where the universities ought to be directing their efforts rather than towards pure scholarship in such studies.

Waddington: Don't you think the universities will have to do a bit of both? They should reach much further down to the general public, but I hope this can be done without losing altogether the forward-looking role that we have also been talking about, which is possibly not confined to the élite but is likely to have more impact on the élite. The combination of mass appeal and high-grade scholarship is the difficult but essential task of universities.

Perry: I was pointing out the difference but I was not suggesting that the scholarship should disappear.

Woodroofe: The universities have the role of looking forward, warning the rest of the community of the dangers ahead, and influencing the decisions that the top people in the community are making. I suspect that they should teach first about the present. My contact with university students, and indeed with some university staff, suggests that they don't understand the present. They do not seem properly equipped to understand what they read in a good newspaper. Many of them do not know the basics of economics, the way industry and commerce work, or the way government works. Before we start teaching the future let us have a good base by understanding the present.

Waddington: But wouldn't you agree that what is happening is always a lot of processes? There is no such thing as the present. Whitehead defined the present as the fringe of memory tinged with anticipation.[11] We can't in fact teach the present without teaching either a bit of the past or a bit of the future, or a bit of both.

Woodroofe: Absolutely. I wouldn't mind if we were teaching ten years behind the times or even longer, but I don't think that we are up to date as far as that.

Kumar: I wonder whether other people are having the same problems about this discussion as I am? The main reason for us getting together is to talk about what kind of contribution the universities can make, in a teaching capacity, to thinking about the future. But the other main thread that keeps coming through is, how do we actually think about the future? What do we as a group think about the various problems and methodologies? I can see that there is a certain overlap here but I find it difficult to concentrate my mind on both simultaneously. As a kind of practising futurologist I have one way of thinking about the sort of problems that Professor Shane listed; and as somebody involved in university teaching I have another way of thinking about how I can put over a way of thinking about the future to undergraduates. It is not an enormously great problem to think about how undergraduate courses about the future might be put on in universities. I teach a course called 'The sociology of industrial societies', large parts of which are concerned with the processes of social change, and one can deal with things as far ahead as one wants to. I know other people are doing this in the sciences. Whether one wants to put these studies together in some sort of school, or have a degree in futures studies, seems to me to be a bureaucratic problem. It may be just a matter of different bureaucratic rigidities at different universities which determines how difficult it is to persuade faculties to allow these courses. I would like some guidance about what kind of discussion you would like us to have about the teaching element in putting on futures studies. What kind of problem and evidence ought we to be talking about? I find that thinking about what the future is going to be is a different kind of mental exercise from thinking about arranging such courses.

Waddington: One question is: are we properly educating our students if we give a somewhat future-oriented course on the sociology of industrialization to those few students at a university who are taking that type of degree, while we give nothing that is future-oriented to those who are doing standard biology or chemistry? As you say, Dr Kumar, it is a bureaucratic question whether we can have courses on futures studies, or have to be content to allow the future to be brought in by any lecturer who happens to be interested in these matters as they concern his specialty. That is the essential question I think we are discussing. Personally I don't think it is adequate to leave individual lecturers to bring in some future-oriented matters only if they feel like it. On the other hand, I don't think we want to have a total degree course in futures studies and nothing but futures studies. My view is that at an elementary university level— and I have chosen the second year for my experimental course—we should have a superficial broad course, mentioning all aspects of the future, for practically all students. Then some of them will go into specialties like industrialization, where they will get a lot more of it. Some of them will study languages and get much less of it, and so on.

Eldredge: It seems to me that we are also discussing the total function of the university in society. I think there are three main audiences for the universities. First there are the students, who are a captive audience. Second, there are the decision makers. Futures studies may play the role of an intelligence officer serving his commander. There are many commanders, or decision makers, in society and the university has a major function in dealing with those decision makers, trying to loosen them up. Finally, in a democratic society, there is a third audience—the people: nobody dares to do anything unless the people, however defined, are at least told what is going on. I think that the Open University attitude of open, popular, advanced education is an absolute necessity. In my own work in urban studies, where we move on to urban planning, we now tend to think in terms of 'alternative horizon scenarios' because in 'multigroup' or 'mosaic' societies one must offer different sorts of possible futures. One of the most difficult is to develop realistic alternative future scenarios.

References cited

[1] SHANE, HAROLD G. (1973) *The Educational Significance of the Future*, Phi Delta Kappa, Bloomington, Indiana

[2] PLATT, JOHN (1969) What we must do. *Science (Wash. D. C.) 166*, 1115–1121

[3] deROPP, ROBERT E. (1972) *The New Prometheans*, Dell, New York

[4] GLAZER, NATHAN (1972) The Great Society never was a casualty of the war, *Saturday Review*, December, pp. 49–52

[5] TYLER, RALPH W. (1975) Can American Schools meet the demands they now face? *Viewpoints: Bulletin of the School of Education, Indiana University, 51*, 2

[6] CHASE, STUART (1968) *The Most Probable World*, Harper & Row, Evanston, Illinois

[7] SEABORG, GLENN (1974) The recycle society of tomorrow. *The Futurist, 8*, 108–112, 114–115

[8] GABOR, DENNIS (1972) *The Mature Society*, Praeger, New York

[9] KRECH, DAVID (1969) Psychoneurobiochemeducation, *Phi Delta Kappan 50*, 375, March

[10] WADDINGTON, C. H. (1975) *The Sources of the Man Made Future*, Cape/Paladin, London

[11] WHITEHEAD, ALFRED N. (1926) *Science and the Modern World*, Macmillan, New York

Additional reading

BECKERMAN, WILFRED (1974) *Two Cheers for the Affluent Society: a Spirited Defense of Economic Growth*, St. Martin's Press, New York

BOULDING, KENNETH E. (1964) *The Meaning of the 20th Century*, Harper Colophon Books, New York

BROWN, LESTER (1974) *In the Human Interest*, Norton, New York

COLEMAN, JAMES S. *et al.* (1974) *Youth: Transition to Adulthood*, University of Chicago Press, Chicago

DICKSON, PAUL (1971) *Think Tanks*, Atheneum, New York

EHRLICH, PAUL R. & EHRLICH, ANNE H. (1974) *The End of Affluence*, Ballantine Books, New York

FREEMAN, S. DAVID (1974) *Energy: the New Era*, Vintage, New York

HEILBRONER, ROBERT (1974) *An Inquiry into the Human Prospect*, Norton, New York

HOSTROP, RICHARD W. (ed.) (1973) *Foundations of Futurology in Education*, ETC Publications, Homewood, Illinois

KAHN, HERMAN & WIENER, ANTHONY J. (1967) *The Year 2000: a Framework for Speculation for the next Thirty-three Years*, Macmillan, New York

KAHN, HERMAN & BRUCE-BRIGGS, B. (1972) *Things to Come: Thinking of the Seventies and Eighties*, Macmillan, New York

KOSTELANETZ, RICHARD (ed.) (1972) *Social Speculations*, Morrow, New York

MESAROVIC, MIHAJLO & PESTEL, EDUARD (1974) *Mankind at the Turning Point*, Dutton/Reader's Digest, New York; Hutchinson, London

SALK, JONAS (1972) *Man Unfolding*, Harper & Row, New York

SALK, JONAS (1973) *Survival of the Wisest*, Harper & Row, New York

SCHUMACHER, E. F. (1973) *Small is Beautiful: Economics as if People Mattered*, Harper & Row, New York

THOMPSON, WILLIAM IRWIN (1974) *Passages about Earth*, Harper & Row, New York

TOFFLER, ALVIN *et al.* (1967) 'Toward the year 2000: work in progress', *Daedalus*, summer

TOFFLER, ALVIN (1970) *Future Shock*, Random House, New York

TOFFLER, ALVIN *et al.* (1974) *Learning for Tomorrow*, Random House, New York

From academic hothouse to professional dugout: a mean free path

JOHN M. FRANCIS

Heriot-Watt University, and Society, Religion & Technology Project, Church of Scotland Home Board, Edinburgh

Abstract This paper deals with the task of assessing new technologies and with the definition of key subject areas for multidisciplinary research within universities. In the United Kingdom, for example, the universities could develop an invaluable network for monitoring land use, food production and energy supply at a regional level. The opportunity to contribute to an overall planning framework which effectively integrates social, economic and environmental factors would be an important longer-term objective. To illustrate this point, the paper refers to the escalating effects of major industrial developments in Scotland resulting from the exploitation of North Sea oil and gas resources. It is suggested that the regional analysis of critical resource potential in land, food and energy would provide a core of relevance for futures studies in the universities and also establish a focal point for departmental interests within each university.

At the start of my paper I make no apology for the fact that my views are a product of my own peculiar path of experience. This can best be illustrated as follows:

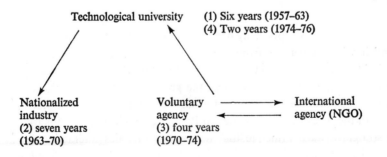

Technological university   (1) Six years (1957–63)
                                      (4) Two years (1974–76)

Nationalized industry (2) seven years (1963–70)   Voluntary agency (3) four years (1970–74) ⟶ International agency (NGO)

Despite our particular form of enlightenment in the West, this is not a well-trodden path. In my case, having returned to base, I am more than ever inclined to believe the old adage—'the more things change, the more they are the same'.

The purpose of my paper is not to register frustration but rather to signal one or two opportunities that I believe are there for the taking among those who can project an integrated view of the future.

In brief, I should like to deal with the task of assessing new technologies, with the definition of key areas for multidisciplinary activity and with the nucleation steps that must be taken in the very near future to provide a planning framework at a regional level which is more appropriate to the age in which we live. The latter part of the paper will obviously bear heavily on my own interpretation of what is happening in Scotland largely as a result of developments related to the exploitation of North Sea oil and gas resources. This problem is one of resource management on a relatively large scale and over a time scale that does not allow the future to be discounted lightly in terms of social and environmental factors. If ever there was a positive need for integrated planning of industrial development embodying new content and new directions, there is ample evidence that this need exists in Scotland under the pressure of recent events. The failure of the academic community to make an effective connection with these problems—apart from highly individual contributions at public inquiries and the like—suggests a degree of improvization and an almost characteristic lack of anticipation. The value of an early warning system in key subject areas, such as land use, food production and energy supply, that could be provided by certain universities on a regional basis and as part of a national network should not be underestimated. In the first instance, this would provide a core of relevance for futures studies and a focal point for departmental interests within each university.

THE ASSESSMENT TASK

General case

In recent years, a supposedly new discipline referred to as 'technology assessment' has been emerging from the shadows. The idea has achieved a certain credibility in the USA with the establishment of an Office of Technology Assessment within the Congress, although the greatest stimulus must have been the statutory requirement to prepare formal environmental impact statements in line with the National Environmental Policy Act.[1] The approach is founded on the straightforward principle that technology includes interacting social and physical components. The combination of physical technologies (the hardware) and the social technologies, embracing organizational and managerial skills, represents a complicated interface that cannot easily be determined. The primary role of the technology assessors is to explore this interface by:

(1) defining the assessment task;
(2) describing relevant technologies;
(3) developing state-of-society assumptions;
(4) identifying impact areas;
(5) making preliminary impact analysis;
(6) identifying possible action options;
(7) completing impact analysis.

In this methodology, the physical technologies are assumed to be causal factors and therefore the logical starting point for assessments.[2] It is also assumed that, starting with the physical technologies, it is possible to trace through the consequences of these technologies for both the social technologies and for society at large. The objective is to identify those points where changes in either the physical technologies or the social technologies would result in significantly different results to those that might otherwise be achieved. Several multidisciplinary teams that have taken this road have ended up with the belief that no method or theory exists which will adequately explain the ability of our society to develop complex technologies.[3] While that problem is not directly relevant to this short paper, some elements of the final analysis must contribute also to the functional task of technology assessment. It is necessary to be specific, and I shall choose the example of a multidisciplinary research team brought together inside a university in the United States to conduct an assessment of Outer Continental Shelf Development.[3] The team consisted of a marine biologist, a lawyer, a physicist, two political scientists and three engineers. The project was funded by the National Science Foundation's RANN programme (Research Applied to National Needs) and it ran for the period from September 1971 to March 1973. The initial task was to prepare a detailed description of offshore operations and accordingly three subsystems were defined:

(A) Exploration.
(B) Drilling and production.
(C) Pipelines, storage and transport.

It was then possible during the data-collection phase of the systems analysis to identify the critical pieces of hardware (the physical technologies)—such as wellhead safety devices—and the social technologies (rules, regulations, procedures and the responsible statutory agencies). The goal was to develop a matrix which would give some indication of how the physical and social technologies interact. It was possible to reach certain conclusions fairly quickly as a result of this procedure:

(1) Physical technology systems in use in the late 1980s would be substan-

tially the same as those in use today. (This does not indicate that the technology is unchanging but that the changes are expected to be evolutionary in character and will take place on a component-by-component basis.)

(2) Information is limited to publicly available sources and the currently stated views of the domestic industry and contractors involved directly in offshore oil and gas operations.

(3) Lack of information leads straight to the difficulty of determining which of the impacts are costs and which are benefits, as well as to the problem of giving these factors specific weightings.

The realization that in this instance the physical technologies were not driving the system caused the team to turn their provisional methodology around and to concentrate on major modifications required in rules, regulations, procedure, etc. It was concluded that correction of all detectable weaknesses in the physical technologies was well within present state-of-the-art capabilities, and that improved regulatory procedures would induce the application of the best available physical technologies. In turn, this would stimulate new research and development activities to make a creative contribution over the next fifteen years. In a comparatively short space of time, this team had made an effective, if incomplete, synthesis of this important area of technology, had focused on the otherwise fragmented appreciation of the problems, and had worked their way out of a job. While this can serve as an illustration of the advantages of a flexible team approach working outwards from a university base, it is a critical part of my argument that in the UK there is an immediate need to deploy some of our university resources in this direction. I shall come back to the specific opportunities later in the paper.

The particular case

During the past four years, I have had the privilege of directing a project sponsored by the Church of Scotland on 'Society, Religion and Technology', which has certainly taken me in some unexpected directions. Since I was appointed to this post in 1970, directly from a research and development background in the nuclear power industry, it will not surprise the members of this seminar that I was soon very much involved in the continuing struggle to understand the problems of population and pollution, peace and poverty, in the period leading up to the UN Conference on the Human Environment held in Stockholm in 1972. Principally through the agency of the World Council of Churches, but also because the project was based in Scotland, I organized and took part in a multitude of study groups, workshops and public meetings at every conceivable level. While this may have been a fairly typical experience for many scientists of my generation, it did persuade me not to go on pursuing these issues at such a high level of generalization. It was necessary to find an appropriate middle path that would allow an element of professional competence to survive alongside these broader concerns. I simply found that a total disengagement from the intensely pragmatic world of the physical technologies was not possible in my case. The chain of circumstances which led me into a 'problem-centred' approach was similar to that encountered by the team already mentioned, but unfortunately without the nicely-balanced constituency of a project team and the ancillary resources. In mid-1972 the problems facing Scotland were immediate and obvious. An entirely new industry was being born, geared to the increasing scale and pace of offshore oil and gas exploration in the northern sector of the North Sea. The planning response was slow and uncoordinated; public sector investment in roads, housing and general community services was heavily time-lagged—not able to match the incoming wave of industrial development projects which swept the country. The conventional wisdom on resource management and integrated environmental planning failed to make a connection with events on the ground. Decisions taken at local authority level were based on rapidly redrafted development plans, and these decisions were subsequently endorsed by Ministers at the Scottish Office. It was happening, it was important, but it was outside the commonly regarded axis for development in Scotland (namely the central belt). It was time to build up a more general appreciation of the significance of these events and to try and place them in a more realistic social and environmental context. Historians will, I feel sure, come to regard that period as a watershed for Scottish industrial development in this century, but it found the country quite unprepared and largely ignorant of the political and economic significance. For the Church of Scotland project, it was not only a vital opportunity to begin some initial stocktaking of the prospects for the offshore and onshore industry but a challenge to make some connection with the ongoing debate concerning the major factors of population growth, resource depletion and environmental hazards. The procedure was improvised and the final report undoubtedly contained many imperfections, but the response to the publication indicated that it did fulfil a clearly felt need on the outside of the industry.[4] Since then, a series of studies have been conducted at a community level and at a regional level; the investment in manpower has been surprisingly small but the analysis that has been generated will, I hope, be of lasting benefit in many situations throughout Scotland. This method of working does however place a large emphasis on the continuity of personnel directing the programme and on a wide network of contacts at many levels throughout the government machine, industry and local authorities. It demands a good deal of application and a certain amount of footwork. In a highly dynamic political and economic situation the outcome is always uncertain, but the discipline of exploring the future choices is certainly never dull.

Many consultancy and planning organizations have now elected to operate in this mode. It has become almost a prerequisite of local planning procedures that a general analysis of the social and environmental impact should be prepared on the occasion of a major development proposal. In some areas, the groups possess no local knowledge and have to begin their task with a sweep of facts and figures relating to the area in question. While this is now an accepted part of the planner's skill in formulating strategic and tactical choices, there has been a very limited diffusion of this technique into other areas of decision-making.

ENERGY AS A KEY AREA

The case against centralization

It should not be necessary to dwell on the connection between events in Scotland and the problems of national energy policy. The task of 'embedding' the energy system in relation to

- — the atmosphere
- — the hydrosphere
- — the ecosphere
- — the sociosphere

underline the enormity of the challenge when taken forward at an analytical level. Fortunately, there is at least one organization in existence that is prepared to encounter this task, even if only as a global dilemma. I recently visited the International Institute of Applied Systems Analysis (IIASA) in Laxenburg, outside Vienna, and met Wolf Häfele, the Deputy Director, who gave me a breakdown of their mode of operation. It is his synthesis of the task ahead that I have to quote to you as the mainspring for my own argument:[5]

'It is necessary to identify and understand all system problems that are inherent in the various options for large scale energy supply. This will be a continuing task and will probably never be completed as energy systems expand further and further. The task is not a matter of algorithm. It is a matter of technological and social substance. Scenario writings and life-style descriptions will probably be among the tools for accomplishing this task. It will be in particular important to identify the various interweavings that become important with the increasing size of energy production. This requires to some extent discipline oriented work but only to the extent that it is necessary for the identification of discipline oriented questions. From then on it is the task of the various scientific disciplines to pursue the questions so identified in connection with the systems analysis'.

This is the technique that has resulted in the first-class appraisal of the US energy situation published by the Ford Foundation Energy Policy Project based in Washington, D.C.[6] Although this operation was probably more generously funded than the previously quoted example of the team based at the University of Oklahoma, it is the style of project management that stands out in this instance. Members of the Ford Foundation team were able to move from and return to the Federal Administration at the end of a two-year term. Indeed some members of the team were in a position to contribute to the Federal Energy Administration Project Independence Blueprint that was published in November 1974.[7] I wish to stress that this is another example of an elaborate multidisciplinary effort that succeeded because of the essential flexibility and consolidated vision of the individuals concerned. Within the UK, it appears that there has been some hesitation on the necessity for such an effort. However, a recent report on Energy Research from the Advisory Board for the Research Councils[8] does register an interest in establishing and supporting multidisciplinary research groups that will undertake exploratory studies: 'Such assessments will have to take account not only of the scientific and technological aspects of the various energy options, but also of economic and sociological features such as the organisation and financing of existing energy-producing industries, fuel marketing strategies and the vulnerability of modern society to energy shortages, however caused'.

This suggestion is a suitable counterweight to the Department of Energy formulation of a large-scale computerized model, which simulates the management and growth of the UK fuel economy at the present time. It has been claimed that this is the most important single energy-planning tool available in the UK, but in view of the highly centralized nature of the technique and its relevance to policy-making, it seems unlikely that many of the results will be widely disseminated. There is an urgent need for independent reappraisal of the UK energy system, but in view of the difficulty of this task, it can probably best be managed on a regional basis. While the Department of Energy model can possibly be interfaced with future models to be developed by the IIASA in arriving at a global synthesis, there is a positive need for energy planning at a regional level in the UK where the planning constraints, including the availability of land, water and manpower resources, are already critical locational parameters far beyond the description of even the most sophisticated model. Independence and precision at this level can therefore be placed at a premium, while the advantages of connecting the energy sub-system with other sub-systems, including agriculture, transport and building industries, also at this level, should be very apparent.

Regional studies

It is at this point that the universities should come into their own as regional centres of excellence, with not only a declared concern for perfecting the standards of undergraduate and postgraduate education, but an equally clearly defined contribution to the social and economic planning processes out of which the future springs. Unlike most other agencies, the universities have a standing complement of professionals who combine effectively in the teaching role, but remain otherwise a largely uncoordinated body of people and ideas. There would seem to be a substantial case for establishing multidisciplinary teams in each university to give regional emphasis to critical areas of assessment— food, energy, housing, transport are the obvious examples. Where there are two universities in reasonably close proximity, then a division of labour according to the available baseline of competence in subject area would obviously have to take place. Alternatively, each university could elect to concentrate exclusively on one or two subject areas of specific interest to the surrounding community.

If this is a pious hope, then by way of contrast I should like to know how it is going to be possible to nucleate 'futures' studies in universities if the more spontaneous forms of interdepartmental cooperation are not available. It may be that my views are far too pragmatic to be taken seriously in such a meeting as this. Either that or my plea to connect with the realities of the planning process, which I see as the inertial devices of the next twenty to thirty years, comes too late for it to make any real difference. I do not hold to such an obviously pessimistic view, but I am apprehensive that as most people inside and outside the universities lower their time horizons so that they can weather the coming economic storm, the relevance of the future as an academic discipline may look increasingly remote.

There is a tangible connection that can be made under some of the headings that I have already mentioned. I should personally prefer to see it happen that way.

Discussion

Waddington: This is a fine introduction to the question of the relevance of research. You are obviously putting forward something considerably broader and more thorough than what has already been done, for instance, by the Department of Urban and Regional Planning attached to the School of Architecture in Edinburgh. Could you say a bit more about how your idea differs from earlier surveys, like the Middlesborough Survey and Plan in the 1930s, on which my wife worked, where the region was surveyed before the plan was made?

Francis: The statutory requirements for planning procedures necessitate modifications on the basis of a short-term analysis, although longer-term projections are frequently attempted. In contrast I am suggesting that, for example, the pattern of energy use within a region needs to be known in some detail so that we can understand how energy is being used in that community and how to anticipate the actual requirements with a much higher degree of precision. It seems to me that this analytical task is an ongoing task. It isn't something that can be done in five or six months so that a development plan can be adapted for a region; it is basically a consolidation of all kinds of resource data at a regional level, representing a pool on which the planners could draw. I believe it would be far better than the improvised superimposition of planning strategies which tends to occur in many parts of the country at present. I am simply suggesting that this requires a large technical and analytical component which is currently lacking, and consequently the planners don't have access to the kind of information that they need. It is quite useless to talk about a 'systems' approach to planning until this situation is remedied.

Eldredge: At the Harvard Business School the instructional method is to analyse one case study after another and let the students draw what they can from these data. Some good reliable futures investigations could come out of a series of case studies which could be either regional or sectoral, or perhaps both. It is a marvellous teaching device, as well as providing research results, because students can play an active part in the surveys. Students often say they don't want to talk about the future but want to *do* the future. They prefer what is now called experiential learning. Case studies can be used first as an active teaching device and then could be generalized at some future date, so that we not only don't have to reinvent the wheel but—as Professor Dror has said—we don't have to reinvent the broken wheel; this would be a step forward.

Dror: I think one should go a little further and not base the idea of futures studies on technology assessment alone, which itself needs a broader base in social futures, international futures and so forth.

The subject matter of this symposium is the future as an academic discipline. This goes far beyond teaching and certainly far beyond undergraduate teaching. One of the main purposes of an academic discipline is to provide knowledge; and, I think, we should emphasize that futures knowledge which is useful for policy-making may be even more needed now than futures teaching among undergraduate students.

Another main function of the universities is to prepare professional people for their callings, and again I would regard the absence of policy professionals able to deal with complex problems as an even more serious and acute problem than inadequate understanding of the future among citizens at large. This doesn't mean that I regard the role of teaching undergraduates as unimportant but I would not regard it necessarily as the most important role, and certainly not as the only function, of the universities.

We may be able to agree more or less on a list of important problems affecting society, like the one Professor Shane presented, but I have great difficulty in seeing a real connection between those lists which are intellectual thinking exercises and the present real agendas of most governments. In other words, putting present decisions and futures perspectives into gear is very difficult. Many people seem to assume that there will somehow be a *deus ex machina* quantum jump. But the social decision-making machinery needed for dealing with these types of problems does not exist either nationally or internationally.

This means that we need new bridges. I would say we need a double bridge: one between knowledge and power, and one between the present and the future. One way of looking at some of the functions of universities is to look at their possible role in providing those bridges. I have spent most of my life at universities and, being rather interested in this matter, I have found much more useful work going on at Rand Corporation-type think tanks than at universities. Some universities do some useful things and some think tanks do a lot of nonsense things, but in general universities have a lot to learn from the structure of think tanks if they are to adopt the bridging function.

I am trying to study the policy-making system in Great Britain. Although interesting attempts at improvement have been made—such as the Central Policy Review Staff Programme Analysis and Review, the special advisers, the work of Political and Economic Planning (PEP), and so forth—there is no policy research organization equipped to handle 'macro-social diagnosis'. This is something that universities should develop by trying to do it themselves, by training policy professionals and by encouraging the establishment of think tanks. In this way the academic discipline of futures studies, if it is intellectually feasible, may fill a real social need.

Waddington: It must be not only intellectually feasible but also administratively feasible.

Shane: Some years ago John Fischer published an article which was most prescient.[9] He suggested, for example, that architects should be taught not only their technical and professional skills but also to question whether, from an ecological point of view, an airport *should* be built in Chicago, when biospheric–ecological problems might ensue. Of course, this leaves unanswered the question of *whose* viewpoints shall be accepted as to what is 'sound' or 'desirable' from an ecological point of view. Conflicting opinion in the academic arena as to whose ideas should be reflected could lead to a lively conflict.

Francis: Many of the problems that I described in my paper were not anticipated and yet they have recently occurred within a concentrated time scale. The problems were not anticipated because it was almost impossible to predict the offshore oil and gas potential in the North Sea without going and drilling to establish the scale of the reserves. Under these circumstances, the planners could relax back into the position that they didn't have to anticipate a particular sequence of events because it wasn't their problem at that moment—there was only a limited frame of reference, there was no contingency plan, there was no alternative strategy. Nearly all of the regional growth-points were in the wrong place when it came to administering the industrial development pattern that emerged with the build-up of offshore production. To that extent we do need to have a base-line study going on at many levels. Land use is a fundamental consideration in determining settlement patterns and almost inevitably too many easy assumptions are incorporated concerning community needs and the need of individuals on that point, particularly when it comes to multiple land-use functions in certain critical development areas. There are many problems in this country of that kind. We really don't know the real asset value of a particular land area until it is already committed and subsequently sterilized. To that extent there has been a total deficiency in strategic planning at a national level. The Central Policy Review Staff, for example, which is working on energy conservation at present, throws all the balls in the air and simply makes blanket recommendations, with no real idea of what the actual contribution can be at the regional level. There is no machinery for making connection with the broad policy decisions or for the actual meshing of these decisions at a particular regional level. Energy requirements over the country as a whole are really quite disparate. Any general energy policy that is smeared over the whole country has an almost unanticipated effect when interpreted by local authority planners and similar concerns. A general policy can create all kinds of problems and for that reason I am very suspicious of any exclusive reliance on central policy machinery.

Black: You said that when the oil development came, it caught everybody napping. I am not a futurologist so I don't have to pretend that I know what the future is going to contain, but it certainly contains change, and change at an increasing rate. Professor Waddington has pointed out many times that, biologically, the success of evolution is to be found in its ability to cope with the unpredictable, and I would suggest that this is true of social evolution too. So what we should be developing in our students is the intellectual ability to cope with change. The old linear thinking whereby we go one step at a time along a fairly defined road is probably no longer adequate, as Professor Waddington has also pointed out today. Increasingly I see general undergraduate education—not specialist education—as developing the ability to cope with the unpredictable. Of course what happened in Scotland was unpredicted, and all the growth points were in the wrong place, but this is what happens in life.

Waddington: Are you saying that the university already provides this ability, or that it should provide it?

Black: I am saying that it *should* be providing the ability. At the moment it does not, and one reason why people get out of date is that they have been educated in a limited way.

Dror: Is this more a question of intellectual or of emotional training?

Black: Both; they can't be separated. I believe that we have been letting our undergraduates down by not giving them the emotional as well as the intellectual basis they need for coping with rapidly increasing change.

Waddington: I don't believe that when he was at Imperial College John Francis was indoctrinated with the notion that he was likely to change his profession radically, from being a professional nuclear power engineer to being whatever he may call himself now.

Perry: That makes me think of what I was trying to do when I taught pharmacology, where the rate of change is more rapid than in almost any other discipline in the medical schools. Although I tried hard to tell the students that they would have to face up to change, there was little I could tell them about how to prepare themselves for it. Change could not be foreseen because one never knew what the chemists were going to come up with. Apart from some general principles in the way of looking at evidence and judging it, what one is really trying to do is to introduce something right outside the subject, that is a state of mind prepared to receive change. I don't know if one department can do that alone. That is a naive remark but it does seem to me that it is quite important to realize this.

Waddington: I think there is going to be an even more fundamental effect. It really signals the end of our classical idea that education goes on until people have a degree at the age of 21 and then stops. At the Open University students can take a course at any stage in their lives.

Stewart: The report of the Advisory Board for the Research Councils[8] to which John Francis referred was really issued to show what research related to energy the Research Councils were funding in the UK and to indicate possibilities for the future. Universities have two principal contributions to make, one in teaching and the other in research, partly in regional problems and partly in general ones. The constraints on universities in building up interdisciplinary teams and breaking down barriers between departments are considerable. These, perhaps, can best be overcome by interdisciplinary teams being built up within a university with outside support. The system of dual support for universities could achieve this in the UK. The Research Councils can fund people who form a unit or a group of some sort within a university, and that group can draw in people from various departments of the university who become interested in the problems the group is dealing with. Sir Ernest Woodroofe made the point that if a research function is to operate together with a teaching function to undergraduates in such fields, a few permanent people are needed, plus a set of people who come in and out of the system. Could one not derive a system where, with a small permanent group, *ad hoc* groups could come in for a time and study particular problems of the day, energy being one such problem?

Waddington: Who should take the initiative in forming such groups? Many universities have quite a lot of people who could form an effective group if they were brought together. Sometimes one person likes organizing things, so he whips up his pals, who work out an interdisciplinary group which may be successful. Quite often an outside planning body, like one of the Research Councils, may know that there is a general problem and would be only too willing to fund an interdisciplinary group. Does the Council have to wait until somebody comes and asks for that? For example, from about the mid-1960s it became obvious to biologists that the world was soon going to run short of animal foodstuffs, and that the oil-seed cake and so on, which we used for feeding cattle in the UK, was going to be eaten in the countries where it is grown. It was clear that Britain ought to rethink its livestock industry. But there was no one in British research or in the science policy set-up to whom this could be said. The problem doesn't really belong to the Agricultural Research Council, which basically deals with British agriculture and not with conditions abroad. So what happened? The British livestock industry went over from feeding its cattle at least partly on home-grown grass to feeding them on home-grown or imported barley and other imported foodstuffs. This turning away from home-grown to imported foodstuffs developed just when everybody who raised their eyes to the world at large saw that imported foodstuffs were going to get scarcer and more expensive. This is what we are caught with now.

The point is that there was no central body looking at the world outside. That would be the most elementary futurology on the world scale rather than on a local scale. And, if there had been such a body, does the British administrative machinery provide any way in which a central forecasting body could stimulate the types of scientific research within the universities that it knows ought to be there?

Stewart: Some of the Research Councils prod the universities into doing work which the Council considers desirable but which is not reasonably covered at present. I think this practice is growing, particularly in the present financial climate. It is important that people in universities and elsewhere should also prod the research councils for money and draw the problems to the attention of the Research Councils. Both responsive and positive approaches are necessary.

Dror: Experience in other countries indicates the need for some redundancies in such institutions. A whole network of bodies is needed, with different perspectives and different loyalties. Some should be nearer and some further from the main policy makers.

Lundberg: Dr Francis, when you called for increased interdisciplinary contacts within the universities you stated that the departments combined effectively in teaching but not otherwise. Actually they usually don't combine even in teaching! It is our experience in Göteborg that interdisciplinary teaching is a good way of establishing contact. Undergraduate or graduate courses like those proposed by Professor Waddington may thus have the secondary effect of creating an interdisciplinary platform for research and external activation.

Waddington: Nearly all our organizations are vertical, either in hierarchies or undivided disciplines. We are bad at horizontal cross-connections. There is inadequate theorizing about such structures, and I think there is a lot to be done in systems-thinking about organizations with both horizontal and vertical links.

Francis: I agree with what Sir Frederick Stewart said about groups as points of nucleation. I also agree that the university has to put its house in order as far as revitalizing its own constituency is concerned. On a subject such as energy there are many contributing groups outside universities who are looking for a meeting point, which doesn't seem to exist. For the past two years I have been a member of the Oil Development Council for Scotland, and there is no way of making contact with the government machine other than by contacting each part of the energy system independently. There is no coordinating link at the regional level.

King: There is something of a paradox in your approach, Dr Francis. You were stressing the need for regional and local consideration of futures and of trends. I think you are right here, and this is true in many ways other than in futures studies. It is certainly true for participatory democracy and decision-making at local levels. But at the same time we have to indulge a lot more in global thinking. One of the problems is how to marry these two apparently contrary needs. For governments the importance of external factors is increasingly great. Recently a man who had been the Head of State of a small, highly industrialized, rich country told me that he had abandoned political life because it was no longer any fun: there was no room for manoeuvre at all and everything was determined from outside by what happened in the United States or in the Arab countries. This may be an extreme case but the influence of external forces is great in relation to contagious inflation, to the monetary system, the balance of payments, and to many other things. The force of these external factors is not yet reflected in the general trend of political thinking.

Waddington: The number of people in the world now who expect they will ever have autocratic power to decide things for themselves is small. I think your friend is suffering from a trend that began long ago in most countries. I am sure Sir Ernest Woodroofe would say that even Unilever has not total freedom to do whatever it pleases all the time.

King: In what we have said about horizontality within universities we are talking a little as if universities were monolithic structures and were roughly of the same pattern everywhere. But we are talking of a certain type of Anglo-Saxon university. In France, a survey of social science research in universities showed recently that there is practically none. Nearly all the social science research in France is done in independent institutes because the university system has been too rigid to accept it, or to find ways of financing it. Different countries have different approaches, and there is a good deal to be learnt from some of these as case studies. In our Anglo-Saxon system the flexibility is marvellous in some ways; on the other hand we haven't explored all the possibilities. In Japan, for example, there is a well-established way of starting serious research for a new subject. The universities get together and form temporary or permanent organizations—they may have institutes or they may not—which act on behalf of the university system as a whole. So instead of fractional work starting in many places, national institutes are created, each for simplicity under the management of a particular university, so that neither management nor resources are fractionated. That institute is able to give doctorates on behalf of the whole system to people from other universities.

Waddington: That is similar to what we have done in this country in relation to nuclear power.

King: That is for certain very expensive equipment, but the Japanese system is used more flexibly and in other ways.

Another experiment is the approach taken by the University of Manitoba, where a Vice-President for Multidisciplinary Studies has been appointed, whose job is to stimulate these studies. He formed institutes which existed only on paper. For instance, one project was on a very practical subject—the total water resources of the prairie provinces of Canada. On the Board of this institute, the Vice-President would probably act as Chairman. The chemistry department, the agricultural people, the law people and so on would join, and all aspects of the subject would be looked at. A programme in common is created and then elements of the programme are undertaken by different parts of the university, with the interdisciplinary discussion in this paper institute. There is even the possibility of giving contracts to other universities inside or outside the country for elements of the work for which the university lacks the skills. We ought to explore, in this country and in others, a large number of alternative approaches.

Waddington: In the University of Edinburgh we have to some extent explored this type of institute by what we call 'Schools'. The School of the Built Environment brought together architects, town planners, civil engineers, lawyers and so on. And there is a School of Epistemology; it was going to be called the School of Experimental Epistemology but nobody could swallow that! These Schools have been quite active in bringing together different interests. They have not yet achieved really large-scale activities, but I think this is due partly to financial stringency, and partly to the lack of research programmes capable of attracting outside funds on a big enough scale. But they are a beginning.

Ashby: Dr Francis said that it is the universities which have failed in Scotland. Universities in Britain have to be regarded as a constellation of anarchies; they are virtually acephalic—that is, without a head. Therefore to approach a university as a corporation and to expect it to do things as a corporate body is not to my mind a practical political solution to the problems you have been raising. However, we do have in this university system a remarkable tradition of *laissez-faire* liberalism for the individuals inside it. What you must ask, Dr Francis, is not that the universities as corporate bodies should take an interest in the oil problem in Scotland, because I think this would be an inefficient way of doing it, but that certain groups of experts in the universities should do so.

I entirely agree that interdisciplinary groups are needed. Alvin Weinberg has been trying to press for these in America for some time. Generally the nucleation force for these groups has been either research councils, or foundations like Ford or Nuffield, or even local stimuli, such as the Sabrina project in Bristol. This project is trying to do for the Severn the sort of thing that you have been talking about for Scotland, although they haven't so far made great progress.

In our experience the difficulty about institutes which exist on paper and not as physical entities inside universities, has been that unless they are well financed —which again means that an outside body is helping to support them—they have to borrow people from departments of biology, history and so on. These people are always being drawn back to their departments; they feel they had better keep their roots there. So 'paper institutes' can't get the full loyalty they need.

I agree that if we are to instil in universities an appreciation of future problems, the case-history method of bringing undergraduates and staff into planning studies is one way to do it. But we must remember that all attempts at forecasting on the microscale have so far been extraordinarily disappointing. If it is true that the present is going to produce the future, then it is the past that has produced the present. The manpower prediction committees that served (or mis-served) the British government for years made deplorable mistakes over comparatively simple predictions such as the production of medical doctors: they only had to look at the age distribution of practitioners to work that out; and yet they got it all wrong. Planning, although necessary, is something which can only be used as a base. If we are to teach planning for the future in universities the key thing we have to get into the minds of the young is something that the staff of the university can't themselves supply. And that is how to build bridges between planning and political decision. If I had to devise a course of futurology in universities I would be cautious about predicting the future because the past is littered with failures in prediction. But I would be enthusiastic about telling the young how to cross the bridge from planning to political action. It is possible to do this: the bridges are in fact being crossed all the time. But this would mean bringing into the universities, on secondment, the people who are making the decisions, and battering them with questions, about (for instance) how a Royal Commission report gets turned into legislation.

Woodroofe: I suspect that in that particular line a good deal of experience is available already, particularly in America. In order to plan in business, people have to make assumptions, define objectives, assign priorities and then decide how to achieve those objectives. The assumptions are really where one tries to predict the future. What is the purchasing power going to be? What are the social changes if women go out to work? Some assumptions are on a long time scale—if you are growing palm oil trees you need about twenty-five years—but most are on a five-year scale. After working this way for a long enough time one is able to monitor the results against the assumptions, so one is learn-ing all the time. This learning process on a microscale, particularly in the short term, probably would provide a lot of experience if it could be tapped. To the best of my knowledge it has not been tapped much by universities.

Ashby: Would you second a very bright young man of 35 from your firm to the universities to explain the processes?

Woodroofe: Fortunately I am retired and don't have to answer that question! Maybe we don't need to second people so much as get them to work together. From time to time Unilever seconds people to universities, but what has happened much more is that some of our scientists have been appointed as part-time professors or associate professors in universities, delivering a certain number of lectures, and responsible for a number of research students. I think this is the way to do it.

References cited

[1] COUNCIL ON ENVIRONMENTAL QUALITY (1973) Guidelines: preparation of environmental impact statements. *Federal Register, 38* (No. 147), Part II, August 1
[2] JONES, MARTIN V. (1971) *Project Summary: a Technology Assessment Methodology,* p. 7. The Mitre Corporation, Washington, D. C.
[3] KASH, DON E., WHITE, IRVINE L. *et al.* (1973) *Energy under the Oceans: a Technology Assessment of Outer Continental Shelf Oil and Gas Operations,* University of Oklahoma Press, Norman, Oklahoma
[4] FRANCIS, JOHN & SWAN, NORMAN (1973) *Scotland in Turmoil: a Social and Environmental Assessment of the Impact of North Sea Oil and Gas on Communities in the North of Scot-land,* St. Andrew Press, Edinburgh
[5] HÄFELE, WOLF (1974) Energy systems. *IAEA Bulletin, 16* (No.1/2)
[6] FORD FOUNDATION ENERGY POLICY PROJECT (1974) *A Time to Choose: America's Energy Future,* Ballinger, Cambridge, Mass.
[7] FEDERAL ENERGY ADMINISTRATION (1974) *Project Independence Report,* FEA, Washington, D.C.
[8] ADVISORY BOARD FOR THE RESEARCH COUNCILS (1974) *Energy Research: the Research Council's Contribution,* p. 11, Science Research Council, London
[9] FISCHER, JOHN (1971) Survival U is alive and burgeoning in Green Bay, Wisconsin. *Harper's Magazine 242,* 20, February

Sclerotic structures and the future of academic organization

J. N. BLACK

Bedford College, University of London

Abstract Universities have developed strong organizational structures that act to inhibit change. Reshuffles of the academic mix can be achieved, though the problems of dealing with redundant departments have not yet been solved and are exacerbated in periods of financial stringency. It is doubtful whether really major changes can be accommodated in existing structures. If universities are to respond to innovations of the magnitude implied in some of the titles of the papers at this meeting, some or all of the following problems will have to be solved: restrictive practices based on departmental autonomy; resistance to change in individual teachers arising from excessive tenure and an implacable 'hands-off' attitude to 'my own work'; wasteful duplication of effort between universities by which less central subjects are taught in small, barely viable units in many places. Resolution of some of these difficulties will involve careful examination of a number of academic sacred cows and is unlikely to be achieved without increased central direction.

Much of the discussion at this meeting has been concerned with the type and style of teaching in universities in the next few decades. Most of us accept that there will be a need for many changes in the type of courses offered, though we may not agree on what they should be. I propose to deal with a different theme —the impediments in the way of introducing innovations into university structures—in the hope that if we can identify the problems in advance some of them at least can be 'short-circuited' in the event.

By structures I mean the basic units of organization into which a university is divided. These commonly incorporate a central Administration; Faculties (broad subject groupings); Schools (narrower subject groupings); Departments (usually taken to be the essential teaching and research grouping); Units (either within departments or outside and across departmental boundaries). It would probably not be usual to find Faculties, Schools and Departments all coexisting; two would normally suffice to provide a structure with academic

107

cohesion but without the additional administrative effort and delays of a further tier in the organizational hierarchy. Nevertheless we can all, I suspect, point to complex groupings introduced more for personal or 'political' than for academic reasons.

I propose to deal basically with the department as the central organizational structure which would be called upon to take the brunt of any changes. From the title of this paper it may be assumed that I am predisposed to the view that academic structures have become rigid, thus preventing free flow of 'bits' of 'information' (however described) through the interdepartmental (or faculty or school) barriers.

This is not to say that universities do not adapt (or have not adapted) to change. To suggest this would be monstrously unjust, and I may refer to Perkin's recent article for an analysis of such adaptation.[1] As Perkin points out, universities have had to deal with students with new and disturbing motives, and there can be no reason for assuming that the trend away from uncritical acceptance of traditional course structures will diminish. I think the trend is more likely to intensify, not so much in demands for relevance, as the shallowness and ambiguity of such a concept becomes more apparent, or by a rejection of logical argument as the basis of intellectual activity, as the tide of social emotionalism retreats, but rather towards a separation of general from specialized education, with the latter becoming increasingly a postgraduate concern.

Similarly, universities have made major strides in altering the balance between staff and students in decision-making fora. It may well be that the concessions towards greater participation have had two results not always apparent to those taking part. First, they have led to a greatly increased work-load for the administration and, since the processes of consultation are time-consuming and open to manipulation of almost Byzantine opportunism, greater power in the hands of the permanent structure. Secondly, I suspect—but cannot prove— that greater participation is a potent factor for the maintenance of the *status quo*; contrary to expectation, it may be easier for an energetic and single-minded operator in a formal hierarchical structure to bring about far-reaching innovations than it is for an army of angry young men in a system of participatory democracy.

It is also true that universities have gone a long way in introducing new courses in response to changing requirements, notably in subject areas which straddle existing disciplines. I do not seek to diminish their significance by saying that these are fundamentally new ways of assembling the academic jigsaw, and sometimes give the impression of being made to work in spite of, rather than because of, accepted structural conventions.

The changes universities may face can roughly be grouped as follows:

(a) New subject matter within a discipline;
(b) New disciplines;
(c) New combinations of disciplines;
(d) New teaching methods;
(e) New links at inter-tertiary level.

To deal quickly with the last two points, it is noteworthy that the only large-scale innovation in British universities for many years has been the setting up of the Open University. As an innovation this has to be compared with the introduction of non-collegiate 'civic' universities in England (for which models existed in Scotland) or the development of federal structures in Wales or London. The possibility of links with polytechnics and teacher-training colleges, thought by many to be one of the most likely as well as the most desirable of the developments in higher education, is now being tested, but there seem to be major underlying problems of regrouping.

NEW SUBJECT MATTER IN EXISTING DISCIPLINES

The pace of development, particularly in the sciences and social sciences, is such that teachers may quickly become out of date, needing to vary their subject coverage as they get older (at an age when to do so becomes harder). The outstanding difficulties for universities in meeting the demands of changing subject matter are twofold. First, the contractual right of tenure—often from the age of 25 or 30 to retirement—denies universities the ability to replace staff as academic considerations would suggest. Reliance upon tenure may sometimes lead the individual to sit back and fail to keep up with his subject, though I do not know whether this would be cured by, say, a system of five-year appointments. More publications might well mean worse, but we all know colleagues whose papers are delayed for incorporation into a monograph, then withheld for a book which itself is eventually earmarked for his retirement and is ultimately condemned to oblivion, along with the author and his reputation.

The second difficulty is one of retraining. Lord Annan has suggested that anyone wishing to remain all his life in an academic career will have to be prepared to retrain at intervals, but I doubt the efficacy of this: first, the older a man, the more scholarly 'capital' he has accumulated and the more resistant to retraining he will be; his status depends on the opinion of his colleagues in the same subject, and to begin again dissipates that status. Secondly, we are touching here on one of the most important factors involved in resistance to change in universities—the divided loyalties of a university teacher, first to the institution in which he serves and second to his discipline. (Lord Ashby's 'Thank Offering to Britain Fund' Lecture of 1969 contains an elegant dissection of this attitude.[2]) When someone says 'I teach philosophy at the University of Mummerset' what he usually implies is that he is a professional philosopher who happens to teach at the University of Mummerset, not that he is first and foremost a university teacher whose subject happens to be philosophy. Of course not, you will say; his subject is the thing he really cares about, and he is never given any instruction in teaching, it being tacitly assumed that a good scholar can automatically communicate his subject. (Any student can give the lie to this and it is odd how quickly one's experience as a student is forgotten when one becomes a scholar–teacher oneself.) From this stems the importance of 'my own work', and the corpus of published work which constitutes the basis of professional status. The tradition of investment in personal intellectual capital, however important as a vehicle for scholarship, certainly brings with it resistance to change.

Besides, do we really want retraining on a vast scale? I have a feeling that those teachers who should be retrained may turn out to be those whose contribution to academic life is small in their present subject and likely to be even smaller in the next, and that those who would respond best to the challenge of retraining are also those who can be least spared from their own subject. The extent of change must surely be limited; apart from the slow build-up over the years of a repertoire of techniques in a given subject, there are 'casts of mind' which, I would think, severely limit individual flexibility. I say nothing of that sacred cow, academic freedom, which encourages an academic in the view that he can do whatever work he wants to do regardless of the needs of his institution or the community at large. May I paraphrase—'Academic Freedom—how many crimes are committed in thy name?'

NEW DISCIPLINES

A comparison of a university calendar of today with one of fifty or even twenty-five years ago reveals the emergence of departments representing subjects that seem to be quite new. Over a long period of time one can discern patterns of construction and demolition, old names being replaced by new ones, departments splitting and lumping in an attempt to reflect the changing state of knowledge. Straight changes in name do not concern us (e.g. in my own college, 'Natural Philosophy' changed to 'Physics' in 1872, while in my last university the change had still not happened a century later), and many changes of name do not really introduce anything new (witness variations on the theme of

English, English language and English literature). More important are subjects which are not so much new as bits of old ones achieving independent status—as, for instance, genetics, which has emerged from other biological departments as a subject in its own right. Such changes are easy to bring about, since the 'core' of the subject and the teaching and other staff are available, and as a subject becomes differentiated the hold of the parent department weakens, so that all that is necessary is a recognition of departmental status reflected in suitable accommodation. Both subject and staff are then safely within their own ring fence.

The problem of dealing with emerging and declining subjects is not difficult to solve at a time of expansion in university finance. A new department can be set up through normal planning by the allocation of enough posts and facilities from 'development' funding. It is possible to short-circuit a run-down department by setting up a parallel department, differently named, which can gradually take over, so that existing staff can be allowed to drift on until overcome by retirement. In periods of financial stringency, however, it becomes almost impossible to justify funds for such exercises—indeed, pressure grows for departments (particularly those not currently favoured by students) to merge and pool their resources. We can then expect a 'closing of the ranks' as each department, fearing that a new post somewhere else may mean the loss of one of its own, tacitly agrees not to pursue competitive policies. There is, too, a size below which a department ceases to be viable. If it cannot be closed down or absorbed, it can, however, be reduced to a care and maintenance basis, thus countering the argument that if it were to be closed it would be hard to re-establish it if there were to be a recrudescence of demand.

The history of forestry teaching in this country illustrates this. In 1960, there were departments at four universities teaching much the same course. An anticipated decline of employment prospects led to changes; one department developed a strong interest in wood science and technology; one changed to forest biology, a unit in a larger programme of biological teaching. One changed to natural resources, teaching forestry along with a number of 'new' subjects, such as wild-life management, against a background of general ecology. The fourth remained basically unchanged. It is doubtful how many of these developments in what is, after all, a minor subject could have been achieved in anything but the period of post-Robbins expansion. Today these departments would probably have been left to wither on the vine.

The problem of changing departmental roles is not so much one of creating new or alternative departments, but of deciding what to do with the old ones. It may be possible to run them down quickly, if the age structure of the staff is favourable, or to disperse the staff to other departments, or to agree a programme of early retirement (although the machinery for this has yet to be agreed and it will never be cheap), but counterarguments based on such premises as possible return of student interest and the maintenance of valuable intellectual diversity, reinforced by considerations of tenure and tradition, are not easy to refute. It may be that resistance to change is greater in large organizations, as is often said, but the close personal links in smaller ones result in all proposals being considered in an emotional way that highlights the problems of the individuals.

NEW COMBINATIONS OF DISCIPLINES

Probably most changes now facing universities come into the category of new combinations of disciplines, and in times of financial constraint there are likely to be pleas, particularly from departments finding it difficult to recruit students, for an increase in the number of joint degrees offered. Certainly there are many more 'unit' type courses available than hitherto, and some of the new universities have constructed their main curricula around courses of this type. If these new general courses are introduced against a background of strong departments, with well-marked territories, a number of problems are likely to arise.

(1) In contradistinction to single honours students, students on joint courses etc. do not 'belong' and have no 'home' in any department, a situation which plays into the hands of the disaffected. (See Lord Annan's report on the troubles of Essex University.[3])

(2) Departments are jealous of the standards of entry of their students, and, unless students are admitted to the Faculty (or School), are apt to set entry qualifications incompatible with free choice of course.

(3) Similarly the construction of unit degrees may be complicated by excessive demands for prerequisite courses. There is considerable and justified pressure against composing a degree from a wide range of subjects without some intellectual 'backbone' to support them, but this requirement need not prevent wide choice.

(4) Strong territoriality in departments can increase overlap between courses, and unnecessary duplication. It is hard to separate departmental from personal factors in such situations, but at the root is the strong feeling of departmental identity and autonomy. Unnecessary overlap is one of the most wasteful uses of academic resources, and is not always easy to identify, let alone correct.

(5) If it can be accepted that good teaching should be illuminated by

cogent and appropriate research, a major difficulty seems to be the paucity of interdisciplinary research. Emphasis on specialization only accessible to the initiated does not provide a pattern which the 'joint' student finds easy to emulate.

(6) Another problem is that of degree standards, for it is often difficult to obtain agreement between departments on classification—even at the pass/fail borderline. The situation is made more difficult by the heterogeneity of the experience brought to a class by students whose course background is different.

So far I have been dealing with departments, and have emphasized the extent to which reorganization is confounded by departmental demarcation. Teaching across faculty boundaries is harder to achieve, not only because of timetabling problems, but because teachers on each side tend to assume a familiarity with basic principles and outlooks which does not necessarily exist. It has been most successful where objectives are limited, e.g. German or Russian for scientists, economics for engineers, etc. Courses of general cultural interest should, one would think, be everywhere available, but it is not easy to tempt students to them unless they carry credit in the examination system. Nor are they popular with those who are asked to teach them.

If it is true that traditional organizations are almost too rigid to accommodate the modest changes required today, it is unlikely that major developments which universities may face in the future will be achieved without rupture. I refer not so much to the intellectual problems of the transmission of experience, the sensing of value judgements and the basis of rationality, but to the way these are manifested in teaching programmes. What will have to be done to ease the introduction of major innovations?

I suspect that there may be two areas of interference with what we have come to regard as necessary props of university and academic autonomy. Firstly, the contractual rights of tenure of individuals, with a possible change in the balance between scholarship and teaching in favour of the latter. Secondly, an end to the scandal of duplication of subject matter between universities—not, of course, in the major academic disciplines but in those where mini-departments are maintained in many places for a relatively small number of students. Today even a federal university like London finds its hands tied when it tries to 'rationalize' departmental structure across the constituent colleges, and the time must surely come when this nettle is grasped, even if it means direction from the centre or the appointment of teachers not to an individual university but to a central pool. One can imagine the hue and cry which would greet this proposal, but it is the only way in which I can see major regroupings coming about without unacceptable and wasteful financial overprovision. The autonomy and independence of universities currently sheltered by the existence of the University Grants Committee is already probably further eroded than many academics suspect by such matters as national negotiations on salaries and conditions of work for all grades of staff, and by the 'earmarking' method in the quinquennial system (a system which is of doubtful relevance anyway in the present financial climate). Few of us, probably, would welcome increased bureaucratic intervention in university matters, but if we find that the changes required of us are of such magnitude that we cannot meet them within existing structures, it is hard to see how our paymasters can be prevented from calling the tune. I do not like the implications of this conclusion, still less do I wish to make recommendations in this direction; rather, I feel that it is inevitable.

Perhaps the greatest difficulty in accepting really radical innovations in teaching programmes will prove to be the task of altering the feeling, widespread within the universities (if declining outside them), that universities have a privileged place in society which protects them from the rough blast of economic blizzards. I have been saddened by the number of times when, in recent months, attempts to instil some measure of financial prudence in the face of inflation and cutbacks have been met by demands to spend to the hilt, and beyond, on the grounds that university spending is not to be questioned, and will always be met by a grateful government. This, despite all the quotations one can muster from the University Grants Committee and the Committee of Vice-Chancellors and Principals. Universities must shed the comfortable illusion that they have a special privileged position in society, and face the fact that like other public enterprises they have to account for their use of public funds, not so much in the book-keeping sense required of us by the Auditor-General, but in relation to the size of the public purse, and their contribution to society. The 'mystique' of the university, and the privileged position of both staff and students have to go—or have to be swept away. If this mystique is seen to stand in the way of desirable innovation the risk is that the universities will be swept away, too, in a babies and bathwater syndrome perhaps to be replaced by institutions of more appropriate structure.

Discussion

Platt: Universities are among the most durable human institutions. They have lasted longer than any others except religions. A number of universities in Europe have lasted through many changes of government and dynasties, and in the US Harvard University has lasted through three systems of government. I don't think they will be wiped out.

Black: The rate of change is getting quicker.

Perry: The Open University has been called the only innovation in the UK but there is a paradox of which you may not be aware. First, the Open University could not have begun in the UK unless it had been started as a new and independent institution on its own. I don't think it would have evolved out of existing institutions. Secondly, we haven't discovered, in the Open University, how to institutionalize innovation; we are liable to become just as sclerotic in a different form. We are caught on the horns of that dilemma.

Regarding unit or modular systems, we require almost nothing in the way of entry qualifications and we leave it to the good sense of students to make up their own coherent package of courses. It works in the sense that they refuse to take a rag-bag of assorted credits, as many people thought they would. They tend to choose sensible patterns. But I think this is only true of our kind of student who is an adult with experience of life and highly motivated in a particular direction. I suspect that it would not be true of 18-year-olds straight out of school.

Jevons: I wonder how far the paucity of research recognized as interdisciplinary is due to the apparently transient nature of interdisciplinarity. Interdisciplinarity is a self-transcending process: as soon as it becomes successful it ceases to be called interdisciplinary because it has become labelled as a new discipline. Take as an example my own former discipline of biochemistry. The name is a verbal fossil which tells us that it originated as an interdisciplinary study, but few people nowadays think of it as interdisciplinary.

Ashby: I think Dr Black's diagnosis is absolutely correct. Unfortunately he may have diagnosed something like Huntington's chorea for which there is no cure. One is comforted by the fact that the British universities, at any rate in the eighteenth century, were in a state that was even worse, yet they recovered. No one has adequately analysed the causes of that recovery. It certainly was not due to a succession of Royal Commissions or interventions from outside— these did occur but all they did was to push at doors which were already open. It was probably largely the influence of Germany on the new universities (London and Manchester); and Oxford and Cambridge revived under the threat that Manchester might become a better place than they were!

Eldredge: We are treating this at the level of the university as an institution, but there is another level—that of personal development. I have been in an interdisciplinary field (urban studies) for over twenty-five years. There is transference of skills in such activity—one doesn't lose one's academic capital by going into something different with mutual cross-fertilization. Loss of academic skill does not occur when one begins to transfer around. Dr Platt, for example, has moved from one field to another in his work. I was a sociologist of revolution and then I became a planner to see how to eliminate vicious revolution. There are all sorts of ways of shifting back and forth as an individual inside the system in the US, which is, as noted earlier, a disorganized system offering more freedom to the individual than the rather tighter systems of England or Sweden.

Waddington: The administrative structure tends to be treated as a cross-country racecourse by the really enterprising person. Most innovations get done by people who find some way to work the system, which they accept as a challenge which is interesting to meet.

Lundberg: In most countries the cost of basic academic research is only 10–20 per cent of the total expenditure for research and development. Have the British universities asked themselves how sclerotic they are relative to other research agencies? The sectoral research agencies are politically directed and generally seeking solutions to short-term problems. In the end they may turn out to be much more inflexible than the universities which have always benefited from changes generated by internal forces.

Waddington: That is a good point. The question of flexibility needs to be considered in relation to the question of scale. In universities things may look difficult to shift, but they are not of the scale of Oak Ridge or even Harwell, or laboratories of that kind, which have outlived their immediate purpose. It is difficult to know what to do with those places, though there has been some limited success with finding new roles for them.

Valaskakis: University reform is important but I am not sure that the tenure system should be severely challenged or removed. The relationship between job-security and poor performance is by no means established. In fact a good case can be made for universalized tenure outside the university system. The Japanese work on the tenure system within industry, and as we know they seem to be very competitive. To keep people on their toes we may have to have a built-in system of incentives and promotions completely separate from tenure. The permanence of employment need not be challenged.

Black: I am not suggesting that we should take away all tenure. It is a necessary part of the commitment to scholarship, though it may need to be modified. Other difficulties arise when administrative responsibilities are linked to tenured positions. In this situation, change can be blocked and the interests of other staff may be prejudiced. That is where I part company with it. Another point: does the Open University accept the faculty/department type of structure for its staff?

Perry: We don't have departments as spending units but as research and recruitment units. I think they are a necessary part of a permanent structure.

Woodroofe: The Japanese system of tenure in industry is breaking down. In the past, many Japanese companies solved the problem by having specific departments, often called general affairs departments, to which they transferred people who were getting in the way.

Waddington: It is probably true that the universities have been neglectful in providing acceptable wastepaper boxes for people who have lost their usefulness where they are.

Ashby: Tenure is a terribly difficult problem. One compromise might be to grant tenure at a 'basic' level in the academic profession after a probationary period, but to promote people above this basic level only for periods of, say, five years. Thus a professorship would be reviewed every five years, and the holder at the end of such a period might well go back to being a lecturer again. That would have a healthy effect on ourselves and our colleagues!

Black: I think this is right. It may even be necessary to appoint academics not to one particular university but to some body representing the academic profession as a whole, so that they can if necessary be moved, and subjects can be grouped. Perhaps what we also need in this country is a University of the Chiltern Hundreds—a lovely old house, lawns, a library, and very deep armchairs!

Eldredge: In America we make failing academics into administrators.

King: We also make successful academics into administrators, unfortunately.

Lundberg: In Sweden only full professors and associate professors have tenure. This makes it very difficult for a young scientist to move outside the accepted border of his discipline. The absence of tenure may be a strong barrier to innovation.

Shane: While I do not disagree with Dr Black, I think that in the US we have reached a point at which we cannot improve the future of the universities just by removing today's problems. There must be more basic changes. Our universities need to become different kinds of institutions. I doubt, for instance, that we should continue to drift towards a universalized baccalaureate degree in the US—at least as higher education is now constituted. I favour a variant of the Open University concept for the US—a form of post-secondary education based on the concept of continuing life-long education. In the future, I hope we can cut the red tape and apply the concept of the Open University in lieu of the 'open admissions' policies now in vogue. We need to satisfy the aspirations of some of the people who quite rightly feel that they have not had fair secondary school opportunities. We need, therefore, to contemplate opening the university to motivated, able, persons and letting them study in our schools even when they lack formal qualifications. Let me give a personal example. My sister was a high-school drop-out—married at 16, divorced at 20. But being a determined, able woman—one who never needed to be liberated—she persuaded the Dean at an eastern US university to admit her to the journalism programme. By the time she was 30 she was an accredited White House correspondent, a member of the *Newsweek* staff, and a member of the staff of the *Baltimore Sun*. In our new emergent university structures we need to find imaginative ways of satisfying the aspirations and needs of enormous numbers of people like my sister in ability, confidence and stamina.

Waddington: Dr Black has drawn attention to the asymmetry in this process. We are loosening up enormously over the age of students and the qualifications we demand of them. We are trying to set up life-long entry and re-entry, with freedom to go in and out of the university all through life. But the life-long tenured appointments on the staff side make the system asymmetrical. Maybe it should be like that. To abolish tenure now, without some substitute, would bring innovation to a halt; no one could afford to do it. If you have tenure, your bread and butter are assured.

Platt: Twenty years ago there was a British book called *Redbrick University* which I thought hit the nail on the head in terms of the sclerotic structures of those days. It discussed the incentives for continued intellectual productivity in different schools. There was a chapter on 'The Professor and His Rose Garden', as I remember it, which I did not find in the American edition. The point was that as soon as a person became a full professor, with tenure, he turned his energies to trying to grow the best roses in the community, partly because he was at the top, then, with no reason to work any more. I would like to suggest that there may be a difference in the positive rewards and incentives which the American full professor still has, to keep his research going full blast, and the rewards the British professor goes on receiving. The American professor may still do research so that he will get to move to Harvard or to California. He may still try to become the president of a national professional society, even though he has never been chairman of the department or Dean of the Faculty. I can think of at least half a dozen academic and prestige rewards of various sorts for continuing research and scholarship in the US, which in a certain sense are not there for his British counterpart because departments are dominated by the professor at the top of the pyramid, whose other rewards are connected to his rank rather than his work. It seems to me that it is safe for a system to offer tenure, as a valuable protection for academic freedoms and for experimentation, only if we also have the other methods of reinforcement for those with tenure at the top—methods which stimulate continuing ongoing research.

Shane: If an American professor is troublesome enough to the administration he is virtually sure to be promoted to being a Dean.

Platt: He can resist that! The flat-topped departments in which there are many professors who are more or less equal (like the Chemistry Department at Oxford in the 1950s) are much more of an encouragement to graduate students. Where there are many specialties, many different points of view, the student may usually escape from one professor to another or find another channel at another university. The single-professor type of pyramidal hierarchy is the source of the sclerotic character in most British and European universities as much as anything else and, I believe, far more damaging than tenure itself.

Waddington: There is something in that. On the other hand, I think it is easier to move, in the US, from partial professorship to chairmanship of a company or something, not by doing research yourself but by organizing a large team of Ph.D. students to do it for you. This can be done in Britain, but with more difficulty. I think that is the other side of what you said.

Perry: Size is a factor too. The average number of staff in British departments is still in single figures.

References cited

[1] PERKIN, H. J. (1974) Adaptation to change by British universities. *Universities' Quarterly,* *28* (4), 390–403

[2] ASHBY, SIR ERIC [now Lord Ashby of Brandon] (1969) The academic profession. Fourth annual lecture under the Thank Offering to Britain Fund. *Proceedings of the British Academy 55,* 163–176

[3] ANNAN, NÖEL GILROY, baron (1974) *The Report of the Annan Enquiry,* pp. 29–30, Essex University

Eclectics: elements of a transdisciplinary methodology for futures studies

KIMON VALASKAKIS

GAMMA, Université de Montréal/McGill University, and Département des Sciences Economiques, Université de Montréal

Abstract Futures studies involve two families of issues: those relating to *forecasting* as such, and those relating to the effective *understanding* of complex reality which in fact is a precondition for forecasting. Other than straightforward mathematical techniques such as extrapolation and envelope curves, more subtle forecasting methods such as scenarios, Delphis and cross-impact matrices depend for their success on an understanding of the present. Eclectics is an attempt to model the present in a transdisciplinary fashion. The starting-point is an extended philosophical notion of *scarcity*, the analysis of which leads to certain basic theorems of choice. These theorems are then made to apply to what we call *quaternary* commodities—that is, abstract commodities not usually treated in economics, such as 'nationalism', 'achievement', 'prestige', 'freedom from stress', 'justice' and 'influence'. The approach involves the definition of *content* from fields such as psychology, sociology, anthropology, political science and the choice of *method* from economics (which is seen here as identical to the theory of choice). The advantage of eclectics is that it provides for rigorous treatment of 'non-economic' variables (and therefore humanizes the economist) while at the same time exporting choice theory to other social scientists (thereby formalizing what have hitherto been imprecise techniques).

The business of attempting to treat the future as an 'academic discipline', i.e. as an activity where the rules and rigour of the scientific method can be applied, leads to two families of issues. The first is concerned with forecasting techniques as such, and we now have an array of mathematical, non-mathematical and quasi-mathematical techniques to choose from. The second is the actual base from which the forecasting will be done, i.e. an image we have of the present, of the past, or of the future. The tempting fallacy would be to entirely separate these two issues. This could lead to results not only incomplete but actually misleading. As Herman Kahn has eloquently put it, in one of his famous one-liners: 'There are two serious errors in forecasting. The first is to assume that a rate of growth is constant. The second is to assume that it will change'.

121

In point of fact, we can assume nothing. Rates of growth may or may not change, extrapolation is often absurd and yet rejection of extrapolation may turn out to be unnecessarily timid. Whether we construct scenarios or use contextual mapping, Delphi or cross-impact techniques, we must, in each case, first attempt a thorough understanding of the 'base'. This is what some futurists and historians have called *synchronic* analysis. Once the synchronic dimension is well understood the *diachronic* or time-dependent dynamic analysis can be brought in. This paper will focus on the analysis of the base and its potential for forecasting. The problems and opportunities of diachronic analysis have been treated elsewhere.[1]

As far as understanding of the base is concerned, it has been the fashion in recent years to consider interdisciplinary studies as a necessary method for the investigation of complex reality. In Gamma we wholeheartedly agree with this view but would like to take the 'faddish' elements out of it and define the approach as precisely as possible. To do this we have to distinguish between the following:

A mono-disciplinary approach is very sectoral and partial. It implies a study involving only one discipline. Such an approach we find very unsatisfactory for the celebrated reason (first given by Kenneth Boulding) that although universities are administratively divided into departments, nature is not. The universe has no 'economic department' working separately from its 'physics' department. To assume otherwise is to court irrelevance.

A multidisciplinary approach involves parallel inputs from different fields in apposition to each other and unintegrated. This is of very little use since the vital interdependences are not identified.

An 'undisciplined' approach although well-meaning leads nowhere. The starting and finishing points are that 'everything depends on everything'. The temptation here is to conclude pessimistically that there are 'imponderables' in human behaviour not subject to analysis, thereby ending the tale without further ado.

A cross-disciplinary approach involves the marriage of two or three disciplines by the establishment of methodological 'bridges'. Examples of such marriages are: political economy, biochemistry, social psychology, astrophysics. They are a distinct step forward, relative to any of the preceding, yet fall short of a completely unified scientific method.

An interdisciplinary approach is an 'intellectual commune' so to speak, in which many disciplines cross-interact. In principle a generalization of the cross-disciplinary approach, it is the penultimate step before the transdisciplinary approach.

A transdisciplinary approach really calls for the unification of science where all existing disciplines are integrated into a super-discipline. It is difficult, yet, we feel, an ultimately attainable goal.

In our perception a 'discipline' is really a generalized theory akin to a 'language'. It will be noted that the etymological origin of 'theory' is the Greek *Theoros*, i.e. a spectator. A theory is a way of looking at things, neither true nor false, but either more useful or less useful. Different spectators have different perceptions of the same spectacle. As in a sports event such as a football game, some vantage points are better than others. The 'better' depends on the purpose. If we are interested in watching passing plays rather than goal scoring, a seat near centre field might be better than one near the goals, and vice versa.

A theory is couched in certain words and concepts which when numerous enough elevate it to the rank of 'discipline'. Hence economics is a 'language' of thought that possesses, like all languages, a vocabulary and rules of syntax. The same is true of each and every discipline. The vocabulary of economics includes perhaps five hundred technical concepts; political science, anthropology, psychology, etc., each contain as many if not more; and biology and medicine probably head all the lists with many tens of thousands of technical words in their vocabularies.

The 'rules of syntax' are different to some degree, since some disciplines pride themselves on possessing a particular methodology made-to-measure for the problems encountered within that discipline. Thus an anthropologist will rely extensively on field work, the experimental psychologist on controlled experiments, the historian on analysis of rare documents and the economist on model-building. We now arrive at the statement of the crucial problem of transdisciplinarity: *To achieve transdisciplinarity we must utilize both a common vocabulary and common 'rules of syntax' (i.e. a common methodology).*

THE FORMAL DESCRIPTION OF 'ECLECTICS' OR 'MEGA-ECONOMICS'

A systemic (as opposed to an administrative) classification of disciplines involved in the study of human behaviour yields five basic hard-core social sciences. In alphabetical order we have:

Anthropology. Presumably the science of culture, anthropology with its many subdivisions overflows into and overlaps with other related fields.

Economics. Presumably the science of scarcity. Up till now the scarcity at the basis of economic theory has always been interpreted as material scarcity. In this study, I shall attempt to show otherwise.

Political Science. Presumably the analysis of power, its ramification, its subdivisions, its organization and manifestation. Obvious overflows can be seen with every other behavioural science.

Psychology. Presumably the investigation of the nervous system. From its obvious biological connection psychology also intrudes into economics, sociology and anthropology and, in some schools of thought, is part of philosophy.

Sociology. Presumably the science of groups and social interaction. Very close to anthropology, it is nevertheless considered distinct by sociologists and, in Auguste Comte's initial conception, is the all-inclusive behavioural science.

History and geography are, in this systemic view, not separate activities but dimensions of the preceding disciplines. Hence we can have historical anthropology, economic history and geography, political history and geography, etc. History introduces a time-dimension to the analysis and geography a space-dimension.

The harder sciences are also related to the behavioural sciences. There is a biological foundation to all behaviour. Biology in turn depends upon *chemical* conditioning and chemistry ultimately depends on the laws of *physics*.

A potential unity of science exists, then, not only as far as form is concerned but also content. If the various linkages between the separate fields of investigation are mapped out and precisely identified, we may achieve interdisciplinarity.

Eclectics is a transdisciplinary approach which features the adoption of the methodology of economics in combination with the terminology of all behavioural sciences. (We hesitated between the two terms eclectics and 'mega-economics'. Our original choice was 'mega-economics' since the approach we will be describing can be viewed as an extension of the subject-matter of economics. We now prefer 'eclectics', which is to signify the combination of the economic theory of choice with non-economic variables derived from psychology, political science and sociology.)

(a) The starting point: an all-encompassing view of scarcity

In traditional economics, scarcity is an objective situation where material resources are insufficient to satisfy unlimited wants. In most standard economic texts, it is the famous trade-off between 'guns and butter' which illustrates the inevitability of choice under conditions of scarcity. However, with the development of economic thought and especially the increasing mathematization of economic theory, the problem of choice was seen to be independent both of *material* resources and *objective* scarcity. In contemporary form, the theorems of choice (which constitute the central part of what is now known as microeconomic analysis and used to be known as 'principles of economics') are purely formal propositions equally applicable to all trade-off situations. Thus the same body of analytical thought can be used to study 'guns versus butter', 'Gross National Product versus Quality of Life' and even 'virtue versus power', 'love versus selfishness'—indeed almost any of the famous dilemmas of philosophy.

In the mind of the proverbial 'man in the street', economics is 'business', and rightly so, for the mainstream of the economics profession still deals with shoes, ships and sealing wax. The eighteenth century Physiocrats viewed agriculture as the only 'true' productive activity. Marx claimed that 'materialism' was the mainspring of history, meaning by materialism the pursuit of primary (extractive) and secondary (industrial) commodities.[2] To this day services are not accounted for in the GNP of the Eastern European socialist countries, under the pretext that tertiary activities are 'unproductive'.[3]

In eclectics we replace these restrictive interpretations by positing the following. Scarcity is a subjective situation that exists in the mind of the consumer. It can relate to the insufficiency of either material or non-material commodities. If we suppose that N stands for subjective needs (whether natural or artificial, real or imagined) and C stands for commodities or resources, then three situations are possible:

(1) $N < C$ (opulence)
(2) $N = C$ (equilibrium)
(3) $N > C$ (scarcity)

The third situation gives rise to choice. The other two do not. It is our contention that the third situation is the cause of most social problems. I shall defend this apparently bold statement later.

(b) The next step: identification of the set of 'quaternary' commodities

The perception of scarcity forcing a choice between guns and butter, or 'wine and cloth', is comparatively easy. Much less so is the perception of scarcities in 'leisure', 'time', 'the quality of life', 'tradition', etc. To deal with such problems we introduce a new set of commodities to be entitled *quaternary commodities*.

Let us suppose that there is some final goal which directs human behaviour.

If human behaviour is purposive then that is tautologically true. If not, we must assume that behaviour is mechanistic, i.e. explainable by the laws of physics rather than the cybernetic laws of information. The overwhelming evidence seems to be in favour of the purposive interpretation (even if some purposes are unconscious) and therefore I shall not belabour this point.

Let us call the final goal of behaviour in humans, 'felicity' (or happiness, satisfaction, pleasure, utility, quality of life, or whatever cliché one prefers). There is, then, a felicity function, at the level of each individual, which would explain this individual's behaviour. It may be the case that some people like Roquefort cheese, others not, etc. The preference functions are individual and we assume consistent.*

Let us now claim that a felicity function can be expressed as follows:

$$F_A = f(p, s, t, q)$$

where F_A is the total felicity (f) or happiness of A, p is the set of primary commodities (those extracted from the soil, the sea, the forest or the crust of the earth), s the set of secondary commodities (transformed commodities involving labour and capital), t the set of tertiary commodities (services), and q the set of quaternary commodities defined in the next paragraph. What the felicity function says is that happiness for A depends on his consumption of various types of commodities in certain doses.†

A quaternary commodity can now be defined as an entity which (*i*) is capable of producing felicity in one person, (*ii*) is scarce, (*iii*) is abstract, (*iv*) is not at present marketed.

Characteristic (*i*) ensures that the entity is indeed a commodity in that it can produce satisfaction. Characteristic (*ii*) ensures that it is not a free good which would then make choice unnecessary. Characteristic (*iii*) ensures that the commodity is neither a primary nor a secondary one. Finally characteristic (*iv*) ensures that it is not a service because services are indeed abstract commodities which are marketed. Only non-marketed commodities can be called quaternary.‡

It is important to note that, in our model, felicity and commodities have their symmetrical opposites. Infelicity is 'disutility', dissatisfaction, unhappiness or illfare, and discommodities are entities producing infelicity in any one person.

---

* More about consistency, transitivity and conscious or unconscious motives later.
† The division of economic activity into primary, secondary and tertiary sectors is attributed to Colin Clark in his *Conditions of Economic Progress*.[4]
‡ Although the 'quaternary' idea has been used in regional economics and planning it is very superficially related to what we are discussing here. The quaternary sector in regional economics deals with high-technology services.

The identification of certain quaternary commodities may involve a roundabout process of *minimizing a discommodity*.

How are we to identify quaternary commodities? First we must bear in mind that quaternary commodities are not necessarily 'good' or 'bad'. In fact we propose a threefold division:

(*i*) Symbiotic quaternary commodities: those whose consumption by A increases not only A's but B's felicity.

(*ii*) Neutral quaternary commodities: those whose consumption by A does not affect B's felicity.

(*iii*) Parasitic quaternary commodities: those whose consumption by A actually decreases B's felicity.

Second, we propose that the actual discovery of quaternary commodities be left to the relevant specialists. Since, in the systemic view of behavioural science there are four specialists other than economists, namely psychologists, political scientists, sociologists and anthropologists, we can classify quaternary commodities as 'psychological', 'political' and 'sociocultural'. All abstract commodities directly satisfying needs arising from the operation of the nervous system can constitute the subset of psychological commodities. Political commodities are those motivated by the need for power and its derivatives. Finally, sociocultural commodities are those that are identified by the sociologist and anthropologist around the notion of the 'group' and 'culture' (the information shared by the group).

There is an interesting symmetry to note here which makes eclectics possible. Psychologists, sociologists and anthropologists have a tendency to refer to desires and wants by identifying them with a prefix 'n', denoting need. They speak of n-affiliation, n-aggression, n-recognition, n-status, etc. Translated into the language of eclectics, n-recognition is a discommodity denoting a state of infelicity for the individual concerned where there is an unsatisfied desire for whatever constitutes recognition. The commodity which will satisfy the desire will be prefixed by a 'c' (for commodity). We will then have perhaps c-prestige satisfying n-recognition, c-power satisfying n-aggression, c-religion satisfying n-rectitude, c-legal justice satisfying n-equity, etc.

(c) The final formal step: developing theorems of choice to deal with quaternary commodities

To recapitulate my argument so far, I present two tables. Table 1 summarizes the subject matter of eclectics: *choice applied to abstract as well as materialistic situations*. Table 2 introduces the key concepts of eclectics in the form of a

TABLE 1
The subject matter of eclectics

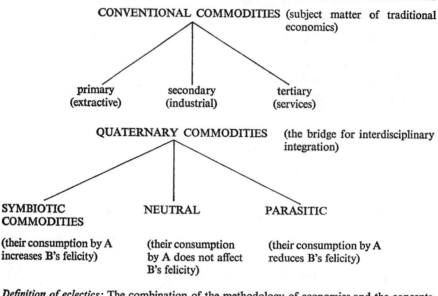

CONVENTIONAL COMMODITIES (subject matter of traditional economics)

primary (extractive)   secondary (industrial)   tertiary (services)

QUATERNARY COMMODITIES   (the bridge for interdisciplinary integration)

SYMBIOTIC COMMODITIES   NEUTRAL   PARASITIC

(their consumption by A increases B's felicity)   (their consumption by A does not affect B's felicity)   (their consumption by A reduces B's felicity)

Definition of eclectics: The combination of the methodology of economics and the concepts of all social sciences to arrive at a general theory of behaviour around the concept of choice.

glossary of terms. Having identified the quaternary commodities and their underlying needs, we then formally represent this in decision theorems with references to a felicity function.

It might well be asked: why is this approach which includes decision theorems more useful than other multidisciplinary approaches? The answer is that it allows (*a*) economists to make use of variables that they usually omit by either politely calling them 'non-economic' or impolitely calling them irrational, and (*b*) other social scientists to think in 'economic', i.e. cost–benefit, scarce, 'can't have your cake and eat it too' terms. The most important conflicts that arise today are of the 'good versus good' rather than the 'good versus bad' variety. It is easy to deal with the latter and most difficult to deal with the former. If we take the trade-off between say c-culture (through restrictive economic policies) and c-GNP growth (through free trade, liberal policies, etc.) the narrow economist will unconsciously assign a zero-value to the non-economic goal, nationalism, and call it irrational, and an infinite value to economic growth. The socio-anthropologist will assign an infinite value to c-culture and a low value to 'materialist' growth. The eclectic approach avoids these two

TABLE 2

Partial glossary of terms to be used in eclectics

Scarcity=a subjective state which exists whenever a person's (or group's) needs exceed the resources at his command. If N is needs and C stands for commodities or resources, then logically we have

        (1) $N > C$
        (2) $N = C$
or (3) $N < C$

      Needs may be real or artificial. They exist in the mind of the consumer. (1) denotes scarcity, (2) denotes equilibrium, (3) denotes abundance.

Choice=decision process made in allocating scarce resources (i.e. commodities) to satisfy needs. Choice implies scarcity. If there is no scarcity there is no need for choice.

Felicity   These two words can be used interchangeably to refer to happiness, satisfaction, *or Utility:* pleasure, or whatever it is, a given individual wishes to maximize. Although there is no formal difference between the two words, utility connotes usefulness and this is not what we have in mind. Therefore in most cases felicity will be used.

Disutility   The opposite of utility or felicity. Refers to pain, dissatisfaction, displeasure *or Infelicity:* or more generally whatever it is that we want the least of.

Commodities: Entities that have the potential of creating felicity in at least one person. They may be concrete or abstract, visible or invisible, private or public.

Discommodities: Entities that have the potential of creating infelicity in at least one person. They may be concrete or abstract, visible or invisible, private or public.

Infelicity cost: The cost in terms of dissatisfaction (or displeasure or infelicity) of choosing one alternative. Infelicity cost includes real cost and opportunity cost.

Real cost: The measure of cost in terms of some material or directly quantifiable thing, i.e. measuring the cost of painting the house in terms of the cost of materials plus the cost of labour.

Opportunity cost: The measure of cost in terms of the felicity of opportunities foregone. For example, I paint the house for three hours and use $10 worth of paint. My opportunity cost is the movie I missed plus whatever I could have alternatively bought with my $10.

---

excesses. Through decision-making techniques like indifference maps, cost–benefit or cost-effectiveness calculi, minimax–maximax game modelling, etc. the *problèmatique* will be accurately represented and an enlightened choice made.*

    Economics has an array of highly sophisticated concepts, laws, techniques and models for choice and decisions. The unfortunate thing is that these powerful

---

* It would be beyond the scope of this paper for me to describe each of these techniques. They will be the subject of a forthcoming book.

tools have been used for trivial problems of everyday life when they could also be used for the really interesting problems of society. In a nutshell, then, eclectics involves convincing both economists and their colleagues of the value of identifying *'quaternary commodities'*.

The emphasis is on 'quaternary' when talking to economists because they already know all about commodities. The emphasis must be on 'commodities' when talking to the other social scientists because they are already aware of the 'quaternary' aspect but tend to forget that all choices, under scarcity, involve costs.

POTENTIAL APPLICATIONS OF ECLECTICS IN FUTURES STUDIES

(a) A guide for the understanding (and therefore prediction) of human behaviour

As was noted earlier, we tend to dismiss what we do not understand as irrelevant, imponderable or irrational. If one adopts the systems view of an ordered universe (cosmos rather than chaos), the irrationality in other people's behaviour is a measure of our ignorance of their underlying motives. There is method in almost every madness. If we were to understand this method we would be able to 'explain' behaviour. Behaviour will be adequately explained when we can accurately predict future behaviour: hence the connection with futures studies.

A common mistake which leads to obviously incorrect predictions is not taking sufficiently into account the relativity of beliefs, ideals and preferences. Consider an example reported by Herman Kahn of two categories of people working the night-shift at a post-office in California. The first category includes hippies, getting the high overtime rates for a few weeks in order to live the rest of the year on the commune. Their demand for money may be about $2000 a year or whatever it costs to live for that period of time on a commune. To earn it they may work overtime for six weeks and then leave. The second category includes lower middle-class people newly arrived in the affluent society. They work overtime to supplement their $10 000-a-year regular jobs and to be able to buy the colour television set which they need to live up to their desired image of themselves. Through quaternary commodity analysis their desires would have been identified and their behaviour explained.

Another example is concerned with people's consumption of c-leisure. Leisure is an allocation of time and although often confused with idleness in fact may involve a greater calorie expenditure than 'work'. In Table 3 I suggest that c-leisure is the commodity that satisfies n-freedom from labour stress. It is assumed that 'labour' which is work solely performed to obtain an

TABLE 3
An illustrative list of quaternary commodities

Type of quaternary commodity	Discommodity or need	Commodity	Identification primarily reponsibility of
Symbiotic (Felicity of B increased by A's consumption of these commodities)	n-communication	c-language	Psychologist, sociologist, anthropologist, linguist, cybernetician, etc.
	n-affiliation	c-solidarity	Sociologist, etc.
	n-affection	c-love	Psychologist, philosopher, anthropologist, sociologist, etc.
Neutral (Felicity of B unaffected by A's consumption of these commodities	n-freedom from labour stress	c-leisure	Psychologist, sociologist
	n-freedom from boredom	c-excitement	Psychologist, anthropologist
Parasitic (Felicity of B decreased by A's consumption of these commodities)	n-aggression/control	c-power/ influence	Psychologist, political scientist, sociologist, biologist
	n-recognition	c-prestige/ status	Anthropologist, sociologist

income involves some infelicity. This infelicity may take the form of stress. C-leisure may replace this stress with either idleness or felicity-bringing work. The professional tennis-player may play the piano for relaxation. The professional pianist may play tennis for the same relaxation. There is nothing intrinsic in either piano-playing or tennis which stresses or relaxes an individual. It is all a question of subjective perceptions which will appear on a felicity map.

Table 3 presents an illustrative list of quaternary commodities that emphasizes the symmetry between the need and the commodity. The first group of *symbiotic* commodities includes the need for communication, for affiliation and for affection, and possible corresponding commodities of language, solidarity and love. The very identification is at this stage an amateur job, since it is the author, *qua* general citizen, identifying these commodities on the basis of readings. The proper identification must of course be done by psychologists, sociologists and others. It is apparent that in each case we have a symbiotic situation, since language, solidarity and love are cooperative activities.

Neutral commodities are those whose consumption by A does not affect the felicity level of anyone else. Leisure and excitement could possibly fall into this group.

In the parasitic category, commodities such as power and influence on the one hand or prestige/status on the other are obviously zero-sum and competitive. A's influence over B's behaviour (i.e. A's ability to determine or change B's decisions) may reduce B's influence on his own behaviour. Similarly if a person desires to have the longest car in his neighbourhood for prestige reasons he is preventing someone else from having the longest car.

(b) A step towards the construction of meaningful welfare indicators

All societal forecasting is hampered by the problem of indicators of societal performance. The familiar GNP measure is really an index of the production of primary and secondary commodities in the communist countries and primary, secondary and tertiary commodities in the capitalist countries. This economic accounting is seriously deficient today. Some proposed recent measures like the Tobin–Nordhaus–Samuelson NEW (net economic welfare) measure merely add to the GNP the cost of antipollution industries and non-renewable resource depletion. It is marginally better than the GNP index. Finally, the recent trend towards social indicators, although a laudable initiative, to be sure, falls far short of the ideal. The plethora of social indicators now current (newspaper per thousand inhabitants, number of surgeries per thousand, psychiatric treatment per thousand, etc.), only reveals their basic flaw: *it is by no means sure what in fact they are indicating.* There is no underlying theory of behaviour, just a mass of statistics.

Quaternary commodities constitute an attempt at identifying elements of a theory of behaviour. Although the endeavour is by no means easy, quantification of these commodities is possible.

Quantification itself, it should be noted, may be done with three separate degrees of precision.

At the first degree, two entities are identified as magnitudes and compared, using adjectives such as 'greater than', 'equal', or 'smaller than'.

At the second degree, two or more entities may be compared and rank-ordered—1st, 2nd, 3rd, etc. This is *ordinal* quantification.

Finally, at the highest degree of quantification, entities are given precise *cardinal* numbers—1, 2, 3 etc.

Although full quantification is only complete at the third level, much information can be obtained by use of one of the other two. Some quaternary commodities are reasonably well-suited to quantification, others much less so.

Some attempts have been made to quantify c-power,[5,6] c-achievement,[7] c-leisure, c-justice, etc. These attempts have often been only partially successful but we feel that the reason for this is incomplete information about the nature of the commodity itself.

Economic theory itself has thrived using ordinal quantification. The key elements of economic theory are usually not fully quantified. Instead concepts such as 'opportunity-cost' have been used very successfully. Opportunity-cost is the measure of the cost of choosing alternative X by computing the anticipated disutility or infelicity of giving up the best other alternative that could have been obtained had X not been chosen. If we apply this to quaternary commodities, the cost of c-nationalism (non-membership for Britain in the EEC, anti-American policies in Canada, anti-Ottawa policies in Quebec) can be a slowing of economic growth—a directly quantifiable index. The idea that 'opportunities foregone' can be a measure of the cost of choosing is, in my view, a most fertile way of approaching complex societal problems.

(c) A guide for long-range planning

Long-range planning involves a decision procedure where goals have to be ordered. A favourite technique for ordering goals in a systems approach is a hierarchy or relevance-tree. I have had the opportunity of utilizing such a technique coupled with the introduction of quaternary commodities in a long-range planning exercise in Africa, entrusted to the University of Montreal. A research centre of the latter institution was asked to prepare long-term orientation for the Republic of Niger. Our chosen starting point was an identification of high-order goals by the Niger government. These goals were implicit and, after some prodding, it was found that the Niger government wished the nation to achieve: 'a high material standard of living with national unity and independence within an interdependent world'.

All policies were to be chosen by reference to this supreme goal. It soon became obvious that there was not one supreme goal but three, and that they were incompatible. The material standard of living goal was easily rewritten as a desire for rapid economic growth. The second goal of national unity was identified after careful analysis as meaning *regional balance and high spatial integration* of the Niger economy. This was particularly important since different tribes inhabited each region of Niger. Centrifugal forces were also working in favour of separatism.

The third goal of 'independence within interdependence' really referred to Niger's desire for a loosening of ties with its two major and overwhelming economic partners, Nigeria and France. Nigeria by its sheer size and proximity also threatened the regional balance of Niger since the Centre–East region of Niger was an economic satellite to Kano in Northern Nigeria. On the other hand, without close ties with Nigeria or France, Niger's economic growth, already slow, would become even slower.

Reformulating the Niger *problèmatique* in *eclectic* terms, we find that this is an obvious trade-off between 'good and good', the perceived good of economic growth versus the quaternary commodities c-independence and c-unity. As usual, the economists would tend to discount the quaternary commodities in favour of economic growth and the more political–social-minded observers would favour the opposite ruling. To deal with the problem we indicated the incompatibilities to the authorities, pointing out that the cost of independence was slower growth, and that the cost of faster growth was less independence.

The need for eclectics is also evident when the planning takes the form of utopian model design. With the acceleration of change we become more and more aware of what we are against and less and less aware of what we are for. The identification of quaternary commodities and their use in an eclectic model would permit meaningful positive thinking. Witness the following course-description found in two Free University catalogues in the US:

(1) The course will be divided into two parts. In the first there will be an opening crying session in which we will knock present day America and indulge in many New Left clichés. Next we will attempt to answer the arch-typical parent's remark, "so what do you want for Christ's sake!" After seeing if we can agree to some notion of a society we want to move toward, we will do some power-structure analysis to see who is keeping us from getting there. Finally if we get this far, we may discuss what tactics have some hope of success and which of the others are fun and irrelevant.

(2) Seminar for those who are tired of capitalism but uncertain and fearful of what may replace it. Can capitalism be junked without violence. Is it possible to secure both the form and substance of democracy under socialism or would it destroy the human potential? Do the Soviet Union, Czechoslovakia, China or Cuba offer guidelines for bettering N. American society...[8]

To construct utopias (and the whole branch of future studies dealing with normative forecasting is directly or indirectly involved with utopian thought), we must fully understand behaviour. Assumption of 'man is inherently good' or 'man is inherently evil' must be treated with circumspection. A full identification of quaternary commodities will help to avoid such tempting pitfalls and allow reasoned planning with full knowledge of the total nature of man.

CONCLUSION

By way of summary I would like to restate the essential points made in this article. First it must be recognized that I am actually reporting work in progress and not offering a finished product—which because of the complexity of the issues involved must take the form of a book. The outline presented here represents more a series of questions, a *problèmatique*, as it were, rather than a series of answers. These questions seem to be meaningful and fertile. They are connected with an all-encompassing view of scarcity and a suspicion that stems from subjectively perceived scarcity. A busy executive under stress, a married man envisioning divorce, a nation at odds with itself—all are experiencing scarcity and the agony of choice between 'good' and 'good', the most difficult choice of all. What the alternatives in this choice really are is the subject matter of eclectics, which is economics plus socio-politico-anthropologico-psychology.

Second, in progressing along our chosen avenue towards a full methodology for futures studies, we must pause before certain obstacles of great importance. These are, the nature of felicity functions, the nature of quaternary commodities and their possibility of aggregation, and finally the nature of the measurement problem. Once these have been solved 'the base' will be well known and the actual forecasting of future states will be a relatively simple endeavour.

In dealing with felicity functions we must delve far into psychology and the theory of motivation. Perhaps some kind of psychological homeostasis may be identified, akin to the biochemical homeostasis in our bodies. Perhaps, too, there is not one felicity function but two. The *authentic* complete felicity function may be hidden in the most private recesses of our unconscious. It would then take a most proficient psychoanalyst to act as midwife and explicate our felicity function for us. In addition, at the conscious level there may be an explicit preference-function easily identified by interview and questionnaire. The direct questions, 'do you like X?', 'why do you like Y?' can have direct answers—sometimes. But when we obtain the frequent 'I really don't know why' response we have to repair back to the *authentic* felicity function of the unconscious. The *overt* preference function is like the tip of the iceberg; it is partial, spotty, incomplete, and rare is the person 'who knows himself', as the Buddhists advise. The overt function may in fact be inconsistent because the real motives are not recognized. One way or the other, much work is needed on the psychology of motivation and also on the psychology of 'pleasure' or 'happiness'. This appears to be a grossly underdeveloped field of study within psychology itself. An eclectics team must do fundamental work in this direction before proceeding further.

The identification of quaternary commodities is a second obstacle along the road requiring the wholehearted assistance of sociologists and anthropologists in addition to the psychologist. What it really involves is a programme of naming, defining and analysing.

There are those of course who would rather not raise these issues. To live in a 'world without names', a world without categories, is indeed a worthy aesthetic goal. Such a world should best be expressed, if expressed at all, by art forms, the literary, poetic, cinematic or musical genres. The scientific method, for good or ill, is taxonomy, categorizing, non-contradiction and logical inference. If man is to study himself by using science he must investigate his behaviour systemically. This implies naming, sub-naming and sub-sub-naming. The tyranny of language is with us anyway, whether we have read Wittgenstein or not. To define is to understand, even if understanding is perhaps anticlimactic in that it eliminates suspense and analysis. However, the stakes are sufficiently high to make the study most interesting and useful. If indeed we want to construct a transdisciplinary language, we must build a meaningful vocabulary.

Finally the last obstacle, but strangely enough the least formidable, once the other two have been surmounted, is formal modelling into theorems of choice describing actual situations. Here the economist, with the close assistance of the political scientist, can digest the inputs and construct decision alternatives with some degree of quantification. Whether this quantification is ordinal or fully cardinal is not the issue, provided that some quantification is realized. Once we have the raw material there are sufficient sophisticated techniques in decision theory, game theory and conflict theory to come up with the full range of alternatives. Then the decision maker—whether an individual choosing between chess and movies, a nation choosing nationalism or internationalism, or human society choosing a conservation ethic or a consumerist ethic—will make informed choices. To predict or to plan we must get away from naive assumptions about the nature of man and encounter the implications of (mega)-scarcity head on. 'Good versus good' must be tackled and an iterative process developed. 'Eclectics' is one of many starting points. But rather than pass the buck and dismiss what we do not understand, we must instead perceive the order that lies in apparent chaos. For it is the basic tenet of the systems view of the universe or indeed of science that there is really no such thing as irrationality. Only ignorance of motives!

Discussion

Waddington: We must be able to think in multidimensional terms, and universities must teach these modes of thought. They will have to show how to go beyond linear cause-and-effect thinking, and the idea that there is one measure of all things. No biologist wanting to differentiate between two species dreams of being able to get one index that will do it; he measures a hundred or more differences. Similarly, there will be not one felicity, but a hundred different felicities, and somehow we have to get used to taking account of all of them.

Dror: I am strongly in sympathy with the fundamental search for ways of dealing with the issues presented here. We need some integrated prescriptive approach which permits us to order our knowledge so that we can make recommendations for future action. Ideas developed in decision theory, microeconomics and systems engineering can, among others, be helpful—if suitably reworked. Indeed the complexity of problems calls for some redundancy or overlapping approaches, so that we have an arsenal of methods and approaches which can be used to reduce bias and ignorance. Neither economics nor operations research nor management sciences in their classical form can deal with the basic societal problems, unless developed into a kind of 'policy science'. Also, in reality we are faced in most situations with a choice not between good and good but between bad and bad. Our main need is therefore often to design new alternatives, not screening tools which can only help us to identify the best of the available alternatives or the less bad amongst the available ones.

Few of the approaches at present available handle the continuous feedback problem, though there are some cybernetic beginnings, which stress that we are dealing with a continuous learning process rather than with determining how to make decision A, then decision B, and then decision C. The classical decision approaches do not usually handle institutional aspects, and cannot handle them. Thus, in the face of real uncertainty, the only way to do something is to improve crisis management, which is an institutional feature quite distinct from comparing alternatives. Another institutional aspect is that even though all political ideologies favour transparent goal decisions, the dynamics of political systems—the need to maintain a consensus—makes opaque decisions much more useful. How to reduce the political barriers to decision improvement is another problem which cannot be handled by classical decision theory. Therefore I agree with your basic search but I think we need a much broader approach to the provision of a systematic intellectual basis for improving decision-making.

Waddington: Decision theory seems to me a rather misty term; I don't know just what it includes. For practical decisions, it is most important to arrange for adequate feedback. In complex situations which we don't understand, it doesn't much matter what you do first, so long as you get adequate feedback on what the results are and react to those. Many situations have certain stability characteristics. They form what I call an epigenetic landscape; that is, they can go in various directions, but once they start to go in a certain direction it is difficult to shift them to another one. They tend to go on and on; but after a bit they will reach their stability limits and break down into two other branches. If there are several pathways of change of this kind, they form a landscape.

You often find yourself confronting a situation which you know has some definite general character, but you have no idea of the shape of the landscape. Gelfand and Tsitsin said it was as though you had landed by parachute in thick fog in a strange landscape and you wanted to discover what the landscape was like. So you make small steps in all possible directions out from where you landed. You find that in some directions you are going uphill and in others downhill, and so you will eventually discover what the slope is in that immediate locality. You then make quite a big jump, not straight downhill or straight uphill and not straight along the horizontal, but down some sort of slope. That is where you have to judge how to jump and in which direction. Testing around by small steps again you may find that you are still obviously on the slope of the same bank. So you then make a bigger jump, and find yourself at the other side of the valley, with the slope going in the opposite direction. It is a combination of little probing movements with adequate feedback, and then a biggish jump, and again little probing movements with feedback. This has always struck me as a convincing recipe for making decisions in unknown situations.

Valaskakis: The eclectics procedure that I have been describing actually stands or falls on two issues. The first is: is there directive goal-seeking—i.e. cybernetic mechanisms in behaviour—or is it haphazard? Are actions purposive—do they tend towards an objective, implicit or explicit—or not? If behaviour is not haphazard but mechanistic (i.e. the billiard-ball metaphor where we predict future behaviour by observing the path of the first billiard ball which hits the second, and so on and so forth), then it is explainable by the laws of physics. If on the other hand behaviour is purposive then there is an entity, X, that we are seeking. Whether we reach it or not is immaterial. In either case it would be possible to identify some of its elements. If we accept that there is such a magnitude, the next thing on which this approach stands or falls would be on the identification of all the elements of this entity X, including what I call the quaternary commodities in the 'felicity function'. The felicity function would conceivably change every hour, but there is reason to believe that it is reasonably stable over time. This stability I suspect is reinforced by *culture*, which teaches people to like the same things, more or less. The trouble I have had so far in trying to convince people of the usefulness of the concept of quaternary commodities is twofold. Economists recognize commodities but they say that I should forget about the quaternary aspect. They say 'Let's talk in terms of guns and butter and shoes and ships, because we know what these are'. Other social scientists say 'Sure, there are also kinship, leisure, prestige, but why call them commodities?' I think the two words are important, 'commodity' because of the cost element—the fact that you can't have prestige for nothing, you can't even have leisure for nothing, in fact there is almost nothing you can actually have for nothing. And the word 'quaternary' emphasizes the abstract nature of certain things we desire that are neither visible nor tangible. I agree with Professor Waddington that there are many individual felicity functions. But, as I just mentioned, anthropologists claim that there is a family resemblance between individual happiness functions in the same culture, and that within the same culture and subculture one can identify similar goals. A middle-class British university professor probably has a lot in common with other middle-class university professors, and so on and so forth. What people want may not be such a great mystery after all.

Waddington: This is what I mean by cluster analysis. I think you will probably find clusters in your multidimensional space.

Jevons: Are there any guidelines to indicate how the coefficients or weighting factors that you applied to the commodities in the felicity function will change over time? Professor Eldredge suggested earlier that there might be such a thing as a theory of cultural change. Of what would such a theory consist?

Kumar: Exchange theory in anthropology tries to take into account things like love, hate, affection, and so on. What seemed to be missing in your methodology, Dr Valaskakis, was a political dimension, which is also part of the problem with some of the other things we have been talking about. We are talking about searching for a common vocabulary, and we want this vocabulary to include values and alternatives and so on. That seems to me to be talking about a political philosophy. Although you mentioned the Quebec Separatists, you didn't really discuss the political dimension. A British example is the third London Airport, where the Roskill Commission went in for something like your exercise, trying to quantify the unquantifiable by putting a value on a Norman church, for example. The whole exercise was absolute nonsense, and it was admitted to be so in the end. This was partly because they were trying to make a decision at a national level for a local community. If that kind of mix of variables had been localized there might have been some kind of rational strategy. As it was, no matter how sophisticated the social science was that went into it, there couldn't possibly have been a satisfactory outcome. In your notion of eclectics, have you got some kind of political contouring or level or scale on which these kinds of calculations ought to be made?

Valaskakis: I would bring in political science very simply through the quaternary commodity of power and all its derivatives—influence and so on and so forth. Power can be viewed as a capital commodity or a capital good, that is as a means to an end, or it can be viewed as a *final consumption* good, in other words as one that would produce direct satisfaction. You could then make a power analysis at the individual or at the subcultural level—whether at a regional level, a class level, a sexist level or whatever—and look at the commodity power as it is effectively desired and do some kind of behaviouristic analysis to ascertain its competitiveness with other commodities.

When I mentioned quantifying the unquantifiable I meant it in terms of an ordinal rather than a cardinal ranking. Economic theory has allowed us to treat such a thing as 'utility' or 'felicity' without having to specify what units it is measured in. We only need to say that we rank a situation, alpha, higher than beta, and beta higher than gamma, but not necessarily alpha higher than gamma. The relationship doesn't even have to be transitive in the overt preference function. Quantifying the unquantifiable is merely using the technique of opportunity–cost and saying that the cost of nationalism is so and so, the cost of so and so is something else, and so on. The cost of Britain leaving the EEC could possibly be measured in terms of other quaternary commodities and other conventional commodities, and vice versa.

It is ridiculous of course to give a monetary value to a Norman church. But if it can be shown that demolishing the church will allow the building of, say, a hospital (and it is wartime and no other possibilities are open), then we must trade off the very real cultural and aesthetic value of the church (which would probably get my vote) against the immediate concern with the wounded and the dying. Such a trade-off is admittedly far-fetched but it dramatizes my main point: it is as misleading to assign an infinite value to a Norman church as it is to assign such a value to an airport. There is a human cost element always to be reckoned with.

Eldredge: We seem to be talking a slightly different language. I begin to recognize felicity functions as similar to what we call social indicators, which have a long and not as yet very successful tradition in what has been termed trans-economic cost–benefit analysis. I prefer the phrase 'societal' indicators because that includes a whole lot more than social indicators, unless you are a sociologist and understand that social means the whole complex of human society and culture.

The System Dynamic Center at MIT uses a completely cybernetic system in decision-making for urban planning which may be relevant here. For the city of Lowell, which I mentioned in my paper, they assigned arbitrary numbers to certain types of goods. They found that it didn't matter much how arbitrary the numbers were, since they showed the interrelationship in their dynamic model and helped people to make decisions.

Valaskakis: My case is that we should adopt the methodology of choice theory which was developed via economics. I accept entirely your point about social indicators. My argument against them is that we don't know what they indicate. What does a newspaper per thousand inhabitants really mean? If we want to go towards meaningful social indicators we must try and find out what is behind them. This is where we come back to felicity functions and quaternary commodities.

Eldredge: I was trying to marry your phraseology to quality of life. I have made an economic analysis where I concluded that heroin was more important to the inhabitants of New York than the Metropolitan Opera, in terms of money spent on the two commodities.

Shane: I met some Montreal businessmen in 1974 who were involved in a controversy about the teaching of French in the schools. They insisted that it should be taught even though the teaching time was at the cost of other fields of study. How do you cope with people like these who were striving to have French required in the schools, to the loss of those students seeking other more general educational benefits? The Montreal spokesmen for French instruction said frankly in newspaper interviews that they thought it would help to strengthen the ascendancy of the French in local business affairs, in competition with the non-French.

Valaskakis: I can give you an even better example than this on multicultural problems. Belgium like Canada has two primary languages, which makes things extremely expensive because everything has to be translated. One person suggested, tongue-in-cheek, that if one language has to be given up and the other adopted as the national language, the people whose language was chosen should pay all the income tax. People would then have to make a choice. The introduction of cost is the key thing in this analysis. Teaching in French in Quebec universities is extremely costly, in terms of having to translate so many new things that appear in English. There is a time lag of many months if not years before the new material is available. Yet it is something people are quite willing to pay for.

Shane: Perhaps what you have to do is to accept the happy assumption that people will be reasonable.

Ziman: Implicit in Dr Valaskakis's approach there is a model of man. We ought to be very worried about such a model becoming too dominant in our thinking. Anthropological evidence for exchange functions etc. was mentioned but that example does not show that this model of man is correct. On the contrary it shows that this metaphor of commodity, which implies exchange equivalence and so on, is forced by anthropologists onto the groups of people that they study. It is by no means clear that this is the full description of human social relations. If you want to start all this, you must first take account of what the poets and other writers have been saying. If I want to discuss the rationality of irrational action, I would turn to Stendhal or to Doris Lessing. Doris Lessing discusses the whole process of what people want and what they haven't got in their personal lives in ways that just don't seem to me to depend on a hidden utility or felicity function, a 'goal function'. What is missing from the Valaskakis model is the notion that everybody, every community, is itself a historical process. Life isn't a steady state, with each person trying to maximize his or her utility function. People arrive in the world with all sorts of backgrounds. If you are going to find what this felicity function is, you must use your analysis to *discover* it, not hypothesize it as a hidden variable. You have to go right into the heart of the lives of each individual in this society. In other words what you are trying to achieve would need far more than a mathematical or logical model that you can deal with in some sort of analytical way. In the end, you are making a model of the whole; you are trying to reconstruct reality. We must face that and not try to push it aside. With horizon analysis you are doing something that is not so bad in this sense, because there you are envisaging certain types of steady state. You are abstracting them from their history, in conditions where certain exchanges, trade-offs, etc., are credible. Classical economics talks about the steady state but doesn't really talk about change, or dynamics. Perhaps that is the use of it; but I don't see how your method is going to deal with getting from here to there and beyond.

Valaskakis: Dynamics is in fact a well-developed branch of economics, at least in the mathematical sense, and I would not fault the discipline on this specific point. Let me express my confidence in the 'eclectics' approach by saying that even the most difficult of behavioural problems could be dealt with successfully through this approach: Hamlet's felicity function could well be discovered through critical examination of his words and deeds—for, like Polonius, I feel there was a method to the madness—and too often we dismiss what we do not understand as not understandable (by anyone).

References cited

[1] VALASKAKIS, K. (1975) Prospective, rétrospective et perspective. *Actualité Economique*, August
[2] QUERILY, J. (1965) *Economic Thought, A Historical Anthology*, Random House, New York
[3] SCHAFFER, H. G. (ed.) (1967) in *The Communist World*, p.99, Appleton-Century-Crofts, New York

4 CLARK, C. (1957) *Conditions of Economic Progress*, 3rd edn., Macmillan, London
5 ROTHSCHILD, K. W. (ed.) (1971) *Power in Economics*, Penguin, Baltimore, Maryland
6 ISARD, W. *et al.* (1969) *General Theory: Social, Political Economic & Regional*, MIT Press, Cambridge, Mass.
7 McLELLAND, D. C. (1967) *The Achieving Society*, Free Press/Macmillan, New York
8 BRONFENBRENNER, M. (1972) A review of radical economics. *Journal of Economic Literature*

Additional reading

BOULDING, K. E. (ed.) (1970) *Economics as a Science*, McGraw-Hill, New York
BOULDING, K. E. (1973) *The Economy of Love and Fear*, Wadsworth, Belmont, California
DEUTSCH, K. W. (1953) *Nationalism and Social Communication: An Inquiry into the Foundations of Nationality*, MIT Press, Cambridge, Mass.
FROMM, E. (1971) *Escape from Freedom*, Avon, New York
GARDINER, W. L. (1973) *An Invitation to Cognitive Psychology*, Brooks-Cole/Wadsworth, Monterey, California
MASLOW, A. H. (1954) *Motivation and Personality*, Harper & Row, New York
MUNDELL, R. (1968) *Man and Economics*, McGraw-Hill, New York
VALASKAKIS, K. (1971) *Quaternary Commodities*, Cahier de l'Université de Montréal/Sciences Economiques

Some fundamental philosophical, psychological and intellectual assumptions of futures studies

YEHEZKEL DROR

Department of Political Science, The Hebrew University of Jerusalem; and The London School of Economics and Political Science

Abstract Futures studies have three operational bases, each supported by a number of assumptions or premises.

The first basis is that something ought to be known about the future. This is based on two assumptions: (1) the future should be known, as a goal or value in itself; (2) knowledge about the future is useful for achieving other values and goals.

The second basis is that something can be known about the future. It is based on four assumptions: (1) the past can serve as a basis for predicting the future because society has some stability or ultra-stability; (2) special senses permit predictions that are independent of the past; (3) the human mind is capable, directly or indirectly, of recognizing stability or ultra-stability and basing predictions on it; (4) knowledge-distorting effects of intense values, emotions and interests can be overcome.

The third basis is that 'futures studies' as a specific endeavour are a preferable frame for producing desirable knowledge about the future. It is supported by three assumptions: (1) futures studies have shared characteristics; (2) the shared features of futures studies are unique; (3) the unique features of 'futures studies' are best developed within a distinct frame.

Altogether, futures studies seem to be based on nine assumptions which are mixed philosophical, psychological and intellectual. Critical examination of these nine premises seems to indicate that most of them can be supported by some parts of futures studies. These subdivisions can, therefore, constitute the elements of an academic–professional discipline or sub-discipline of 'futures studies'.

Interest in the future may well have accompanied humanity since its very beginnings. Certainly, organized societies have had future-probing institutions from early history, such as seers, prophets, fate-questioning devices, oracles, etc.[1,2] Whether motivated by curiosity or caused by the dependence of all conscious decision-making processes on contingency predictions, attempts to foresee the future are nothing new. Therefore, if indeed contemporary futures studies belong to a different species of endeavours, the distinctions must be sought not in subject matter but in methodology and paradigms and their underlying foundations (for the term futures studies see ref. 3, p.45).

The problem is made all the more difficult by possible differences between appearance and reality. A superficial look at contemporary futures studies reveals many features of modernity, of professionalism and of scientism, all of them recent. A large and rapidly growing professional literature, international and national associations and conferences, special research organizations, university chairs and teaching programmes, special units in private and public organizations, and a large set of tools, techniques and methods—all these characterize contemporary futures studies. These characteristics seem to set futures studies in their modern form apart from their historic ancestors and present a *prima facie* case of scientific–professional legitimacy. The trouble is that alchemy and demonology could develop similar features, given suitable support and interest. External symptoms and presenting signs must not, therefore, be relied upon when one is diagnosing the validity and usefulness of futures studies: a more thorough examination is needed.

Evaluation of the quality of an intellectual endeavour such as futures studies can proceed on different levels, with the help of a variety of criteria. In particular, three levels of investigation are relevant: (*a*) the pragmatic; (*b*) the paradigmatic and (*c*) that of basic assumptions. For futures studies to be accepted as a valid scientific–professional endeavour, or at least as a worthwhile intellectual activity, some criteria for all three dimensions must be satisfied. At the very least, the endeavour must meet requirements on one of these levels.

The trouble with futures studies is that both pragmatic and paradigmatic tests are hard to apply. At the pragmatic level, the utility of futures studies outputs (never mind how arrived at) has to be examined. But this is unproductive for the following reasons. (1) Predictions on complex issues are probabilistic and open-ended; therefore, often actual events cannot prove or disprove the validity of the predictions in the absence of statistically significant sets of similar events, which usually do not exist for socially important phenomena. (2) Human action is influenced by images of the future, which in turn are influenced by futures studies; self-fulfilling or self-negating effects of predictions may be among the useful outputs of futures studies, but they are hard to identify and they distort the objective validity of the predictions themselves. (3) Long-range predictions are among the important concerns of futures studies, but their accuracy cannot be evaluated for a long time. (4) The youth of futures studies may be one of the reasons why they do not meet the pragmatic tests, rather than any inherent defects. (5) To disagreements among those working on futures studies about desired outputs and even about the qualifications needed for engaging in futures studies must be added the difficulty of applying the concept of 'objective knowledge'[4] to the domain of futures studies.

I do not want to overstate my argument. Any good book on futures studies methods (e.g. Martino[5]) includes some pragmatic evidence on the usefulness of some techniques and tools. But for futures studies as a whole, pragmatic tests are in part inappropriate and in part impossible or too difficult to apply at present.

The paradigmatic level of investigation, too, seems inappropriate for futures studies. It involves evaluation of the paradigms used in futures studies in terms of those of other sciences or of contemporary sciences as a whole.[6] But, as I have argued elsewhere at length,[7] futures studies can, and perhaps should, be regarded as part of a 'scientific revolution' which involves substantive changes in their paradigms. Therefore, the paradigms unique to futures studies (on which there is a lot of disagreement) cannot be evaluated through comparison with other sets of paradigms but must be examined and justified in terms of their own foundations.

Medicine, engineering, applied physics, chemistry—these and other disciplines registered significant progress in terms of pragmatic results before achieving validated paradigms and before improving the assumptions on which they were based (though validated paradigms and improved bases became essential for their advancement into the post-pragmatic stage). Futures studies cannot follow a similar road, because the pragmatic and paradigmatic tests cannot be applied or are inappropriate. Validated assumptions are, it follows, already essential for futures studies while they are in their *status nascendi*. This conclusion is all the more important because this dimension has been neglected in published futures studies and is disliked by many of the mission-driven scholars and advocates of futures studies.

Futures studies, in all their varieties, have three operational bases:

(1) Something *ought* to be known about the future.
(2) Something *can* be known about the future.
(3) 'Futures studies' as a specific endeavour are a preferable frame for producing desirable knowledge about the future.

To justify futures studies and, indeed, everything concerned with 'the future as an academic discipline', these bases must, in the main, be supported by viable philosophical, psychological and intellectual assumptions.

Without trying to distinguish strictly between 'philosophical', 'psychological' and 'intellectual' facets, I would like to turn now to a critical, though concise, examination of some such main assumptions of futures studies.

(1) THE FUTURE SHOULD BE KNOWN, AS A GOAL OR VALUE IN ITSELF

Behaviourally, curiosity about the future is a widespread phenomenon, though not a universal one. For example, various primitive societies without time perspectives, or with different time perspectives, show little curiosity about the future. Similarly, fatalistic *Weltanschauungen* and perhaps some existentialistic variations may tend towards non-interest in the future. But, in most contemporary and many historic societies, curiosity about the future is intense.

Independently of the distribution of interest in the future among various populations, every scientist must choose for himself, value-wise, his own area of interest.[8] If one accepts the ideology of the autonomy of science from society and social needs, knowledge about the future is as valid a value for pure-science concern as any other subject. If one introduces considerations of social utility of knowledge of the 'technology assessment' type, the next assumption is reached.

(2) KNOWLEDGE ABOUT THE FUTURE IS USEFUL FOR ACHIEVING OTHER VALUES AND GOALS

In this assumption, knowledge about the future is seen as instrumental for achieving other, undefined, values and goals. This assumption is closely tied in with assumptions about decision-making. Clearly, every conscious and goal-oriented decision-making process depends on knowledge about the future when the probable results of different alternatives have to be compared (ref. 9, chapter 12). Therefore, if such decision-making is accepted as possible and desirable, the assumption about knowledge of the future being instrumentally useful is acceptable. Decision-making itself can be negated either by an extreme deterministic and steady-state point of view or by doubts about the capacity of the human mind to achieve more good than bad through decisions. Also, if one regards human decisions in any case as being incapable of warding off some terrible future, then ignorance about that future can perhaps be regarded as useful, under some conditions.

Another instrumental argument against futures studies relates to their self-fulfilling potentials. Predicting possible undesirable scenarios, so the argument may go, increases their probability of occurring. This, for instance, was a main line of argument against strategic studies dealing with the possibilities of survival during and after a nuclear war.[10,11]

To meet such objections, one can either rely on existing consensus among many scientists on the possibilities of improving human fate through conscious decisions,[12,13] or allow that both positions are equally plausible, so leaving each scholar free to choose sides on the basis of extra-rational beliefs. A stoic philosophy which demands that we try our best, whether it helps or not, can also serve as a foundation for futures studies, as part of policy sciences as a whole.[7]

The first operational basis of futures studies, that something *should* be known about the future, seems therefore well based on philosophical and other assumptions. These assumptions are open to doubts, but not more so than those of most sciences and disciplines.

To continue with the main assumptions of futures studies, we reach now a few that are relevant for the second operational basis of futures studies.

(3) THE PAST CAN SERVE AS A BASIS FOR PREDICTING THE FUTURE BECAUSE OF SOME STABILITY OR ULTRA-STABILITY OF RELEVANT PHENOMENA

Without some regularity of phenomena no nomographic rules can exist, and such rules, in various ways, constitute the base for predictions. In other words, without continuity in the time dimension, no futures studies are possible. Continuity does not have to be deterministic, linear and fixed: probabilistic dynamics, complex continuities, ultra-stability with constant change and even a limited amount of discontinuities—all these can be handled by sophisticated prediction methods. Nevertheless, all knowledge (with one hypothetical exception, to be discussed under the next heading) is based on the past and can, therefore, serve to probe the future only in so far as the future is in continuity with the past.

This is so important an assumption as to justify some further clarifications:

(*a*) Dependence on the past is obvious in the simpler prediction methods, such as extrapolation. But more advanced methods also depend on the past, because models and theories have been verified in the past.

(*b*) Intuition, on which the Delphi method relies, also depends on experience and tacit knowledge accumulated in the past.

(*c*) Even utopian schools of futures studies depend on the past, which shaped concepts and ideas and limited the domain of imagination. Some imaginative creativity may escape these fetters—but, however important for prophetic activities and artistic expression, creativity cannot by itself serve as a main basis for futures studies.

The assumption of continuity in the time dimension is shared by all scientific knowledge related to the physical world and creates few difficulties in the physical sciences, where regularity is assumed on a cosmic scale. In life sciences and medicine there is more awareness of possible non-continuous changes in the objects of inquiry. When we come to the social domain, discontinuities appear frequently and may become dominant during the approaching epoch. Paradoxically, it is the accelerated rate of change itself which pushed the development of futures studies as an aid to dealing with increasing uncertainties, while simultaneously imposing rigid limits on the domain of predictability open to futures studies.

Again, overstatement must be avoided. When we are dealing with short time spans and limited sets of phenomena, sufficient continuity exists to permit predictions, at least if they are in stochastic form and open-ended. Also, explication of the limits of predictability can be helpful by leading to the adoption of uncertainty-absorbing (as distinguished from uncertainty-reducing or uncertainty-patterning) modes of decision-making, such as planning for uncertainty[14] and institutionalized learning.[15,16,17] Nevertheless, dependency upon continuity and past-based knowledge imposes limits on futures studies of non-stable phenomena, so reducing the usefulness and feasibility of futures studies as a whole. Another implication is that futures studies need to be tied in with uncertainty-absorbing modes of decision-making and therefore at least parts of futures studies should be integrated into policy sciences as a whole (ref. 3, chapter 5).

(4) SPECIAL SENSES PERMIT PREDICTIONS INDEPENDENT FROM THE PAST

A logical, but unacceptable, alternative to assumption (3) is a belief in precognition. Even people who accept some parapsychological phenomena as true reject precognition, which contradicts assumptions fundamental to all sciences and to most philosophical systems about time, the cosmos and the nature of human life. Therefore, such an assumption must be rejected, though some persons active in futures studies seem tacitly to believe in precognition, without saying that this is the basis for what they are saying.

(5) THE HUMAN MIND IS CAPABLE, DIRECTLY OR INDIRECTLY, OF RECOGNIZING STABILITY OR ULTRA-STABILITY AND BASING PREDICTIONS ON IT

Within the domain of validity of assumption (3), futures studies are in principle possible if and as far as assumption (5) is also correct. It is not enough that some continuity in the time dimension exists—we must be able to recognize it (either directly or indirectly, e.g. with the help of pattern-recognizing computers) and utilize it for futures studies.

This assumption is related in part to epistemological considerations, in part to psychology, especially the psychology of thinking and perception theory, and in part to intellectual considerations concerning the availability of scientific methodologies and their limitations. Full consideration of these issues would lead us too deep into the philosophy of science, where they have been quite fully considered[4,18,19] though not applied to the specific problems of futures studies. Let me, therefore, limit myself to a few comments.

(a) Subjects which futures studies share with other disciplines present no special problems for this assumption.

(b) When we are dealing with complex phenomena, such as social macro-change, we begin to doubt our ability at present to arrive at valid perception and understanding of the phenomenon. Less ambitious attempts, in the social sciences, to explain specific cases of social macro-change have not so far been very successful, which raises doubts about the capacity of futures studies (which depend on knowledge of different subjects supplied by appropriate disciplines) to do much better in the near future.

(c) Nevertheless, futures studies may do better than expected, thanks to novel packages and methodologies able to handle dynamic, complex and non-deterministic phenomena—such as scenarios, alternative futures, unexpected occurrences, structured imagination, and others.[5,20]

(d) There is no clear and immediate limit to human capacity for understanding complexity, if necessary with the help of intelligence-amplifying devices. Even if an absolute limit exists, futures studies still have a long way to go before it is reached, as demonstrated by ongoing advances in methodologies for futures studies.

(e) Even if an optimistic view of human ability to develop futures studies is adopted, the many difficulties in doing so must be acknowledged. As a minimum, methodological care and sophistication are needed. Simple tools and naive images cannot be expected to go far in futures studies.

Subject to these observations and reservations, assumption (5) seems to be, in the main, acceptable. But a strong barrier, relevant to (5) as well as to (3) and (4), remains: futures studies deal with a subject that is emotional, intensely value-loaded and related to vested interests. Therefore, the need for assumption (6).

(6) KNOWLEDGE-DISTORTING EFFECTS OF INTENSE VALUES, EMOTIONS AND INTERESTS CAN BE OVERCOME

Futures studies deal with a highly emotion-sensitive, value-sensitive and interest-sensitive subject—the shape of the future. All of us have values, the only hope for realization of which lies in the future; all of us have emotions which shape our perception of the future; and many of us have interests whose present fate may depend on accepted images of the future. If the self-fulfilling and self-defying effects of images of the future are added to the above-mentioned forces, then the strength of their distorting effects on futures studies is clear. This effect is fully shown by the present state of much of futures studies, in which hopes for the future, hopes for the present, emotions about both the future and the present, and efforts at identification of probable and possible futures, are often completely mixed up. (This situation is fully reflected in the proceedings of the various international and special world conferences on futures research. For detailed discussion of such weaknesses of futures studies, as reflected in the world conferences, see refs. 21 and 22).

The present state of much of futures studies, therefore, does not supply much factual evidence for the validity of this assumption. But, although psychological factors undermine this assumption, intellectually it is tenable: modern methodology for value analysis permits some separation between futures studies and emotions, interests and values;[23] explicit methods for futures studies help this separation to be made[5] (e.g. see the many methodological articles in the two professional futures studies journals in English, *Futures*[24] and *Technological Forecasting and Social Change*[25]); suitable institutional arrangements can push this separation beyond psychological barriers, through pluralism, positive redundancy and mutual set-offs. Therefore, the conclusion seems to be that in principle assumption (6) will be sustained if—and it is an important 'if'—futures studies in fact are methodologically sophisticated and evolve within a suitable structural setting.

From the combined examination of assumptions (3), (4), (5) and (6) it seems that the second operational basis of futures studies, namely that something *can* be known about the future, can be supported conditionally. The conditions involve some characteristics of futures studies that lead directly into the third operational basis for futures studies, namely that futures studies as a specific endeavour are a suitable frame for producing desirable knowledge about the future.

This operational basis in turn depends on three assumptions, to the examination of which we now turn.

(7) FUTURES STUDIES HAVE SHARED CHARACTERISTICS

The very use of the term 'futures studies' in the plural demonstrates my image of pluralistic features of this activity. Indeed, books, articles and ideas presented under the flag of 'futures studies' have many divergent elements, which do not form a meaningful mosaic. Revolutionary exhortations, utopian and anti-utopian prophecies and plain hallucinations can be found hand-in-hand with careful studies of possible futures, design of desirable and feasible futures, and stimulating counter-probabilistic scenarios. (In addition to the already-mentioned conferences and journals, the more popular monthly *The Futurist*[26] provides a good sample of the various elements that go under the name of 'futures studies'.)

Behaviourally, the seventh assumption is, therefore, not too well supported. Only if one excludes from the legitimate domain of futures studies some of the fringe activities, including—in addition to those already mentioned—strong 'action-oriented' quasi-political activities aggregating around the standard of futures studies, can one identify a meaningful shared characteristic that can serve as a basis for a 'futures studies' frame. Interest in the future by itself is not a meaningful characteristic, being much too diffuse. The shared characteristic of those futures interests which can constitute elements of a discipline, inter-discipline, subdiscipline, supradiscipline, of futures studies etc., must be that they have an explicit methodology for dealing with the future. This common denominator of futures studies returns us, in part, to assumption (5). As indicated there, a methodology for futures studies is possible and, in fact, already exists in part.

(8) THE SHARED FEATURES OF FUTURES STUDIES ARE UNIQUE TO THOSE STUDIES

To justify a specific frame for futures studies, it is necessary to show both (*a*) that there is a common denominator, as considered just now; and (*b*) that this denominator is unique, at least in some aspects. All disciplines of knowledge are interested in the future, prediction being a main test of a valid theory or model. The question is whether predictions and futures studies, and their methodologies, have something special which justifies their advancement as a distinct endeavour.

This question can probably be answered positively. No existing discipline focuses mainly on predictions and futures treatment as such. If one includes all the special features of methodologies for futures studies (e.g. utilization of intuition, important role of futures invention with the help of creativity and imagination, special relation to planning and policy-making, and others), 'futures studies' seem to have a unique domain of concern, which is specific but not exclusive.

(9) THE UNIQUE FEATURES OF FUTURES STUDIES ARE BEST DEVELOPED WITHIN A DISTINCT FRAME

Given the features of the organization of knowledge and the structure of universities and of research, the need for distinct frames in which futures studies can develop seems both reasonable and experience-based. The analogue of the dependence of policy studies on novel institutions which fit their special characteristics seems quite convincing (see ref. 7, especially Part Four). The differences between some of the methodological features of futures studies and those of most 'normal' academic endeavours reinforce the conclusion that distinct frames are needed for futures studies. This does not imply that those frames must be separate and unique for futures studies. Perhaps, some parts at least of futures studies have a better chance of developing in conjunction with policy sciences or policy studies as a whole—never mind the name. But the requirement for a distinct frame for futures studies seems well enough supported to justify at least some serious experimentation with it.

In the aggregate, assumptions (7), (8) and (9) seem to support the third operational basis, at least in respect to some sorts of futures studies, which in turn should be open-ended and innovative but not completely anarchic.

To sum up this examination of the nine main assumptions on which futures studies rest, it seems that for parts of futures studies, as constituted now, these assumptions are sufficiently well supported to justify a *prima facie* case for 'futures studies' as an academic–professional endeavour. But, if they are to live up to the assumptions of this ambition and claim, futures studies must transform themselves and upgrade their qualities. For actual moves in these directions, suitable institutionalization, designed to build up the foundations of futures studies, is necessary, as discussed in this paper. The details of appropriate institutionalization need separate enquiry.

Discussion

Waddington: In the academic context, futures studies should be compared with the discipline of history. Nobody really pretends that history leads us to an exact definition of the facts, or an account of all the facts. History is a normative exercise. The evidence is never complete, and the best historians give a personal interpretation of the way people were feeling and the way they were acting. Historians are, of course, constrained by what facts are known, but the best historians are also great moralists. The sort of truth they are aiming at is not the same as scientific truth, and even scientific truth is not absolute truth.

I am sure that students of the future should not be regarded as simple seekers after the truth. I don't believe in futuristics as prediction: they have always turned out to be wrong.

One characteristic of futures studies is that, in today's immediate context, they are much more multidimensional than most other types of studies. Just looking at telecommunications and asking how soon we are going to get the video-telephone isn't 'futures study'—it is the future of a specific technology. Futures studies must be as totally multidimensional as they can be, trying to look at everything. That is a distinct difference from nearly everything else in the academic world now. The academic world has gone through a hundred years of sub-division, and it is fairly difficult to find anybody anywhere who really looks at the world in a multidimensional way. Historians perhaps do so, and lawyers to some extent, but it is against the general trend of academia in the last hundred years.

The practical justification of futures studies is that they are an attempt to draw a picture of the present, from the point of view that the present is not just the existing instant but really consists of processes. We can't have a picture of the present without knowing what has been going on for the last thirty years—in fact we may have to go back to Magna Carta to get some of the relevant dimensions—and we also need to look ahead five, ten, twenty or thirty years. Futures studies are an attempt to draw a picture of the stage on which we are going to take the next step; and the next step must carry us away from where we are now towards somewhere. Futures studies try to give us some idea of whether we are going to fall down a chasm in the next few years or not. And this has to be done in a multidimensional sense, not just two-dimensional.

Those seem to me to be the three major characteristics of futures studies: they can only aim at the sort of truth historians aim at—a truth involving a great element of normative moralizing; they must be exceedingly multidimensional and their basic relevance is as a dynamic analysis of today.

Platt: It is worth remembering that three different kinds of problem-solving were needed in evolution. The first is problem-solving by survival: the creatures that didn't solve the problems died off. That kind is encoded in the DNA. The second is problem-solving by learning, with the nervous system. That kind is encoded in the neurons: you don't have to fall over the cliff before you draw back. The third is problem-solving by anticipation; this can only come with science, with the knowledge of laws and regularities, so that one can predict things that have never happened. The Sputnik is a good example of these differences. The first Sputnik was not one of ten thousand that were shot up at random and only one survived; nor was it something which flew too high and then too low until it learned the right orbit. No: it was designed by anticipation—programmed with a feedback-stabilization program to go into the right orbit on the first try.

In the same way, the human race collectively is now encountering families of hard problems that have never been encountered before. We cannot solve them by learning because it would require living through them; and we cannot solve them by survival, because we have in a sense only one world for one trip. We must therefore solve them by anticipation. This requires us to understand the laws of social dynamics so that we can anticipate all sorts of things that have never happened before. It will require many sensitive little feedbacks all along the way: tiny indicators, fluctuations which show whether we have got the rules right or whether they are going astray, advance warnings or 'feed-forwards'. We will need all sorts of special little methods that give us indications short of catastrophe to help us to go rapidly but as cautiously as possible in solving this global problem that has never existed before.

Nevertheless, there is another sense in which knowledge of the future is impossible, simply because of its interaction with our choices. Here the analogy I would suggest is something like the steering of a bus. For this, we need not a narrow knowledge of one single possible path or rut, but knowledge of the total visual field, the total set of alternative paths, so that you see the old ruts here and the good roadway there, and the dangers somewhere else. You choose among them in a cybernetic way and the result is that you cannot predict your own choices until you know what the whole field is, and it continues to change as your vision changes, and your choices as you move along.

The role of futures studies, it seems to me, is to describe this total visual field, this total multidimensional family of alternatives within which we choose. It is, in Harvey Cox's sense,[27] a prophecy—that is, it is an 'if–then' procedure rather than 'prediction'. Prediction says that we *will* do so and so, at least with a certain probability. Cox says, on the other hand, that what we need instead is the Judaeo-Christian tradition of prophecy, not probabilistic but *conditional: if* you make love to your neighbour's wife, *then* you will roast in hell; but *if* you love God, *then* you can create the Kingdom of Heaven around you. The old prophets were never predictors but made prophecies in this conditional sense. So a view of futures knowledge, it seems to me, is a description of conditional knowledge—that is, of a range of alternatives such that *if* you do this, *then* with fair probability *that* will happen. This makes it very operational, but different from the deterministic findings of science, not like physics but cybernetics.

Oldfield: Even after Professor Dror's interesting philosophical, psychological and intellectual analysis of futures studies I am still very much the worried outsider. As an empirical ecologist and certainly not a philosopher, I find it difficult to express the problems that I see, but there are at least five aspects of futures studies which worry me. I think I would label them identity, cost, shift of mode, the question of responsibility or escapism, and the question of positive feedback.

Identity—Professor Waddington encouraged us to think in terms of history, so let us think briefly of African history. Until recently this was essentially colonial history, with which the African had little identity. I fear that some futures studies are perhaps tending towards an even more worrying and more dangerous kind of intellectual neocolonialism in which the majority become alienated not merely from the real experiences of the past but from all the alternative articulated images of the future.

Cost—scenario models cost money and I think they are usually funded by people who have cash and a belief that they have options. People who have neither, don't or can't fund them.

Shift of mode—when we contemplate the idea of the future as an academic discipline, I think we are saying by implication that we can study the past and we can study the future. But 'study' means such different things in those two contexts, different in terms both of what is available for our empirical examination and different in terms of what is amenable to change. In practice there seems to be, within futures studies, an emphasis on the positive evaluation of methodology, no bad thing in itself. However, I suspect that it is a self-generating thing, that it heightens mystique and jargon, and that it helps to diminish communication outside the subject.

Escapism—some of the points I suppose are McLuhanesque and they are by way of saying that the study of the future is a different medium. Therefore I suspect that it will be perceived and decoded by people outside the study in ways which we might find difficult to anticipate. My fear is that, all too often, it will tend to promote despair or irresponsibility or escapism. T. S. Eliot, who said wiser and more beautiful things about time than any of us, said that 'humankind cannot bear very much reality'. For myself I am forced to wonder in what sense, if any, it is still possible to affirm that the future is not something to be predicted or anticipated, but to be worked for?

Feedback—my final point is that I suspect, partly from the little reading that I have done and partly from our discussions, that it is going to be difficult for futures study to avoid reinforcing the great socioeconomic disparities in the world. I think it is difficult for it ever to become a vehicle for doing the reverse. It is more likely to be a mechanism for positive feedback in socioeconomic divergencies and disparities.

I am not trying to discredit futures studies. I am merely expressing a lot of worries and I would be happier if some of these things were discussed in a meeting of this kind.

Waddington: Why do you think futures studies are necessarily going to encourage the development of disparity in different parts of the world?

Oldfield: I suspect that by revealing the range of possibilities and the range of choice they will be most clearly perceived and acted upon by those who can profit from the range of alternatives presented.

King: Like all knowledge?

Oldfield: Sadly, yes.

Dror: Edmund Burke, I think, said that the present is a bridge between the past and the future. In this sense I certainly agree with Professor Waddington. But I think there are radical differences between futures studies and studies of the past. Thus, there is one past but many alternative futures.

Waddington: Are you sure there is only one past?

Dror: There are different perceptions of the past, but there is only one past.

I agree that in principle anticipation and learning must be tied in but the problem is more complex. For example, even though few areas of learning from information have received such large inputs of money and high quality manpower as military defence intelligence—which certainly has had much more attention than social indicators—the history of military intelligence is full of extreme failures because all data were perceived in the mirrors of the past. A main danger is, therefore, that even when the future already gives warning symptoms we cannot recognize what is going to happen. Therefore, one main problem of futures studies is how to jump out of our own skins, how to broaden our perception of the future. This is a main intellectual challenge which leads us to the question of learning, anticipation and so forth.

I would completely disagree with what Professor Oldfield said about methodology (p. 157). Methodology is difficult for those who don't study it. Indeed, in a new endeavour where we can't test the results the only thing we can do is to test the methods and the underlying assumptions.

If the Zionist movement had had an excellent institute for futures study sixty years ago, it would probably have failed. In a movement that was trying to do the nearly impossible, the knowledge that it was nearly impossible would have made it completely impossible. It is different in Israel today, where good futures studies are very necessary. Futures studies are useful for most societies today, but for some types of social movements they are dysfunctional.

Oldfield: I didn't want to imply that a careful regard for methodology is bad. I was saying that a preoccupation with methodology has certain sorts of implications for people outside the methodology.

Waddington: Nobody could possibly deny that professional futurologists have invented some pretty awe-inspiring jargon, which inspires more awe than the subject can really carry off. Some of the methodologies are definitely useful, but there has been, as you said, too great a proliferation of methodology, and the promises held out have been too great. Delphi sounds a wonderful method, but it is simply systematized guessing, though it sometimes pretends it is a lot more.

Eldredge: Futures studies are really a problem-oriented field. I have worked in a number of problem-oriented areas, and we never did like the word 'discipline' because it suggests a body of knowledge, with well-worked-out theory and methodologies. 'Field', on the other hand, suggests an area of interest that hasn't yet grown up; moreover it doesn't sound quite so pretentious. One of the worst things that futures studies at this point can do is act in a pretentious fashion. We don't use the term 'discipline' for urban studies, which are very interdisciplinary, or for women's studies or black studies.

Waddington: You are possibly right but I would say that, on your definition, history should be a field.

Ashby: I think the opportunity costs which Dr Valaskakis discussed are relevant to the main theme of our discussion. I am uneasy about their use, for various reasons. First, it tempts the worker to put a money value on something which many people believe can't be measured, and then to slip the money value into a cost–benefit equation as though it were as valid as the other numerical data. This is exactly what was done by the Roskill commission; they did a cost–benefit analysis for the third London airport at a cost of £1 million, and its conclusion—to put the airport in Buckinghamshire—was promptly rejected by the Minister. The only relevant question about opportunity costs for our discussion is: can you use this technique, and are you prepared to do so, to estimate what people are prepared to give up in the way of present benefits for the benefit of their great-grandchildren. The relevance of discussions about the future, in so far as they bear on policy-making, depends on how much we are prepared to sacrifice now for the benefit of coming generations. Without knowing how we stand on that question, we cannot be clear about what kind of future we want for people not yet born. A future of the kind we want now may not be at all what our great-grandchildren would want. They might not even want to go around in cars. There might be quite different means of inter-communication then, and people might not want much to travel. I think we have to distinguish the study of the future—which is immensely interesting and which has great potentialities—from the application of the study of the future to present political policies. I am suspicious of those who are tempted to calculate numerical discounts on the future.

Valaskakis: I shall resist the temptation you referred to. Opportunity–cost has in essence nothing to do with money, because one can measure opportunity–cost with this idea of felicity without mentioning money at all.

Another example shows that money does not have to enter into the subject at all. The sociologists say that we seem to be moving towards a singles life-style as opposed to a married life-style. Many people argue about this but they can't seem to explain why. If we could identify not the material but the abstract advantages of the marriage situation, including some form of emotional security, and then trade this off against the liberty or freedom that is perceived in the so-called 'singles' situation, then we would have the quaternary commodity trade-off that I am talking about. No money enters into the picture, but what seems to happen is that people make changing choices: they have alternative goals depending on their position in life. In the Californian model, a person marries six or seven times in a lifetime because of a continuous change in the hierarchy of values. At times the need for emotional security seems to be stronger than the need for so-called freedom, and vice versa. I shall give yet another example of non-monetary opportunity cost as an explanation of behaviour. Kenneth Boulding has written a fascinating book called *The Economy of Love and Fear*[28] where he substitutes for the notion of exchange the notion of grants, which are unilateral movements of goods with no counterpart. It is the *quid* without the *quo*. Implicit grants occur when such a transfer of commodities arises as a by-product of certain actions. If we deplete non-renewable natural resources, we are actually exacting a tribute or an implicit grant from future generations to ourselves, because we are reducing the anticipated felicities of future generations. This is not measurable in any cardinal terms, but we could speak in terms of orders of magnitude, or of the magnitude of anticipated effects. To deplete this now is to help our grandchildren at the cost of lower present consumption. The opportunity-cost tool thus helps us to decide.

Waddington: This opportunity-cost argument doesn't necessarily apply only to the future. It applies also today. You are loading onto the shoulders of the people doing futures studies one of the insoluble problems of today. It is today that you ask a man living in Berkeley, would he go to Los Angeles for so many thousand dollars more? The problem of comparing incomparables is a present-day problem. Of course, it is also a problem that arises in the future, but it is not the responsibility of the future to raise it: it is a problem of today.

I am much more modest than Lord Ashby about what I would give up for my great-grandchildren. I am worried enough about what I would give up for my own present-day children. I don't think I can see the future for the whole of their lives, let alone their children's lives, or their children's children's lives. You are a terrific optimist if you think you could get much idea of what your great-grandchildren will want.

Ashby: I am not optimistic at all. I am dealing with the need to approach the problem as objectively as possible. To do that, one has to minimize personal involvement. One can do that for one's grandchildren, not for one's own children.

Waddington: The point I wanted to make is that with futures studies one can hope to say what sort of things are going to be the important variables—the non-comparable variables, I am sure. But one of the things to explore is, what sort of questions will you be asked? That is by no means obvious. I don't think we can get more than indications of it.

Valaskakis: An excellent common denominator which is much better than money is time. Time is a scarce commodity. If we think in terms of an evening out where we have a choice between the theatre and a concert, money need not enter into the picture. The two tickets cost the same. It is at the felicity level that we compare either allocation of time.

Shane: Studies of interventions in the future are present realities—at least in the sense that a great deal of money is being spent on plans for new commercial products. Could you list some practical reasons that you feel are valid ones for deciding quickly whether futures studies should be deemed to be a discipline, Professor Dror?

Dror: If I were given a few million pounds to do something to improve human capacity for influencing the future, I would establish integrated policy research institutes with comprehensive interdisciplinary teams. These would work for a number of years, say between five and ten, on the main problems, with predictions constituting an integral part of the analysis as a whole. If I had to decide on a new programme at a university I would establish demanding and advanced programmes for graduate and postgraduate students, preparing them for dealing professionally with complex decisions.

Woodroofe: Ought one in the first instance to concentrate studies of the future on the short term rather than on the long term, and then proceed at some later date to the long term? If we concentrate on the short term, we can validate some of the methodology and so have a firm base. We talked about looking back and saying that most of the predictions were wrong, and we also say that the purpose of looking at the future is to make our decisions better. If, then, our predictions in the past have been bad, we must have been taking bad decisions. If we now concentrate on the long-term future which we are not able to validate, we may continue to excite interest in this particular area, making predictions which are wrong and taking wrong decisions. Why not work on the short-term scale, say five years, and validate; then work on a ten-year scale and so on; and proceed in that way?

Shane: The US Office of Education had an interesting experience in that line when they commissioned two educational policy centres. Within eighteen months they had moved from a focus on developments thirty years hence to a focus on immediate future developments.

Dror: That certainly should be done, but the prediction problems are even more serious for three to six years ahead, because one cannot assume linear continuity. Also, for many decisions the lead time needed to have any impact on reality is rather long. It takes two to four years, and sometimes much more, just to start changing something complex like a transit system or an educational system.

Woodroofe: Some years ago I asked my staff what they could do about telling me about the next five years. They said the next five years were difficult but they could be much more confident about the next twenty-five years!

Francis: The renewal of the capital stock, for example, on which our society depends, can't be achieved on that kind of time scale, given the constraints as we now see them. The reason that we can be so certain is because there is a great deal of inertia already incorporated in the present system. I really don't understand how you can suggest that there is such a wide spectrum of possibilities and that these possibilities still exist in an open-ended way, Professor Dror.

Dror: It depends on the time stream. The longer the time stream, the more hypothetical the possibilities are, and the more uncertainties there are. This is the basic dilemma. A main problem in top-level decision-making is that good predictions replace subjective certainty with objective uncertainty. If the decision maker has to consider what the Soviet Union will do, he may think A, B or C are possible, so he calls in his prediction experts. The prediction experts will probably say—after suitable studies—no to A, B is possible, C is possible and D, E, F, G are other possibilities which the decision maker forgot. Most decision makers will then kick the experts out of the door. Therefore, for applied purposes, as aids to decision-making, futures studies or predictions are of little use unless they are tied in with uncertainty-absorbing decision methods. For this, different and new modes of decision-making are needed; classical decision-making patterns which assumed a lot of certainty are hopeless and even counter-productive under contemporary and future conditions.

Waddington: In operational research in the war, cost was a major factor. Was it worth changing a weapon, say, and retraining and re-equiping a squadron?

Woodroofe: This also applies to information. You can improve your decisions by getting more and more information, but information costs money and there comes a time when it costs more to get the information than an improved decision is worth.

Perry: I can only go along with cost–benefit analysis when we are talking economics. I can't see how we can relate all values by such means. We can do it, perhaps, with those values which money can buy, but it can't buy all the values that are built into a felicity index, either now or in the future. I come to a complete impasse there.

Waddington: The trouble is, we relate values all the time. We decide we want to go to the opera or have dinner.

Perry: But if it is to be an academic discipline, we can't compare like with unlike. A decision to go to the opera is a political decision, not an academic or a scientific decision.

Ziman: If there is to be a rationale of decision-making in terms of futures, it must displace some other way of taking decisions or acting. Human beings have taken actions and made decisions throughout the whole of history, and we want to be very careful that we do not displace a not very good method by a worse one. Intuition based on experience, which cannot be rationalized in a formal way, should not necessarily be replaced by something that is mechanized.

Waddington: Aren't all students in universities now told that it can be?

Ziman: I am saying that this is a folly. For example, a good general knows that up to a certain point he can trust his staff plans; but to carry that trust too far is dangerous. Such misplaced confidence produces bad generals.

Dror: I agree. It is a question of adding to intuition so that better decisions have a higher probability of being made. Decisions by many generals and other decision makers in the past show a history of stupidity, ignorance and mistakes. Most methods for improving decision-making are not very good. But the strong justification for using them is that most real-life decision-making is even worse.

Woodroofe: One ultimately makes decisions on the basis of judgement, after getting as much information as possible, including predictions about things likely to happen in the future. At the end of that, there is still a large element of uncertainty.

Ziman: Is it justified to hope that the stupid generals will make better decisions if they have better staff plans?

Dror: No. The decisions will only be better if the decision structure of the army is changed. It is not enough to give the same person, if he is no good, more information.

Ziman: They might be better generals if they read a great deal of the history of war.

Waddington: You make better generals by giving them feedback, as the results of operational research.

Dror: If they are not very good, even though they are aided by suitable structures, they don't learn correctly. Learning is a very complex process which cannot be relied on as spontaneously successful.

Eldredge: An interesting aspect of technological forecasting is where one knows more or less surely that something is going to appear, but not quite how it is going to appear. We knew that the speed of transportation was going to increase before we knew about jet engines or rockets. In 1946 Ogburn[29] thought it would be possible soon for aircraft to fly under imperfect conditions and at night. He spoke of using fog dispellers, flares and fog-piercing lights, but he didn't then know about radar, although he believed that it was pretty certain to happen. That is technical technology forecasting. I think there is now going to be trans-economic cost–benefit analysis (societal technology). Nobody yet knows how to do this, but it is so important that someone is going to find a way. Trans-economic cost–benefit analysis will not be very reliable initially but it will be better than some of today's intuitive guesses. In planning, one has to value any loss of amenities against economic costs. The aircraft industry in the 1930s had to get those unlikely miserable crates up and down on runways. We have to find some method for decision-making which helps us to weigh apples against opera. I really feel that someone is going to break through within the next few decades in a cost–benefit analysis which will be trans-economic. This is an act of faith. This is an umbrella curve—technological forecasting in societal technology.

Waddington: Work is going on on that sort of question in evolutionary biology. How do species cope with having two or three different environments making different demands on them for natural selection? There is quite a lot of theoretical or mathematical work on how they do it. It depends on the scale of the mix—is it a big-scale mosaic or a small-scale mosaic of different environments? It is the beginning of an intellectual mathematical analysis of adaptation to disparate demands. Something will eventually come out, which will provide more understanding of what can be done about it. I don't think we will get a prescription to tell us how to solve the problem. I think what we will get will be more understanding of the logic of the situation.

References cited

[1] DAVID, F. N. (1962) *Games, Gods and Gambling*, Hafner, New York

[2] LEWINSOHN, R. (1961) *Science, Prophecy and Prediction*, Harper, New York

[3] DROR, Y. (1971) *Ventures in Policy Sciences*, American Elsevier, New York

[4] POPPER, K. R. (1972) *Objective Knowledge*, Clarendon Press, Oxford

[5] MARTINO, J. P. (1972) *Technological Forecasting for Decisionmaking*, American Elsevier, New York

[6] KUHN, T. S. (1962) *The Structure of Scientific Revolutions*, University of Chicago Press, Chicago

[7] DROR, Y. (1971) *Design for Policy Sciences*, American Elsevier, New York

[8] POLANYI, M. (1962) The Republic of Science. *Minerva*, *1*, 54 ff.

[9] DROR, Y. (1968) *Public Policymaking Reexamined*, Intertext, New York

[10] GREEN, P. (1966) *Deadly Logic*, Ohio State University Press, Ohio

[11] KAPLAN, M. A. (1973) *Strategic Thinking and Its Moral Implications*, University of Chicago Press, Chicago

[12] ETZIONI, A. (1968) *The Active Society*, Free Press, New York

[13] LASSWELL, H. D. (1971) *A Pre-View of Policy Sciences*, American Elsevier, New York

[14] MACK, R. (1971) *Planning on Uncertainty*, Wiley, New York

[15] BEER, S. (1975) *Platform for Change*, Wiley, Chichester

[16] SCHON, A. D. (1971) *Beyond the Stable State*, Temple Smith, London

[17] DUNN, E. S., Jr. (1971) *Economic and Social Development: A Process of Social Learning*, Johns Hopkins University Press, Baltimore, Md., and London

[18] POLANYI, M. (1958) *Personal Knowledge*, Routledge & Kegan Paul, London

[19] NAGEL, E. *et al.* (eds.) (1962) *Logic, Methodology and Philosophy of Science*, Stanford University Press, Stanford, California

[20] KAHN, H. & WIENER, A. J. (1967) *The Year 2000*, Macmillan, New York

[21] DROR, Y. (1973) A third look at futures study. *Technological Forecasting and Social Change*, 5, 109–112

[22] DROR, Y. (1974) Future studies—quo vadis? in *Human Futures*, pp. 169–176, IPC Press, Guildford

[23] DROR, Y. (1973) Scientific aid to value judgment, in *Modern Science and Moral Values*, pp. 257–264, International Cultural Foundation, New York

[24] *Futures: the journal of forecasting and planning*, IPC Science and Technology Press, Guildford, Surrey

[25] *Technological Forecasting and Social Change*, American Elsevier, New York

[26] *The Futurist*, World Future Society, Washington, D.C.

[27] COX, H. (1968) *On Not Leaving it to the Snake*, Macmillan, New York

[28] BOULDING, K. E. (1973) *The Economy of Love and Fear*, Wadsworth, Belmont, California

[29] OGBURN, W. F. (1946) *The Social Effects of Aviation*, Houghton Mifflin, Boston

Universities as nerve centres of society

JOHN PLATT

Mental Health Research Institute, University of Michigan, Ann Arbor

Abstract The smartest brain is made of ignorant cells. They achieve intelligence and complex differentiated responses by multiple inputs, parallel processing, extensive cross-connection with common biochemical excitation, hierarchical stages of abstraction and differentiated parallel output, and feedback restimulation for goal-seeking. The parallels with effective action for a national or global society deserve exploration.

Television is the adrenaline of the body politic, producing instant outrage, instant imitation and instant demands. In a high-education society with free news media and participatory checks and balances, this can lead to immediate expert debate and the creation of interest groups and pressure groups in any area of information, forecast and concern. 'Social lag' turns to social pressure for change, with revaluing and restructuring—often with technological lag instead. This constitutes a new form of revolution—informational and structural rather than military.

The universities, as the primary repositories and transmitters of knowledge, become abstracting centres and catalytic combination and forecasting centres, offering information as desired to the community, farmers, industry, business, government, policy makers and change agents, the young, the curious, and the leisured, often through their mutual interests in participatory action. The universities will expand problem-oriented research and their interconnected network-outputs of research reports, news organs, radio, television, and community education.

THE ELECTRONIC SURROUND: HOW IT CHANGES SOCIAL INFORMATION AND ACTION PATTERNS

In the course of evolution, every change in the mode or speed of communication has led to a step-function jump in the organization and competence of organisms in relation to themselves and to their environment. We see successive steps of this kind in the development of the chordate nervous system; in encephalization, with the grouping of sensory and decision functions into a brain; in collective signalling; in symbolic language and speech; in the invention of

167

writing; in mass printing of books and newspapers; in the compression of knowledge by mathematical symbolism and scientific laws; in photography; and today, in the invention that has given us for the first time simultaneous global aggregate consciousness—television.

This is what Marshall McLuhan in recent discussions has called the Electronic Surround. Probably neither he nor anyone else of this generation has realized or can realize how this new medium will change our view of reality, our habits of mind, our intellectual and social development, and our mode and success of interaction into more integrated or more differentiated human organization. But in the United States and other nations with almost universal television, we can see some of the changes already and we can see the probable lines along which further changes will carry us.

The first of these changes is that television eliminates distance and direction. The same news commentator is two metres away, in the direction of the box, whether we are on the top floor in Seattle or rocking in a boat in a Miami marina. This will also be true of videocassettes, just as it is true now for electronically amplified rock-music concerts or for self-chosen stereo records or quadraphonic tapes in the home. 'I am *inside* the music', Janis Joplin said.

This is just the beginning of the ways in which television eliminates reality, or rather, changes what we have called reality to another and more public reality, simultaneous for everybody. We all watch the late-night murder movie together, and it becomes more real than the murder in the street outside our window, because we can validate it the next day in conversation with a dozen people. We all share the nation's or the world's grief and joy, not only with shared in-jokes that every stewardess knows, but with going to the Kennedy funeral together, walking on the moon together, and seeing the Olympic games in Munich together, and the terrorist murders there. It has been estimated that 1500 million people, or 38 per cent of the world's population, saw those Olympic games and their aftermath by simultaneous or delayed satellite broadcasts.

Television expands to fill the available leisure time. This is a corollary of Parkinson's law of the expansion of work. Surveys show that the average set in the United States is on for more than six hours a day. Even allowing for different viewers at different times in the same family, this may represent well over half of the available free-choice time for the average person. With good programming, this could even be good—a collective and enlarging experience for all, as dancing once was, and epic myths and poetry, when we watched and listened around the fire in the cave.

Television will spread quickly to the poorest corners of the world, because it is the cheapest way of spending time that the human race has ever invented.

The total cost, including sets, power and programming, is about two cents per person per day, even at American prices; that is, hundreds of times cheaper than a car and a thousand times cheaper than a schoolteacher. Indeed it is the poorest countries that may find television the cheapest investment for rapid economic growth, because it can bring literacy, rural and urban skills, family planning knowledge and images, weather reports, and government exhortations and plans, and hope. For these reasons, it seems likely that 80 per cent or more of the world's population may be linked together, at least by village television, by about 1980. The effect on global consciousness and global unity of these steady daily messages shared by everybody cannot help but be immense.

For McLuhan is right again, in saying that the medium is the message. Just as automobiles transform road systems and cities and food distribution and family structure, regardless of the economic system and the design of the cars, so television will transform consciousness and human interaction in many of these ways, regardless of the programming. Yes, it is better not to have continual violence or raw government propaganda or censorship; but even with these, the medium—the flashing box itself—is saying: There *is* high technology; There is human communication and organization and planning; These ideas, like these weather fronts, may cross all boundaries; There is one world and one set of human problems; and Those people live like *that*, so why don't you? It is no wonder that closed societies fear television.

For television is the real revolutionary of our times. It produces instant outrage, instant imitation, and instant demands. The conventional intellectual view, that belittles television as an idiot box, offering mainly football or late-night movies to passive beer-drinkers who are taken in by the advertising, is only partly true. For many viewers who are concerned people, it is not a pacifying or coercing medium, but an activating medium. My own scanning of television programmes in the San Francisco Bay area in 1973 indicated that a large fraction of programmes implied responsive action by the viewers, such as setting-up exercises, yoga, TV auctions, French cooking, Japanese brush-painting, language learning, and Sesame Street with the children dancing and singing around the box. In addition, political activism in the news or problem-analysis can lead to 100 000 letters to Congress the next morning, or to thousands of people going down to help picket City Hall. The only way to talk back to the box—so that it becomes two-way *com*munication—is to exert political pressure or to get out in the streets so that you get on television yourself.

The somewhat surprising result has been not uniformitarianism but the sudden development of powerful differentiated movements, with group images and group communication leading to group unity for protests or demands.

These include the civil rights movement, the student movement, ecology, consumerism, birth control, black power, the ethnic movements, the anti-war movement, women's liberation, and the limits to growth, as well as the political pressures connected with Watergate, all in the last decade or so. Each of these movements, of course, had its own special causes and dynamics and timing, but I believe that it was television in a high-education society that gave each of them a national simultaneity, spread, speed of development, and impact, that went considerably beyond the effects of the older media of the press and the radio.

And I think television gave these movements their 'participatory democracy', with none of them being directed by a single central committee, but with leaders and issues springing up in a hundred cities at once. Television becomes the adrenaline of the body politic, so to speak, exciting the concerned groups to put immense pressure on policy makers and administrators for a change of attitudes and the correction of old inequities. The old hierarchical methods of government and business direction and planning by managers and manipulators, 'the best and the brightest' of the Kennedy and Johnson and Nixon administrations, with their technological élitism—pro-male, pro-natalist, pro-growth, pro-hierarchy, pro-Vietnam War, pro-supersonic transport, pro-auto —have gone down again and again before the power of these new movements of consciousness. It is a new politics of shared consciousness that is loose in the world.

This ferment has made television the primary educator for adults. Today, in the United States, there are probably several millions of people who could give good lectures on ecology or Watergate and the US political process or on world population or world food or energy problems or on the limits to growth or women's rights, yet who never learned about these subjects in college. By a good lecture, I mean one that includes material and arguments that professors themselves did not know five years ago. These are all subjects which are not usually taught, even now, to university undergraduates, but which are vital for democratic voting and policy making and for the world's future. How did we all learn them?—By television debates that called in the concerned and the expert for public confrontation. It has taught not only adults but young students, who frequently know more than their teachers now, and who transform the classrooms as a result.

Such an analysis of the role of television in powering these new movements of consciousness must not neglect the supportive and analytical role played by other recent inventions, such as photocopying and cheap lithoprinting and university FM radio and even the jet plane. Television may generate the simultaneous emotion and concern, but it is print and the lecture circuit that give the structural details and subtleties of analysis and action. Tens of millions of Americans have been so disgusted by the admitted lies and 'inoperative' statements of government and the establishment media that they will believe any opposing statements of counter-cultural media and critics, even sometimes when they are no more accurate. This creates a receptive seed-bed for thousands of alternative communications, counter-cultural newspapers, house organs, movement magazines, pamphlets from small mailing groups, books, and lectures on FM radio, with movement leaders and speakers flying continually between centres. In many Californian cities today, a downtown street corner may have fifteen or more newspaper vending machines representing competing political opinions and social interests.

These alternative media get read and analysed by local groups in all kinds of mass meetings, retreats, or Tuesday evening consciousness-raising sessions. The result is probably a more widespread, diverse and critical assessment of society and of our alternative futures than any society has ever had. This is much of what the French observer, Jean-François Revel, talked about in his 1971 book *Without Marx or Jesus: The New American Revolution Has Begun*.[1]

These new technologies, with this new consciousness and political interaction, have led to a remarkably rapid reversal of the attitudes and laws of many decades or centuries. The reason for the reversals has been described by Jonas Salk in his book, *The Survival of the Wisest*.[2] He points out that when exponential growth approaches limits and begins to level off—passing the 'watershed', where we take our foot off the gas and put it on the brakes, so to speak—then our ethics and attitudes must also turn around in many areas. In population, for example, the injunction of the Bible to 'go forth, be fruitful, and multiply' must change to 'Zero Population Growth' if we are not to destroy ourselves. The increase of energy consumption and the use of non-renewable resources was good in the growth phase, because it got rid of slavery and gave leisure and new potentialities. But it becomes bad when it leads to the overheating of all our cities or the dispersal of resources our children will need to make a decent life.

What is remarkable is the speed and number of these reversals today. I believe that more than forty major changes of this kind can be demonstrated in the United States and in significant new world structures since, say, 1968. They include

— several détente agreements ending the Cold War;
— the first international money not based on gold or a national currency;
— new national and international laws and organizations for pollution control and ecological protection, with the banning of such disruptive

developments as the SST and new jetports for the first time in western technological history;
— the changes in sex laws, in the US, Italy and France, on homosexuality, pornography, abortion and contraception, with more permissiveness for sexual acts between consenting adults than in western Christian history;
— the reduction of birth rates to 'replacement level' or below, in the US and eleven other countries, through the free choice of tens of millions of families;
— and the reversal of numerous other laws, decriminalizing drunkenness, auto accidents, and divorce, and increasing the rights of prisoners and the mentally ill.

There is also
— the greatest reform in the universities, in the treatment of students as adults, since the early 1900s;
— the greatest reform in western religions since the Protestant Reformation, according to several observers;
— the greatest reform in the rights and opportunities of minority groups and women in several generations;
— the greatest reform in American politics, in election laws and accountability, in this century;
— and a turnaround in attitudes towards (*a*) science, (*b*) energy, (*c*) space exploration, (*d*) the global future in the next century, (*e*) the limits to growth, and (*f*) systems analysis studies of global problems and alternative futures.

These are the fastest and most extensive peacetime reversals of attitudes in the whole intellectual history of humanity. It all makes this the most responsive society ever known. It is a new kind of revolution, an information and consciousness revolution that works by changing ideas rather than by killing off the old leaders.

It is worth looking at the dynamic sequence of some of these reversals to see how they happen and how fast. A classic example is the ecology movement. In its current form, it started essentially with the 1962 book by Rachel Carson, *Silent Spring*,[3] which put together, in a readable and gripping way, many of the trends and threats to air, water, land, the network of plant and animal life, and human survival. This can be called catalytic analysis, because of its self-multiplying power as others take up the same concern. But many such analyses, even true ones, are neglected by the public because they are not related to real and obvious events. Carson's book, however, was followed by a series of catalytic crises that came to public attention, such as DDT in the rivers, the California oil spills, and the increasing Los Angeles smog. The term refers to crises that are not quite catastrophic, but are dramatic and important enough to mobilize human concern and the money, time, and energy to do something about it. When such crises erupt, people organize picket lines and study groups and call for lecturers and pass around the book, saying, This shows why it happened and what we have to do about it. The fastest way to radicalize a Republican rose gardener is to put an oil spill on the doorstep.

So concerned constituencies build up rapidly, like the Sierra Club and the rest of the ecology movement, and they elect legislators and throw out 'The Dirty Dozen'. The *New York Times* identified ecology as the main ideological issue affecting the elections in 1970, 1972 and 1974. By 1974, of course, the new laws had been passed, the new agencies such as the Environmental Protection Agency had been set up, and they were in the Federal Bureau phase, with all the ongoing checks and balances of the Federal power structure. The transition from catalytic analysis, isolated and derided, to an established government structure to deal with the problems in an ongoing way took about ten years. We can see an exactly similar but even faster chain of events in several other areas. These include the sequence of action starting with Ralph Nader's *Unsafe at Any Speed*[4] in 1965 and going on to the major auto safety and pollution-control laws of 1972; and a large-scale consumer movement by that time with hundreds of activist lawyers. Another sequence is that beginning with Paul Ehrlich's *The Population Bomb*[5] in 1968, and his Zero Population Growth [ZPG] campaign, which may have accelerated the downturn in birth rates, so that they dropped below replacement levels in 1971, 1972 and 1973. (Note that this very rapid change did not require centralized or radical government birth control measures, but only many independent democratic consciousness-raisings and decisions in tens of millions of families.) The fastest case of all is the sequence starting from the MIT–Club of Rome book, *The Limits to Growth*,[6] by Donella Meadows and coworkers in 1972, and going on to a city-wide, nation-wide and world-wide recognition of such limits, especially in oil and energy and other resources, by 1974.

We see that for this responsive society, when analysis is coupled to dramatic evidence of the need for change—evidence most compellingly presented through television—the turnaround times for old ideas and laws are now in the range of two to ten years. This reverses not only our old ideas of revolution, but our conventional ideas of 'social lag'. In the 1920s, the sociologists of social lag supposed that society took twenty-five years to adapt to the electric light or the automobile because the old people with the old ideas had to die off. But for this present high-education television society, the ideas turn around suddenly and simultaneously in young and old alike ('co-figurative learning', as Margaret Mead calls it); and it is technology that now lags, with pleas that it will take twenty years or more for improved contraceptives, or mass transportation, or fusion or breeder power, or coal gasification, or solar energy. But this is what is to be expected in a cybernetic society which is consciously choosing its own values and steering its own future and shaping its own research and development, instead of being helplessly overrun by the technological juggernaut of greedy companies or unheeding inventors.

It is interesting to show the close parallel between these sequences of rapid change and the revolutionary sequence of proletarian revolution as outlined by Karl Marx. The catalytic analysis is done by the Intellectual Vanguard, who have knowledge, concern, and leisure to study, but who are traitors to their class. Their writings are then used to awaken the proletariat when oppression, or catalytic crises or confrontations occur. The workers are further educated by reactionary responses from the system when they attack it. Even when they have to go underground, the movement grows. But the old structure is rotten at the core and is unable to solve its problems or to keep the allegiance of its own people or to go on opposing the workers' movement; so that finally the workers take over easily, although they must go on fighting the bourgeois remnant who are sabotaging the new structure for selfish purposes.

Ecologists will find some glee in these parallels. The difference is that the socialist revolutions, with underground pamphlets, took a lifetime; while these television revolutions of consciousness and laws have achieved major structural rearrangements in a decade or less.

It seems probable that many of these rearrangements of attitudes and laws in the United States are now approaching a limit. There is still an extensive process of consolidation to be carried out in all these areas, but further changes on the same scale may be rarer in the future, unless some more encompassing war occurs, or some larger revolution in philosophy and belief systems, comparable in scope, say, to the Maoist revolutions in China.

Except for such dramatic deep changes, the next step today may simply be the extension of many of these new characteristics of social innovation and action to other societies as rapidly as they get universal television. This may rapidly change many patterns of elections and the structure of democracies and dictatorships. The potentiality for such sudden changes in response to perceived problems and inequities will continue indefinitely into the future as long as we have instantaneous global video electronics of any kind.

In the last two years, many of the high-speed and participatory-pressure aspects of these television-induced movements could be seen in such countries as Italy and Japan, in their debates over political accountability and ecology and pollution; and in Italy and France in the reversals of divorce and abortion and contraceptive laws. In dozens of countries, the sudden awareness of limits to growth is a typical consciousness-raising process that was made possible by the standard sequence of events: the confirmation of the catalytic-analysis book on *Limits*[6] by the catalytic crisis of the rise in oil prices, which seemed to prove the thesis.

Nevertheless, the change in global laws and policy-making among the 150 countries of the world will not be as easy or fast as the change within individual countries. National differences and slanting of television presentations will support self-righteous national differences on policy, and all the dilemmas of non-zero-sum game theory and the Tragedy of the Commons will hinder agreement or solution. It is in this context that the role of the multinational corporations must be seen as useful and even benevolent, since they will exert a steady pressure for common television programmes and parallel interest groups in many countries, easing a parallel approach to global problems. Even when such approaches are not concordant with the larger world interest or human interest, the competition between multinationals will make such discrepancies visible and will spur the growth of television debates and of multinational labour movements, consumer movements, ecology movements, and multinational-control movements. The success of the new movements in the United States, in changing policies and laws, will be a powerful example for similar interest groups in other countries, especially since these laws now apply to the head-quarters operations of the largest of the multinationals. Because of these various considerations, the rate of change in reversing old and dangerous nation-state policies and in getting more effective solutions of global problems is hard to predict, but it may be much faster than is generally supposed, and it could lead to massive transformation of world management structures in the decade of the 1980s.

Note that many of the futurist electronic innovations frequently proposed, such as shopping by cable television, or instantaneous electronic voting, are either irrelevant or dangerous for the participatory debates and consciousness movements described here. They may need careful watching and anticipatory control.

THE ROLE OF UNIVERSITIES IN A GLOBAL ELECTRONIC SOCIETY

To understand the role of the colleges and universities in the kind of national and global television-informed society which we see developing, it may be helpful to think of the systems-theory analogy between society and the human brain. The smartest brain is made of ignorant cells. How do those cells achieve collective intelligence? The answers are not all in, but it is clear experimentally and theoretically that they involve several major features, such as

— multiple sensory inputs with parallel processing and intercomparison;

— extensive cross-connection with common neural and biochemical excitation of many centres at once, depending on the body's overall state of deprivation or excitation;

— hierarchical stages of abstraction, with higher centres controlling the goals and feedback-settings of lower-order sub-goals;

— differentiated parallel output, with coordinated sequences and cycles of action in thousands of glandular and motor outputs; and

— feedback restimulation or reafferent stimulation for fine-tuning and success in overall goal-seeking.

It is always dangerous to apply such systems-parallels too literally between a biological body and the body social or the body politic, or between the brain and our collective intellectual and social enterprise of information, values, decision and action, but the parallels nevertheless raise questions that are suggestive and that deserve exploration.

In the total intellectual enterprise of human society, it is clear that the universities are the primary repositories of available knowledge, the centres of analysis of that knowledge, and the generators of basic or abstract new knowledge. This is particularly true in the twentieth century, since the time when science and basic research and development were brought into the universities, although government bureaus and laboratories and industrial and agricultural research groups also play a major role in the generation of new and practical knowledge.

When all of its historical and recent functions are added up, the university comes to be a sort of five-legged animal. The left hind leg could be thought of as traditional scholarship, the knowledge and library storage of everything that humanity has known or said or thought. The left front leg is then traditional teaching, the communication of this organized and filtered knowledge to the next generation. The right hind leg would be the creation of new thought or knowledge, basic studies in the natural and biological and social sciences on how the world works, its laws and predictions. The right front leg is then the transmission of this knowledge for human use, with writing or consulting or broadcasting to farm and industry and business and government and the community.

(Note however that the humanistic creation of fiction, poetry, plays, art or music, is not usually located at universities except in token form, being more individualist and more closely tied to outlets in publishing or the entertainment industry. If four great creators, Michelangelo, Shakespeare, Newton and Mozart, were living today, only Newton would be likely to work regularly at a university. Of the humanists, only the philosophers, the critics and the teachers have been university-based—typically being derided by the creative humanists, from Chaucer to Goethe and Browning.)

The fifth leg of the university is then the trunk of this wise elephant, so to speak, grasping the future. It is the seminal creation of world-changing inventions or paradigms or critiques, such as cybernetics or atomic energy or feed-back theory or ecology or the negative income tax or the concept of limits to growth. These are not merely services to industry or government in the existing structure, but fundamental intellectual and operational reorganizations that change the whole structure. They have been major sources of funding and influence for the universities in the last forty years. Nevertheless they tend to be 'in the university but not of it', using its resources of expertise, libraries and laboratories and leisure, but located outside regular departments, in more project-oriented centres such as the Manhattan Project, or the MIT Research Laboratory of Electronics, or the Sloan Institute of Management.

These five functions are fully displayed only at a few of the great universities, such as Harvard and MIT, but the functions support each other, and schools which are lacking two or more of them frequently find themselves in financial or operational difficulties. Thus the schools that only teach, without research opportunities, cannot attract strong science faculties; while the schools that specialize in research to the neglect of teaching often have disaffected students as well as weak public or alumni support. And schools that make no contribution to the fifth leg, to catalytic analysis and invention that can change large-scale social problems, now find themselves less and less relevant to government and the community, and less and less interacting with the rest of the active university network and the intellectual community.

One further point needs to be noted, namely the scale of college and university operations in a high-information society such as the United States. At present there are some nine million college students, nearly 50 per cent of all the 18- to 21-year-olds in the US. Together with their three-quarters of a million teachers, and supporting staffs of some two million and their families, they make up a much larger group than the family farm population. It is no accident that for the last couple of decades, American politicians have made their major policy addresses at universities, with their audiences of professional experts and with this great body of young adult students, relatively uncommitted politically and with time and energy for grass-roots political effort. Over 70 per cent of male high-school graduates now go to college, and the figure is over 80 per cent in the high-income states, and over 95 per cent in the Jewish community. These numbers are near saturation, at least for males, and will probably come down as higher education is postponed or fitted into longer-range life objectives, but they make an order-of-magnitude change from the 5 per cent college population of the 1930s, and a correspondingly enormous change in every aspect of American leadership, democracy, business and government, decision, management and policy, as well as culture. The revolutionary changes of the last ten years, already noted, were surely due to the impact of television—yes, but especially to its impact on this tremendous new group of college-educated adults who already had a larger vision and more training for leadership than their local high school provided.

Looking back at the comparison between our social intellectual networks and the brain, therefore, we can see the university as, not a small social organ, but a large and influential one, an organ having a role somewhat like those higher nerve centres in abstracting and combining and analysing and reassessing all the other information of the society—in short, in *thinking*. The schools are now centres for the development of novel concepts and the examination of goals and values, which can persuade the other segments of society by illuminating what they are doing and what the consequences are. They are lookout centres for warnings and for the development of alternative policy options. Traditionalists may object that these functions are not the primary business of the teaching university, or that they are too programme-oriented and not basic enough, and that they should be left to other groups, such as business or industry or government. But knowledge is for use, as Bacon said, and as the pragmatic Americans have always recognized, and should we let it 'fust in us unused'? What other group than that of the universities has the breadth of vision, or the libraries, the laboratories and the leisure for analysis, to look at the concerns and needs and goals of the *whole* of society rather than some narrower sector of profit or bureaucratic concern? Society will and must use the universities for this integrative and future-directed purpose, even if it goes beyond traditional roles—just because no other agencies have yet been created to do it. And even if such separate and specialized agencies were created, they would generally have to be placed close to great universities for all the reasons just given.

The result is that alongside their traditional disciplinary education, the universities will probably expand their social research-and-development centres. This will inevitably feed back into more problem-oriented education which for students may become much more involving, more integrative, and more like a practical apprenticeship for adult participatory leadership and management.

In addition to these changes in university structure and functions and methods, there will surely be radical changes in their range of community services for the high-education television-consciousness society we have been describing. For one thing, the age range being served by the schools will change, and there are already strong pressures to provide education from age 2 to 82, coextensive with life. Schools of education will probaby expand into still more extensive university experimental programmes and nursery schools for small children. At a higher level, they already run their own experimental grade schools and high schools, and they may begin to compete commercially for running such schools in other communities on commission or contract, with performance-testing of their educational success.

For adults over 18, there are developing already increasing numbers of community colleges specializing in part-time or night-school education. An increasing number of older adults may come back for summer courses or one-year sabbaticals, for 'retreading' and getting up to date again in teaching and business and engineering and biology, where information and methods are changing very rapidly. With increased leisure or unemployment, other numbers of adults may come for courses or lecture series on global problems or personal development or general culture. In some communities in the United States, 5 to 20 per cent of the adults over 25 years already are enrolled in such night-school programmes or lecture series—more than half of the college enrolment.

The universities may also continue and expand their recent roles in generating and disseminating new information and analyses for farmers, industry, business and government, whether this is done by published research reports or by part-time private consulting by the faculty and staff. The élitist role of this kind of advice and expertise, or its possible controversial advocacy, may have to be examined more carefully than in the past, if there is not to be widespread political backlash against these activities.

A solution to this problem of the narrowness or special interests of the experts may be the development of 'adversary science' by university scientists and consultants, as a kind of parallel to adversary law. The idea would be that major public issues, such as environmental or energy decisions, frequently have public pros and cons, related to the values of different groups in the society. Scientific experts on a problem, either for policy decisions or judicial decisions, might then come to be hired by the opposing sides, as lawyers are, with each group attempting to make the best possible case for their clients, although they might be arguing on the opposite side in the next case. This kind of semi-public or public confrontation might be expected to lead to better-informed decisions, which could find ways around the objections and dangers more successfully than our present partisan and often secretive decision methods.

The development of improved ways of this kind for bringing all of our knowledge to bear on our problems could also lead to the rapid development of new clienteles for the universities. These could include more public policy makers, plus international civil servants and designers of new international structures, as well as change agents and leaders in the new movements and pressure groups. All these groups that work with large-scale social problems are struggling with the lack of complete and coherent and relevant information, and they always seem to benefit from work at short-time university conferences or permanent conference centres.

It is worth emphasizing that these knowledge-services to society and its sub-groups are not simply retrieval problems from a computerized data bank in the sense of information sciences. Our great public decisions today have to be made on the basis of incomplete and uncertain data, by fallible and emotional decision makers often limited by old habit, but guided by feedback consequences —like the brain itself. This gives a human and humane and ongoing cybernetic character to our social decisions, with continual re-evaluation and often a change of fundamental values as new consequences become more apparent, and it makes the role of the universities and their knowledge in such decisions more involving than that of input–output data-processing or search and re-trieval, even of the most sophisticated kind.

In addition to all these direct services to students and clients, the universities have a more general role in raising the consciousness and culture of their whole communities. There is a level where their research reports or new discoveries are of general interest, and new channels may be found to reach an interested audience, from journalists and businessmen to factory workers, farmers and housewives. They operate newspapers and radio and television stations, and this, combined with their more traditional lecture courses and public lecture series, can make a continuous dialogue for the enrichment of a very large public, like the Chatauqua lecture-series and networks that educated adult audiences throughout the United States a hundred years ago. There are more than 2300 colleges and universities in the United States, and about 1000 of these are the principal industry of their city or town, so that almost all of the US population could be within radio or television range of university cultural pro-grammes. Rightly used, this could be as valuable an audience for public support of enlarged university programmes as the commercial audience is for the sup-port of broadcasters and advertisers. This is not to say that all these schools will be or should be in agreement on their knowledge or their advocacy, but that most such programmes are likely to be a contribution to raising the level of dispassionate discussion and understanding of any problem.

In all this, it should not be forgotten that the universities are all part of a close-ly linked network of knowledge. It is 'the great university in the sky', as some of the jet-set professors call it. They are linked not only by real computer networks and telephone networks, but also by widely distributed cassette and videotape exchanges of lectures, and art-film exchanges, as well as by the lecture and music series of the academic and cultural lecture bureaus, the inheritors of the real Chatauqua network of a hundred years ago. What is even more important with respect to the growth and utilization of knowledge is their linkage through the hundreds of 'invisible colleges' of the various academic disciplines. It is these in-groups of close friends and competitors who telephone daily across the country, who share the prepublication reports fresh off the typewriter in a hundred photocopies, and who are continually visiting each others' laboratories and lecturing to and hiring each others' graduate students. In large US universities in the 1960s, one-third of the scientists would be out of town on any given weekday, while an equal number were presumably visiting from elsewhere. In most such cases, the business of this travel was the business of the invisible college, whether lecturing or consulting or on sabbatical leave at some other colleague's laboratory, writing a book.

These networks and invisible colleges of knowledge have always been international. Their contribution to shared knowledge and culture and concerns and decision-making around the globe may be as great in the intellectual sphere as the contribution of the multinational corporations is in commerce. And when the leaders of a dozen major countries have been educated at the London School of Economics or Harvard or MIT or Stanford, these intellectual networks resonate at the political level. The networks carrying new ideas become, and are, worldwide channels of change.

What finally clinches this change role for the universities is that they are now seeing themselves, and being seen by governments, as the primary place where those catalytic analyses of present and forthcoming problems must be carried out. Some 80 million dollars, one-third of the research budget of the National Science Foundation, now go into project RANN—Research Applied to National Needs—of which the larger part is being done in the universities. Rachel Carson and Paul Ehrlich were academic biologists with a side concern with ecology and population problems. *The Limits to Growth*[6] was a computer study at MIT. The Academy for Contemporary Problems in Columbus, Ohio, is a joint venture between Battelle and Ohio State University. Once such university studies have pointed the way, other bureaus and institutes and foundations may take up the work and diversify and improve it, like the sixteen-nation International Institute of Applied Systems Analysis (IIASA) in Austria. But these groups with a well-defined mission have usually not been as flexible as university groups in identifying and working on new problems on the horizon. It follows that it is to the universities that society and the world must turn for major lookout and warning functions, except for the occasional cases when self-appointed groups like the Club of Rome take voluntary action. And when the warnings have been raised, it may be only the universities that can do the tedious work of analysis of alternative futures and the consequences of policy decisions or game-playing, in the detached and careful and complete way that is necessary for success. In the near future, academic and research departments may come to spend a good deal of their time making needed studies of this kind.

These intellectual networks of thought and change will interact in a powerful and symbiotic way with the consciousness-raising role of television, with which I began this paper. The universities, like the higher abstract nerve centres of the brain, collect their information and feedback monitoring from thousands of parallel inputs, but their resultant conclusions are then fed simultaneously by television to millions of output actors, to make the analogy very crude. How does this happen? By the expert analysis and debate which is called forth by television within a few hours after any problem or concern becomes visible and important. Who are the movement speakers, who fly from one group to another, worrying and explaining? Frequently they are the university researchers or synthesizers who have been in the forefront of analysis or concern. Even when the concern is initiated from outside the universities, as it has been in the black power and ethnic movements, the women's movement, the Nader auto safety and consumer movement, and the Club of Rome limits-to-growth debate, it now leads quickly to responses within the universities, such as black studies programmes and women's programmes, or poor-law programmes, or academic computer programs; and a hundred academic hands take up the cause, because they are the ones whose knowledge and analysis are needed.

All this is a rather tentative description of the interplay of these complex groups and forces for change in our time. It is uncertain and has to be pieced out by theories and guesses, because this fluid and participatory information-interplay in the new electronic surround has little precedent in the rather fixed institutions and hierarchical management structures of a low-education society. There will be room for debate over how far these trends will continue, especially under the disasters of the next decade, with famine and oil wars, and terrorist Hiroshima bombs, and back-lash dictatorships and censorship and television barriers, and possibly violent anti-scientific and anti-intellectual movements. But, as H. G. Wells said, 'Civilization is a race between education and catastrophe' and if the trends I have identified are real and can continue and expand, and if these disasters can be anticipated or postponed or contained a little bit, then there is a chance that these forces may yet move us into a more participatory and democratic and humanely conscious global future before the next century. Progress is being made, I think, and we must work with those forces to extend it in the next few years as fast as we can.

Discussion

Valaskakis: You said that the technological–social gap had been reversed, with society now asking for things and technology reacting, but some people might distort that to mean something other than what you have in mind. Before the limits-to-growth controversy the traditional and orthodox economist would have said that if the price system were allowed to react to whatever scarcities or whatever shortages occurred, i.e. if prices rose when there were shortages, people would automatically take corrective action by consuming less. However if we are dealing with an overshoot and collapse system we cannot take corrective action in time. When the signal has been identified it is too late to do anything about it. You seem to be suggesting that with television we can quickly identify certain problems like pollution, and that our reaction time is so fast that there is no such thing as social lag. This might lead to some unintended optimism about the possibilities of solving our problems, which I am sure you are not advocating.

Platt: I think a 'man on horseback' with the right kind of charisma, another Hitler, could leap in and use the medium in the same way. But so far the medium has been part of the checks and balances in the US. It was television that brought McCarthy down in 1953, and it was really television of the Watergate investigation that brought Nixon down. On the whole I think its influence has been helpful and healthy in politics rather than the reverse. But somebody who knows how to use it more subtly, or has a better organized pressure group, could perhaps use these fast time-constants for a disastrous outcome. On the other hand it does seem to bring us both sides, in controversies and debates. Once some influential person stands up and says 'A', then there will be a thousand people in the community and in the universities who will jump up and say 'not-A'. Television, at least in the US where it is relatively free of government censorship, will bring this debate to people and will inform them because they can see the confrontation before their eyes.

Klimes: The use of television as a communications medium and as a new tool for societal engineering depends, obviously, on social conditions. The projections you made are based on a certain kind of society that is relatively open and free. In another kind of society the same technology can be used to halt, slow down or otherwise manipulate social change. A much more important question about this new communications medium is, who controls it? How is it manipulated?

Platt: This is a real and important fear. But in fact it is 'closed societies' that fear television; and the reason is that while the first-order effects may be directly manipulatable and damaging, this is fairly visible manipulation. The second-order effect is criticism and at least some private reply, on subjects that are now opened for discussion, so that in some important sense the medium is the message, as McLuhan said, and as I tried to show in my paper.

Dror: You underrate the capacity of governments for controlling television. If Nazi Germany had had television its propaganda would have been even more effective. A free global broadcasting network might operate more as you say, but as long as television can be controlled technically, it will be used in a totalitarian country to indoctrinate people. In a free society television may help to perpetuate freedom. In a totalitarian society it will probably reinforce the totalitarian system. In other words television *per se* may not lead to a specific form of society; it depends on the starting point.

Platt: This is the conventional view but there are things to be said on the other side. Television is dangerous for a totalitarian society. People see how other people live. It raises questions and changes goals. Just to show a sports event, with athletes from other countries or races, just to show the dictator arriving in his Cadillac or Zis, is to spread ferment and revolution.

Dror: In a totalitarian country they show what they want to show, not what you like them to see.

Klimes: This illustrates to me how some projections, even if they aim at presenting a global picture with a generally valid view of the future, are just based on one particular kind of imagination corresponding to the sociocultural environment of its originator. While I agree entirely that as the information system opens things up, it won't actually be possible to keep any information absolutely closed, the point is that regardless of the technology employed, there is a certain dialectical contradiction in the use of information, and consequently in the types of information society. Can we identify that contradiction? Can we see both sides so that we can point out the dangers?

Shane: About two years ago I worked on a television programme, a 90-minute special in the US called 'Give Us The Children'. The young man responsible for directing this presentation had a large sum of money to spend on it, yet he felt that he was responsible to no one for the programme content. When I asked who did determine policies for the network, the 24-year-old director and his 26-year-old associate assured me that the owners of the television station were concerned with advertising, with mollifying customers, and with new accounts. The persons who presented the newscasts had their material prepared for them. In short, a group of 'unknowns' working like gnomes seemed to be making policy as their judgement dictated. Presumably they were not responsible to anyone—but they often do a great deal to shape what goes out on television. Do you see that as a threat to our culture, and is it something we can take steps to remedy?

Platt: I see this as a great danger. I dislike much television programming. I was just making the additional point that beyond the programming itself there is another message, a meta-message, the message of the medium. This produces effects beyond and counter to any direct attempts at manipulation of the programming, at least for some thoughtful and concerned sections of the population.

Shane: Then you will agree that, when a news commentator says 'And that's the way it was today', that the 'news' really was what a group of TV people decided was most interesting or important to show during the brief time available on the screen. In the Selma, Alabama, Freedom Marches, for example, a number of persons who had been rather dispiritedly walking along at the end of the day began behaving in a most lively fashion as the television cameras turned on them. Thus an image is created on the television screen that is or can be distinctly different from what actually existed or took place. I wonder how great a danger it is, and how we can whip it.

Waddington: Professor Platt has brought out the importance of catalytic crises. It is no use writing *Silent Spring*[3] unless something happens to bring it home to the public mind. There happened to be an oil spill in Santa Barbara, just where it would catch the public mind and would have to get on television; it would be a very dictatorial state indeed that could keep it off. But it might have been something quite different—many books could be as catalytic as *Silent Spring*, if a catalytic crisis happened to bring a particular event to the fore. You can't get a great public movement unless a body of public opinion can be mobilized about something, but which movement happens at which time depends on very chancy events.

Oldfield: I accept that the medium is a message, but I think that the television medium is perceived in different ways by different people. With our ethnocentric viewpoint we tend to underemphasize the different ways in which it is perceived by people who can neither generate nor control what they see. The metaphor of the global village is a soothing one for us, but most people must feel more as if they were in a global aquarium. In a public aquarium, a limited number of people control what a much larger range of organisms see. In a village the intervisibility is more mutual. In an aquarium many barriers inhibit the passage from one condition to the other perceived and unperceived conditions.

Waddington: The metaphor of a zoo might be better. In a zoo the animals are in cages while in an aquarium one gets at first the exact opposite impression; an aquarium is normally transparent, with no opaque walls. I think you are suggesting that the world system is closely controlled, and that people are not absolutely free to move in all possible directions.

Francis: Your thesis seems to imply that an accepted principle of universality comes out of these levels of prophecy, Professor Platt. Instead it seems to me, particularly from my own experience when travelling in Asia, that there is a wall of resistance against exactly these viewpoints. Virtually everything you illustrated was based exclusively on North American experience. How long is it going to take for universities in developing countries to achieve their own catalytic analysis and become receptive in the way you have described? Any real change will take much longer than the three to ten years that you have given for the current North American experience, and that situation has benefited from the consolidated experience of the universities.

Platt: Some countries will move up the path of development at one time and others will move up it later. Some countries will already be facing the problems of saturation, the turnaround and so on, while others are still in the growth phase. But the time between them is now coming down into the five- to ten-year range. For example, Italy has reversed its divorce law. Who would have thought this possible two years ago? France reversed the open sale of contraceptives, and the old abortion law. Who would have thought this two years ago? In Japan and Italy the major themes in the last two years on non-political radio and TV programmes have been ecology and pollution. The fall of Tanaka over financial accountability was probably assisted by the parallel to the US-Nixon Watergate case which they had followed on television. The spread happens just as fast as television arrives.

Francis: Those are all industrialized countries.

Platt: Yes, because they are the first in this; but when there is village television in India I think they will also begin to have television-type awareness. I guess I should emphasize, as I did in the paper, that my opinions and insights here are not dogmatic or final, and are presented more hesitantly than perhaps I sound; but I felt it worth while to try to state clearly a different point of view that may offer some useful corrections to the more conventional ideas.

Francis: I think you are dismissing the cultural elements too lightly, particularly in Asia, which I believe is much more resistant to television than North America.

Waddington: Television brings a revolution of expectations, though this may come more from the movies than from television. You see people living in the style of the affluent industrial society, and you think, why the devil shouldn't we live in something like that? Surely that has had an enormous effect in the whole of Asia.

Oldfield: Professor Platt said that in an affluent society pollution is a catalytic crisis that can promote a sensible response. But in a poor society starvation is a catalytic crisis that can promote death. I don't see how what is essentially a sigmoid curve for population growth, which is density-regulated, can be used as a basis for so many (to my mind) ethnocentric generalizations about crisis and response in the whole of the contemporary world.

Ziman: The Italian divorce laws are fifty years behind the times, by any Anglo-Saxon standards. Relating the change in that law to television seems to be a misplaced historical analysis of the situation.

Eldredge: It is much easier to construct a gadget than it is to construct a societal structure. Societal structure today still cannot cope, even remotely, with the gadgets of nuclear fission and fusion which made a spectacular entrance on the world scene in 1945. The original rather primitive atomic bomb has given rise to a whole family of nuclear weapons, with $n+1$ countries having the bomb and reactors proliferating all over the place. Professor Platt has taught me that public opinion can be mobilized concerning some fringe societal technologies, but I don't really believe that television can produce real détente. There are certainly no institutions to ensure détente, though there are public speeches lauding progress and so forth. I don't see any societal institutions in the immediate future that will cope with the technology of taking oil out of the North Sea and balancing that against oil from the Persian Gulf! Hiroshima happened in 1945 and in 1975 we are in a much more dangerous situation—in a noisy spring rather than a silent one. I am a societal technologist, but I don't think that societal technology is remotely capable of coping with those dreadful technical technologies that keep spewing out new gadgets which I simply don't know how to cope with.

Platt: One thing that amuses me about this particular kind of analysis-and-change sequence is the parallel I mentioned in my paper with the old Marxist analysis of revolutionary change—but moved into a high information society. But in this kind of high-education television society it is not a bloody revolution, but an information revolution, a revolution that is consciousness-raising, and it takes place in this short time of ten years instead of in a century. It is not a revolution in the streets but in the minds, including the minds of cabinet members and Boards of Directors. Our methods of revolution today are as changed from those of a hundred years ago as our methods of television are from print.

Eldredge: But so is the counter-revolution, which is also a part of our society.

Waddington: Some technical changes have been easier for society to cope with than others. It is easier to pass anti-pollution laws than to know what to do about nuclear power. Eldredge has a good point when he says that we have been aware of the nuclear power problem for a long time without having decided what society should do about it. Pollution has been with us for a much shorter time but it is much easier to deal with.

Dror: Political science had quite a lot of published work, usually pessimistic, on the idea of the mass society before television came along. Most writers thought that technological devices permitting rapid mobilization of mass support would work more for the bad than for the good. I wouldn't go as far as that but the question must be put. You say that if television represents a balanced point of view, pro and con, the population will adopt a balanced view. Behind that idea is the underlying or tacit model of citizens having a reasonable pattern of behaviour. I don't see any reason why the mobilization of mass opinion should work for the better rather than for the worse. In some cases it may be for the better, but in other types of situations, such as crisis—an energy crisis, a nuclear war crisis—a different kind of culture may result from the same mass mechanism, one turning in what you and I would regard as a negative direction. This may be partly because, as Professor Eldredge indicated, television communication mechanisms change the message and the speed but don't change the institutions. That is, the interfaces between public opinion and political institutions are not basically changed. Different messages flow through the channels but the channels themselves are not changed. I don't see the evidence for your thesis that the very existence of television assures a radical change for the better in the institutions themselves.

Platt: Yes, we have, and have had, a group of manipulators and would-be manipulators, in Washington and in the military and in industry—manager-manipulators, the best and the brightest. They operate on the old hierarchical system, the old pyramid, the idea that there is a small group at the top who know what is best for the people and who can manage and direct any plan. But I tried to say in the paper that in the last ten years, these managers and manipulators have gone down again and again before the power of these new movements of consciousness, these participatory movements. Somebody in San Francisco sees Germaine Greer and says 'We can do that too'. The result is that a hundred centres spring up all over the country, on women's liberation or black power and so on. The managers and manipulators don't know what the score is. It is a new political phenomenon in the United States. The only person from abroad who saw it coming was Revel, with his book *Without Marx or Jesus*.[1] He saw this as a revolution of communications in the United States which would produce a political, cultural and social revolution. He is right on target: these old structures with the managers and manipulators will have to change their pattern towards participation and decentralization and diversity under the pressure of this new form of power.

Dror: But your underlying assumption is that this new consciousness will always be for the better. What historical or psychological evidence do you have for that?

Platt: More information *is* for the better! More sharing of consciousness between people *is* for the better!—At least, on the average!

Dror: It may be for the better if we absorb and understand it correctly.

Eldredge: That is simplistic eighteenth century rationalism, Professor Platt. One must do better than that!

Platt: It is *human* rationalism—an interconnected brain, a set of eyes seeing the alternative futures, is being created instead of the human race crawling along like disconnected amoebas.

Valaskakis: Your underlying value assumption that change itself is a good thing is probably shared by all of us at this meeting, but it is by no means self-evident. You might have a heated argument with an anthropologist on that count. For example, according to some anthropologists, television has had a disruptive effect on Eskimo societies in northern Canada, where it has produced the kind of social change or catalytic transformation that you have been talking about. It has been successful in creating discontent by providing models that cannot be achieved or approximated by the indigenous Eskimo population. It seems to have destroyed the native culture without replacing it with a viable alternative paradigm. I tend to share the idea that change is a good thing in itself, and that if television accelerates the process of change then television is good. But I feel nevertheless that it is a very western culture-bound idea that is by no means universally accepted.

Eldredge: The 'managers' will soon learn how to manipulate the development of consciousness for good or evil. This is an interim period, while they learn how to manipulate the new types of organization.

References cited

1 REVEL, JEAN-FRANÇOIS (1971) *Without Marx or Jesus: The New American Revolution Has Begun*, Doubleday, New York
2 SALK, JONAS (1973) *The Survival of the Wisest*, Harper & Row, New York
3 CARSON, RACHEL (1962) *Silent Spring*, Houghton Mifflin, Boston
4 NADER, RALPH (1965) *Unsafe at Any Speed*, Grossman, New York
5 EHRLICH, PAUL (1968) *The Population Bomb*, Sierra Club, New York
6 MEADOWS, DONELLA H., MEADOWS, DENNIS L., RANDERS, JØRGEN & BEHRENS, WILLIAM W., III (1972) *The Limits to Growth*, Universe, New York; Earth Island, London

Patterns of education for the future

SIR WALTER PERRY

The Open University, Milton Keynes

Abstract   There are three facets to the probable role of universities in the future: maintaining scholarship, providing general courses for students and the general community, providing continuing education. Whereas scholarship requires a permanent structure based on discipline groups, general courses are best produced by 'course teams' as pioneered by the Open University. These teams bring together subject-matter experts in related fields, educational technologists and media specialists; although making great personal demands, as well as demands on time and resources, the resultant course is of high quality.

A speculative pattern for future education might include a shorter, general school education followed by a period of work to develop self-reliance; then a basic degree and a second interval of service to the community, of a vocational kind. Return could then be made to a second period of university education in a specialized field. Finally there would be specific refresher programmes.

The question of 'The Future as an Academic Discipline' within such a framework can be considered either from a research and advanced teaching viewpoint, based on individuals and groups, or as service courses. Here one of the important functions of basic degrees should be to introduce complex problems which are the stuff of futures studies. Such courses can best be produced by the creation of course teams. A balanced view is then presented, resulting in an increased awareness among the community. Thus the university indirectly affects national political processes, through the constituents.

To be the last speaker in a symposium of this kind offers the great advantage that one has heard all that has gone before; but there may, of course, be a countervailing disadvantage in that all that one had hoped to say has already been said! Thus, in some respects, my contribution will be a summary of what has gone before.

I would like to consider, first, what the role of universities in the future is likely to be; second to suggest a possible pattern of education provision for the future; and, finally, to look at the subject of this symposium

'The Future as an Academic Discipline' within the context of that pattern.

THE ROLE OF UNIVERSITIES IN THE FUTURE

There are, I think, three main facets to the probable role of the universities in the future:

(1) The traditional role of the universities in maintaining and nurturing scholarship through research and advanced teaching (honours and postgraduate) must, I believe, continue. It is vital that what Ashby has called 'the thin clear stream of excellence' be provided for in this way; and that provision is made thereby for the preservation of values through whatever political vicissitudes may lie in the future. Universities have an honourable record of preserving values through just such vicissitudes in the past.

To maintain and nurture scholarship requires, I believe, a continuation within the universities of a permanent structure that is firmly based upon disciplinary groups, although new disciplines may emerge and some older ones may disappear. There are a number of reasons underlying this assertion. In the first place any attempt to abolish a structure based upon disciplines is in a very real sense self-defeating; mathematicians will consort with other mathematicians however dispersed they may be by an alternative structure. Second, it is both necessary and desirable to use a senior mathematician to recruit junior mathematicians. Third, if there is anything that defines a 'discipline' it is, at least on the scientific side, a common body of research technique; so that, over quite a wide range, research activities can be adequately funded only for a disciplinary group and not for individual workers. Finally, the ultimate goal of advanced teaching is the reproduction of one's own kind; and only mathematical scholars can breed a new generation of mathematical scholars. It therefore follows that disciplines must be the permanent organizational units in a university that is adequately to fill this first role in the future.

(2) On the other hand, disciplines are already faced in the university by the necessity of providing 'service' courses for students who require an elementary grounding in the discipline; and such students greatly outnumber those who are being trained as the next generation of scholars. This second role of the universities is likely to increase, as a proportion of the total effort of universities, in the future. 'Service' courses will be needed for an increasing number of undergraduates and, in addition, for the general community through the growth of external or extramural teaching.

My second assertion is that the provision of such 'service' courses should *not* be controlled by the disciplines themselves. This assertion cuts right across the normal customs of most universities and I must clearly justify it. I shall try to do so first on general grounds and then by reference to our practice in the Open University.

On general grounds

    (*a*) Courses prepared and delivered by one man can be splendid when it is the right man and horrid when it is not.

    (*b*) Even when the right man is chosen from the point of view both of academic excellence and of brilliance in presentation, the course may tend to be too inward-looking—stressing the development of scholars in the discipline rather than looking outwards towards the actual needs of the students.

    (*c*) 'Service' courses tend to be regarded by many academics as dull chores. Thus even members of a faculty of medicine may regard the course for dental students as a punishment rather than a challenge.

    (*d*) There is, as has been pointed out many times at this meeting, a very real problem in mounting any real interdisciplinary course when the control of all courses is vested in the individual disciplines.

By reference to practice in the Open University

Our courses are all produced by groups which we have called 'Course Teams' and I think that the concept of the course team is possibly the most notable of all our innovatory ideas. A course team consists of the academic staff, from one or more disciplines, who are experts in the subject matter of the course, together with academics from related disciplines by whom the course may be used as a 'service' course. The course team also has, as full members, first, experts in educational technology who can advise on such matters as the definition of the course objectives, the methods of assessing whether the students have attained these objectives, and the manner of presentation of the course materials; and, second, experts in the media through which the course will be presented—in our case the radio and television producers who will create the audiovisual course materials. Each team is created *ad hoc* by the Senate, is given control of the content and structure of the course, and is disbanded when its task is completed. The academic members then return to their permanent homes within their discipline.

The course team approach makes considerable demands upon the individual members of its team, and, indeed, upon the institution. It is justified, I believe, by the high quality of the resulting courses and by their suitability for acceptance by the target student audience.

Among the demands that are made are:

(a) The primary loyalty of the members to the aims and objectives of the institution: In our experience it is very difficult for even distinguished academics to make as efficient a contribution if they are on a part-time seconded basis from other universities to which their primary loyalty is naturally given.

(b) The commitment of a long period of time to the preparation of the course: It requires a minimum of fifteen months, and preferably much longer, to create a high-quality course lasting thirty-four weeks and occupying a student roughly half-time. In the early months there is a necessary period of settling down and getting to know one another—a sort of group dynamic must be evolved. Later there can be a severe level of criticism from colleagues in the team, more often of the presentation than of the content of material. I once met a Professor of the Open University looking rather woebegone. It turned out that he had just been sent away by his course team to write certain material for the seventh time. Perhaps even more significant than the fact that he had been asked to do it was that he was going to do it!

(c) The resultant commitment of a lot of resources: Our courses are very expensive to create, compared with traditional university courses, largely because of the number of people involved in the team and the length of time that is spent. This cost is increased, of course, by our use of the mass media, which involves heavy production costs. This heavy initial cost is, of course, offset by the large number of students we serve; but it presents a formidable difficulty to smaller institutions.

(d) The loss of complete academic freedom implicit in the course team concept: It is clear that no individual academic can teach exactly what he wants in exactly the way he wants if the control of courses is given to a team. (It is, of course, true that, in the context of the Open University where the courses are transmitted on open circuits and in the bookshops to a public much wider than the students in a closed class-room, this demand of the course team concept offers certain safeguards.)

I would conclude from these arguments that the course team approach is the right one for all service 'courses' and that such courses should not be controlled by individual disciplines. I would further argue that only a course team approach can produce good quality interdisciplinary courses. In respect of the inevitably high cost of the course team approach, I would suggest that there is a strong case for the exchange of courses between institutions in order to spread the cost more widely. While I would be the first to resist any move towards a dull level of uniformity in the teaching programmes of the universities, I believe that the exchange and consequent sharing of 'service' courses would do little to invoke this. Such courses require the interpretation of individual tutors for credit in individual institutions and this in itself would obviate uniformity; and the quality of 'service' teaching would undoubtedly rise.

(3) The third role that I envisage for the universities in the future is that of providing for programmes of continuing education rather than just for initial education. I have developed this argument at length elsewhere.[1] Initial education has been the pattern from time immemorial. It is based on the idea that a man can be fitted for a lifetime in his chosen career and this was largely true until comparatively recent times. It is still true of the small band of natural scholars. For all the rest, the large majority, it is no longer adequate as an overall educational pattern. The quantity of knowledge is now so large that our young are almost middle-aged before they emerge from the ghettoes of education to be of service to the community; and, even worse, the pace of acquisition of new knowledge is now so fast that, even then, their initial education is out-of-date when they are in mid-career.

Most authorities now pay lip-service to the idea that a new pattern of continuing education must come, but little actually happens. This seems to me to be for three main reasons which make the introduction of continuing education very difficult:

(a) We cannot spare people from productive work to go back for further spells of full-time education.

(b) There is bound to be a shortage of teachers competent to deal with new knowledge and those who are available are wholly occupied with initial education.

(c) There is an enormous vested interest in the maintenance of the present pattern of initial education, which calls for such a vast expenditure that little resource is available to add to it the provision of continuing education.

The Open University offers one way of overcoming all these difficulties to a limited extent; it could therefore act as a catalyst to the introduction of the new pattern of continuing education. Further development will require a concomitant reduction in the provision of initial education.

A POSSIBLE EDUCATIONAL PATTERN FOR THE FUTURE

I would like now to take a speculative look at what might be a desirable overall pattern of education in the future. I will not stick my neck out quite so far as to suggest the possible duration in years of the various phases of such a pattern, but will content myself with giving general indications. Thus there might be six phases in the new pattern, namely:

		Duration of education	Duration of interval
(1)	Initial school education	X	
(2)	'Deschooling'—experience of life		A
(3)	Basic higher education—'general'	Y	
(4)	Service to community		B
(5)	Specialist higher education (honours and postgraduate)	Z	
(6)	Periodic updating courses		

I would like to see a move to compress phase (1) into a shorter period—primarily by removing from it the element of specialized studies designed as a preparation for the usual type of English honours degree. Thus there would be a move away from the 'A-level' pattern of school education which forces decisions about career patterns far too soon for the majority of children. For a few natural scholars rapid progress at school should, however, be possible; but these are themselves the very people whose rate of progress is currently retarded to the pace of the slower members in their classes and who, *a priori*, might be expected to complete more advanced work within the shorter, more compressed, phase (1). I am very conscious of the difficulty of the problems associated with such 'streaming'; but I am certain that, in any new pattern of education that caters better for the needs of the majority, provision must be made for the needs of the minority who comprise the 'thin clear stream of excellence'.

There has been a great deal of discussion of the idea of 'deschooling'—which is, in itself, a horrid word; but the idea is far from horrid. There is a great deal to be said for the argument that higher education is of much greater value to people whose experience embraces not only a period of school education but also a period of work in a wholly different ambience where self-reliance is more important than group activity. Furthermore, motivation amongst students is, by common consent, intensified by such experience, as is evidenced both in the Open University and amongst ex-service students.

Phase (3) would consist of a basic degree programme of a very 'general' character. I am not here suggesting a programme *common* to all students but a series of general programmes each pertinent to, say, one particular faculty. Thus, as I have argued elsewhere, a basic medical degree leading to a limited licence to practice under supervision in hospital or in general practice could be a highly vocational example.[1] General programmes within science or within the humanities are other examples more akin to the current degree programmes of the Open University.

Phase (4) would represent a second interval between periods of education, an interval of service to the community. Such service would be of a vocational kind, as suggested in the field of medicine, or of a much more general kind, as, for example, where those trained basically in the humanities could spend a period of time in industry, commerce, or in the public services. As a result of such a period of active work, some would discover a particular field in which they wished to make their careers. They would then return, in phase (5), for a second period of university education in that specialized field. To pursue my two examples, the doctor with a limited licence might discover or reinforce an interest in surgery and return for a specialized training therein (but avoiding any specialized training in all the other branches of medicine), while the graduate in humanities might discover an interest in management studies or in school teaching of history or in librarianship or in any other of a host of possibilities and return to pursue such a specialized course. Finally, phase (6) represents the periodic updating refresher programmes that I have already discussed as a necessary feature of future education.

This whole schematic pattern is, as I said, wildly speculative. It would, I believe, offer great advantages both to individuals in relation to their personal fulfilment and satisfaction and to society in the gains that it would make. There are, however, two enormous practical difficulties. The first, which I have already mentioned, is the need of the minority, of the scholars of the future. Clearly they do not require the intervals from study built into phases (2) and (4); and there must therefore be bridges between phases (1), (3) and (5) that they can cross. There must also be bridges that allow for the late development of scholarship, but most of these are provided within the suggested new pattern itself. The second practical problem is that any educational pattern of this kind requires radical changes in employment practices to enable a proper utilization of the manpower available from the introduction of the intervals of phases (2) and (4). Otherwise these intervals become meaningless and wasteful. If for no other reason, it will be clear that this suggested pattern can only be achieved by a national programme devised to achieve the goal.

THE FUTURE AS AN ACADEMIC DISCIPLINE

Finally, I would like to turn to the question of 'The Future as an Academic Discipline' *within* a future pattern of educational provision of the kind I have described. There seem to be two main ways in which this can be considered:

(1) *Research and advanced teaching in futures studies*

There are, I think, three ways in which the universities of the future could become involved in research and advanced teaching in futures studies:

    (*a*) Within a permanent structure based upon individual disciplines, each discipline could indulge in futures studies; but these, as has been pointed out, could be of great depth but of limited width. Perhaps even more important, however, is the fact that individual members of the staff of the universities could, as they do now, continue to serve on external groups created to study specific problems. Such 'think tanks' offer one way in which an individual can affect the processes of decision-making at a political level. The idea that a university, as an institution, can affect decision-making in this way is one that I feel should be resisted. Universities are after all communities of scholars and should have room for all shades of political opinion; they should not seek to promote institutional political policies.

    (*b*) On the other hand, within the universities, *ad hoc* groups to study particular problems can always be set up; but they should not be part of the permanent structure of the universities. Views expressed by such *ad hoc* groups should not, as the views of individuals should not, be represented as institutional views.

    (*c*) Possibly futures studies will emerge as a new discipline in its own right but, at the moment, I think that the time is not yet ripe for such a development.

(2) *Service courses*

I believe that one major and important function of basic university degrees (my phase 3) should be to introduce students to the complexity of the global problems which are the stuff of futures studies. It is also true that such an introduction would be more valuable and more easily comprehensible after some experience of life during phase (2) of the educational pattern.

Such basic service courses in futures studies, being necessarily interdisciplinary, can best be produced by the creation of course teams created *ad hoc* for the purpose. This is a very expensive way of providing courses in individual small universities; and the need for the exchange and sharing of such service courses between many institutions becomes paramount.

There is also a clear need to involve a wider public in the community at large by attracting them into service courses of this kind. Because the courses would be produced by course teams they would tend to present a balanced view of the complex problems; and in producing an increased awareness of the nature of these problems among the community in general, the university, as an institution, would be indirectly affecting the political processes of decision-making: for it is ultimately the constituents, educated and aware or not, who determine the shape of all political decisions. This is one ultimate and valid goal of a university.

Discussion

Waddington: One of the most important functions of futures study is at the service level in the university. Certainly such a service course ought to be provided by a team, but how does one get the team? The Open University has a mechanism for getting a group together, for funding them, and for allowing them to generate their own enthusiasm in the time that is necessary to produce a good course. In an ordinary university, there is no real mechanism for liberating people's interests sufficiently for a course team to function like your teams do. My one-man course was written simply to provoke somebody else to do something better. It was the only practical way for getting anything done.

Shane: Is the old saying 'the hungry dog hunts best' relevant to the search for the right teams? How do you motivate people so that they do not feel submerged when they become part of a team? Many of our young American assistant professors and associate professors are struggling valiantly to stand for something for which they can be known among their colleagues. Would there be in the Open University a potential submerging of the people who have drive and who struggle for identity? Or do you see the Open University as a launching pad from which they move to some other academic arena?

Perry: I think the answer is both. I would hate it not to be a launching pad because staff can perform a catalytic function by carrying these ideas to other places. I don't think they lose their identity. They are quite free to express their own views, even as polemic if they want to, within the course material. The course team seldom say 'You musn't do that'. All they say is 'We must have somebody else with an opposite view' or 'You must put your views in context'.

I don't think they are stultified in that sense. I think the people in our teams are carried forward primarily by the sheer excitement of doing something that is innovative. A very real problem looming on the horizon is that after something has been done for the first time it it not quite so exciting the next time. The best way of meeting that problem is by exchange and by bringing in new people. That is not easy with the present low mobility of academic staff.

Black: You touched on academic freedom. The view that academic staff can teach what they like, how they like, when they like and if they like isn't a recipe for academic freedom but one for academic anarchy. Academic freedom is only freedom within the constraints of some loyalty to the institution and to the objects of the courses taught, however these may be manifested. I was not in the least worried when you spoke about abrogating some academic freedom because in the situation you outlined you are not really abrogating it but building it in, by substituting a loyalty to the wider concept of your course structure. This means more to me than a rather abstract academic freedom.

Francis: As a teacher at the Open University it seems to me that one functional level has been missed out, perhaps understandably. The course team in Buckinghamshire certainly puts the course together competently and efficiently, but there is an element of good will in the teaching itself. The course is taken as a package by a group of students and then it has to be seen virtually through the eyes of one person who has contact with the students in the teaching situation, who has to get them over their hurdles and has to integrate the package. The package as it comes out through the media is essentially a linear programme and there is still the problem of overcoming the individual idiosyncrasies and difficulties of students. Sometimes the teacher is dealing with broadly based courses of the kind that a futures course might represent. Often the tutor is the least qualified person in the group on certain aspects of the course. In fact, self-help becomes an important element of the teaching process, as I said earlier. Often in my tutorials somebody with considerable industrial experience can take over the class at a certain point because they have far more experience of the point that is being communicated in the group. I don't know how much this is taken for granted.

Waddington: You are saying that however much the high technology media are used, an input of personality remains. But would you wish to eliminate the input of personality?

Perry: I wouldn't. This is the safeguard, as it were—the way the dead hand of uniformity is avoided. Otherwise we would be back in one room with closed walls. Somebody can say precisely what his interpretation is and that is a good thing. The student at least has a balanced view for judging that opinion, and if he is any good he is going to take it with a grain of salt.

Lundberg: You said that the courses cannot afford to be polemical, and it is easy to see why. But isn't there an inherent danger in this in the long run?

Perry: There are inherent dangers in both directions, of course. If we indulge in courses which are not balanced, which are more polemical, we run the risk of evoking government interference because we are a public institution. Governments could close down and impose their will on any of the universities tomorrow. They have the power but by convention they don't use it. We could upset that convention because we use the power of the mass media. I don't think we can take the risk. On the other hand, there is an undoubted inherent risk of just becoming dull, flat and uninteresting.

Lundberg: Isn't there a built-in polemical element?

Perry: Many of the courses have material, written by one man, which is straight polemic, but attached and bound into the same volume is somebody giving the opposite view. You just can't put polemic in on its own and not bother about it.

Platt: In the US, as I said in my paper, we are beginning to have something called 'adversary science', where scientists speak on public issues, doing their best, like lawyers, for a particular side, and then in a later case perhaps doing their best for the opposite side. The hope is that in this kind of open confrontation, as in a court of law, one comes closer to the truth than by having just accidents of committee structure or unanswered polemics decide the matter.

Waddington: I would strongly oppose that as a way of advancing science.

Platt: But somebody should make the total case for a nuclear plant, and somebody should make the total case against the plant for environmental reasons, so that we can see all of both sides before we decide.

Dror: Why shouldn't the two sides make two balanced presentations for and against? Why total? The judge is highly professional and trained to understand the lawyers. This does not hold for the amateur audience, which cannot draw correct conclusions from extreme positions. The analogy of the judicial adversary process is completely misleading. The jury system applies only to limited questions, is controlled by the judge, and is very doubtful.

Platt: Do you know a better system?

Dror: Yes, reliance on professional judges in courts; and careful policy analysis on television for the public.

Platt: Who judges the judges?

Dror: Who judges the juries?

Waddington: That is a piece of politics, not a piece of learning. Learning is not advanced by legal procedures.

Perry: The courses that we are talking about in science don't get to that advanced level of judgement. In futures courses you are dealing with issues of judgement because you are dealing with global problems. A confrontation situation should be expressed within that course material but is not usually necessary in the elementary science that we are teaching.

Eldredge: Could you do specialist or advanced work in the Open University?

Perry: We can in the liberal arts, but I don't think we can in science. I don't think it is possible to teach nuclear physics by the media. We can teach advanced mathematics.

Valaskakis: How would you and Dr Black treat professors who are truly outstanding, innovative and perhaps even geniuses—somebody like an Einstein or a Wittgenstein—but who at the same time are bad teachers? It is said that Wittgenstein never taught in a classroom but always at home, and that if he happened to be inspired he would go on inexhaustibly for hours, while if he happened not to be inspired he would just dismiss the class and declare: 'I have nothing to say'. If the university demands too much from these undisciplined professors, the dynamic elements that they represent might be lost to the university.

Perry: I would have them in the university.

Waddington: I don't think Wittgenstein would have taken a job with the Open University.

Perry: I would like a Wittgenstein as a part-time tutor.

Black: If a university is so rigid in its procedures that it can't take into account the waywardness of such people, then it is really on the way out.

Lundberg: In Sweden there is now strong emphasis on mid-career university education at the expense of initial education. It is probably fair to state that a large section of the academic community favoured initial education. Nonetheless the politically enforced new education policy has been very quickly accepted.

Waddington: The general view of academia until quite recently was that its purpose was producing scholars. It is only gradually sinking into the minds of university staffs that in the present world 80 to 90 per cent of their task consists essentially of providing service courses. Many people regard this as a downgrading of the function of the pure university scholar, but of course one can see it instead as an up-grading of the university's service to the community. But people don't change their minds very fast, so they are bound to oppose it for some time.

Woodroofe: In business we look at what the assumptions are about the future and what kind of world we are going to be working in. We have objectives and priorities about how we carry them out. Do universities ever set down their objectives? You are already saying that some think the main objective is teaching, others say it is advanced studies, research and so on. And there is much talk about academic freedom and little about common objectives, but why should academics be free? Nobody else is.

Waddington: I have rarely heard objectives being discussed by a university senate. I have heard them continuously discussed by groups of individual academics.

Ashby: My answer is that the purpose of a university should be directed to the students, not to the possible jobs awaiting them. It should be concerned with men, not manpower. It should give one student the chance to become a historian, another a doctor, another a psychologist, if these are the disciplines they are interested in, even if there aren't any jobs awaiting them. It was Mark Pattison in Oxford who declared that his aim as a tutor was to produce 'not a book, but a man'.

Waddington: Some people who work in universities would say that, but many others would not.

Woodroofe: That might be a good objective for three universities. I am not sure that it is the right objective for forty-seven universities in a country the size of the United Kingdom.

Perry: We have to differentiate between the overall objectives, and what academics are actually doing from day to day. We need a much more closely defined set of objectives within those overall objectives. That is what is missing.

Waddington: The tradition so far has been that universities don't, as organizations, have overall objectives. The universities consist of conglomerates of individuals, and different individuals have different objectives. Many people in universities say that their reason for being in the university (their objective) is that it gives them the best position for pursuing their own research. For a historian there is probably nowhere else where he can pursue his research, and that is his objective. Other people would say that their objective is to improve individual people according to their desires. Yet others would say their objective is to serve society by turning out the specialists that the society needs. Walter Perry's argument is that universities should have much more defined overall objectives and a certain amount of freedom within those objectives. I am not quite clear whether they need to have those objectives.

Perry: Clear institutional objectives are recommended in the charters of those universities which have charters. Oxford and Cambridge don't have charters.

Waddington: 'Education, religion, learning and research' was the accepted formula when I was at Cambridge.

Woodroofe: Universities also have responsibilities. If we are to have more university education, the idea is not just to improve the fullness of life for the people who go through university but also to make a contribution to the community. A community can afford to have a certain number of scholars searching for knowledge for the sake of knowledge, but it can't afford to have all the scholars of forty-seven universities doing that. They must contribute to the community. In present economic conditions the universities are going to suffer. For their own preservation they should be thinking about making a greater contribution to the community.

Waddington: You don't think universities serve the community sufficiently simply by keeping young people out of labour exchanges?

Robson: I really must protest at this suggestion that disorganized anarchy is the normal state of universities. In this country all forty-seven universities at regular five-yearly intervals have to be extremely specific about what they are doing, what they propose to do, and what they have done. Statistics on university activities are published in great detail, to an extent which is unknown in industry. People in this country can get every piece of information they could possibly want about what universities are doing. If they don't know what that information is, it is simply because they have not read it!

Platt: In my analogy (p. 176) of the university as a five-legged animal, the fifth 'leg' of this wise elephant is its trunk, which is the grasp on the future. As I said in my paper, those universities which neglect futures studies are dropping out of the total network of discussion of world problems and failing to contribute what they might to the total society. And I think there might be useful parallels here, or anticipations, of the futures-role of other universities in other countries.

Waddington: Admittedly the whole university system has to deal with all these functions. But we must find an ideal mix—or can we leave this to work itself out by the forces of interplay between the universities and society?

King: There is no single uniform mix. It must depend on the particular university.

Shane: If you were looking forward to a next step which was as significant a break-away from the present situation as the Open University was thirteen years ago, what would you suggest that this next dramatic step beyond the Open University might be, Sir Walter?

Perry: I see another step for the Open University, and I see another step in the whole pattern of education in Britain. The really deprived people who are not ready for the Open University need an open system of pre-university teaching. I don't think the Open University itself can do it but it ought to be done. Secondly, we haven't even begun to break into the continuing educational field properly. We can do a lot of short courses for periodic 'retreading' that other people can't do. This catalytic move towards continuing education is an exciting prospect for the future, but it hasn't really begun yet.

Eldredge: The 'futurized' part of your scheme for the Open University is excellent. After exploring all sorts of futures courses, I have come to the tentative conclusion that courses outside universities are doing a remarkable job in retreading or 'futurizing' the learning of lots of people and leading them to find their way in the Brave New World. Most people have high motivation when they come in for retreading. The World War II veterans whom I taught had magnificent motivation. We should explore fifty different ways of providing retreading, not necessarily through the university itself. There may be new types of institutions which are better at it.

Woodroofe: One type of retreading is that whereby university teachers come into particular companies in industry and take part in courses. This is beneficial for the people in industry. It is part of retreading. It is also beneficial for the university professor, because he gets contact with reality. Somebody in his audience may know more about some aspect of his subject than he does, and he gets this feedback.

Waddington: Could you explain a bit on the general relation between re-treading, technological innovation and technological unemployment? Can retraining be regarded as a way of using people at a time when they have no definite jobs?

Woodroofe: I don't see it that way. I certainly see that the interrelationship between the universities and industry should grow stronger as time goes on, to the benefit of both. Obviously, the intake into industry in the management field comes largely from universities. Some of those people have had a generalized and not a specifically business-oriented education.

Waddington: That is in the management field, but in America there is a great intake of operatives from universities into industry. Are we going to get much more of that in this country?

Woodroofe: Industry would like it. In the US, college people become supervisors. The result is that, in the US, industry in general is less management-intensive than it is in this country—and this country is higher in its intensity of management than the rest of Europe. The reason is that in the US and elsewhere they delegate more power, so they need fewer layers of management. This would be fine, and with forty-seven universities in this country we ought to be doing the same. But the people who go to universities in this country expect to become managers, not supervisors. In many cases their expectations cannot be fulfilled.

Waddington: Dockworkers or miners now earn more than junior managers. With the change in wage patterns the purely financial inducements to go into management rather than operation must be less. Will students continue to expect to go into management?

Woodroofe: There are three features to that. First, there is concertina-ing of incomes all the time, from top to bottom, and it is much greater in this country than in any other. Secondly, a man who goes into management doesn't get paid the rate for the job immediately but he gets increases year by year until he reaches the full value for the job. That is the tradition. A man who becomes a dockworker gets his full rate for the job plus his overtime and all the other things straight away. Thirdly, if a man comes in as a manager, he comes in on the bottom rung of the ladder, but with the hope that he is going to climb up the management ladder to jobs of greater responsibility. So, although he might be on the same sort of level as a supervisor who has worked his way up from the shop floor, he will nevertheless when he gets further up the ladder be higher than that man. The problem of the compression of differentials in management pay is really getting quite intense. I think universities will experience the same problem.

Reference cited

[1] PERRY, W. (1975) *Higher Education for Adults: Where More Means Better (Rede Lecture 1974)*, Cambridge University Press, London

General discussion

Ziman: Views of the future are too important to be left to the futurists. Our view of the future is a dynamic image of life and of man. Futures studies as an academic discipline inevitably emphasize the analytical techniques. Part of being an academic discipline is that the things on which people can be made to agree by strongly persuasive arguments have to be talked about. It depends on sharp, formal, logical discourse—what we envisage, in the limit, as mathematical proof. That is at the expense of the informal imaginative view of the dynamics of life. This emphasis on analytical method transforms or modifies our view of life from the poetic towards the technocratic view. Because that view influences action, because the dynamics of life include the idea becoming practice, futurism tends to some extent towards a self-fulfilling prophecy. That is, there is a tendency to create a society which warps human life in the direction of the view seen by academic futurologists. The worry that I have in this whole discussion about the creation of departments, specialists and experts on the future, is that their view becomes the image of the future in the same sense that the physicist's image—his technical image—becomes the whole view of nature. The human view of nature should be much broader than the physicist's concepts and constants. Physicists are supposed to be the academics who have the duty of looking at nature as a whole, so everybody says that what the physicists have learned is 'reality'. This is not a deathbed repentance by a mathematical physicist! On the contrary, experience in mathematical physics has taught me the defects and difficulties of generalized mathematical modelling, even in the sphere of the natural sciences.

I want to give two examples of the sorts of things that can go wrong. In classical thermodynamics a maximizable function, the 'Gibbs' free energy', is the standard quantity from which all the properties of statistical mechanics can be derived. It is just like Dr Valaskakis's felicity function. But all theoretical physicists know that this is a very special property of the types of system that we are dealing with in thermodynamics. We know, for example, that the existence of such a function depends upon the intermolecular forces being conservative, and the whole system being very close to equilibrium. I do not see any proof that these conditions apply in the types of human systems we are discussing. This sort of analogy seems highly naive to the theoretical physicist, who knows how difficult it is to get to the genuine parameters and functional relations of a valid model. The theory that such a possibility exists is not proven. That doesn't mean to say that it is chaos. On the contrary, an assembly of atoms might be a perfectly deterministic system, with every particle in the system following its own course under the influence of the others, and yet there would still not be such a maximizable function from which the whole motion could be deduced by variation. I am talking technical mathematics, because this is precisely the sort of thing one has to get right.

The other example comes from the theory of plasma physics and the problems of controlled nuclear fusion.

Back in the 1950s people said that if we set up a system of a big tube containing a low density gas in a strong magnetic field, then we would get a stable electrical discharge at a high temperature. This is a simple system mathematically; the whole behaviour is described by three or four linked partial differential equations, all absolutely deterministic and straightforward. But when the switch was turned on something else happened. The experimental physicists asked the theoretical physicists what had gone wrong. They thought about it again, discovered their error, and suggested modifications in the experimental conditions. Alas, the plasma was still very unstable—more corrections had to be made in the mathematical analysis. There have been several cycles of that process; I am telling that story to show why I have no faith in mathematics as a system of calculating what is going to happen under circumstances where one hasn't already a fair idea of what to expect. They didn't know what the phenomena were—they hadn't done the experiment before—and that made it almost impossible to work it out in advance. Computational techniques have improved since then, but the systems to which they are to be applied are far more complex and poorly comprehended than a plasma discharge. So the worry I have in this whole meeting is simple enough: how are we going to bring a *poetic* view into the *problèmatique*?

Waddington: My suggestion originally was that the *problèmatique* should be treated as history, and we should bring in a few historians. When we talk about interdisciplinarity, why do we mean only inter-scientific disciplines? We need, as you say, to bring in the humanists too. (But, incidentally, the fact that mathematical theorists don't always get it right the first time, or even the

second or third time, is not a good argument for not letting them have a shot.)
I am a great believer in always having orthogonal views: never believe in a
thing unless you believe its opposite at the same time, or never adopt one
principle of ethics unless you adopt an orthogonal principle at the same time.

King: The Club of Rome has a new project being worked out now by Ervin
Laszlo on exactly the lines you have just indicated.

During this meeting my prejudices have perhaps become a little more rigid
than the reverse. We have come round to the fact that at undergraduate level
there is a good deal to be done, but I don't think it is futures studies and futures
teaching in the narrow sense. It is much broader than that. Your own book,
Professor Waddington,[1] is not exclusively on futures as such. There is a desperate need to create a much deeper understanding of the nature of the world,
how the global system works, what its interactions are—the *problèmatique* if
you like, the question of complexity, the global problems, the need for local
participatory approaches in other ways. If we are going to succeed in the next
generation with the management of complexity, change and uncertainty there
has to be a great deal more understanding than we have now, and this has to
be greatly generalized. The political leaders with whom we have had discussions
in the Club of Rome apparently understand that many changes should be
made, but these would be extremely unpopular and they are unable to make
such changes until the general understanding of the world situation on the
part of the public is much greater than it is today. Therefore I think there is a
great deal to be done at the undergraduate level in universities. The prospective element, the futures element, is important but not the totality. To concentrate exclusively on the future as such is perhaps unwise at this level. At the
postgraduate level the needs are quite different. The needs of the decision
makers, the needs of society, the needs of our own search for new knowledge,
call for a great development of techniques and methodology, a great deal of
specific work. I am sure that Professor Dror is right in indicating that this has
a place in the university. Where it should be I couldn't say, but in many cases
it ought perhaps to be associated with policy science. The key to the utility
of futures studies lies first in the methodology, which requires a realistic understanding of the problems, and secondly in its applications. I would put great
stress on the need for communication between the universities and the decision
makers. From my own observations the decision makers are more open to this
than they have ever been before, out of desperation.

Lord Ashby brought in the question of how much we are willing to sacrifice
for our great-grandchildren. This raises the fundamental human problem of
the extent to which human beings, and their societies and governments, are
capable of acting in anticipation of events rather than merely reacting to them

post facto. One of the characteristics of *homo sapiens* is that he can look ahead. We can prepare for the winter just as well as the squirrels, perhaps a little better. We even prepare to some extent for our old age by taking out insurance policies, by supporting geriatrics and all kinds of things. We prepare for military onslaughts—not very well, because there is insufficient futurology in our thinking, so that we remain too traditional, constructing the Maginot Line generation after generation. Professor Dror has supported the idea of research on 'heresies', and I think it is very necessary to question the traditional. This is one part of the futures approach. There is however, also tradition in favour of anticipatory action. The classic example was Noah's Ark. Is there a possibility of a contemporary equivalent to that? I don't know, but I think that the rate of change brings in a new factor and makes anticipation even more necessary.

I am not sure that for the adoption of a futures approach to politics it is necessary to look as far ahead as to our great-grandchildren. In effect the speeding up in the rate of change means that long term has become medium term. So one of the reasons for taking an anticipatory approach is that we ourselves, or our children and people we know, may live long enough to see quite a number of difficulties which are already foreseeable. In other words, because of this shrinking of time, anticipation of difficulties becomes long-term self-interest. And where self-interest is still involved, there is a chance of people taking anticipatory precautions. This is less probable as the degree of self-interest is diluted by the time span from our children to our grandchildren and then to generations whom we don't know. In a period of rapid change such as the present, therefore, self-interest may drive us to anticipatory action to prevent disasters and, perhaps, to take painful decisions which will contribute to the survival of the human race.

Waddington: You are assuming that the rate of change will continue to accelerate. At the moment we don't know whether it will do so, or start slowing down. When Lord Ashby first mentioned them, I said I was not bothered about my great-grandchildren, but the time may come when we can again think about our great-grandchildren.

King: The prospective aspects of research and development are very important at present, particularly with regard to energy, conservation and the like. The lead time for R & D is very long and, taken together with the time required for capital accumulation, construction, etc., the general application of a major technological innovation takes up to thirty or forty years. With the present rapid rate of change, the time between two distinct sets of circumstances which represent radically different situations is now less than the lead time of R & D into production. The power of technology in solving many of the problems that we are up against therefore becomes very dubious. It could often come too late. It is implicit in much economic thinking that a technology 'fix' will in fact provide for a solution. The economists have always taken the view that technological innovation is essentially caused by the inter-action of economic forces, which is the opposite point of view from that of the scientist. One of the biggest questions is whether there is time for the tech-nological fixes to be developed. These matters are not properly appreciated in political and policy-making circles, where the time factor in change is seldom discussed. In France a quarter of a century elapsed between the first experimen-tal pile going critical and the first power station opening. Yet France is relying on having nuclear energy within ten years so that a great number of major energy bottlenecks can be removed. The need to take decisions on quite long-term needs, because of this lead time for research and development, is very great, and seldom appreciated. An awful lot of nonsense has been talked in political circles about the energy question. There is a special need to take the prospective approach to research and development and to persuade the decision makers to make decisions now on major R & D projects whose results will be required thirty years from now.

Robson: I still have two basic anxieties. First, it is unlikely that the graph of any aspect of human affairs would be a smooth curve or a straight line. It would probably be a jerky line, with breaks and discontinuities. Major changes occur as a result of sudden and frequently unpredictable events. If groups of highly informed people in the past had tried to predict what was going to hap-pen, I suspect that their success rate would have been extremely low. One can only predict on the basis of experience already experienced. The chances of predicting one of these massive discontinuities which switch the whole pathway of human affairs must be vanishingly small. People at a point in time don't have the information or the experience. If that is so, then futurology is clearly going to be not only difficult but only occasionally successful.

My second basic anxiety is that setting up futurology as a discipline is surely only one part of the equation and alone would be a sterile academic activity. If it is to have any value there must be some way of ensuring that the decision makers pay some attention to the predictions. At present, I see extremely little evidence that anybody would listen. Even if they did, how would they know which predictions were accurate?

King: I strongly disagree.

Robson: You mentioned Noah's Ark: I believe that according to legend some-body had to tell Noah to build his ark. People have been making predictions about population problems for years without anything being done.

Platt: Prediction alone is not enough. It has to be ratified by a reality prin-ciple—by a real and catalytic crisis—because that is when people begin to put in time, money, effort and organizational skills to meet the problem. It is important to make the prediction so that you have the intellectual tools in advance, as far as possible. It is important to do the homework and the critical analyses, but for society to get moving on these problems people have to come in contact with them in a real way.

Dror: Sometimes it is the other way round. Good analysis recognizes problems, while direct contact distorts understanding.

Waddington: Dr King mentioned that futurology in the sense of prediction is only one element in what we are talking about, and rather a minor element at that. I agree, but I find it difficult to know how any other word but 'futures' could act as a focus. Our interest is really in a dynamic analysis of the present, the present as a set of processes rather than as a state of affairs. It is difficult to express this in just one word without using some word like futures. Admittedly the word future has been largely spoilt for this use by the invention of things like futurology and futuristics, and by premature attempts to be more precise than is possible. Actual attempts to predict are not likely to be successful, and they are only a part of what one is interested in.

Another point was raised by Sir Hugh Robson—how do we get decision makers to pay any attention? Decisions of course are normally taken with some sort of future in mind. If one has to decide to invest in a plant for manufacturing something which will take years to build, one does this in relation to some idea of the future. Whether by studying the present as a dynamic system one can at all improve one's predictive power, is perhaps not so clear, but it is quite certain that among the people who are going to make predictions are the decision makers. They have to make them. Predicting is what decision-making essentially is.

Robson: They are going to base their assumptions on a continuation of the present.

Dror: Advisers say that top decision makers never listen to them. Decision makers say their advisers never say anything useful. Often, both claims are correct. One way to open up decision-making is by public pressure. Other decision makers feel the need for help because they feel uneasy, being unable to solve pressing problems. An additional way is to try and make predictions and other futures studies relevant to the concrete decision agenda of politicians. This requires a set of innovative structures in government itself.

Waddington: Let us consider Mrs Gandhi's problem when faced with the problem of the population of India. If she is to do anything about it at all, she has to do it in relation to the way the future seems to be unfolding. What she needs is not a more precise prediction, but an analysis of the dynamic factors affecting the population. The problem may be to reduce the desire for a family of more than two children: is that the major thing she has to do? Or has she got to disseminate birth control methods more widely and freely, or pay people to be sterilized? She needs a dynamic analysis of the situation much more than an actual prediction. But whatever she does, her decision must be taken in relation to the future.

Platt: It is important to emphasize that there is a historical process of change, or what was once called a dialectical process. The first dramatic presentation by a professor or a wild man or woman isn't enough; it isn't the end of the process. The ideas of those people need to be opposed and debated, because in many cases they will be false and dangerous prophets, whose warnings are simply wrong.

Many people do not understand or accept this historical process, these time constants for redirecting a big social system. For example, some people don't really believe in change at all, or progressive change. They are either young radicals who say the system is so rigid it will never change, or older conservatives who say that a system is going to go on because it has gone that way for all of human history. Then there is the kind of utopian who expects change immediately, as soon as the new truth has been proclaimed. All of these are wrong. Change occurs in a certain time scale, and in a first approximation the system won't change tomorrow or next year or the next. But in fifty years, and nowadays even in ten years, it may be totally different. We have to appreciate these time constants of change and what they really are today if we are to reconcile the different points of view of those who believe that change cannot happen, or that it will happen right away. On different time scales, both of them are entirely correct.

Valaskakis: I would like to expand on some of the points made by Professor Ziman and share some of the experiences I have had in doing interdisciplinary research with hard scientists, soft scientists and people from the humanities. In interdisciplinary teams I have found that it is the anthropologist, the sociologist, or perhaps even the literary critic, who argues for the computer, and it is the computer expert, the mathematical physicist, who argues against the computer, saying quite cogently that there is a 'garbage-in garbage-out' rule. My position would be that we should make sure that we do not feed garbage into the computer, rather than that we should necessarily junk the computer. Two concepts of the uses of mathematics are inherent here: the hard scientist sees mathematics as a tool for finding answers, while others see it as a way of defining problems in a heuristic and meaningful way. When I write an equation on the board I do not always expect to solve it. I am reminded of a billboard seen in the US Midwest with a giant 'Jesus is the Answer' on it. In much smaller graffiti was the irreverent rejoinder 'Yes, but what is the question?'

What we need are good questions even if good answers are not forthcoming. Mathematics can be one way of formulating questions. Insoluble equations measure our ignorance. Their absence makes our very ignorance incommensurable. There is much to be said for the notion of a *'problèmatique'*. Because what is in fact a *problèmatique*? In the technical sense the *problèmatique* is a hierarchy of questions and sub-questions, of problems and sub-problems. It is a systematic process, not a haphazard one, and it can benefit from formal mathematical expression. On the other hand I certainly think that the formal model should be tempered by the humanities. In our Montreal think tank we will endeavour to have a so-called 'scenarist in residence', a person who will produce scenarios. He will not be a physicist or an engineer but a playwright. He hopefully will take a societal model and develop human, rounded, realistic characters around it. This touch of humanity should, we hope, complement the formalism of theory.

Oldfield: For me this symposium has sharpened some personal dilemmas in education. I sense that a tension emerges between education for *adjustment* and education for rational, autonomous, *altruism*. The way in which one steers one's course between these poles depends on the relationship one sees between notions of positivism, questions of values, considerations of empirically knowable reality, and the power of the conceptual frameworks and theories which one uses. It still seems to me that futures study tends too often towards a dissociation between personal or collective value formation, and the generation or evaluation of projective images. It thus embraces a positivism which I still mistrust *vis-à-vis* the future. It tends to rely on theories, tools and concepts which are more impressive for their elegance, sophistication and precision than for their accuracy, validity or relationship to empirical reality. It becomes a sort of non-participatory mystique. Yet I am bound to confess that the frames of reference which I as a blinkered scientist find more authentic, valid and robust—for example, the ecosystem—are only partly integrative. The ecosystem is a powerful framework in empirical study as well as in pragmatic and normative terms. Thus one can try to use it as an axial concept in education for value formation, for judgement and, if you like, for democratic participation. However, working and thinking within an ecosystem framework, I am still forced to admit that I have developed only a partial perspective and I cannot fit it into a global, complex, holistic totality. Therefore I sense a tension between developing the holistic perspective and fostering realistic participation in democracy. That strikes me as being an uncomfortable point to recognize.

Waddington: You have put your finger on one of the difficulties of life. Life is not easy. But it is there and people have to cope with it.

Woodroofe: It seems to me that 'futurology' is a bad term and I would agree that the subject should be considered as the long-term implications of current activities. This is really what we are discussing. And I would again make the plea: let the time scale be as short as is practicable. If it is made long term it will be regarded as futurology in the worst sense and the community will not regard it as credible. Then, if the time scale is kept short, one can validate. Obviously one will have the discontinuities, the unexpected, but at least one will be able to tackle the unexpected better if these factors have been considered beforehand.

The effect of politics has not been thoroughly discussed here. The whole discussion was really on what are the long-term implications of what we are doing now. Politics on the other hand has a very short horizon. The politician has to get himself elected every five years or less. He has to promise goodies in order to get the vote, and he has to promise goodies which are often not achievable or which are borrowing from future generations, even from Eric Ashby's great-grandchildren. How do we get the political system as it is now, democracy as it is now, to agree to take decisions, in the interests of the long term, which are unpopular at the moment?

Perry: I wonder whether looking at the microcosm helps with the macrocosm. In 1969 and the few years afterwards I was having to make more decisions that would have a direct effect than anybody should ever have to make. Nearly all the decisions that I took about forming a new institution were wrong. It wasn't that the ideas or the policies were wrong, but the decisions, which were really not decisions of what policy was but of how to implement the policy, had no evidence to back them up. That applies to the macrocosmic decisions as well. Fortunately most of them are either reversible or, if not wholly reversible, modifiable by feedback. That kind of feedback may be where participatory democracy comes in. Can participatory democracy ever make the decisions through the democratic process or does it actually act as the feedback? Some decisions will be so wrong and so irreversible that they might have awful consequences for the preservation of scholarship. Maybe we should create universities so that they can be Noah's Arks through bad periods. It has happened historically and it may well happen again.

Francis: Universities have a caretaker function which is essentially complementary to that of the political process, and they provide an element of continuity that is not provided by other institutions. Although we have all stressed the essential value of an early warning system we haven't really talked about the assessment of risk, which has come up in a rather roundabout way when we have been talking about nuclear power or something like that. In many areas at present we are able to put down the equation: infinite potential equals infinite risk. We are tending to assume somehow that decisions made inside the political process involve the assessment of risk, and we are not sure how the politicians arrive at their assessment. This independent and complementary function can be provided, I believe, through the universities in their appraisal of the future, working in close contact with other institutions.

Reference cited

[1] WADDINGTON, C. H. (1975) *The Sources of the Man Made Future*, Cape & Paladin, London

Concluding remarks

C. H. WADDINGTON

As Walter Perry pointed out, he, being the last designated speaker in the symposium, had the opportunity to present something of a summary of all the previous contributions. He brought out several aspects of what has seemed to me a rather surprising consensus of opinion which has emerged during our meeting. We all seem to be agreed that universities are finding new responsibilities thrust upon them by the historical events of our present period, and that they will need to show a great deal more flexibility and a greater capacity for imaginative innovation, than they have been exhibiting in the last few decades. The days are long gone by when they could be contented to be mainly Noah's Arks preserving and handing on the wisdom of the past. Even if one adds to this the task, which they have gradually become accustomed to in the last hundred years, of making some modest contributions to the discovery of new knowledge, those two endeavours are by no means enough for the universities of the present day, though I think we can all agree that they remain essential aspects of university life which certainly should not be allowed to deteriorate.

Walter Perry drew particular attention to two further tasks. In the first place, universities have to provide a general background education, covering some broad fields not in great depth or detail, but sufficiently to provide a basis on which more thorough and narrower specialized studies can find a firm ground to stand on. Perhaps in the old days such background could be provided by the schools at pre-university age, or by informal communication between university students themselves. Nowadays the need has grown beyond the capacity of that type of instruction and calls for the provision of 'service' courses, specific-ally designed with this aim in view. Further, Walter Perry also stressed the important changes that have followed from the rapidity with which knowledge advances and older ideas or even alleged facts become out of date. Education, whether we like it or not, cannot be confined to an early period in life, but

217

must continue throughout the years of adult experience. Exactly what form this continuing education should take is still unclear, but it seems fairly certain that the universities must play an important part in it.

I should add, to these university functions, that of providing a forum for wide-ranging discussions between people who are interested in ideas and who bring with them differing points of view and background. I am not thinking only of discussions between academics of various disciplines, but of discussions between academics, industrialists, politicians, civil servants, trades union leaders, and the many other types of people in our world who feel the need to think things out and to learn other peoples' points of view. Again, of course, there are many such 'talking shops' which are not primarily connected with the universities, but it seems to me that the universities are in a favourable position to set them up and operate them.

It is against this background of the changing structure of university activities that we have been considering the relevance of the broad field which we have referred to as 'the future'. There seems to be a general agreement amongst us that it would not be sensible at present to think of this subject mainly in terms of specific prediction of what is going to happen, or even of a series of weighted bets on possible future situations or events. 'Futurology', in so far as it concerns itself with telling us what life is going to be like in the year 2000, is not robust enough to take any place in university concerns. It can at best provide a few vivid illustrations for arguments of a more firmly based character.

In fact there was, I think, general agreement that the 'futures' which might have relevance to universities would perhaps better be described as a multi-dimensional dynamic analysis of the present. It would be concerned with discovering the nature of the processes which are going on at the present time and how they interact with one another. This involves, of course, a consideration of the recent past, and also, since we are thinking of processes, a consideration of the near future. Woodroofe emphasized that the decision makers of today have, of course, to think in terms of processes of change which their decisions will effect; but at one point he was urging that we should keep our considerations to as short a term into the future as possible. Of course, if we never had to look any further ahead than one year, even in the present hectic times, one could hope things would not have changed too much in the interval. But, very often, policies take longer than that to come into effect; consider for instance the population problem. One cannot predict with any certainty what will happen in ten or twenty years' time in almost any field, but large-scale investors of capital, or initiators of major social policies, may in effect have to gamble on their hunches for periods of that time. What can be done, however, is to assess the character of the processes which are going to be operating. It seems to me that it is this aspect of the matter which is of interest to universities. Moreover we are realizing more and more the interrelatedness of the many factors involved. We are dealing with multidimensional interactions, many of which are non-linear and involve highly complex controlling systems of both positive and negative character. New disciplines of thought, such as cybernetics, are called for.

The impression I have received during these days is that there are at least four types of university activity in these fields, which many of us here feel to be valuable.

There is in the first place the straight research project. We have mentioned the designing of a world economic system as proposed by Jan Tinbergen, or the modelling of interactions on a world scale by Mesarovic and Pestel, as activities which are eminently suitable for the academic environment, and which through their interdisciplinary character may require that the environment should give up some of the rigidity of its conventional departmental organization.

Secondly, there is the provision of service courses, which would describe the existing state of knowledge about the processes affecting the main problems of the world—population, growth of cities, provision of food, transport, the natural environment, human aspirations and what people conceive of as 'the good life', and so on. As Walter Perry and John Francis have reminded us, the Open University has already organized a course of this kind and they are both deeply involved in it in different ways. I have myself written a book which I would like to believe could form a textbook for such a course, and I have attempted to organize this in Edinburgh, although still on an unofficial basis.

Thirdly, there is a different type of service course which would seem desirable, namely one which describes the newer types of thinking and theorizing about interacting complex systems. One hears a lot in the semi-popular press about cybernetics, information theory, control theory, decision theory, games theory, and a whole list of theoretical developments aimed at increasing our capacity to understand such matters. Sometimes I feel that the names are perhaps more impressive than the content, but even if one retains a healthy scepticism, one is bound to admit that considerable advances in understanding complex systems have, in fact, been made in the last few decades. Unfortunately most of them have not yet crept through into the general education of the ordinary educated citizen. They remain arcane secrets of mathematicians or the one or two specialist types of engineers who *have* to use them. I believe that here again a new type of service course should be made available to wide circles of the university population.

Finally, there is the possibility of the university acting as a focus and organizer of discussions on the kind of topics we have referred to as futures, not only between different disciplines within the academic world, but between the academic world and the many other interested parts of society. Here I think the University of Göteborg has provided us with a wonderful example. Professor Lundberg has described in some detail the great success they have had in using the university background to stimulate debate on such matters within Sweden. I think we have all been very impressed with this, and I suspect that many of us share my view that many other universities in Britain and elsewhere should try to follow their example. This has, of course, already been done by many universities in the United States, but my feeling is that, perhaps because Sweden is a smaller and more coherent country, the Göteborg experiment is the most successful that has yet been carried out along these lines.

Biographies of the participants

ERIC ASHBY (Lord Ashby of Brandon), born in 1904, is Master of Clare College, Cambridge. He was for 13 years Professor of Botany, in Sydney and Manchester, and for nine years Vice-Chancellor of the Queen's University, Belfast. He was chairman of the Royal Commission on Environmental Pollution in Britain. His books include *Technology and the Academics* (1958), *Adapting Universities to a Technological Society* (1974), and *Portrait of Haldane* (1974).

JOHN BLACK, born in 1922, is Principal of Bedford College, University of London. His academic career started in Agriculture, and has moved through Natural Resources, General Biology and Human Biology into university administration. He has written many papers and one book: *The Dominion of Man* (1970)

YEHEZKEL DROR, born in 1928, is Professor of Political Science and director of public administration programmes at the Hebrew University of Jerusalem. He is a policy consultant to governments and international organizations and a former senior staff member of the Rand Corporation, Santa Monica, California. His books include *Public Policymaking Reexamined* (1968), *Design for Policy Sciences* (1971), *Ventures in Policy Sciences* (1971) and *Crazy States* (1971)

H. WENTWORTH ELDREDGE, born in 1909, is Professor of Sociology Emeritus at Dartmouth College, Hanover, New Hampshire. An urban specialist, he is the editor of *Taming Megalopolis* (1967) and *World Capitals: Toward Guided Urbanization and Urbanism* (1975). Recently he has published a series of papers on long-range planning and futures study courses.

JOHN M. FRANCIS, born in 1939, is Senior Research Fellow in Energy Studies at the Heriot-Watt University in Edinburgh. He is currently also Director of the Society, Religion and Technology Project of the Church of Scotland and a consultant to the World Council of Churches. He is co-author of *Scotland in Turmoil* (1973)

221

FREDERIC R. JEVONS, born in 1929, is Professor of Liberal Studies in Science at the University of Manchester. His books include *The Biochemical Approach to Life* (1964), *The Teaching of Science* (1969), *Science Observed* (1973) and (with others) *Wealth from Knowledge* (1972)

ALEXANDER KING, born in 1909, is Chairman of the International Federation of Institutes of Advanced Study and was formerly Director-General for scientific affairs and education, OECD. He is a co-founder of the Club of Rome. He has written books and papers on physical chemistry, science policy and education.

IVAN KLIMES, born in 1935 in Prague, is the editor of *Futures: the journal of forecasting and planning*, and an associate editor of *Energy Policy* and *Science & Public Policy*. He has written *The Art of Criticism* (thesis, 1958), *A Young Theatre* (1960), *Via Exploratorium* (1964) and numerous articles and studies on literary criticism, history and science writing.

KRISHAN KUMAR, born 1942, is Lecturer in Sociology at the University of Kent at Canterbury. During 1972–3 he was a Talks Producer at the BBC. He has written *Revolution: The Theory and Practice of a European Idea* (1971), and is at present writing a book on the future of the industrial societies.

ANDERS P. LUNDBERG, born in 1930, is Professor of Physiology at the University of Göteborg and a member of the board of the Centre for Interdisciplinary Studies of the Human Condition, Göteborg. He is the author of many papers on neurophysiology.

FRANK OLDFIELD, born in 1936, is Director of the School of Independent Studies and Professor of Geography in the University of Lancaster. He has written articles on ecological themes.

SIR WALTER PERRY, born in 1921, is Vice-Chancellor of the Open University. He was formerly Professor of Pharmacology at the University of Edinburgh and has written numerous papers on pharmacological subjects.

JOHN PLATT, born in 1918, is a research scientist at the University of Michigan, and author of *The Excitement of Science* (1962), *The Step to Man* (1966), and *Perception and Change* (1970)

SIR HUGH ROBSON, born 1917, is Principal of the University of Edinburgh. Formerly Vice-Chancellor of the University of Sheffield, he was before that Professor of Medicine in the University of Adelaide.

HAROLD G. SHANE, born in 1914, is University Professor of Education, Indiana University, Bloomington. Among his 120 books are *Linguistics and the Classroom Teacher* (1967); (with Robert H. Anderson) *Bending the Twig* (1970); *Guiding Human Development* (1971); *The Educational Significance of The Future* (1973); (with Alvin Toffler et al.) *Learning for Tomorrow* (1974).

SIR FREDERICK STEWART, born in 1916, is Professor of Geology in the University of Edinburgh. After a period as Chairman of the Natural Environment Research Council he became Chairman of the Advisory Board of the Research Councils in 1973.

ROBERT D. UNDERWOOD, born in 1945, is research fellow at the School of the Man Made Future, University of Edinburgh.

K. VALASKAKIS, born in 1941, is Associate-Professor of Economics and director of GAMMA (an interuniversity futures-oriented think-tank of the University of Montreal and McGill University). He has written various papers and two books on economic development and futures studies in general.

C. H. WADDINGTON, born 1905, has been Buchanan Professor of Animal Genetics at the University of Edinburgh since 1947. After ten years as a Lecturer in Zoology at Cambridge, he did Operational Research for Coastal Command, Royal Air Force, from 1942–1945. He has published numerous scientific articles and books on embryological development and evolution, and also a number of books about the relations between science and society, addressed to the general reader, such as *The Scientific Attitude* (1941); *The Ethical Animal* (1960); *The Nature of Life* (1961); *Behind Appearance: The Study of Relations between Art and Science in this Century* (1970). Between 1969 and 1971 he spent two years as Einstein Professor in the State University of New York at Buffalo, and during this time devoted himself to considering how the university curriculum should be developed in relation to the present problems of the modern world, and in studying what is being done in this connection in American universities.

MAURICE WILKINS, born 1916, is Professor of Biophysics at Kings's College, University of London and Director of the Medical Research Council Cell Biophysics Unit. His Department provides various interdisciplinary undergraduate courses linking physics, biology and biochemistry, and has developed a student discussion course on social relations of biology. He is President of the British Society for Social Responsibility in Science. His research has been mainly on molecular biology, e.g. the structure of DNA (joint award of Nobel Prize 1962).

SIR ERNEST WOODROOFE, born in 1912, is a physicist turned businessman who in 1974 retired from the Chairmanship of Unilever Ltd., an international corporation. He has given a number of lectures on business economics and is a Visiting Fellow of Nuffield College, Oxford. He is a Trustee of the Leverhulme Trust.

JOHN ZIMAN, born in 1925, is a Professor of Theoretical Physics at the University of Bristol. He is also the author of *Public Knowledge* and a variety of articles on the sociology of science.

Index of Contributors

*Entries in **bold** type indicate papers; other entries refer to discussion contributions*

Ashby, Lord   104, 106, 115, 117, 159, 160, 203

Black, J. N.   62, 100, **107**, 115, 116, 117, 200, 202

Dror, Y.   16, 30, 49, 63, 64, 65, 68, 69, 97, 100, 102, 137, **145**, 158, 161, 162, 163, 184, 188, 189, 201, 212

Eldredge, H. W.   **5**, 17, 32, 63, 69, 70, 86, 97, 115, 117, 140, 141, 159, 187, 189, 202, 205

Eriksson, K. E.   **19**

Francis, J. M.   32, 63, **89**, 97, 99, 102, 162, 186, 200, 215

Jevons, F. R.   30, **53**, 63, 64, 65, 66, 83, 115, 139

King, A.   **35**, 47, 48, 49, 51, 103, 104, 117, 158, 204, 209, 210, 211

Klimes, I. F.   183, 184

Kumar, K.   85, 139

Lundberg, A.   **19**, 30, 33, 50, 102, 116, 117, 201, 202

Oldfield, F.   49, 156, 158, 185, 186, 214

Perry, Sir W.   31, 84, 85, 100, 115, 116, 119, 162, 163, **191**, 199, 200, 201, 202, 203, 204, 215

Platt, J. R.   15, 49, 50, 66, 69, 70, 83, 114, 118, 155, **167**, 183, 184, 185, 186, 187, 188, 189, 201, 204, 211, 213

Robson, Sir H.   204, 211, 212

Shane, H. G.   51, 69, **73**, 83, 99, 117, 118, 141, 161, 184, 185, 199, 204

Stewart, Sir F.   63, 101, 102

Valaskakis, K.   16, 47, 64, 65, 82, 116, **121**, 138, 140, 141, 142, 159, 161, 183, 189, 202, 213

Waddington, C. H.   **1**, 15, 29, 31, 33, 48, 49, 50, 51, 81, 82, 83, 84, 85, 86, 97, 99, 100, 101, 102, 103, 104, 116, 117, 118, 119, 136, 137, 139, 158, 159, 160, 161, 162, 163, 164, 185, 186, 187, 199, 200, 201, 202, 203, 204, 205, 208, 210, 212, 214, **217**

Wilkins, M. H. F.   33, 64

Woodroofe, Sir E.   31, 50, 64, 85, 105, 106, 116, 161, 162, 163, 202, 203, 205, 206, 214

Ziman, J. M.   48, 49, 66, 68, 69, 81, 82, 141, 163, 187, 207

Indexes compiled by William Hill

225

Subject Index

academic freedom
110, 194, 200
academicism
48
academic organization
107–119
adversary science
179, 201
Africa, history of
157
age range of students
178
Agricultural Research
Council
101
alternative groups
33
altruism
214
American Institute of
Planners
12
anthropology
123, 139
anticipatory action
210
anti-science
56
architects
99
atomic energy
14, 27, 208

behaviour
132

goal of   126, 138
modification   76
understanding of   130
utopias and   134

Canada
41
catalytic analysis
172, 185, 186
cause and effect
2
Centre for Interdisciplinary
Studies of the Human
Condition
19–29
change
189
historical process of   213
in world structures   175
rate and direction of   35,
36, 38, 40, 54, 100, 210
world-wide   171
characteristics of futures
studies
152, 155
choice
125
quaternary commodities
and   127
climate control
68
Club of Rome
1, 43, 47, 49, 51, 173, 181,
182, 209

commodities
129
in felicity function   139
need and   131
symbiotic   131
commodities, quaternary
125, 132, 135, 139
choice and   127
identification of   136
illustrative list of   131
communication
84, 167
television and   183
community
service courses and   199
complexity
understanding   151
consciousness
62n
cost
129
of research   116
of scenario models   157
university   31, 111, 112,
114
cost–benefit analysis
160, 162, 164
course teams in Open
University
193, 199, 200
courses
23, 66, 108
available   5
preparation of   194
'service'   192, 198, 202

creativity
  10, 11
cross-impact analysis
  10, 69
culture
  patterns   24
  television and,   186, 188
  universities and   180
curricula
  74
curiosity about future
  148

decisions
  to be made   76, 80, 81
decision-making
  49, 65, 76, 137, 139, 162,
    212, 218
  basis   148
  improvement in   163
  in terms of futures   163
  in universities   108
  in urban planning   140
  science and   64
  uncertainty-absorbing
    modes of   150
decision theory
  137
degrees
  future programmes   196
  standards   113
  unit   112
Delphi techniques
  10, 149, 159
democracy
  37
demography
  6, 15, 37
deschooling
  196
development of futures
  studies
  154, 186
diachronic analysis
  122
disasters
  potential   83
disciplines
  new   110, 112
discommodities
  129
  minimizing   127

eclectics
  121–143
  definitions   123
  need for   134
  potential applications of
    130
  subject matter of   128
  terms used in   128
ecology
  33, 66, 174, 185
  architects and   99
  growth of   172
economics
  50, 83, 123, 124, 183
  concepts   129
  quantification   133
economic growth
  24
economy
  subsistence   33
education
  continuing   195, 217
  developments   78
  expansion   61
  for adjustment   214
  function of   60, 75
  future change   80
  future pattern   191–206
  general   217
  mid-career   202
  objectives   203
  pre-university   204
  self-discipline and   78
  sense of direction   75
  techniques   7
  television and   170
  vitality of institutions   77
  weakness and strength in
    74
educational change
  social decisions and   73–
    87
educationalists
  6
electronic surround
  168
electron society
  universities role in   175
emotional training
  100
employment and unemploy-
    ment
  20, 37

energy
  24, 94–96
  centralization   94
  conservation   99
  economy   95
  nuclear   14, 27, 208
  planning   95
  regional studies   96
  research in   101
energy crisis
  5, 15, 25, 37, 95
environment
  37, 66
  conquest of   56
escapism
  157
ethics
  4, 20, 75
evolution
  100
experiential learning
  10, 97

feedback
  2, 49, 156, 157, 215
felicity
  126, 135
felicity function
  138, 139, 140, 142
food problems
  3, 23, 77
Ford Foundation Energy
  Policy Project
  95
forecasts
  categories of   38
  techniques   121
  uncertainty of   39, 84
forestry teaching
  111
France
  social sciences in   103
freedom of university
  27

goals
  133, 134, 138, 148
governments
  controlling television   184
  future studies   14, 37, 41
  role of   40
graduate courses
  23

growth rates
122

historical process of change
213
history
124, 154, 157, 208
human affairs
trends in   35

incomes
205, 206
India
population problems
212
village television   186
industrialization
sociology of   85, 86
industry
41
in Scotland   93
relationship with
university   205
tenure in   116
infelicity cost
129
innovations
origin of   83
institution of futures studies
41
intellectual assumptions
145
intellectual networks
182
interdisciplinarity
208, 213
definition of   30
interdisciplinary contacts in
universities
102
interdisciplinary courses
25, 31, 102, 103, 104
interdisciplinary teams
161
International Federation of
Institutes of Advanced
Study
43
International Institute for
Applied Systems Analysis
43, 181

Japan
42, 116
justification of futures studies
155

Kahn, Herman
39, 130
knowledge
153, 178
advancing   217
alternative systems   56,
59
classification of   45
evolution of   60
limitation of   55
limits to change in   54
network of   180
new systems of   61
plasticity of   59
synthesis of   21
universities as repository
of   176
views of   53–71
Kuhn, T. S.
55, 57, 60

land
use of   99
learning process
137
leisure
130
television and   168
lifeboat theory
6
limit calculations
69
limits to growth
183
livestock industry
101
living standards
133
see also quality of life

malnutrition
23
manpower
105
Marx, Karl
125, 174
mass media
77

materialism
125
media
alternative   171
medical technology
14
mega-economics
see eclectics
message of the medium
185
methodology
158, 161
millennium
36
models
9, 49, 207
money
159, 160
motivation
135, 196
multicultural problems
141
multinational corporations
51

nations
interdependence of   37
natural resources
see resources
Netherlands
42
Niger
national goals   133, 134
North Sea oil
90, 93, 99
nuclear energy
14, 27, 208
nuclear warfare
6, 83, 187

Office of Technology
Assessment
42, 90
Oil Development Council for
Scotland
102
Open University
12, 31, 109, 115, 116, 117,
219
courses   193
course preparation   194
course teams   193, 199,
200

Open University, *continued*
  future degree programmes
    196
  future of 204
  service courses 198
  technology in 32
operational bases of futures
  studies
  147
operations research
  49, 50, 137, 162
opportunity
  129
opportunity costs
  159, 160
Organization for Economic
  Cooperation and Development
  42
Outer Continental Shelf
  Development
  91

paradigmatic level
  147
past
  158
  as basis for prediction 149
peace
  82
pharmacology
  100
phenomena
  stability of 149, 150
philosophical assumptions
  145
planning
  12, 13, 27, 105
  see also urban planning
  alternative 28
  cooperation in 96
  energy resources 95
  long-range 133
  of research 24
  prospective 39
  systems approach to 97
policies research
  73
policy centres
  161
policy making
  98
  science and 64

world wide 175
political science
  124
political scientists
  7
politics
  215
  influence of television on
    183
pollution
  186
Popper, K. R.
  55, 60
population increase
  15, 37, 38, 171, 173, 211,
    212
pragmatism
  146
precognition
  150
predictions
  146, 156, 211, 212
  stability in past and 149,
    150
present
  definition 85
pre-university teaching
  204
problèmatique
  1, 3, 47, 208, 209, 214
problem solving
  kinds of 155
problems of futures studies
  teaching
  16
processes
  218
projections
  39
prophecy
  156
prophylactic futurology
  39
prospective movement
  47
psychological assumptions
  145
psychology
  124

quality of life
  9, 12, 24, 77, 126, 141
  definition 77, 82

indices 9, 13

Rand Graduate Institute
  10
RANN (Research Applied to
  National Needs)
  181
regional studies
  96, 103
research
  45, 65
  activities 27
  cost of 116
  expansion of 46
  in energy 101
  in futures studies 198
  interdisciplinary 115
  long-term motivated basis
    28
  operations 137
  operational 49, 50, 162
  planning of 24
  relevance of 97
  teaching and 16
  university 118, 177
research and development
  40, 210, 211
  social 178
Research Councils
  101
resources
  37, 54, 160
  consumption and use 79
  sharing of 76
  use of 79
responsibilities of universities
  203, 217
retraining in academic careers
  109
revolution
  82, 84, 187
  television and 169, 173

scarcity
  all-encompassing view of
    124
scenarios
  10, 11, 153, 214
  horizon (normative) 47,
    48
  projective 47
  cost of 157

scholarship
  maintaining 192
scholasticism
  48
schools
  social change and 74
science
  alternatives within 57
  classification 46
  futures approach in 40
  national policy 63
  pace of development in
    109
  policy-making and 64
  public view of 19
  reaction against 20, 29
  social responsibility and
    20
  specialization 21, 45
  technology and 63
  theories and effects 57
  unity of 124
science fiction
  6, 13, 39, 82
scientific knowledge
  55
  popularization of 23
Scotland
  Oil Development Council
    102
  problems of 93
self-discipline
  education and 78
self-fulfilling potentials
  148
service courses
  198, 202
social applications of
  technology
  68
social change
  85
  schools and 74
social decisions
  education change and
    73–87
  wisdom of 76
social indicators
  140
social lag
  173
social macro-change
  151

social progress
  53
social sciences
  46, 103
  types of 123
social unrest
  20
societal forecasting
  13, 14
societal structure
  187
societal technology
  164
society
  moral decisions 75
  problems affecting 98
  sense of purpose and
    direction 80
  technology and 59n
  universities as nerve cen-
    tres of 167–189
  use of universities in 26
society, religion and
  technology
  92
sociologists
  7
sociology
  85, 124
specialization
  45, 46
speculative approach to
  future
  39
stability
  predictions and 150
  recognition by human
    mind 150
stability in past
  prediction and 149
starvation
  186
students
  age of 118, 178
  importance of 203
  motivation 196
  service courses for 192,
    198, 202
subsistence economy
  33
Sweden
  42

Centre for Interdisciplinary Studies of the
  Human Condition 19–29
mid-career university
  education 202
synchronic analysis
  122
systems analysis/systems
  dynamics
  9, 13
systems theory
  13

teachers
  divided loyalties 110
teaching
  in futures studies 198
  research and 16
techniques for education
  7
technological forecasting
  6, 8, 11, 13, 39, 163
technology
  5, 76
  absence of 56
  alternative 54
  autonomy 57, 59
  behavioural 63, 69
  decisions 64
  definitions of 58n
  futures approach in 40
  in Open University 32
  low-energy 33
  rate of change in 36
  power of 210
  science and 63
  social applications 68
  social determinist view of
    58
  society and 59n, 63, 69
technology assessment
  6, 8, 11, 13, 39, 42, 65, 90,
    97, 148
television
  70, 77
  as cause of change 168
  as communications
    medium 183
  as revolutionary influence
    169
  culture and 186, 188
  disruptive effect of 189
  education and 170

television, *continued*
  expectations and   186
  governmental control of
    184
  in India   186
  leisure and   168
  political influence of   183
  revolutionary influence of
    173
  role of   170, 178
theories
  123
think tanks
  30
time
  162
  continuity in   149
Tobin-Nordhaus-Samuelson
  NEW
  132
transdisciplinarity
  123
transformation times
  66
trends
  67, 68
triage
  6
truth
  55, 154

United Kingdom
  fuel economy   95
  livestock industry   101
  policy-making system in
    98
  research councils   101
undergraduate education
  3, 29, 100
  future teaching   209
  human ecology   33
universities
  adaptation to change   108
  as innovators   43
  as mirrors of society   82
  as nerve centres of
    society   167–189

as repository of knowl-
    edge   176
caretaker function   215
change in   50, 109
change in structure   178
changing departmental
    roles   111
culture and   180
divided loyalties of
    teachers   110
duplication of subject
    matter   113
durability of   114
finance   31, 111, 112, 114
flexibility of   31
freedom of   27
future role   191, 192
horizontality in   103
interdisciplinary contracts
    in   102
interdisciplinary studies in
    102, 103, 104
mid-career education
    202
new clienteles for   179
new combinations of
    disciplines   112
new courses   108
new disciplines in   110
new subject matter in
    existing disciplines   109
objectives   203
organization   107–119
place of futures studies in
    44
reform in   172
relationship with industry
    205
research in   118
responsibilities   203, 217
retraining of staff   109
role in electronic society
    175
role of 21, 28, 29, 82, 84,
    85, 86, 96, 98, 176, 179,
    215, 219
reform   116

scale of operations   177
structures   107
tenure of staff   113, 116
unit degrees   112
use of society   26
University Grants Committee
  114
urban dynamics
  13
urban growth
  37
urban planning
  12, 17, 24
  decision making in   140
urban studies
  115, 159
utopianists
  6
utopias
  39, 149
  behaviour and   134

value analysis
  152
value problems
  30
values
  148
  knowledge-distorting
    effects of   151
  preservation of   192

wage patterns
  205
welfare indicators
  132
Wittgenstein
  136, 202
women's liberation
  83, 188
world structures
  change in   171, 175

zero population growth
  campaign
  171, 173